I0631156

Novels

But the Children Survived

Dangerous Stranger

Their Best Dreams

Where's Audrey?

A Tender Heart

Don't Look Back

What She Deserved

A Lethal Legacy

When Daisy Disappeared

The Silver Stag

Novellas

The Ladies of Lavender Lane

Shorts

The Room in Grandma's House

Kevin Chandler and The Case of the Missing Dogs

The House on the Shore

The Little Cottage by the Sea

A Christmas Mystery

Sisters and Whiskers

Divine Detective Agency Mystery Shorts:

The Body in the Bungalow

The Devious Dame

The Kid at the Candy Counter

Libby the Psychic Dog in:

Libby the Psychic Dog

Mystery in the Mansion

Quandary on the Quay

The Nefarious Neighbor

The Cat's Confession

WHEN DAISY DISAPPEARED

A. L. JAMBOR

Woofie

Visit A.L. Jambor's website to read Kindle samples of her books.

ISBN: 978-0-9964373-9-4

AUTHOR'S NOTE

This is a work of fiction. Names, characters, places, and scenes are either the product of the author's imagination or are used fictitiously, and any resemblance to actual persons, living or dead, business establishments, events or locales is entirely unintentional.

Cover design by: Amy Jambor; Photo credit: © Can Stock Photo / thomasmalesse; © deposit photos / kuikson

CONTENTS

Everybody, sooner or later, sits down to a banquet of consequences.

Robert Louis Stevenson

1

TUESDAY

Ben Arntz woke up as the aroma of coffee filled his room. He stretched, rubbed his eyes, sat up, and gripped the edge of his bed as he thought about his mother, Beth. Ben had been avoiding her as he worked out his plans, plans that would raise her ire, and he felt like a coward about to face a firing squad. Since she hadn't seen him in days, she would be waiting for him, and even though he slept well, he felt drained.

In all his twenty-three years, Ben had been a dutiful son following his mother's plans for his life as she dictated both his academic and leisure activities. Bethany Arntz alone knew what was best for her only child, the one who would carry on the legacy of the Friedlander family.

Ben knew well the story of his great-grandparents and their struggles following WWII, how they'd come to the United States after surviving the Holocaust and built a successful business in New York City's garment district. They had overcome adversity, and Ben's life would be a testament to their sacrifices. That burden, along with his mother's ambitions, had brought Ben to a crossroads, and he knew that today was the day he would have to tell his mother that her dreams weren't going to come true.

Ben had graduated from Princeton two years ago with a degree in U.S. History. Before he began college, he and Beth had had several spirited arguments over the path his life should take – business or academia. Ben had no interest in the company. He wanted to teach, and since she had been unsuccessful in changing his mind, she allowed him to follow that course.

While Ben studied the history of the United States, Beth talked about the merits of earning a master's degree. When he graduated, she suggested a higher degree would look good on his resume, and Ben knew she was right. He began classes the following autumn. While he earned his master's degree, Beth talked about the doctorate program and how he was still young and earning his doctorate would give him more options. Her arguments were convincing, and soon she won Ben to her side. Now, two months into the semester, Ben knew without a doubt that he was ready to follow his own dream, and would have to tell Beth he was quitting the doctorate program so he could teach middle school kids the history of their country.

Ben got up, showered, and dressed before heading downstairs. He braced himself as he gripped the railing, deliberately stepping on each step with both feet to delay his progress.

Beth would be dressed for the day and seated at the dining table with a folded newspaper next to her plate. Her only reason to linger at the table was so she could ask her son about how things were going at school.

As Ben stood at the bottom of the stairs, he braced himself for the argument that was about to take place and recalled a conversation he'd had with his Uncle David, Beth's younger brother. David had advised Ben to stick to his guns.

Ben adored David, a man who had suffered a nervous breakdown in his twenties, which ended Jacob Friedlander's dream that David would take over the family business. Beth ran the company now, and under her hands, it had grown far beyond what Jacob Friedlander could have imagined. Unfortunately, Jacob hadn't lived to see the breadth of her success, and while he lived, he never told Beth he was proud of her, but would often mention how sad it was that David would never be able to follow in his father's footsteps.

Beth's bitterness over her father's rejection had led to a contentious relationship with her brother, and Beth expected Ben to side with her, but he refused to sever ties with his beloved uncle. Ben would see David often, but he wouldn't speak of him in Beth's house.

Ben had been practicing what he would say to Beth and decided to emphasize his desire to get on with his life. He would also tell her that he had been offered a teaching job in California. Ben was twenty-three. It was time to spread his wings. It all sounded very reasonable in his head. He took a deep breath and headed to the dining room.

Beth lit up when she saw him. At sixty, gray streaks mingled with her dark blonde hair and her green eyes sparkled in anticipation. She gave Ben one of her rare smiles. He returned it but kept his composure.

"Sit," Beth said. "You have to tell me what you've been up to. I haven't seen you in days."

Ben sat across from his mother and then Maria, their housekeeper, came through the kitchen door with a pot of coffee. They were silent while Maria poured Ben's coffee and waited until she returned to the kitchen to resume their conversation. Beth tilted her head to one side.

"Something's wrong."

Ben took a deep breath.

"I want to talk to you about something that's important to me." He ran his hand through his hair. "I've decided to leave the doctorate program."

Beth straightened her head and hardened her expression.

"What do you mean?"

Ben lowered his eyes and then peered up at her.

"I mean I'm not going to work on a doctorate anymore. I'm going to teach middle school history."

Beth pursed her lips. "That's absurd. You're just tired of school. Why don't you take a few weeks off and go back during the next semester? You've always wanted to go abroad..."

"Mom, I'm done with school. I've been offered a job with a school in California, and I'm considering taking it."

"You can't take a job in California. I won't hear of it. You have an obligation here. You've known that all your life."

"It wasn't my choice to be your only child, but I do have a choice about what I want to do with my life, and what I want to do is teach kids, young kids, history."

Beth's shoulders shook as her face turned red.

"I can't believe this." She stood, put her hands on the table, and leaned forward. "Your great-grandparents suffered terribly. They watched their families die. They did unspeakable things just to stay alive, and you want to throw it all in their faces? You want to reject the future they sweat blood for?"

"This is a future they'd be proud of," he said.

"This is his doing, isn't it?" she asked.

Ben shook his head. "Uncle Dave has nothing to do with this. This is all me."

"No, it's not. You always wanted to be a professor."

"You wanted me to be a professor, Mom. It was never my idea."

"Just because he had a bad experience."

David's words echoed in his ear. *Don't let her get to you.*

"A bad experience? He had a nervous breakdown. He was hospitalized." Ben looked her in the eye. "He doesn't even remember being a professor, so why would he try to talk me out of it?"

"Because he's insane. He's always been crazy. He ruined this family."

Ben pushed himself away from the table and stood.

"He's not crazy, and he didn't ruin this family."

"We were fine until he came along. We didn't need him."

"Jesus, Mom! That was fifty years ago."

"It's not something you forget." She wrapped her arms around herself and began to pace. "He was always the one, the boy. He needed to go to college. He was going to be in charge one day."

Ben fell into his seat and drank his coffee while Beth recounted a litany of David's sins. He gripped his mug and felt his stomach tighten as she ranted about the day her parents brought him home.

"He wasn't even their child. He was the bastard of some teenager who found herself in trouble. For all we know, his father was a serial killer."

As Beth carried on, Ben remembered his grandmother, Linda, and how she liked to touch Ben's cheek whenever he came to see her at the nursing home. She told him she adopted David because he had a sweet nature. When she and his grandfather met him, he was the two-year-old son of a drug addict. He was in foster care. David's foster parents had treated him well, but they couldn't adopt him, so Jacob Friedlander's lawyer had been contacted by an adoption agency.

"He called and said they had a boy, and we didn't even have to think about it," Linda said. "Oh, he had blue eyes and blond curls. He laughed so easily."

"Why does my mother hate him?" Ben asked.

Linda's smile faded. "Beth was jealous of him from the day we brought him home. She never adjusted to us having another child." His grandma had tilted her head forward and looked him in the eye. "She doesn't hate him. Beth has always exaggerated. She's just a high-strung girl. She had big dreams and fate didn't always treat her kindly."

That's not how Ben saw his mother right now. He *knew* she hated David and Ben had spent the last eleven years defending him to her. He was tired of it - the petty jealousy, the constant haranguing that led to arguments, and all because a little girl couldn't accept having a little brother.

Ben drank the rest of his coffee as Beth continued her diatribe on David's shortcomings, and then he got up and walked toward the foyer.

"Where are you going?" she said. "We haven't finished discussing this."

Ben grabbed his jacket from the hall closet.

"I have to be somewhere," he said. "I'll be back later."

She was still talking when he went out the front door.

2

TUESDAY

B en drove to the university to let them know he was taking a
break. He visited some of his old professors, and by the time
he returned to his car, it was already past noon. Every day he
stopped by Uncle Dave's house to check on him, and to see if he
needed anything from the supermarket.

Ben parked in front of David's house and looked at the narrow
two-story home his grandparents had bought for him the year
David got out of the hospital. Built in 1880, the Queen Anne style
house was in need of a facelift. The paint on the shutters had blown
away leaving patches of darkened wood and forest green. The
white vinyl siding had kept the exterior of the house from deterio-
rating, which allowed the façade to retain its dignity. A long
driveway ran next to the house ending at a detached garage in the
back yard. David's old Ford Escort, a car he'd bought twenty years
before, was kept there. A newer model Ford Escort that Ben had
bought him was in the driveway. Ben had suggested to David that
he could have the old car hauled away, but David refused to part
with it.

As he stepped out of his car, Ben heard classical music blaring
from inside the house, and he glanced at the house next door.
David's old friend Harlan Monteif lived there. Ben saw Harlan's car
in the driveway and wondered how long the music had been
playing.

Ben let himself in through the unlocked front door. Stacks of old
newspapers and plastic bags littered the living room floor, all meant

for the recycling bin, though they never made it to the street for pickup. Magazines and junk mail were on the sofa.

Ben waded through the debris to an old stereo in the corner near the stairs and turned down the volume. He worried that David might have gone off his meds as playing loud music was one of the things he did when he was feeling manic. Ben walked to the kitchen and found his uncle busily scribbling on a sheet of paper at the kitchen table.

"Hey, Uncle Dave," he said.

David looked up and smiled. "Ben!"

"The music was really loud."

"Oh, was it? Sorry. I hadn't noticed."

"Did Harlan complain?" Ben asked.

David waved a hand. "Oh, he doesn't care. He likes classical music."

David's small table had two chairs. Ben sat across from him, and then looked at the dishes in the sink.

"You could wash your dishes once in a while."

"You know I use paper plates."

"Then why is the sink so full?"

David glanced at the sink. "I ran out of detergent."

Ben exhaled sharply and sat back, his hands on his knees.

"I went by the library, but you weren't there."

"I only work part-time now," David said.

"But you need to get out and see people," Ben said.

David shrugged.

"Anna told me they're worried about my heart." He looked up from his scribbling and glanced at Ben. "I told them my heart is fine, but they still insisted I cut back on my schedule."

Ben leaned forward, elbows on the table. "Your heart is not fine, Uncle Dave. You had two heart attacks." Ben saw a half-empty pack of cigarettes on the table. "And you're not supposed to smoke anymore."

"I can't stop smoking, or I'll have a stroke." David shook his head. "Honestly, Ben, you should know better."

Ben got up and opened the fridge. It contained a half-gallon carton of milk, a stick of butter, and a Big Mac box. He picked up the milk, shook it, and then looked in the freezer.

"What are you eating?" Ben asked.

"What I've always eaten."

"Hamburgers and ice cream," Ben said.

"And you know I've always taken good care of myself. I don't need anyone telling me what to do."

"Are you taking your meds?"

"Only because you want me to."

"What if you get so sick you can't take care of yourself?" Ben asked.

"I've made my wishes known to Harlan."

Ben looked at the paper in front of David as he sat.

"What's that?"

David put his hand over it.

"You'll find out after I'm dead."

"I can't read it now?"

"No. I'm giving it to Harlan, and when the time comes, he'll give it to you."

Ben folded his hands on the table and rested his forehead on them.

"So, you're working part-time now. What do you do with the rest of your time?"

"I'm catching up on my reading and sorting through some things upstairs."

Ben lifted his head.

"Have you kept it clean?"

"Just as you left it last summer," David said. "I sleep down here now."

"But that's why I cleaned it so that you could sleep up there."

David shook his head.

"I like being closer to the front door."

"Damn it, Uncle Dave. I worry about you."

"Don't worry about me, Ben. I'm just fine."

Yeah, you're fine because you don't know what the hell is going on half the time.

"So, Harlan got back from Europe," Ben said.

"Yes, he did, and we sat on his porch last night and talked about old times."

"You've known him a long time."

David sat back and dropped his pen.

"We met when we were freshmen in high school. He was my best friend."

"I'd like to talk to him about something," Ben said. "Do you think he'd mind if I dropped by?"

David waved his hand dismissively.

"He won't mind at all."

"I did it, Uncle Dave. I quit school."

David's expression grew solemn.

"Did you tell your mother?"

Ben nodded. "She's...not happy."

"I'll bet she blamed it on me," David said.

Ben smiled. "She did, but I told her it was my idea."

David sighed. "She was always a pain in the ass. Nothing was ever good enough for her." His expression hardened. "She's the reason I'm living here and not in my own home. Beth made my parents buy this house."

Ben had heard this story most of his life and had even asked his grandmother about it. It was true. Beth had insisted they make him live away from the mansion.

"But at least you don't have to see her every day."

David's shoulders slumped.

"That should have been my house."

"Did you really want it?" Ben asked. "I always thought it was too big."

"That's not the point. Beth was supposed to get married and leave, and I was to run the family business and live in that house." He glanced at Ben. "That's what my father told me. He promised that one day I would represent the family."

Ben reached out and put his hand on David's.

"You still do, Uncle Dave. You're the last Friedlander."

David was quiet for a moment, lost in a memory, and soon a tear rolled down his cheek, but he wiped it away and pretended it hadn't happened.

"She called me," David said.

"Who, Mom?"

David nodded. "We argued. That's what we always do."

"What did you argue about?"

David smiled. "Nothing for you to worry about. Just the same old same old."

A moment passed while David gathered his thoughts.

"Right you are."

"About what?" Ben asked.

9

"I am the last Friedlander."

David began scribbling again. Ben sat back and looked at the old, grease-stained wallpaper.

"You need milk. Do you want me to pick some up before I come by tomorrow?"

"You don't have to visit me every day, Ben."

"I have to know you're all right."

David grinned. "Yes, you can bring milk, but not that skimmed kind."

Ben rolled his eyes. "Right, only whole."

Like you don't tell me every time I ask if you need milk.

Ben got up and looked into the cabinets.

"You're out of Cheerios."

"I want Rice Krispies this time. And some of that fluff stuff."

"You want Rice Krispy squares."

"I make them myself with the fluff. Just enough for me." David squirmed in his seat. "I put it in the microwave."

"Okay. I'll get the fluff stuff, too."

"And butter. Can't make them without butter."

Ben left the kitchen and went upstairs. The place was as clean as he'd left it after cleaning it out during the summer, all but the spare room where David had laid things on the bed. Ben went inside and scanned the items - magazines and photos. He noted that the magazines were from the 1980s. The photos were of David, Harlan, and Anna, a woman who worked with David. In the photos, David had a full head of dark blonde hair, and Harlan was thin.

Ben saw a photo of a young woman sitting under a tree near one of Princeton's iconic buildings. She had her arms wrapped around her knees and was smiling broadly, but her eyes were squinting from the sun. Ben looked at the back, but there was nothing written there. She must have been someone special for David to keep her photo so long.

Ben went downstairs and stood at the kitchen door.

"I'm going now."

David didn't look up from his writing.

"Take care. See you tomorrow."

"Bye."

When Ben got outside, he looked at Harlan's house, but the car was gone. He'd have to see him tomorrow when he brought David his fluff.

Ben went into Logans Grove and spent some time looking through the stores on Artisan Row, a strip of King's Highway that had once provided goods to local shoppers. It's conversion from a mom and pop type local shopping area to a high-end tourist spot had taken place in the early 2000s, and now it had amenities designed to lure city dwellers to the quaint country shops, which included a café with a coffee bar.

Once he had sampled all the Row had to offer, Ben still didn't want to face another confrontation with his mother, so he went to The Ugly Badger, the oldest tavern in Mercer County, sat at the bar, and watched the local news.

Ben ate his dinner at the bar and watched most of a football game until ten ensuring that he would get home after Beth went to bed. He paid his bill and walked out of the bar. A cold wind made him shiver as he got into his car. He sighed, laid his head back for a moment, and then thought about David and Beth. An ache in his neck that had started when he was sitting at the bar was worse, so he started the car, and stopped at a 24-hour pharmacy for a bottle of Ibuprofen before he went home.

3

WEDNESDAY MORNING

M addie Brady stretched and groaned as the sunlight from the bedroom window hit her eye. Larry was at the side of the bed pressing his cold, wet nose against her outstretched hand.

"I know you want to go out. I'm getting up."

The old, black Labrador Retriever went and stood by the door as Maddie put her feet on the floor. She rubbed her eyes and looked at the old digital clock on her dresser. 8:00 a.m.

"Ugh."

She put on a pair of slippers, got up, went to the front door, and took her jacket off the old brass coatrack before opening the door. Larry usually walked to the back yard and did his business while Maddie waited near the side of the house, but this morning, he took Maddie by surprise as he bounded toward the old Fenway place.

"Larry!" she cried. "Get back here!"

The dog had caught the scent of something and wasn't about to stop. There was a half-mile between Maddie's house and the Fenway place, and her slippers weren't going to protect her feet from the morning dew, so she went back inside to put on her father's ancient rubber galoshes.

Her feet slid inside the boots as she walked through the tall, dead grass, and she almost slipped before reaching Larry, who was sitting at the center of the yard behind Fenway Manor. The tall grass concealed his body, and Larry's head looked as if it were floating above the yard.

Larry was eleven. His arthritic joints usually kept him from roaming too far from his back yard, so it was strange to see him jumping with excitement as she approached him.

"What's gotten into you," Maddie said. "You've never done that before."

She was moving toward him and bending down to put the leash on Larry's collar when her foot hit something. Maddie looked down. It was a foot in a sneaker. Her eyes traveled up the leg to the waist, and then she saw blood. The man was lying on his stomach, his head turned to one side, and his eyes staring at the grass. Maddie gasped, stepped back, and fell onto her butt when a boot slipped off her foot. She crawled backward until she was at a safe distance and stared at the man's legs.

"Shit," she said softly. Maddie reached into her jacket pocket for her phone, which she'd left on the end table beside the bed. "Larry." The dog woofed. "Come."

He obeyed this time, and she attached his leash. She pushed herself off the ground, put on her boot, and pulled Larry across the yard while he sniffed the ground for a place to do his business. When they got home, Maddie went to fetch her phone and dialed 911. As she spoke to the operator, she turned on the burner under the teakettle.

"What's the nature of your emergency?"

"My dog…found a man in the yard behind the old Fenway place." She paused. "I think he's dead."

"Why do you think he's dead?"

"There was blood on his jacket, and…his eyes were open. He wasn't moving."

Maddie answered the woman's questions and then gave the woman her address.

"I've contacted the police, and they are on their way," the woman said. "Stay there until they arrive."

The teakettle whistled, and Maddie made a mug of instant coffee. She took it to the bedroom, placed it on the dresser, and then went into the bathroom to take a shower. She heard someone knocking on her door when she stepped out of the shower and dried off quickly.

"I'm coming!"

Maddie got dressed while Larry barked at the door, and got there just as the cop was trying the doorknob. She opened it while holding Larry's collar.

"Sorry. I was in the shower. Come in." She saw flashing lights in the driveway of the old Fenway place. "Would you like some coffee?"

"No, ma'am," he said.

"Well, I'm gonna have mine. We can sit in the kitchen."

She retrieved her coffee from the bedroom and found him sitting at the table with an open notebook and pencil. She sat and cradled her mug.

"Can you tell me how you found the body?"

"Larry woke me up and I let him outside. Usually, he goes to the back yard and does his business, but when I opened the door, he took off. I went after him, and that's when I found that man."

"Did you know the victim?"

"No. I've never seen him before."

"Did you hear anything?" Maddie thought for a second and then shook her head. "No gunshot?" She shook her head again. "And you didn't see him there before today?"

"No, never."

The officer jotted down everything Maddie said, asked her for her full name, phone number, and then closed the notebook.

"Will you be home for a while?" he asked. "I think our detective may want to speak to you."

"I work in town. I own the used bookstore on Artisan Row. The Daisy Chain."

"That strip with all the artsy fartsy stores?" He smiled.

"That's the one."

"So, the detective can find you there."

"Between ten and five," she said. "I'm there every day but Monday."

The officer wrote this down.

"Well, I guess that's it for now. Thanks for calling it in."

"No problem," she said.

Maddie got up with him, walked him to the door, watched him walk to his car, and then looked across toward Fenway Manor. There were more vehicles there now, and Maddie shuddered as she thought of the dead man's eyes.

"I didn't like seeing that, Larry," she said. The dog was lying on his bed in the corner of the kitchen, and he lifted his head. She smiled at him. "Are you ready to go to work?"

Larry, moving slowly, got up and walked over to her, his nails clicking on the linoleum floor. He stood while she put on his leash and they walked out the door together. He barked once at the lights across the field and then got into the back seat while Maddie held the door.

She kept her eyes on the scene across the way as she went to the driver's side of the car, and wondered who the man had been and why she hadn't heard a gunshot.

4

WEDNESDAY

C andy Burke placed her new real estate license on the wall of her cubicle. She stood back and put her hands on her hips as she admired it, and then began to sort the things on her desk.

She pulled the sign she'd bought for her desk out of the plastic bag and put it at the front of the desk. "Candace Burke," was written in black letters on a brass plaque affixed to a wooden base. She then put a small wooden holder next to the sign, took a box of business cards out of the bag, and put some in the holder. The business cards had the office landline and her cell phone number along with her photo and a slogan, "Own the Home Meant for You."

Candy examined her photo. Her mother had taken it with her cell phone. Candy's shoulder-length blonde hair had cooperated that day, and it looked good. She had been careful not to use too much makeup and was happy with the results.

Candy was working for, Ross Carpaza, owner of Carpaza Real Estate in Logans Grove. His face was all over the small town. Ross's late mother had started the agency in the forties. He was a broker, and Candy, an independent contractor. He had employed Candy when a friend of her mother's recommended her.

"You understand that you will only be paid if you sell a house," Ross said the day he hired her. "You're gonna have to hustle."

This was the way Ross did business. He'd let some green kid with a new license use the desk and the office the way new hair-dressers rent a chair in a beauty salon, only he didn't ask for rent. Ross would use them to help the receptionist with clerical duties as they learned the business. Candy didn't tell her mother about this, but she did tell her about the need to sell in order to get paid. Her mother's advice was to check the obituaries.

"Old people die," Nina said. "If they leave a house behind their kids might be anxious to sell."

Candy sat in the armless office chair and folded her arms on the desk. Paintings of houses with tiny real estate signs on their lawns had been hung on the walls. A combination umbrella stand and coat rack stood in the right corner behind her desk, and a metal folding chair was in front. Candy sighed and booted up her laptop.

She went to the Newark Star-Ledger website to look up the obituaries posted since the beginning of the year. One struck her immediately - Carl Brady, the father of an old friend, Maddie Brady, whom Candy had known since middle school. They'd had a falling out during their senior year in high school, and Candy hadn't spoken to Maddie in years. Still, she wrote down Carl's name and then thought about the house on King's Highway. It was near that disgusting old mansion.

Images played in Candy's mind – a bonfire, a darkened stairwell, and Maddie's boyfriend…

Candy's hand quivered. Fear crawled up the back of her neck, and she dropped her pen. Her breathing became shallow, her chest tightened, and her heart pounded.

"This might happen now and then," her therapist, Sandy, had said. "Remember your mantra."

Candy closed her eyes, concentrated on breathing in and out, and then said aloud, "I'm safe. I'm in a safe place." Her heart stopped pounding. She began to relax, grabbed the bottle of water out of her purse, and took a few swigs.

Her forehead was damp with perspiration, and she took a tissue from a box she had put in the drawer to wipe it away. She felt the sweat on her back, got up, and ran to the bathroom near the back of the office.

Stains had formed under her arms and on the back of her blouse. Candy's mother had warned her not to wear the silk blouse alone and to wear the new suit she'd bought, but Candy was so sure she wouldn't have a panic attack that she wore her pink silk blouse with a slim, short black skirt. When her mother saw her at the breakfast table, she frowned and shook her head.

"That skirt is too short. You're a professional now. You should dress like one."

Candy had dismissed her mother with a laugh, but now, as she looked at the stains spreading across her chest, she wished she'd listened. She was thirty-years-old now, not sixteen. Candy had to start dressing like an adult.

Fortunately, the bathroom had an electric hand dryer, so she took off the blouse and held it under the dryer. As they dried, the stains were less visible, but she could still see them. She thought of sneaking home to change, but then Candy would have to face her mother and admit she'd been right.

"Girl, what are you doing in here?"

Trini, Ross's Jamaican receptionist, walked in and saw Candy holding her blouse. Candy loved the cadence of her voice and smiled when she saw her.

"I'm a little nervous."

"Well, get your clothes on and get out there. The boss will be here soon."

Candy held up the blouse.

"Can you see the stains?"

Trini shook her head.

"I don't see a thing."

Candy bit her lip, and then put on the blouse. She looked at her reflection in the mirror, but all she could see were the outlines of the stains. Trini came out of the stall and washed her hands.

"You look beautiful. Now get out there."

Candy took a deep breath and went out the door. She walked past Ross's office without looking inside and went straight to her desk so she could resume her search through the obituaries. She saw an ad for Artisan Row and a list of the stores under that banner. The Daisy Chain, the bookstore Maddie's father had owned was still there. Carl had died, so who was running the store?

Candy went to the lobby and gave Trini the number of the bookstore.

"Call and find out who owns the store now," Candy said. "Please don't say anything about me. Just say you work for a real estate office and you heard the store might be for sale."

"Girl, I know what I'm doing."

Trini smiled broadly as she dialed the number and talked to someone for a few minutes before hanging up.

"Well?"

"The owner is Madelyn Brady," Trini said.

"Oh, shit," Candy said.

"What?"

"Nothing. We went to school together."

"Oh, and she was one of the bad girls."

"Maddie? No, never, but something happened that she…misunderstood."

"So, maybe it's time you talked to her," Trini said.

Candy sighed.

"It's been thirteen years since I spoke to her."

"But you're all grown up now, and so is she. She won't bite you."

"You're right. I have to talk to her."

"That's the spirit."

"Maybe she forgot all about it," Candy said.

"There you go," Trini said.

"But I want to ask her about selling her house. She's gonna think the only reason I'm making up is so I can list it."

"Is that the only reason you're making up?" Trini asked.

Candy bit her lip.

"Well, I heard she was back in Logans Grove, and I never stopped by to see her."

Trini sat back and clasped her hands in her lap.

"So, this *is* the only reason you're going to talk to her."

"Now I feel awful. Why didn't I go and see her before? I didn't even know her father had died."

"It won't look good. Maybe you should go and see her first, and then go back another time to ask about her house."

Candy took a deep breath.

"So, I just go over to see how she's doing." Trini nodded. "And just act like I saw her in the window and wanted to tell her how sorry I was to hear about her father."

"That would be nice."

"And see how she reacts to seeing me again."

"There you go. Now you have a plan." Trini leaned forward and looked at Candy through her lashes. "And just be yourself."

Candy's chest tightened, and her throat felt parched as she went to get her coat and purse in her office. She would keep her coat on when she talked to Maddie in case the stains on her blouse were too obvious.

The idea of talking to Maddie filled her with dread. Perspiration dotted her forehead, and she cringed as she thought about her blouse, but Candy put on her coat, grabbed her purse, and walked past Trini with as much positive energy as she could muster.

5

WEDNESDAY

The aroma of coffee roused Ben from his sleep. He got up, put on a T-shirt over his pajama pants, and went to the kitchen where he found Maria standing by the stove flipping pancakes.

"Good morning," he said.

Maria glanced at him, smiled, and then put some pancakes on a plate for him. He saw a place set on the kitchen island.

"So, we're eating in the kitchen, which means my mother isn't here."

"She left for the city first thing this morning," Maria said.

Ben narrowed his eyes. "She didn't say anything about it when I saw her yesterday." He opened the refrigerator door. "She took her insulin."

"She always takes it when she goes to the city in case she decides to stay overnight."

Ben sat at the island and Maria set the plate down in front of him.

"What exactly did she say?" he asked.

"She said she had an appointment in the city and wouldn't be back until tonight."

"What kind of appointment?"

Maria shrugged. "She didn't say." She went to the coffeemaker, grabbed the pot, and brought it to the island.

"That's not like her." Ben watched as she poured the coffee, and then he took a swig. "She would have left a note or something, especially after the way we left things yesterday."

Maria looked at him and shook her head.

"You worry too much, and you're too skinny. You haven't been eating right."

"I've been eating just fine."

"No. You haven't. Eat all those pancakes."

Ben made a face after she turned around. He stuck his fork into a pancake just as the doorbell rang. Maria went to answer it and then reappeared a moment later with an odd look on her face.

"What is it?" he asked.

"It's the police. They asked for your mother, but I told them she wasn't here."

A man and a woman in plainclothes were waiting for Ben when he went to the foyer. The female looked to be in her mid-forties. She had short brown hair in need of a trim and looked tired. The man was older with a gray buzz cut and wore a faded London Fog raincoat. Judging by their grim expressions, Ben braced himself for bad news and thought of his mother.

"I'm Ben Arntz."

"I'm Detective Janet Worthington." She gave him a business card. "And this is Detective Gaines. Can we sit down somewhere?"

"Sure."

Ben led them to the living room where he sat on the sofa. They sat in a pair of chairs across from him. Janet took out her notebook and a pen.

"We are looking for Bethany Arntz," she said. "Your housekeeper said she left for the city early this morning."

"She was gone when I got up."

"Do you have any idea when she'll return?"

"She told Maria she would be back tonight," Ben said.

While Janet wrote this down, Ben's heel was moving up and down.

"Do you mind if I call you Ben?" she asked. Ben shook his head. "I'm afraid I have some bad news." Ben's heel stopped moving. "We found David Friedlander's body this morning behind the old Fenway place."

Ben's mouth felt dry.

"You what?"

"He was shot from behind."

Ben shook his head.

"No. I just saw him yesterday."

"I know this is hard to hear, but he had his wallet with him. His driver's license was inside."

She took the evidence bag bearing David's wallet out of her large purse. Ben recognized the old leather wallet David had carried for years and his lip trembled.

"When…"

"It happened sometime early this morning. The medical examiner estimates that he'd been there for approximately two hours."

Ben looked at the old grandfather clock in the corner. It was nine-thirty a.m.

"Do you think you could come and identify the body?" she asked.

"You said you knew it was him," Ben said.

"It's a formality. We need someone who knew him. Do you think you can do it?"

Shot. She said David had been shot.

"He was harmless."

Janet glanced at her partner, and then looked at Ben.

"You said you saw him yesterday."

"I went to his house around noon," Ben said.

"Did he say he had any plans for today?" she asked.

Ben shook his head.

"What time did your mother leave for New York?" Gaines asked.

"I don't know. Maria was here when she left."

"We'll have to talk to her before I leave," Janet said, and then she made a note in her notebook. "So, can you come down the station and identify him for us?"

Ben looked younger than his twenty-three years. His pained expression made her look away.

Gaines stood. "I'll go and talk to the housekeeper."

When he left the room, Janet stood.

"We'll drive you to the station."

"I can drive myself," Ben said.

Janet looked unsure, but let it go. She stayed in the foyer as Ben climbed the stairs.

He felt numb as he walked into his bedroom and changed into a pair of khakis and a button-down shirt. He fumbled with his wallet as he tried to put it into his pocket, and then couldn't get his foot into his Nikes. His shoulders shook as he sat on the bed and began to sob.

A few minutes later, Janet appeared at the door.

"We can drive you there if you don't think you can handle it."

"I'm fine."

Ben swallowed hard and put his sneakers on while she waited in the hallway. He followed Janet down the stairs where her partner waited, and then he saw Maria, her face wet with tears, and he choked back his feelings. Maria had her arms wrapped around his jacket.

"Thank you," he said as he took it from her. He put it on and hugged her.

"This won't take long," Janet said.

Ben pulled away from Maria and looked into her eyes.

"I'll be right back."

Maria nodded, and then Ben followed the detectives out the door.

Ben followed their black sedan down King's Highway to the county medical examiner's office near the county courthouse. He parked next to them, and then Ben followed Janet into the lobby and through a set of double doors that led to the rear of the building. A chemical smell grew stronger as they neared the double doors marked "Morgue." Janet slowed her pace so she could talk to Ben.

"The M.E. will do an autopsy after you do the ID."

Ben was quiet as they walked through the doors to a large window. Behind it was a tiled room. A table sat near the window, and the outline of a body beneath a white sheet made Ben shudder. Another grim-faced man stood ready to pull back the sheet.

"You tell me when you're ready," Janet said.

"Now," Ben said.

Janet nodded, and the man lifted the end of the sheet. Ben clenched his teeth when he saw his beloved Uncle Dave's still, pale face.

"Is this David Friedlander?" she asked.

Ben nodded, and then he turned and laid his forehead against the wall. His tears flowed freely now, and the detective left him for a few minutes. Janet stood by the doors, and when she saw he was pulling himself together, she came over and put her hand on his arm.

"I need you to come to the station with us. We have a few more questions. Can you drive?"

Ben nodded, wiped his face, and then followed her back to the parking lot.

When they got to the Logans Grove P.D., Ben followed Janet to a windowless room with a table and four chairs. He sat, and she took a seat across from him. Her partner was absent.

"So, Ben, what time did you leave David's house yesterday?"

"Around twelve-thirty."

"What did you do after you left?"

Ben's head was muddled. He tried to remember what he had done the night before, and then it came to him – walking around Artisan Row, eating dinner at The Ugly Badger, and then watching a football game to avoid seeing his mother.

"I went to Artisan Row for a while, and then to The Ugly Badger. I had dinner and watched a football game until ten." He leaned forward and put his arms on the table. "It doesn't make sense."

"What doesn't make sense?" Janet asked.

"Why anyone would kill Uncle Dave," he said.

"Did he have any enemies?"

"No." Ben clasped his hands and rocked in his seat. "Everybody liked him."

He avoided her eyes.

"Are you sure everybody liked him?"

Ben closed his eyes and put his forehead on his folded hands.

"Maria gave us your mother's cell number, but she's not answering her phone."

Ben lifted his head. "She always answers her phone, even when I tell her she can let it go to voicemail."

"Does your mother own a gun?" Janet asked.

Ben sat up. He tried to read the detective's face, but her expression revealed nothing.

"My dad had a hunting rifle, but I don't know what happened to it." He sat back. "It disappeared after he died. I think my mother got rid of it."

"Do *you* own a gun?"

Ben shook his head.

"I don't like guns."

Janet looked at her notes.

"What did you and David talk about when you saw him?"

"Not much. He needed some stuff from the supermarket, and I told him I would get it for him."

"Would you say he was depressed?" she asked.

"No, Uncle Dave was bi-polar. When he didn't take his meds, he was manic, not depressed."

"Did he ever talk about ending his life?"

"Not my Uncle Dave," Ben said. "He was a happy guy, what my grandmother used to call *lustik*, joyful."

"Did David own a gun?" she asked.

"Not that I know of."

The detective looked at her notes.

"What do you do for a living, Ben?"

"I've been going to school to become a teacher."

"So, you're not working," Janet said.

Ben shook his head.

"So, where do you get the money to eat at The Ugly Badger?"

Ben eyed her closely. "I have a trust fund set up by my father when I was born. I don't need money if that's what you're asking."

Janet scribbled something in her notebook and then stared at it for a moment.

"Okay." She closed her notebook. "I guess that's it for now." She stood. "We have your number. We'll call if we have any more questions."

"So, I can go?"

"Yes."

Ben got up and headed to the door.

"Oh," Janet said. "Do you have any plans to travel?"

"No."

"Do you have a key to David's house?"

Ben took his keys from his pocket and took off David's house key. He handed it to her, and then followed her to the lobby. She stayed at the door and watched him walk to his car.

It was a gorgeous, cloudless, Indian summer day, and Ben took off his jacket before getting inside the car. The weight of his loss was heavier now that David's death was beyond a doubt, and a terrible thought crept into Ben's mind - did Beth still have his father's gun? He dialed Beth's number, but she didn't answer.

He started the car, drove to Harlan Monteif's, and parked in the road in front of his house. Ben tried calling Beth's cell phone again, but it went to voicemail. Uniformed officers were waiting at the door of David's house. As he got out of the car, Ben saw Detectives Worthington and Gaines arrive.

Ben knocked on Harlan's front door, and when Harlan didn't answer, he walked to the back yard. He found Harlan reading the newspaper on his screened porch. Ben wondered if he had heard about David and braced himself for the older man's condolences. As if sensing Ben's presence, Harlan looked up, saw Ben standing at the screen door, and smiled.

6

WEDNESDAY

Harlan was a large man with a balding pate who walked with a cane. His students often compared his appearance to that of Jabba the Hutt, a rotund, slug-like character in the movie "Star Wars." Harlan was a law professor and maintained a license to practice law.

"Ben, come in." Harlan noticed his ashen pallor and reddened eyes. "What's wrong? Is it your mother?"

Ben shook his head as his lip quivered.

"You didn't see the police next door."

"No. I grabbed the paper when I woke up, and I've been sitting on the porch ever since."

Ben lowered his eyes.

"It's Uncle Dave. He's gone."

"Gone?"

"He's dead, Harlan."

Harlan's shoulders slumped.

"Did he have another heart attack? I saw him last night, and he looked fine."

"It wasn't a heart attack."

"Let's go sit down," Harlan said.

As he led Ben through the kitchen to the back porch, Harlan offered him some coffee.

"No, thanks."

There was a round table with four matching chairs on the porch.

A newspaper was open in front of one seat. They sat, and Ben slumped in his chair.

"When did this happen?" Harlan asked.

"He was found behind Fenway Manor this morning. Someone shot him."

Harlan leaned forward. "Who would shoot David?"

Ben shook his head and peered at Harlan.

"The cops asked if we owned a gun."

Harlan straightened his back and narrowed his eyes.

"You spoke to the police?"

Ben nodded. "I was careful. I told the truth."

"That doesn't always matter to the police. The next time they want to talk to you, you call me."

Ben nodded and then leaned forward.

"You said you saw him last night. What time was that?"

"He knocked on my door around eight-thirty. He had a letter he wanted me to put in my safe with his will. He seemed a bit agitated, and I wondered if he was off his meds."

"I wondered the same thing when I saw him yesterday."

Harlan sat back and put his hands on the table.

"And your mother? What was her reaction when she found out?"

Ben shrugged. "She doesn't know. She left the house early this morning, and she's not answering her phone."

Harlan raised his eyebrows.

"What time did she leave the house?"

"Maria was up, and she saw her go, so it must have been early, like seven or eight. She told Maria she was going to the city for an appointment."

"And she's not answering her phone. Is that something Beth normally does?"

Ben shook his head. "She always answers when she sees it's me."

Harlan sat back and looked at his back yard.

"I must say it strikes me as odd that you can't get her on the phone. Did the police ask about her?"

"They talked to Maria."

"What did you tell them when they asked if you had a gun?"

"I told them my dad had a hunting rifle and that my mother hid it after he died."

Harlan screwed up his mouth as he pondered this.

"Did she ever tell you what happened to it?"

Ben shook his head again. "I have no idea where it is." Ben looked at Harlan. "I can't stop thinking about him." His lip quivered. "Why would someone kill him?"

Harlan shrugged. "David was odd. He always talked to strangers. Someone might have taken offense at something he said. I've heard him get into arguments with students, but it seems a stretch to think one of them would go so far as to kill him. And behind Fenway Manor, no less." Harlan folded his newspaper. "You don't believe Beth was capable..."

"She didn't kill him," Ben said.

"Of course, not," Harlan said. "She adored her brother."

"That's not funny."

"Neither is denying the nature of their relationship."

"My mother couldn't have done this," Ben said.

"Listen, Ben, I understand how you feel, but as a lawyer, I have to warn you that sometimes people do things that you would never think they could do. You must prepare yourself just in case..."

"Oh, for God's sake. She didn't kill him."

Ben stood, and Harlan grabbed his hand.

"Sit." Ben kept his eyes on the kitchen door. "Please."

Ben returned to his chair, but he averted his eyes.

"We have to discuss David's will," Harlan said. "We looked it over last night while he was here. He wanted to make sure you knew what he wanted. He didn't want to be placed in the Friedlander mausoleum."

"Why?" Ben asked.

"He said he's not a true Friedlander, but I think he was trying to protect you. He didn't want you to get into an argument with Beth over it, so he said he wants to be cremated."

Ben's lip trembled. "Shit."

"He left all his worldly possessions to you." Harlan smiled. "He loved you very much."

Ben folded his arms on the table and rested his head on them.

"I'm getting more coffee," Harlan said. "Are you sure you don't want some?"

"No, thanks."

When Harlan returned, Ben sat up.

"When did he start showing symptoms?" Ben asked.

Harlan sat and adjusted his bulk for a moment as he thought about Ben's question.

"He started having mild episodes during our senior year in Princeton," Harlan said. "At first, I thought he was drinking too much coffee, but after a while, I noticed he was having trouble focusing on his schoolwork, and that was a big red flag. David was an excellent student. His academic career was the most important thing to him. For him to earn less than an A was inexcusable."

"My grandmother told me once that she was worried that he might be moving too fast."

"He was seventeen when he graduated. The next semester, he was working on his masters." Harlan sipped his coffee. "Linda might have been right, but Jake would have disagreed."

"Did my grandfather put a lot of pressure on him?" Ben asked.

"David knew that Jake wanted him to run the business. It wasn't David's desire, but I'm sure he felt an obligation to please his father." Harlan glanced at Ben. "It's also why he and Beth never got along."

"I know," Ben said.

"When he had his first breakdown, she saw it as an opportunity." Harlan sighed. "She told Jake that David was weak, but your grandfather was old-fashioned and resistant to change. Boys ran businesses; girls got married. Jake had no idea who Beth was."

"What a waste," Ben said. "They could have been friends."

"Everybody, sooner or later, sits down to a banquet of consequences."

"Who said that?"

"Robert Louis Stevenson."

"So, this is our banquet of consequences?" Ben asked.

"Let's hope it's more of a light supper," Harlan said. "So, I will file the will in probate. In the meantime, just take care of David. When I need your signature on the paperwork, I'll let you know."

Ben took a deep breath and then exhaled sharply.

"Did he really leave everything to me?" Ben asked.

"He did."

"God, it's sad. That house is full of junk. He had nothing but that job at the library."

"That's not exactly true," Harlan said. "When David became ill, his parents formed a trust. Jake knew one of the board members at the university. He arranged for David to work in the library, but his salary was paid through the trust. Officially, it was an unpaid research position, but David didn't know that. Anna was working as the dean's secretary at the time. I bought these pay envelopes at the office supply store, and I would put a weekly wage in them from the trust. Anna would fill out the taxes, etc. to make them look official, and would give it to David as his pay."

"And he never knew?" Ben said.

"Not for a long time. A few years ago, though, he figured out that his job at the library wasn't a real job at all and that's when I told him about the arrangement. He was hurt, but I think by then he understood why his father had done it." Harlan sat back and sighed. "He continued to suffer bouts of mania over the years, which would keep him from work, and he knew that would have made employment elsewhere very difficult."

"Poor Uncle Dave."

"Precisely, though I don't think he wanted anyone's pity." Harlan leaned sideways toward Ben. "And I think he delighted in putting something over on Beth."

"She didn't know?" Ben asked.

"Jake felt it was better if she remained in the dark. She had told her parents at the time that it would be best if David simply disappeared. She suggested they send him far away. I believe she mentioned California."

"You're kidding."

Harlan shook his head.

"Beth was afraid David's illness would present itself in public. She was worried about how it would look. She often spoke of protecting the family name."

"I heard them fighting about that once when I was a kid," Ben said. "It was the last time he came to our house."

"As I said, Beth had her reasons for feeling the way she did, but I always wondered why she found it so hard to forgive. It only made things worse for her."

"One of my friends told me that they would rather die than suffer the wrath of Bethany Arntz," Ben said.

"It's a miracle you turned out as well as you have," Harlan said.

"Uncle Dave helped me a lot. He listened to me." Ben's shoulders slumped. "I still can't believe it."

Harlan took a deep breath.

"It will take time, Ben."

"I don't even know what to do next."

"I'm sure your mother had a list of contacts. She might even have an address book in her desk where you might find the name of a funeral home. They're very good at taking the burden off your shoulders."

"She does have an address book."

"Listen, Ben, the police will be talking to people. They'll say he didn't get along with his sister. I know you feel you must defend Beth, but be careful. Don't give the police more than they ask for."

"She didn't do this," Ben said.

"I understand that's what you believe, but we're talking about the police. Just be careful and call me if they want to interview you again."

"I'm not worried about them."

"Well, you should be." Harlan leaned forward. "As a member of the family, they will suspect you, too." Ben's shock at the suggestion was genuine, and Harlan felt a twinge of guilt, but the boy had to understand where he stood with the cops. "Just remember to call me before speaking to them again."

"I will."

"The police will hold the body until the coroner is through with the autopsy. Contact the funeral home now so they can handle things when the body is released."

Ben cringed. "Did he say what he wanted me to do with his ashes?"

"No." Harlan clasped his hands over his belly. "You can think about that later."

Ben looked at the fence that separated David's property from Harlan's.

"Did you put up the fence?"

Harlan shook his head.

"My parents put it up when I was a boy."

"Why did my grandparents choose that house?" Ben asked.

"Jake was looking for a place that would be close to the university so David could walk to work. My grandparents had just put that one up for sale so they could move south." Harlan looked around the room. "This is the house I grew up in." He smiled. "Jake bought

33

that house sight unseen. He was grateful to have me right next door."

"It must have been a nice house."

"It was, and it was close to the campus. Jake was afraid to let David drive, but David managed to get his license and that Escort on his own."

Ben smiled. "He defied them."

"He did, and he enjoyed every minute."

Ben sat back. "My mom will want me to sell the house."

"It's not up to her. You're a grown ass man, Benjamin."

Ben tilted his head forward and smiled.

"Where did you hear that expression?"

"I overheard a couple of my students saying it once."

"Well, it fits. I am a grown ass man, and I don't want to sell his house."

"I'm sure she will bow to your wishes."

"No, she won't, but it's all I have left of him." Ben sat up. "I think I'm gonna go home now."

They got up, and Harlan followed Ben to the front door.

"Call me if you need anything," Harlan said.

"I will."

Ben stood at the door for a moment watching the lights on the police cars. Harlan put his hand on Ben's shoulder.

"As I said before, give it time. This too shall pass."

"I wish I could get my mom on the phone."

"Maybe she went to the foundation. Perhaps they called an emergency meeting. Those things can go on for hours."

"And she wouldn't take a call in the middle of one."

"You should call them and ask if they've seen her," Harlan said.

"Right. I should have thought of that."

"Well, your mind is a bit muddled right now."

Ben turned and hugged Harlan.

"Oh, do you have a key for his house? The cops have mine."

Harlan took a key off the holder on the wall near the door. Ben took it and then looked at Harlan.

"Thanks for taking care of him," Ben said.

Harlan felt tears sting his eyes as Ben went out the door. He watched Ben walk away, and then went up the stairs to his office. He stared at the picture that hid his safe and thought about David's visit the night before. He had written Ben a letter that he wanted

Harlan to give him after he died, but Harlan had read it, and now he wondered what had driven David to write it.

As David's attorney, it was Harlan's duty to follow his client's instructions, but he also felt an allegiance to Ben and knew that the contents of that letter would break Ben's heart. As he heard Ben's car go down the road, Harlan decided that he would not give that letter to Ben while his mother was still alive.

7

WEDNESDAY

As she drove down King's Highway, Candy gripped the steering wheel and recalled the last time she and Maddie had spoken to each other. It was thirteen years ago during a Halloween party held behind the old Fenway place. She also remembered what she saw that night inside the old mansion.

"I'm safe," Candy said. "I'm in a safe place."

As Candy neared Fenway Manor, she kept her eyes on the road, but her imagination conjured up the image she saw that night. She gripped the wheel tighter until she was past the old mansion, and then pulled to the side of the road and closed her eyes. She was shaking, and sweat covered her forehead, but Candy summoned the courage to look at the rearview mirror.

"He wasn't real," she whispered.

Candy had passed the old place many times in the last few years without incident, but knowing she would see Maddie must have triggered the panic attack. She closed her eyes again and visualized a calm lake on a cool, spring morning. Birds sang in the trees and a dog barked in the distance. Everything was peaceful, and Candy felt her muscles relax. She took a few deep breaths, opened her eyes, pulled back onto the road, and then turned on the radio.

"A body was found behind Fenway Manor, an old, abandoned mansion on King's Highway." Candy's back stiffened. "Authorities say they are withholding the name of the victim pending notification of the family."

Candy pulled to the side of the road again. She was now across the street from Maddie's house. The sounds and images of the party began to play in her head. The senior classes always gathered behind old Fenway Manor on Halloween night. It was a Logans Grove High tradition, and Candy had planned to meet up with Maddie there. Maddie was going with her boyfriend, Kevin, a handsome jock with a roving eye.

Candy was a beautiful girl. Before he and Maddie started dating, Kevin often made remarks to his football teammates about what he would like to do with Candy. She got wind of it and tried to ignore it, but when Maddie started dating Kevin, Candy longed to tell her about what he'd said, but Maddie was head over heels in love with Kevin. Candy couldn't bear the idea of breaking Maddie's heart.

As the night of the Halloween party drew near, Maddie confessed to Candy that she wasn't excited about going to Fenway Manor.

"I hate that place," Maddie said. "But I feel like I have to go because Kevin wants to."

"You don't have to go, Maddie," Candy said. "I'll stay home with you."

"I'm worried that if I don't go, he'll find someone else to be with."

"Why would he do that?"

"I don't know. Sometimes I wonder if he really cares about me."

Candy had taken Maddie by the shoulders and looked her in the eye.

"He cares about you. I can see it when you're together."

"Yeah, when we're *together*."

Maddie did go to the party with Kevin, and they were sitting in front of the bonfire when Candy arrived. She had driven herself in her mother's old sedan. Maddie's discomfort was clear by the way she kept looking toward the old mansion as if something were about to come out and attack everyone like in movies.

Candy had a weakness for alcohol. She always drank too much. She didn't think it impaired her and she had made some questionable decisions while under its spell, such as sleeping with a football player who liked to brag about his conquests. That wasn't enough to keep her from drinking again, though.

Alcohol always softened one's moral code as it softened the brain, and as Candy grabbed her second beer, she noticed that people were walking toward the mansion.

A. L. JAMBOR

"Let's go inside," one of the boys said.

The other boys followed him, but Maddie held onto Kevin's hand as he got up.

"You don't have to go," he said. "I'll be right back."

She let go reluctantly, and then turned to Candy when she saw some of the girls going inside.

"Please go with him," Maddie said.

Candy was a little buzzed, but she understood that Maddie wanted her to keep an eye on Kevin.

"Sure," Candy said.

Candy went to the porch and peered into the doorway. She'd never been this close to the decrepit manor, and a wave of fear washed over her. She glanced back at Maddie, who was relying on her to keep the other girls away from Kevin, took a deep breath, and went inside.

It was so dark that she had to follow the other kids' voices to a stairwell. Some of the kids carried lit cigarette lighters, and Candy saw dim lights at the top of the stairs. She climbed the stairs with her hand on the wall until she reached the top. She saw the back of Kevin's varsity jacket and went past the dark rooms until she was close to him.

"This is creepy," Candy said.

"Did Maddie come with you?" he asked.

"No."

She barely saw his smile as he turned to face her. He moved her toward one of the rooms.

"Stop," she said as she tried to go around him.

"You afraid?"

She didn't like the sound of his voice or the way he kept his hand on her arms.

"Let go of me."

Kevin shoved her into a room and then grabbed her, forcing his mouth on hers. Candy struggled and was able to push him away, but Kevin persisted.

"Stop that," she said.

"You know you want me to."

"No, I don't."

He pressed himself against her and wrapped her in his arms. She pushed against his hard chest, but he wouldn't budge.

"Come on, Candy. I know you screwed Joe."

Anger replaced fear as she kicked Kevin's leg. He backed away.

"Right," he said. "Now you're gonna get it."

He pushed her, and she fell onto her back. He was on top of her before she could move and pulling at her jeans. Kevin was heavy, and Candy felt as if she couldn't breathe. When she tried to scream, her throat felt constricted, but she managed to get her knee between his legs and shoved it into his groin as hard as she could.

"You bitch!" Kevin cried as he rolled off Candy.

She got up and went toward the door. At that moment, Candy saw an illuminated figure hovering near her. He looked like a handsome, long-haired pirate. Candy stared at him. Was it possible he was smiling at her?

Kevin got up and pulled her by the hair. This time Candy screamed, and two of the boys came running. Kevin let go of her hair when he saw them. She pushed past them and ran down the stairs and out of the house. She looked for Maddie, but she was gone. Candy saw the light of a flashlight off in the distance and knew that Maddie had decided to walk home.

Kevin came out of the house. He was limping, and when one of the boys asked him about it, he said he'd screwed Candy. She denied it, but they all laughed, and his words stung. She knew the boys would choose to believe Kevin because of what had happened with Joe. By Monday, everyone would know, including Maddie.

Candy had grabbed a six-pack before getting into her car. She drove to a small park near King's Highway and drank them all while she tried to figure out what to do. She should have gone to Maddie's house and told her what had happened. She shouldn't have had so many beers.

When the beers were gone, she turned on the car, got onto King's Highway, and turned right. She could barely focus on the road.

According to the police report, a passing motorist saw the car's headlights off the road and stopped to see what had happened. Candy's car had crashed into a tree. The car was totaled, and Candy was hospitalized with two badly broken legs, a broken arm, serious cuts and bruises, and by some miracle, a *mild* concussion. She underwent several surgeries on her legs and missed the rest of her senior year during her extended recovery.

Some of her friends from school visited her at home, but Maddie didn't come. One of the girls told Candy that Kevin had talked about screwing her in the mansion. Maddie broke up with him and told one of the girls that she was no longer Candy's friend.

Candy was heartbroken. She endured months of physical therapy. Bitter and angry at the loss of her senior year and her best friend, Candy took her frustration out on her mom, and she often wondered why her mother had put up with her. Since she wasn't able to graduate with her class, the school gave her the option of repeating the twelfth grade and graduating with the next class, but Candy refused. Instead, she fell into a depression, which led to a prolonged period of psychological therapy. During one of her sessions, Candy told the therapist, Sandy, about seeing what she described as an angel at Fenway Manor.

"He appeared as I was trying to get away from Kevin," Candy said.

"Like a guardian angel?"

Candy nodded. Sandy knew the story and how Maddie had refused to talk to Candy after the incident.

"Have you ever talked to Maddie about this?"

Candy shook her head.

"I couldn't…I wouldn't know what to say."

"Why?"

"Because no one believed me at the time."

"Candy, this wasn't your fault."

"It was my fault for letting him get me into that room. I should have screamed. I should have fought harder."

Sandy leaned forward and looked her in the eye.

"This was not your fault. He was stronger. He tried to rape you, Candy and you were no match for him. And what was wrong with Maddie that she believed him over her best friend?"

Candy had thought about that for a long time. Maddie had believed him and the boys who backed him up. What was wrong with their relationship that Maddie never once tried to talk to Candy?

During another session, Candy again brought up her "guardian angel." One Halloween while she rode past Fenway Manor with her mother, he was standing by the mailbox. Candy began to shake, and she had shortness of breath.

"It sounds like you had a panic attack," Sandy said. "This figure appeared while you were still dealing with a traumatic incident. You associate him with what happened to you. It was Halloween. It's not uncommon for the mind to generate images when we are under stress." Sandy leaned forward. "Maybe you conjured up a strong man, a pirate, to protect you."

Candy remained silent. She knew she hadn't conjured him up. She knew the ghost was real.

"What we need to do is find a way to counteract the panic attack. I've found that focusing on something peaceful can help calm you down, or repeating something like, 'I'm safe. I'm in a safe place,' will help because you can only think one thought at a time." She took Candy's hand. "Reinforce the thought that helps alleviate the fear."

Candy tried repeating the phrase with some success, but fear still lingered and would emerge during times of stress. Hypnosis sessions with Sandy had helped Candy to come to terms with what had happened to her when Kevin pushed her into that dark room, but she was still uncomfortable around men.

"Not every man is like Kevin," Sandy said. "The next step is letting yourself get to know someone."

"I don't know if I can," Candy said.

"You don't have to do it right away. Nobody is forcing you. It's is all about what you want when you're ready for it, Candy."

Candy went on to finish her GED and earn an associate's degree in English from the local community college. She wasn't sure what she wanted to do with her life. She had wanted to teach, but with a DWI on her record, it would be very difficult to find a school willing to hire her, so even the idea of working toward a bachelor's degree filled her with dread. While she didn't rule it out, finishing her education would have to wait until she knew where her life would take her.

The DWI court order had taken her driving privileges away for ten years. She was twenty-eight when they were restored, and with her mother's help, she bought a used car. She landed a series of retail jobs, but the pain in her legs made standing for long hours nearly impossible. For two years she floundered, and then her mother suggested she take some real estate courses.

Candy embraced the idea of working on her own and helping people find their dream home. When she got her license, a friend of her mother suggested she go to see a local real estate broker named Ross Carpaza. Carpaza Real Estate had been in Logans Grove for decades, and Ross had mentored agents who later went on to get their broker's license. When Ross hired Candy, she glowed with excitement.

As Candy drove into the public parking lot for Artisan Row, her hands began to shake. Candy hadn't seen Maddie since that fateful night. Would she still be angry, or would she be willing to listen to what Candy had to say?

Candy got out of the car, took a deep breath, buttoned her coat, and then took her first step toward reconciling with her old friend.

8

WEDNESDAY

Maddie dusted the shelves as she thought about the man Larry had found that morning. Living next to that awful house had been difficult when she was a child, but now it meant that her property would be harder to sell. She felt the tension in her shoulders as she thought about all the times she'd told her father to sell the place and get something smaller, but he always gave some excuse to stay.

Maddie knew the real reason he wouldn't go was the belief that his wife would one day return, and he wanted to be there when she did. Daisy Carter Brady had gone missing in 1991. On Maddie's second birthday, Daisy took their dog for a walk before the birthday party began and had never returned. The dog was found tethered to a newel post on the porch behind Fenway Manor. Carl called the police. They did a cursory search and then told Carl to come to the station and fill out a missing person report.

Carl and the others who had come for the party searched the area themselves but found nothing. For weeks afterward, Carl called the police regarding his missing wife. Their answer was always the same; they had placed her on a list of missing adults, and no one had reported seeing her.

Maddie had learned the details of her mother's disappearance on her own when she went to the public library and looked up old newspaper articles about Daisy. She grew up seeing photos of her mother, but Carl refused to talk about her. It took Maddie years to understand that Carl still believed Daisy would one day return to

Logans Grove. It was the only explanation she could find for the tenacious hold he kept on the store and the house.

When Carl died six months ago, Maddie had slipped into a cocoon of numbness that allowed her to ignore the realities of her situation. She had taken a leave of absence from a high-paying job in NYC to care for her dying father. She hadn't counted on his death affecting her so deeply, and she was unable to push herself into returning to her old life.

And then there was Larry. She had promised her father she would take care of the old dog. How could she take him from the only home he'd ever known?

So, Maddie lost the job, and her landlord was suing her for back rent. She had hit a new low where her emotions were concerned, and she liked to indulge in pints of chocolate marshmallow ice cream.

As she gazed at the holiday festoons strung across the road on the streetlights, Maddie hoped the holidays would put her in the black. The last of her savings was in the bank, enough to last at least six more months, but time was forcing her to face facts. She had wallowed in a pit of indecision long enough.

Maddie stood at the door and folded her arms while watching the road crew put up the rest of the holiday decorations.

"I should put up a tree," she said.

Larry groaned.

Maddie tossed the duster over the counter and stepped outside. She took a few steps toward the road and then turned to look up at the sign over her store - The Daisy Chain. Her father had changed the store's name when he married Daisy. He hoped it would change the store's fortunes and bring in new customers, but most of the people who lived in Logans Grove still called it Brady's Books.

Some accused Carl of betraying his father, the man who had built the business up during the seventies, and they would walk by without coming inside after making sure Carl saw them. Then Daisy disappeared, and these same folks took pity on him. They began coming inside. They even revived the book club Carl's dad had started, and for a while, it was just like the old days.

Then the town began to change. People from the city started buying up the old stores. Soon, the feed store became a restaurant and the old coffee shop, a "cafe." That strip of King's Highway became known as Artisan Row. Gone was the small town feel Carl had so loved, and the constant calls for him to "freshen up" his store's appearance just added to the stress he was enduring over his lack of sales.

Maddie believed the stress caused by the pressure had triggered the prostate cancer that took his life. Carl couldn't afford health insurance. He never visited a doctor, but when he was dying, he qualified for hospice care. His death was brutal, and whenever an image of her dying father came to Maddie's mind, she banished it quickly. She couldn't cry during working hours.

Now that Carl was gone, Maddie heard the same things from her fellow shopkeepers. When she began running the store, she contemplated making a go of it, but the constant jibes regarding her "sad little store" pissed her off. That's when the thoughts of selling the store began and grew until Maddie could no longer ignore them. The time had come to make a decision - she would work through the holidays and then put it up for sale while she decided what to do with the rest of her life.

Maddie came inside and scanned the store. It hadn't changed in over fifty years. A counter with a cash register was on the right. Rows of bookshelves ran from the counter to the back of the store forming aisles, each assigned a genre. An old, round kitchen table with four battered chairs sat in front of the display window to the left of the front door, and Larry's bed was part of the display so he could watch people walk by.

There was little in the way of decoration. Carl had placed some abstract paintings on the walls that a local artist had given him in exchange for books. They clashed with the dingy crown moldings of the Victorian era, and the wall sconces made to look like candles, each with a flame-shaped bulb. Those bulbs did little to illuminate the store, giving it the feel of a cave at sunset.

Maddie sighed as she thought of her father and of the hours he had spent inside these walls. Carl didn't care about how things looked. His house hadn't changed since the seventies. It never occurred to him to buy a new rug or chair, or change the curtains. As long as his TV came on, Carl was happy.

Some teens walked by the store with their phones in hand, and Maddie remembered gazing out the display window as a teenager. She had worked there on weekends for pocket money, but her mind was always on something else - the ecological fair she'd created or the homecoming committee, which she headed along with the class president. And then there was Kevin.

"Piece of shit," she said softly.

Whenever Maddie thought of Kevin, she thought of Candy Burke. When Maddie heard that Candy and Kevin had sex, it broke her heart. For a long time, she couldn't think of Candy without anger. But over time, loneliness replaced the anger, and for years Maddie had wished she'd swallowed her pride and contacted her old friend. Now, as she looked at her closest companion snoring in his bed, she decided to call Candy. Maybe they could have a drink, or go to lunch on Maddie's day off.

Most of the time, though, Maddie thought about her father. She wished she'd been kinder to him. She'd left home at eighteen believing he had done all he could for her, and over time, when she was alone in NYC, she began to think that maybe *he* was to blame for her mother's departure.

Carl was not an ambitious man. He was content to live out his life without leaving Logans Grove, and his lack of motivation was astounding. Daisy had gone to college. Her grandparents had told Maddie that Daisy was smart and ambitious, so her attraction to Carl was a mystery. If this is the way he was when Daisy lived with him, then she might have had a good reason for walking away.

But when Maddie came home to care for him, she felt nothing but compassion. He was so thin, so ravaged by that awful disease that she decided to forget the past and all the things Carl had done because he didn't know what else to do. They had spent a lot of time getting to know each other, and he had finally talked about Daisy. His halting words were full of emotion, and as he outlined the details of her disappearance, Maddie realized that there was something wrong with the way police had handled things. She almost said something about it to her dad, but then chose not to. He had made peace with what had happened, and she wasn't about to ruin his last days on Earth.

It looked like rain, and Maddie had forgotten to bring Larry's kibble from home. She would have to go to the café across the street and get him a hamburger. She went behind the counter to grab her wallet and keys.

"I'll be right back," she told Larry, and then locked the door behind her.

The café was quiet between breakfast and lunch, so she didn't have to wait long for her burger and coffee. She was back at the store in fifteen minutes and put the bag and cup on the old kitchen table. Larry was in his bed. He smelled the burger, stood, groaned, and came to the table. She sat, and then he put his head on her leg.

"Sit," she said.

Larry obeyed. She unwrapped the burger, broke it into small pieces, gave him one at a time, and then she drank her coffee and checked Instagram on her phone. When the burger was gone, she got up and went to the back room to get a clipboard she used to do inventory. While she was back there, she heard the bell on the door ring and then heard a female voice greeting Larry.

"Hello, boy."

Maddie thought the voice was familiar and went to the front of the store. She stopped when she saw Candy.

"Hi, Maddie."

Maddie smiled.

"I can't believe this. I was just thinking about you."

Candy smiled broadly.

"Really? I've been thinking about you, too. I just heard about your dad, and I wanted to say how sorry I am."

Maddie moved closer to Candy.

"Thank you. Dad was sick a long time."

Candy put her hands into her coat pockets and bit her lip.

"Maddie, we never got to talk about what happened."

Maddie held up her hand.

"And we don't have to. It was a long time ago, and Kevin was a jerk."

Candy put her hand on Maddie's arm.

"I know what you heard, but it wasn't true."

Maddie studied Candy's face. She saw the scar on Candy's neck from the intubation. She saw other scars on her face from broken glass, scars that couldn't be concealed by makeup alone. It was the first time she'd seen the damage Candy had suffered that night.

"I wanted to come to the hospital," Maddie said. "I tried, but I was so hurt. I wanted to see you before I left of college, but it had been too long…"

"Forget about it. None of it matters now."

Maddie looked at the table and chairs.

"Why don't we sit for a minute?"

As Candy walked to the table, Maddie noticed a slight limp

when Candy stepped on her right leg. She sat, and Candy sat on the opposite side of the table.

"How are you?" Maddie asked.

"I'm okay."

"How are you, physically I mean?"

"I'm good. My legs hurt sometimes, but it's not too bad." Maddie saw Candy's hands shaking as tears rolled down her cheeks. "I never would have done anything to hurt you, Maddie. I loved you."

Maddie tried to stem her tears, but they ran down her cheeks, too. Candy reached across the table for Maddie's hand.

"I'm sorry," Maddie said softly.

Candy nodded. "It's okay."

"It must have been awful for you."

"I was in therapy. It helped a lot. I still have some problems, but my therapist thinks they will get better in time." She glanced around the store. "It's dark in here, isn't it?"

"It's those stupid flame bulbs. I think they're like 25 watts or something." Maddie wiped the tears off her cheeks. "We should go out sometime."

"I'd love to." Candy smiled broadly. "God, this feels good. I really missed you."

"I missed you, too." Maddie folded her arms on the table. "I'm so sorry I listened to those boys."

Candy leaned forward. "It's okay. We don't have to think about it ever again."

"Is it that easy?" Maddie asked.

"I don't know. We'll have to see."

Maddie rocked in her seat.

"The store is closed at night," Maddie said. "Do you want to meet somewhere later on?"

"We could meet at that Italian place down the street," Candy said.

"I have to take Larry home first. I could be there by seven."

"It works for me."

Candy glanced at the old school clock on the wall between the abstract paintings.

"I didn't know it was that late." Maddie and Candy got up, and Maddie followed Candy to the door. "I'm so glad I stopped by."

"Me, too."

"See you later."

"At seven."

Candy waved at Larry as she walked out the door.

Maddie spent the rest of the day moving books and cleaning years of dust off the shelves. Making peace with Candy was like removing a burden she hadn't known she was carrying.

When the clock struck five, Maddie locked the door and turned the "Open" sign around. She took the till to the safe and was about to put it inside when she spied a stack of papers. She saw them every day but had never looked through them. They might be legal papers pertaining to the store, so she pulled them out and stuck them in her purse.

Maddie called Larry to the back door. They went outside, and she let him in the car. She felt guilty about leaving him home alone to eat with Candy, so she stopped at a drive-thru on the way home and bought him another small burger.

9

THURSDAY

Ben looked at his phone and sighed. Three a.m. He rolled onto his back and stared at the ceiling wondering who could have killed David. It played like a mantra in his mind, a constant loop of disbelief intermingled with grief. He stretched, sat up, and put his feet on the floor. The floor was cold, which meant the temperature had dropped, and he guessed rightly that Indian summer was over.

Ben put on his jeans and a shirt. As he passed his mother's bedroom, he paused at the door. Beth's bed was empty. Ben had called the foundation when he left Harlan's house, and they told him they hadn't seen Beth. A knot had formed in his stomach, and as he descended the stairs and walked to the kitchen, it returned. He went to the garage door and looked for her car as if she might be hiding somewhere in the house. He saw only his car, and the knot twisted.

Ben wondered if Maria had misunderstood Beth when she said she would be coming home that night. His mother hadn't returned any of his calls or Maria's, and that wasn't like her. Beth was a good driver and smart enough to pull off the road if she felt tired. So why hadn't she called?

Exhaustion lay on him like a shroud. His body didn't want to move, but his mind wouldn't rest. Ben didn't want to think about Beth or David, for the unavoidable pain associated with her absence and his death were tearing him apart, yet he couldn't stop thinking about them. Since he knew he wouldn't sleep, Ben made himself a cup of instant coffee in a travel mug, left a note for Maria, put on his coat, and then checked the lock on the front door before driving to David's house.

David's street had few lights and none near the house. Ben parked in the driveway behind the Escort and sat for a moment before exiting the car. The heated air dissipated quickly, forcing him outside before he was ready to leave. The wind chilled his face making him shiver as he walked to the front door.

When he got inside, Ben flipped on the light switch next to the door and looked around the room to see what the police had been up to while he was talking to Harlan. Considering how it had looked the night he came to visit David their investigation hadn't changed a thing.

Ben took off his coat and stared at the unholy mess. He wondered how long it would take to get the place cleaned up if he decided to sell. It would take a crew to wash thirty years of tar from David's cigarettes off the walls, not to mention dust, mold, and whatever else lurked underneath the plastic bags and piles of news-papers. With sadness, Ben thought of how David had lived, as a hoarder who found safety in accumulating junk, surrounding himself with useless things he treasured for reasons he alone understood.

Ben went to the second floor. David had kept it clean by sleeping downstairs. Another wave of sadness washed over Ben. His uncle had done it to please him.

He went to the first bedroom, the one David had used when he moved into the house almost thirty years ago and began opening the dresser drawers. Underwear and socks filled the top drawer of the tall dresser, some of them still creased from the packaging they came in. They had been thrown into the drawer without care. The second drawer contained button shirts still in the dry cleaner's plas-tic, and the bottom drawer held several pairs of Jordache jeans.

The closet was full of business suits David had worn when he was an associate professor at Princeton. They had wide lapels with pinstripes, and wide ties hung over the shoulders. It must have been years since he'd worn them. Why hadn't he gotten rid of them?

The top of the low dresser held photos of David's parents. The top drawer was full of bills from the early 1990s, and the second drawer held photos of David with young people, perhaps students, and some with Harlan when they graduated from college.

Ben's back began to ache, so he sat on the bed. He laid down, closed his eyes, and woke up three hours later. When he got up and sat on the edge of the bed, he heard the springboard scape something underneath the bed. Ben got on his knees, looked under the bed, and found a suitcase.

He pulled it out, put it on the bed, and then opened it. There must have been a hundred photos inside - all of one model, the girl with long, dark blonde hair he'd seen in a photo on David's bed the day he came to see him. Loose curls surrounded her head, framing her pretty face. She must have been David's muse for he captured her at every angle. It was obvious by the look on her face that she cared for him, and Ben could only surmise that David had felt the same way, so why had he never mentioned her?

As far as Ben knew, David hadn't dated much if at all. He didn't talk about women in his past or being in love with anyone, and Ben had often wondered if he was gay, but these photos were evidence that there was someone in his past, and maybe she had broken his heart so badly that he never wanted to feel that way again.

Ben checked the back of each photo for her name, but David hadn't labeled any of them. One portrait, though, was a close-up of her face surrounded by a chain of flowers with long white petals and yellow centers. Daisies.

"Was your name Daisy?" Ben asked.

The suitcase also contained an old Nikon camera in a case, which David must have used to capture each pose. Ben held it up and tried the mechanism. It still worked. He put it back into the suitcase.

Ben shut the suitcase and put it in front of the low dresser. He then explored the rest of the second floor to see what lay inside each drawer and closet, and they were all filled with old bills, clothing, and newspaper articles. Ben's eyes were too tired to go through them all, but he wanted to see why David had kept them. Reading them would be like having a conversation with David again, something Ben longed to do, especially after seeing the photos of the girl he now called Daisy.

Unfortunately, most of the articles were about the university or Fenway Manor. Ben left them where they were until he had the energy to clean them out.

It was nearly eight when Ben drove up the driveway of his home, and when he opened the garage, he saw that Beth was still away. He parked his car, lowered the garage door, went inside, and found Maria putting the teakettle on the stove.

"So, you're back," she said.

"Yes, I am." Ben took off his coat and hung it on a hook by the garage door. "Mom's not home yet?"

"I tried to call her, but it goes to voicemail."

"I'm worried," he said.

Maria glanced at Ben. "Maybe we should call the police."

"If she had been in an accident, they would have called us, but I just feel like there's something wrong."

"Then call them."

Maria's eyes were bloodshot from a lack of sleep. She held onto the edge of the island as if her life depended on it. Ben nodded, and then left her and went to the living room.

Beth had taken her car, which meant she would have taken the turnpike. He Googled the state police number with his phone. He spoke to a woman and said he thought his mother might have been in an accident. He gave her Beth's name and heard her typing.

"There have been no reports filed under the name Bethany Arntz."

"She may have pulled off the road."

He heard her typing again.

"No one has called in reporting her tags. Would you like to file a missing person report?"

Ben hesitated. Was Beth missing? The knot in his gut tightened.

"Yes, ah, no, I...ah…"

"You can do it with your local police department."

"Right, okay, I'll do that."

Ben hung up and returned to the kitchen.

"They haven't gotten any reports on her," he said. "They asked if I wanted to file a missing person's report."

"Do you think someone took her?" Maria said.

"No, not at all, I just don't know what I think anymore." He looked at Maria's troubled expression. "The woman on the phone told me I could file one with the police here so maybe I'll talk to that detective about it."

Ben sat at the island and drank the coffee Maria had put near his seat. She was chopping vegetables, slamming the knife on the cutting board with ferocity. He closed his eyes and saw his mother passed out behind the wheel of her car. He opened them again and shook his head.

As he had been concentrating on taking care of David's things, Ben had avoided thinking about the way David died, but now the timing of his mother's departure and her subsequent absence were playing on his mind. It was too coincidental, and for a moment, instead of seeing Beth in her car, he saw her behind David holding his father's rifle.

10

THURSDAY

M addie had been too tired to look at the paperwork from the safe when she got home from her dinner with Candy. They had talked for hours, and it was as if they'd never been apart. It felt good to talk to someone other than Larry.

The papers were on the kitchen table, and Maddie read them as she had her coffee the next morning. She immediately understood why he had kept them there but was still annoyed that he hadn't shared them with her when she was older.

They referred to the 1991 disappearance of her mother, Daisy. There had been a party for Maddie's birthday, and friends of her mother were waiting at the house. They helped search for her after the police left. The papers were reports Carl had sent to the FBI. Carl's desperation drove him to believe he could convince those in charge that his wife might have been kidnapped and taken across state lines, making it a federal crime. As he was unable to produce any new evidence to support his claim, the feds had referred him to his local law enforcement agency. They did, however, add Daisy's name and description to a national list of missing persons.

When Maddie turned eighteen, she had ordered a copy of the Logans Grove police report without Carl's knowledge. She found out that Harlan Monteif had been at her party along with Anna Freeman. She went to see them at Princeton, but they had little to add to Carl's account. Harlan believed the police were reluctant to give her disappearance the import it deserved because Daisy was an adult and had, perhaps, left of her own accord.

"I said to the police, 'Why would she take the dog if she intended to run away?'" Harlan said. "They blew me off with some flimsy excuse about her rights as an adult."

Anna had placed the blame on Daisy for the way the police had handled things.

"I thought it was odd that she would leave on your birthday, but then again, Daisy could be a bit flighty. It seemed logical that the police would wait before calling out the dogs, don't you think?"

Now, Maddie wondered why the police hadn't done more considering the facts at hand - the dog tied to the porch, her mother's purse left on a chair in the living room, and nothing missing from the house like a suitcase or clothing. A woman planning to leave would have taken her purse, wouldn't she?

Maybe she hid one at the old house, Maddie thought. *Maybe the dog was just a cover.*

Anger pricked at her, causing her to ask herself questions Carl Brady might have been too afraid to ponder such as what kind of person leaves their two-year-old child on her birthday? How could she leave when there were so many things yet to come - graduations, a wedding, and grandchildren? If she went away on her own, why hadn't she ever tried to contact Maddie? Would Carl have told her if Daisy had tried to see her?

Among the papers, Maddie found a sheet outlining the things Carl intended to do if the police refused to investigate Daisy's disappearance. There were names of town officials he was going to call and newspapers he hoped would help him by keeping Daisy's name in the papers. He must have worked on it during his last couple of years in the store when Maddie was in the city.

She got dressed, put on her coat, and attached Larry's leash, but the anger persisted. What kind of person does something like that? A selfish bitch is what, a sociopath, a person who left someone else with the responsibility of raising their child.

Maybe Daisy was on drugs, had gotten into trouble with the law, or had met another man. Maybe she had a criminal record. Maybe Daisy Carter wasn't even her real name when she married her dad. She had stolen the Social Security number of some dead child and used it to form a new identity. No, that was ridiculous. Maddie had known her mother's parents and had heard stories about Daisy. She wished she could ask them what they thought had happened, but they were both gone now.

Maybe, maybe, maybe. It's the maybes that will drive you crazy. While Maddie sorted the books in the store, she couldn't stop thinking about her mother. Maddie wasn't maternal. She had never felt the need to have children, though she hadn't ruled out the possibility. What if Daisy had found out that she wasn't cut out for it after the fact? She might have thought that leaving was the best thing she could do for Maddie.

Maddie went back and forth about Daisy all afternoon, and by the end of the day, she was more confused about her mother than ever. She decided it was time to go online and search for her on one of those websites that helped you find lost relatives.

Maddie bought some take-out on the way home and with more than a twinge of guilt, ordered a plain hamburger for Larry. The vet had told her to watch his weight, but he was still mourning Carl, and it broke her heart when the dog climbed into Carl's chair and groaned. He missed him so, and she was a poor substitute so she would buy him a damn hamburger if she felt like it. Besides, Larry would smell her food and he would give her that look if she didn't buy him one, too.

The house was cold and dark when she got home. She tried the light switch, and the lights didn't come on. She put her hand on the old, iron radiator and it was cold. If it got too cold, her pipes could burst, so she got on her phone and dialed the number for Carl's electrician. A woman answered.

"What type of fuse box do you have?" she asked.

"I have no idea."

"Well, you might have blown a fuse or tripped one," she said. "If it blew, you just have to replace it."

"I have no idea if my father even had a replacement."

"Well, you might not need one. Go and see what type of box you have."

Maddie thought the fuse box was in the garage, so she turned on her phone's flashlight and went outside. The garage was added to the original structure in the 1930s. It was a doublewide with two sliding doors in front and a side door across from the kitchen door. An overhang protected the area between the garage and the house. Carl had stored books in the garage - boxes, and boxes of them - and Maddie had been avoiding it since she came to live there.

Carl had used the boxes to create an aisle that ran from the side door to the other side of the garage. Another aisle was created to go to the fuse box at the center of the back wall. Maddie glanced into the boxes as she walked by. They were full of used textbooks. When Maddie got to the fuse box, she opened it.

"These don't look like fuses," Maddie said.

"He might have had to replace the old glass fuses with the plug-ins. They are like switches."

"That's what they look like."

"See if there is one that doesn't line up with the others."

"Okay."

Maddie cringed. In the city, someone else had taken care of such things, and when she was at home, Carl took care of the house. She never thought to ask him about this before he died, and now, as she held up the flashlight to look for an out of whack switch, she felt incompetent. Then she saw the switch and smiled broadly.

"I see one!"

"Flip it back until it's even with the others."

Maddie flipped the switch. She went back down the aisle to look out the door and saw that her kitchen lights were on.

"Yay!" she cried. "The lights are back on."

"Great."

"I can't believe it was that easy," Maddie said.

"I'm glad it's only a tripped fuse," the woman said. "I'm Joan, by the way. I knew your father. I'm so sorry for your loss."

"Thank you," Maddie said.

"Normally I would have to charge you for this call, but this time is for Carl."

"Oh, thank you. That means a lot to me."

"So, if you have any more problems, just give us a call, but that should be all right."

"Great. Thanks for your help."

Maddie went back to the house and looked at Larry, who was on his bed.

"That's the kind of job I want," Maddie said. "Someone calls, and you tell them how to flip a switch." Larry groaned. "Absolutely."

While she was grateful the woman hadn't charged her Maddie found it hard to believe that just telling someone how to flip their fuse would cost anything.

Maddie had never worried about money. She pulled down six figures in the city and lived a careless life. Of course, she had a

401K, and she had always meant to open a personal savings account, but never got around to it. She had enough to pay her rent, to buy a latte on the way to work, rent a movie on demand, or go anywhere she wanted to regardless of the cost. She had traveled, eaten in fancy restaurants, and bought clothes without looking at the tags. All that went bust when the hospice called to tell her that Carl was dying.

Maddie had taken money from her 401K after Carl died and opened a bank account in a local branch. She was still living as she had since coming to care for her father - stopping at drive-thrus for dinner, $5.00 coffees from the café across the street, and spending money for *on-demand* movies. She'd used her father's death as an excuse to ignore reality, and now the money in her bank account was dwindling fast.

Larry had cost her money, too. His teeth needed extensive dentistry, which had cost her a thousand dollars, but at the time she didn't even think about the money. She just wanted him to be okay.

Now, though, she understood that Larry was another impediment to her leaving Logans Grove. Wherever she went, she'd have to find a place where they allowed pets. It would also mean that he'd be alone all day, something Larry had never dealt with before.

All these things would work their way into her thinking at least once a day, and she'd slam the door on them so she could buy another take-out dinner on her way home.

When she finished eating, Maddie made a cup of tea, which she took to the living room and sat on the sofa while Larry climbed into Carl's old recliner. The laptop was on the coffee table, and as it booted up, she wondered where to start her search for Daisy Carter Brady.

She started with Google and put her mother's name in the address bar. Several pages popped up, including the Newark Star-Ledger's archives. The stories of Daisy's disappearance had been news in 1991, but the articles said nothing more than what she already knew.

Since the dog was found behind Fenway Manor, the name of its owner, Friedlander, was connected to Daisy's story. Maddie clicked on an article from 1993. It mentioned that the property had been "... transferred from Jacob Friedlander to his daughter, Bethany Friedlander. Jacob Friedlander owns Carefree Garments in New York

City. Ms. Friedlander was reluctant to share her plans for the property."

Maddie wondered if Bethany Friedlander still owned the property next door. She had never heard Carl mention them as being their neighbors and as far as she knew, none of the Friedlanders had ever lived there.

The other pages were for DNA sites that must have caught the algorithm for the search. Maddie clicked on them and discovered that one, Ancestry.com, had Daisy's name. She created an account and typed Daisy's name in the search box. Her name appeared on her Aunt Sylvia's family tree as her brother Carl's wife. Maddie's name was on the tree under Carl's. There was no leaf indicating another connection to Daisy's name.

Maddie closed her laptop and turned on the TV. After watching what she called the "Home Renovation" network, she put on the local news. The big story was about the body found behind Fenway Manor.

"The body of a man found behind Fenway Manor on King's Highway has been identified as David Friedlander, the son of the late Jacob and Linda Friedlander of Logans Grove. Police are still investigating his death."

"He was related to them," Maddie said. "Do they still own it?"

"The property on King's Highway belongs to the victim's sister, Bethany Friedlander Arntz."

"Did he just answer my question, Larry?" Maddie said.

"While David Friedlander's death is still being investigated, there is speculation that it might have been caused by a stray bullet from the woods. Though hunting season doesn't start until December, some take advantage of the mild temperatures and begin hunting illegally in the woods behind the old manor house. Police are asking you to contact them if you know of anyone who might have been in those woods early yesterday morning."

11

A s Maddie was lying in bed that night, her thoughts drifted to Candy. For years, Maddie had believed Candy had betrayed her. It had been easier than believing the boy she loved was a jerk who cared little for her and would even assault her best friend without giving it a second thought.

What was wrong with me?

All these years she and Candy could have been friends, but instead, Maddie had wasted time on people who could help her climb the ladder. Her focus had been on getting there, not on what happens after that.

Maddie hadn't discovered what her true talents were until she went to college. After being so involved in extracurricular activities through high school, she sat back in college and let others take the lead. She began to notice things and ask questions like why did her roommate buy that blouse, or when did the boy down the hall shave his head?

Maddie would share her opinions with her roommate about what she thought would be the next big thing. More often than not, Maddie was right. Her intuition for discovering the latest trends before people knew what they wanted led her into marketing. When she graduated, she lucked into a job with a small firm that led to a job at a bigger firm, and soon she was at the top of her game discerning what people were watching, and wearing, and following. She instinctively knew what caught people's attention and would exploit it.

It had worked well for her in the marketing firm, but not so much in real life. Her dogged pursuit of other people's hopes and dreams had caused her friends to grow weary of her feigned interest in their lives.

When Maddie left the city, she didn't leave one close friend behind. Even her roommate hadn't been upset when she told him she had to leave. They had been lovers, but there was no real emotional connection, so when she packed her bags, he whispered a sad goodbye in her ear, but Maddie understood that it meant nothing.

She had learned early on how to hone her focus to avoid maudlin feelings, placing disappointment in a special box at the back of her mind behind missing mothers, pets that had passed away, and friends that had betrayed her. As she had little to occupy her mind over the last six months, the tape holding the lid on the box had loosened, and some of that disappointment was wielding its way into her conscious mind. She soothed herself with food and had gained twenty pounds.

In high school, Maddie had genuinely cared about things like ecology and animal rights. She'd abandoned those things when she crossed the bridge into the city. She felt free. Her life in Logans Grove had been confining. She believed she'd spent too much time on others and that now it was time to spend it on herself.

Then life changed the rules. Her father got sick, and she was thrust into the role of caretaker. She had been unprepared for that role, and while she dealt with the responsibility, she also refused to think about what would happen when he was gone. Maddie's focus was on Carl, and her old life seemed less important. She let it all slip away and avoided thinking about what she wanted to do with the rest of her life.

After Carl died, Maddie saw the life her father led, a life of poverty and broken dreams, and feared she might be headed down the same path. Grief weighed her down. It was like living underwater for months, and now she wanted to breathe fresh air again. It was time to reconnect with her fellow man, and when Candy walked into the store, she found someone who understood what Maddie was going through.

When she met Candy at the Italian place, they were just as they'd been thirteen years ago, and it felt so good to share her grief with someone who truly cared about her. Maddie found out that Candy was selling real estate, and that led to a conversation about what Maddie might gain financially from selling both the house and the store. Maddie was thrilled by the idea and was happy that someone else was helping her make the decision.

Now, Maddie shook her head as she thought of David Friedlander's body lying in the grass.

"I'm such an idiot," she said. "Nobody's gonna buy this place."

A rotting old mansion had been bad enough, but now a body had been found on the property.

Maddie closed her eyes and imagined the zeros in her asking price slowly disappearing. If she was lucky enough to get anyone to even look at the house, she had to be prepared to take less than what she knew was fair market value. She would be what they euphemistically called a "motivated" seller.

The trick would be to find something about her house that would make it so desirable that even a dead body next door wouldn't keep someone from snatching it up. Maddie knew little of the history of the house, but she had learned a few things from her aunts. She recalled a conversation she'd had with her father's sisters, Aunts Joanie and Sylvia when they came from South Carolina to her father's funeral.

"Our house was built in 1789 by Alastair Fenway," Joanie said. "It was for his son. The boy disappeared sometime in 1790 something, so he never lived here."

"He wasn't a boy, Joanie, he was at least twenty-five or so."

"Well, whatever, this house hadn't been lived in so when Alastair got this sixteen-year-old girl pregnant, he finagled a marriage between her and his son so Alastair could bring her back to Fenway Manor. The girl lived in this house for a while."

"He had a wife," Joanie said. "She refused to have the girl in her house."

"It was a real scandal back in the day," Sylvia said.

"Didn't Alastair murder them?" Maddie asked.

"Not exactly. Alastair did shoot his wife, but *she* pushed the girl over the balcony. The girl broke her neck."

"I heard he shot his son, too," Joanie said.

"No, Joanie. Nobody ever found the son's remains."

"Yes, they did. That Friedlander guy found them. Don't you remember? It was in a Sunday supplement."

Joanie screwed up her mouth and then smiled broadly.

"I do remember that. They buried the bones next to his parents' in that cemetery behind the Presbyterian church."

"Right, now what was his name?" Sylvia asked.

"I can't remember his name. Did they say he was shot, too?"

"That must have been where I read it."

"The kids always said there was a ghost there," Maddie said.

"Well, now that would be silly, wouldn't it?" Joanie said.

Joanie went on to tell Maddie the history of her house after the Fenway family died. It had belonged to one of her father's ancestors, a hardy soul who bought it for a song back in 1900 when the mansion was still presentable.

"The people in the mansion were land rich. They had to sell the land in parcels so they wouldn't starve. The estate used to be much bigger." Joanie sighed. "When I was a kid, I wanted to live there for the rest of my life. I thought the old mansion was so romantic. I used to see myself gliding down that big old staircase in the foyer and dancing around that ballroom. It was like some northern ante-bellum fantasy."

"I found her in the garage dressed up in a set of mom's old curtains once pretending she was Scarlett O'Hara," Sylvia said.

"Don't tell her that," Joanie said. "Anyway, mom and dad decided to give Carl the house because he was willing to work at the store and he had you. I admit I was upset at first, but then I saw your father digging snow from that driveway so he could get his truck on the road. That's when I told Uncle Jim that we were moving south."

She slapped her leg and cackled along with her sister, and then they remembered they had just buried their brother.

"Sorry," they said.

"It's okay. He would have laughed, too."

Maybe Maddie could use the history as a selling point. Maybe someone with a macabre sense of humor would find it all fascinating.

She sat back, and a thought moved to the front of her mind. Had the proximity of the house put off prospective buyers, which meant the Brady's *had* to pass it down from generation to generation?

"And I'm the lucky winner," Maddie said. "The last woman standing."

Her father had loved the place. He had never lived anywhere else in his entire life. He never wanted to live anywhere else either, not even when his wife abandoned him.

Maddie didn't want to think about the Fenway family and their grisly fate. She wanted to go to sleep, but when sleep didn't come, she began to think about visiting her aunts for Thanksgiving. She could drive down there with Larry after closing the store on Wednesday. She loved them and missed them, and she was always grateful that they had laughed off the idea of a haunted Fenway Manor.

12

FRIDAY

en was able to fall asleep on Thursday night but woke up again at around 3 a.m. He left the house and drove the length of the parkway looking for Beth's car. When he came home, he went into the kitchen and found Maria sitting at the island with her head in her hands. She looked up and was upset to see how he looked.

"You have dark circles under your eyes," Maria said. He grabbed a mug out of the cabinet and was going to pour himself a cup of coffee when she got up and took the pot out of his hand. "You have to try and get some sleep."

"I slept," he said.

She sighed. "You still look tired."

"I just went up and down the parkway looking for my mother's car."

"I can fix you something to eat."

"I'm not hungry. I think I'm gonna call the police and report her missing." Ben opened the refrigerator and looked for Beth's insulin. "I wonder how much insulin she took with her."

"She was going to the city," Maria said. "Probably just enough for one day."

When Ben called the Logans Grove Police Station to report his mother as a missing person, an officer was sent to the house to take a report. Ben took him to the library, closed the door, and then they sat in chairs by the fireplace.

"The protocols have changed," Officer Kendall said. "Have you heard of Patricia's Law?"

Ben shook his head. "No."

"Simply put, we are required to take any report of a missing person without delay. There's an extensive list of questions, and we take a sample of the missing person's DNA. That DNA is added to a database of missing or unidentified persons."

"So, if she's in a hospital somewhere, you could find her through the DNA?"

"Yes. And if your mother is unconscious, whoever has her will contact local law enforcement, and they would check the database for missing persons. And since she requires medication, she will be designated as at risk."

Ben sat back and sighed.

"This makes me feel so much better."

The officer went over the list of questions with Ben. Beth's physical description, her age, the make and model of her car, and all known associates were entered into the report. The officer also asked for her hairbrush.

"How long will it take to get this out there?" Ben asked.

"I'll enter the information today. Other agencies will be able to see your mother on there today, too."

Ben walked Officer Kendall to the front door and watched him drive away. He felt drained but relieved. He went to the kitchen to tell Maria about the report, but she wasn't there. He found her resting on her bed watching TV in her bedroom, and when he knocked, she turned her head to look at him.

"They're going to put her in a database. If she's in a hospital somewhere, they'll find her."

"Oh, that's good," Maria said. "That's better than you running all over the state looking for her."

Ben went up to his room, took off his shoes, and fell onto his bed. He was asleep within minutes of his head hitting the pillow. A few hours later, the text ringtone on his phone woke him up. It was from Janet Worthington. David's body had been released.

Ben rubbed his eyes, got up, and sat on the edge of the bed. After leaving Harlan's house the day David died, Ben found his mother's address book, an old, leather-bound artifact from the sixties, in her desk and found a funeral home. He had called them, and they assured Ben that as soon as the body was released, they would take care of all the arrangements. He called them to let them know where to pick up David's body.

"If you are agreeable," the man said, "we can hold the viewing tomorrow."

Ben was agreeable, and the man again expressed his deep sympathy. He then added, "And will your mother be there?"

"I'm not sure," Ben said.

"No worries. We will have everything ready for a four o'clock viewing. I see that the deceased has chosen not to be interned in the family crypt."

"That's right."

"Very well. That's all we need for now. Your uncle will be ready for your private viewing at three."

Will your mother be there?

The question echoed in Ben's head. While he doubted his mother would want to go to David's funeral, she might do so for the sake of appearances. He hit her number on his phone, and when it rang, he heard the muffled sound of Michael Bublé's "Haven't Met You Yet," the ringtone for his mother's phone. He followed it into her room. He found her phone in the drawer of the end table next to her bed.

"Shit," he said. "She left it here."

Ben was furious. Beth never forgot her phone. She had to have left it on purpose so no one could find her.

He took the phone downstairs so Maria would see it when she woke up. Before he put it on the island, he scrolled through the calls and found that Beth had called David Tuesday night around ten. That was late for her, and he wondered what they had talked about.

Ben's phone rang, and he saw Janet Worthington's number.

"Ben," she said. "Do you have some time this afternoon to come in and answer some questions?"

The hairs on Ben's neck prickled. He remembered Harlan's admonition.

"What's this about?"

"I'm just following up on things we talked about before. I'd like to get some more details."

He put the phone on his chest and exhaled sharply. Should he call Harlan? Ben didn't feel nervous about talking to the detective, but Harlan was adamant. Still, he could always say he didn't have much time because he had to be someplace else.

"Okay," he said. "I'll stop by on my way to the funeral home."

A lie, but one they would believe considering the circumstances.

Maria was sleeping when he left the house. He put a note by the phone and told her he might not be home for dinner. Half an hour later, Ben was sitting across a table from the detective. She had her notebook open, and she offered him a sad smile.

"You look beat," Janet said.

"I haven't been sleeping."

"I saw that you filed a missing person report."

"She's been gone too long."

"Just so you know, we already put an APB out on her."

Janet noted Ben's shocked expression.

"Why?"

She looked at her notes.

"Because she took off the day your uncle was killed, and you mentioned your father's rifle when I interviewed you."

Ben's expression hardened. "She didn't kill him. She just didn't like him."

"You said you don't remember what happened to that gun," she said.

"No."

"You've never seen it around the house?"

"Not since I was seven."

He lowered his eyes and stared at the file on her desk. He thought of the phone Beth left in her end table.

"My mother is not a killer."

"But it is weird that she's disappeared," Janet said.

Ben's face was red. "She's diabetic. For all we know, she could have gone into shock and was taken to a hospital."

"Then they will find her, but listen, Ben, this doesn't look good for her. I've talked to a lot of people, and they all agree on one thing – she hated David Friedlander."

"The news said it could have been a stray bullet from a hunter," he said.

"It's a theory." She leaned forward and put her hand on his arm. "Tell me why Beth didn't like David."

Ben shifted as he pulled his arm away.

"She was jealous when my grandparents adopted him."

"But that was what, over fifty years ago?"

"She was six when they brought him home."

"Yeah, but people usually get over something like that when they get older. Why did Beth hold onto it for so long?"

"I don't know." He sounded weary. "Her father didn't think she could run the company. It pissed her off, and then David got sick. They did everything they could to help him so he would be able to take over the business even though she ran things while they took care of David."

"Which was totally unfair. Beth must have resented him terribly."

Ben kept his eyes away from hers.

"And did your grandparents expect Beth to take care of him after they were gone?"

"I don't know."

"She must have thought of him as a burden."

Beth had, but Ben kept this to himself. No need to add fuel to Janet's fire.

"He took care of himself," Ben said.

"Was he still on medication?" Janet asked.

Ben nodded. "Sometimes he would forget, but I always checked on him."

"When he forgot, did he do things that embarrassed your mother?"

Ben screwed up his mouth. He stood and buttoned his coat.

"Look, my mother and my uncle didn't get along, but she had no motive to kill him."

Janet stood. "I disagree. I think David was a thorn in her side all their lives and she had had enough. Did you know he had a separate trust that would revert to her upon his death? And it didn't matter if he was murdered or not. Your mother would inherit that money."

"She didn't know about that trust," Ben said.

"What are you talking about?"

"I spoke to the man who arranged it. He said my mother didn't know about it."

Ben was satisfied by the perplexed look on her face. She hadn't known that.

"Besides, my mother has more money than God. She wouldn't kill for money."

"Then who gets that money?" she asked. Ben was quiet. She exhaled sharply. "That APB is out there now along with your missing persons. We will find her."

"That's what I want too."

Ben went to his car and sat for a few minutes. Memories of the arguments between Beth and David played in his mind; the old hurts rehashed over and over until one of them would storm off and slam doors while a young Ben sat at the top of the stairs. She would always insist that they talk in the living room, and then the fight would ensue.

Ben tried to remember what they fought about, but he was young and didn't understand most of it. Why would David even come to the house in the first place? After Ben's grandmother died, there was little reason for David to come there, especially when he knew Beth hated him.

A chill ran through his body. He closed his eyes, but then all he could see was Beth raising a rifle and aiming it at David's back. He opened them and started the car.

As he drove home, the numbness he felt on and off since losing David returned and comforted him. For a moment, he was able to forget his loss. A few moments later, something else mingled with the numbness, and it took him a moment to understand what it was. Ben was an introvert who was happiest when he was alone, as his mother had been for most of her life. He never thought he'd *need* anyone, but now he felt lonely, and the reality of that revelation was humbling.

Ben didn't want to go home, so he stopped by The Ugly Badger for a beer. The tavern had been at the crossroads of King's Highway and SR 635 since 1730. It had begun life as a coach stop and inn, but only one building remained, and it had been refurbished many times since then. The historical society had supervised the work, which had maintained and strengthened the original brick walls, windows, and shutters. The inside still looked as it had when a German named Shultz built it. It had seen the likes of George Washington and Benjamin Franklin and had survived the Revolution and the War Between the States. Candlelight and violin music provided ambiance, and the hostess always greeted him with a smile.

"Hi, Ben," she said.

"Can I sit in Uncle Dave's booth?" he asked.

She turned away from him for a second.

"It's free."

She held out the menu, but he shook his head.

Ben walked to the last booth, one of several lining the front wall underneath the windows. Opposite the booths was a bar the length of the room that separated them from a large room with tables.

David had introduced him to The Ugly Badger and to the booth where he showed Ben the initials carved into the wood.

"That's ALF," David said. "Alastair Louis Fenway."

"You said he died in 1795," Ben said. "That would make this table over two hundred years old."

"Older than that. It was made in 1730. They kept the tabletop when they refurbished the place. The historical society insisted." David's eyes had glowed with excitement. "Imagine Ben, sitting where Alastair Fenway sat."

Now, Ben ordered a beer and ran his finger over the initials. Would anyone other than Ben remember why those letters were here or who made them now that David was gone? The thought was another layer of sad added to a dismal day, and Ben drank his beer quickly.

He ordered another and nursed that one while he contemplated his future. He would have to decide what to do with David's house. He would have to decide whether he would teach. A few days ago, there would have been no question about it; now, he felt at loose ends.

Where was his mother? Why hadn't anyone found her yet? She had a car with tags and a driver's license. How could she simply disappear?

During times like this, Ben would have gone to David. He thought of stopping by Harlan's house but didn't feel like seeing him. He always felt he had to match Harlan's enthusiasm for life. He didn't have it in him to rise to the occasion today.

When he finished his beer, Ben felt a bit buzzed, so he called for an Uber to take him home. He told the hostess he was leaving his car, and she made a note of it for the owner.

13

FRIDAY

When she woke up on Friday morning, Maddie gazed around her bedroom. She sighed as she thought of spending the day at the store when what she wanted to do was clean out the house so she could sell it. She was eager to get on with her life, and that meant getting rid of the things that tied her down.

At four, the weekenders were still strolling past her store when Maddie turned the "Open" sign around. They had kept her busy all day, which made time pass quickly, but she had already decided to visit Candy at her office after work. She closed the store and drove to Ross Carpaza Realty.

Maddie had Larry with her, but since the real estate agency didn't offer food, she thought it would be fine to bring him inside. They walked through the double glass doors and into the lobby where a slender black woman sitting behind a counter greeted her. Her nameplate read, "Trinidad Whalen."

"Hello." Her soft Jamaican accent and big smile were soothing, and Larry must have liked it too for when Trini came from behind the counter, he wagged his tail so hard it hurt Maddie's leg. Trini came to him and stroked his head. "Oh, he's beautiful."

"Thank you," Maddie said.

"He's an older gentleman, isn't he?" she bent over and kissed Larry's head. "And he's so friendly." Trini stood up. "So, what brings you here today?"

"Is Candy here."

"She's right down the hallway." She bent over to Larry. "Follow me."

Maddie followed Trini with Larry beside her.

"So, what's your name?" Trini asked.

"Maddie Brady."

They went to a door at the end of the hallway, and Trini stuck her head inside.

"You have a visitor, Ms. Burke. Maddie Brady is here."

"Oh, thank you, Trini," Candy said.

Trini stepped aside so Maddie could pass, and then took the leash from Maddie's hand.

"He can stay with me while you talk," Trini said.

Candy got up and came to Maddie.

"Hi."

"Hey. I've been thinking about what we talked about the other night. I want to sell the house and the store."

Candy grinned.

"Great, well, then let's sit down."

Maddie looked around the tiny office. Candy went to her seat behind the desk while Maddie sat on the metal folding chair in front of it.

"So, what do we do first?" Maddie asked.

"Well, there are things we need to do like a title search and I would want an inspection. It's an older house, which means there might be leaks in the roof or bad pipes, things like that."

"I think my dad took pretty good care of the place."

"Oh, I'm sure he did, but you never know with an old house."

"Who pays for the inspection?" Maddie asked.

"The seller, but you can always postpone the payment until the close of escrow."

"I feel like an idiot."

"Why?" Candy asked.

"I know nothing about this stuff. The other night, the lights went out and I didn't know that all I had to do was flip a switch in the fuse box to get them back on."

"Well, you lived in an apartment for a long time. You had no reason to know."

"Yeah, you're right, but that doesn't make me feel any better."

Candy folded her arms on the desk and leaned forward.

"Maddie, this is a big step. You don't have to worry about what to do to sell your house. That's why I'm here. All you have to do today is sign a listing agreement. In fact, why don't you take it home and read it? Go online and do your homework. You can sign it when you're ready and then we'll get started."

Maddie's shoulders relaxed. "That sounds good." She exhaled sharply. "So, what about the store?"

"I didn't look at it closely when I stopped by the other day, but you shouldn't have to invest that much in fixing it up. You'll need to paint it and maybe rearrange the bookcases. Whoever goes in there will redo it anyway so I wouldn't spend a lot on it. We have to show its potential, though, so we'll have to use our imaginations."

"My father told me he owned the building and the land."

"That's one of the nice things about Artisan Row. All those shops were individually owned when the place was built in 1900."

"I'm worried about the Fenway place," Maddie said. "It's bad enough by itself, but that guy was murdered there, too."

"I wouldn't worry about the house," Candy said. "They're holding a meeting in a couple of weeks to move forward with the condemnation of the place."

"They've done that before. It always gets postponed."

"I looked up the court files. Every time the town voted to condemn, an Order to Stay Proceedings would stop it from happening. There was no order filed this time. I think that means they're going to go through with it."

"Really? Oh, that would be nice." Maddie bit her lip. "It's owned by the Friedlanders."

"I know," Candy said.

"I wonder why they didn't tear it down years ago."

"I remember standing at the counter in your father's store, and we'd see her pass by. She always gave me the creeps."

"My dad used to say she had hard eyes. I was glad she didn't come into the store."

Candy opened a drawer and pulled out a listing agreement. She slid it across the desk.

"Take it home and read the fine print," she said. "I can come by the store, and we can talk about it."

"Okay. I'm good with that," Maddie said.

"So, what will you do after you sell?"

"I thought I would go back to New York, but now I'm not sure," Maddie said.

"Where else would you go?" Candy asked.

"South Carolina, or maybe New Mexico. The southwestern style appeals to me."

"That's far away, though. You've always lived on the east coast."

"To tell the truth, it's mostly about what Larry wants." Maddie smiled. "I'm not sure he could travel so far." Maddie looked at Candy's nameplate. "So, how much do you think I can get for the store?"

"Let's take a look at it. It's part of Artisan Row, which is a big plus." Candy started searching on her laptop and pulled up the county website. "There are no liens against it, and your father always paid his taxes, so nothing's due on it until the first of next year. The appraisal from last year was for 152K, but I think we can get more than that because of its size and location on the Row."

Maddie's mouth gaped.

"You're kidding," Maddie said.

Candy shook her head.

"That strip brings in people from the city every weekend. It's a gold mine."

"Wow. I had no idea." Maddie bit her lip. "Do I have to close it to sell it?"

Candy shook her head again.

"It'll be better if they see customers coming in."

"Right. Then we'd have to show it on Saturdays when things are busy."

"Great."

Maddie smiled. "I feel good about this." She stood. "Then I guess I'll see you when?"

"Read the agreement, and then call me. I can come over whenever you want."

Candy stood and came around her desk. She hugged Maddie. They walked to the lobby and stood in front of Trini's counter.

"Thanks for watching him," Maddie said to Trini.

"He's been a very good boy," Trini said.

Maddie called Larry to her. When he came around the counter, she picked up his leash, and then she turned to Candy.

"I'll call you."

"Take the weekend."

Candy returned to her desk and ran a search on Maddie's house.

Google bought up several pages regarding the history of the building that had once been a part of the Fenway estate.

A man named John Brady had purchased the property in 1900. It had come with an acre of land. There was a photo of John and his wife standing in front of the house that looked remarkably similar to the house of today. John was a blacksmith, and at that time, it had a barn.

She found another photo in an archival database for the Newark Star-Ledger. The photo, taken in 1935, showed an attached garage that had replaced the barn. The owners at the time were Burt and Georgiana Brady.

After printing out the pages for Maddie's file, Candy realized it was almost five, and shut down her computer. She put it in the laptop case her mother had given her for her new job, grabbed her coat off the hook beside her desk, and headed for the lobby. Trini was putting on her coat when Candy walked by.

"Have a good weekend," Trini said.

"You, too," Candy said.

She walked out the double doors and into the parking lot. The sun was setting, and the temperature had dropped. Candy ran to her car and threw her stuff inside before putting on her coat. She hated this time of year and the random highs and lows that made it hard to know what to wear. No wonder everybody got sick just before the holidays.

Candy had always wanted to move south, to Miami or South Beach, but the accident had put off her dreams. Now, though, she had a real estate license, and the old dream of getting out of the frozen north seemed more like a possibility than a dream. After she sold Maddie's properties, she would have a better idea of her financial situation, and that would help her decide what to do next.

Candy shivered as she put the key into the ignition. As she tried to start the car for the third time, she prayed for it to start, and it did.

"Thank you, God," she said.

Her relationship with a higher power had grown over the last few years, but she didn't think of herself as religious. She didn't go to church, but she always gave God credit for the good things that happened in her life. Candy knew, though, that their relationship might never be more than it was right now and she believed God was okay with that.

As she pulled onto King's Highway, she decided to pass by

Maddie's house before it got dark. She was pleased when her hands didn't start shaking. Maybe she had conquered her fear at last.

Traffic through Artisan Row was moving slowly as the shops closed and everyone was pulling out into the street. Candy glanced at The Daisy Chain, Maddie's bookstore, and shook her head. The store had no charm whatsoever and compared to the other shops, whose artistic owners had embellished them for maximum effect, it looked like a neglected child. A coat of paint and a new door would do wonders for its appearance.

When she reached the end of the strip, traffic moved faster, and soon she was parked in front of Maddie's house. She left the car running when she got out and walked up the driveway. She avoided looking in the direction of the old mansion. There were no lights on in the house, and Maddie's car wasn't in the driveway.

The house was about a half-acre from the road. The left side faced King's Highway. The driveway went past the front of the house and ended at the garage. The rest of the property was wooded. A stonewall marked the property line between the house and the mansion, and it had a gap at the center that used to have a wooden gate. Candy dictated a note into her phone to ask about the gate.

The colonial style home had one floor and a loft. The kitchen door had a window and faced the garage. There was a small octagonal window on top for the loft, and three windows on the bottom floor – one in the kitchen and two to the right of the main entrance in the living room.

She walked to the front door and examined it with her phone flashlight. It needed a power wash, maybe even paint, but it looked solid. The window and door frames had peeling paint, the bushes under the windows on each side of the door needed trimming, and the stones that served as a walkway to the front door were almost buried in the dirt.

It was an unusual house, but she might find a buyer if she emphasized the historical significance of the property.

"Be positive," her instructor had said. "Always say you *will* find a buyer, not that you *might* find a buyer."

"I *will* find a buyer," Candy said aloud.

She smiled, turned to walk back to her car, and that's when she saw him standing near the gap in the stonewall. Her heart pounded, her hands shook, and her mind froze as he smiled at her. So much for conquering her fear. But as Candy stared at him, he didn't look frightening; he looked gorgeous. They stared at each other for a moment, and then she closed her eyes and willed herself to speak.

"Go away," she said softly.

She opened her eyes to see the man's smile fade, and she thought he looked disappointed. He seemed oddly human, and she felt curious about him. He moved away from the wall, and she had the urge to call him back. She raised her hand but remained silent.

Candy was thrilled. She had faced up to him, ordered him to go, and he had obeyed her. She had control over him, and it made her feel powerful.

14

As Ben looked at the peaceful countenance of his Uncle Dave, he smiled. Seeing him in the casket wasn't as bad as he'd anticipated, but when he touched David's arm, it felt as if he was touching a piece of wood. He quickly took his hand away.

Maria had contacted his mother's caterers so David's mourners could come to the house after the service. He knew Beth would have a fit when she found out he'd brought them there, but he didn't care. He'd deal with her...later.

Harlan arrived at the funeral home with Anna Freeman as soon as the doors opened. They embraced Ben and offered their condolences while others filled the chairs behind them.

"Don't be surprised at how many people show up," Harlan said. "David was well-liked."

"I miss him," Anna said. "The students he helped with research miss him, too."

"He'd love to hear that," Ben said. "He wanted to be cremated so we won't be going to the cemetery. If you want to come to my house, we'll have food."

"We'll be there," Harlan said. He glanced around the room. "Is your mother coming?"

Ben shrugged. "I still haven't heard from her."

"Since when?" Harlan asked.

"Since Wednesday. I filed a missing person report."

"It's odd that she hasn't called you," Anna said.

"That doesn't sound like Bethany," Harlan said.

"No. It doesn't."

Harlan leaned on his cane with two hands.

"How are you holding up, Ben?"

"Not so good. I still can't believe he's gone."

Anna patted his shoulder.

"It will take some time."

Ben nodded and then stepped aside so a mourner could go to the casket.

"Why don't we let you go for now," Harlan said. "We'll see you at the house."

"Thanks for coming," Ben said.

Ben took a seat in the first row of chairs and watched people come to the casket, sigh, and then walk away. He wished he could hide in a corner until it was over, but David had no one else to stand for him, so Ben stayed in the chair while people came to offer him their condolences.

The service was short, and Ben gave a eulogy that painted his Uncle Dave as a kind, gentle man who loved his nephew and his country's history dearly. He kept watching the door, but when the service ended without Beth's appearance, he told everyone that they were welcome to stop at the house. After the mourners had gone, the funeral director approached Ben.

"We will have the urn ready by Wednesday. Would you like me to have it sent to your house?"

"Yes, please."

"It was a lovely service," the man said. "And again, I'm so sorry for your loss."

"Thank you."

The man left Ben alone with David. He approached the casket and looked at David's hands. The last time he saw them, they'd been holding a pen and madly scribbling something. He'd forgotten to ask Harlan about it. He made a mental note to ask him when he saw him at the house.

Ben's eyes went from David's hands to his face. He looked as if he might open his eyes and say something.

How can he be dead?

It still didn't make sense to Ben. He reached out to touch David's hand but pulled it away. He wanted to remember David as a warm-blooded human being, so he grasped the side of the casket instead and took a deep breath.

"I hope this is what you wanted. I hope I did this right for you. I'm sorry my mom was so hard on you. God, there are so many things…I just miss you so much."

Ben started to weep again. He wiped his face with his hand. He tried to stop the tears so his eyes wouldn't be red when he arrived at the house.

"Don't let anyone know how you really feel." It was Beth's voice in his head. "Never give them the advantage."

Ben pushed himself away from the casket, and after one last look, he left his uncle for the last time.

Maria had wanted to go to the funeral to be with Ben, but she had to supervise the caterers. She felt she had let Ben down by missing the funeral, but now, as she led the first guests into the living room, she felt tired and raw from lack of sleep and too much anxiety. Maria tried to smile and remain polite, but if one person said the wrong thing, she might take their head off.

When Ben came into the house, she was in the kitchen supervising the staff they'd hired to serve the guests. His mind had been vacillating between worry and grief for the past two days. He'd have to choose which one he'd give himself to today, and since he had just left his uncle's dead body, he chose grief. He'd let the police worry about Beth.

Ben was glad to see Harlan and Anna when he went into the living room and braced himself for the onslaught of condolences from the same people who'd already given them at the funeral home. Once the initial press of bodies had subsided, he went to Harlan to ask him about the letter David had left with him.

"I don't recall that," Harlan said.

"We talked about it on Wednesday. You said Uncle Dave brought it to you the night before."

"Sorry," Harlan said. "I must have confused it with something else. I was a bit overwhelmed when I heard the news, so it's possible."

"Okay. Well, yeah, I know the feeling." Ben stood back on his heels. "Maybe you can check your safe again, and I can get it the next time I come over."

"Yes, I can do that," Harlan said.

"Thanks." Ben smiled wanly. "Well, I've got to make the rounds. Thanks for coming."

After he left them, Anna turned to Harlan.

"What was he talking about?" she asked.

"Nothing," he said.

She looked up at him and into his eyes.

"I know your lying. I can always tell."

Harlan closed his eyes.

"It was a long rambling letter he'd addressed to Ben."

"So, why didn't you give it to him?"

"David was Ben's hero. He doesn't need to know."

"Harlan." Anna stared up at him, and then her eyes widened. "Is it what we always…"

"Yes."

"Oh, dear." Anna's face turned pale. "After all these years." She held onto Harlan's arm, and then looked him in the eye. "He wanted Ben to know. You have to give it to him."

"Ben's got enough on his plate."

"That's not for you to decide. You can't keep this from him."

"I'll give it to him…someday."

"You'd better, or I will tell him about it myself."

"You don't mean that. Let me handle it, please."

Anna took her hand away.

"Harlan. Ben deserves…"

"Stop. He's coming this way."

Ben walked by them, and then Anna glared at Harlan.

"I mean it, Harlan. I will talk to him." She leaned closer. "If David gave you that letter, then you as his counsel must give it to Ben as per his wishes."

"I will, Anna, but only after I feel he can handle it."

"But who can handle something like that?" She shook her head. "You are the most stubborn man I've ever met." She folded her arms. "What gives you the right to decide when he's ready?"

"I know him."

"Well, I know him too," she said. "And I think he can handle it."

"Well, it's not up to you." Harlan grabbed her arms. "David gave it to me. That's what gives me the right to decide."

He let go of her, and her lip was trembling.

"I've never seen you this way."

"I'm sorry," he said. "I just think that until we know what happened to his mother, we have to put this aside."

"Very well." She folded her arms again. "He is going through a lot right now."

"So," Harlan said. "I guess we'd better start mingling or people will talk."

Harlan left her to join some of the students who had come to pay their respects, and Anna watched him talk to them as he had talked to so many young people over the years. She watched Ben and admired the way he, too, handled people. She remembered David at that age and recalled the first time she met him.

Anna was the dean's secretary when David Friedlander walked into his office. He was seventeen and about to graduate with his bachelor's degree, and he wanted to talk to the dean about his options. She smiled and told him that there were others he could consult and took a list of names from her drawer.

"But my father told me to see the dean," David said.

"I know, David, but I'm sure they can help you with any questions you might have."

David had looked at her and tilted his head.

"My father said I shouldn't take no for an answer."

Anna smiled at the memory. He hadn't said it the way other young men had when they showed up at her desk demanding to see the dean, too. He was mimicking his father, a man Anna was well acquainted with, for he was one of those who demanded an audience with the dean, and David's lack of confidence was endearing.

David was still so innocent back then, not at all like the man he would become - a charmer who had a certain young lady wrapped around his finger.

Tears stung her eyes. David had been bright and full of hope and was too smart for his own good. Anna felt the tears rolling down her cheeks now and took a tissue from a box on a table in the foyer. She went to the powder room and sat while she cried for David and all those whose lives he had affected

15

SUNDAY

The house was quiet the next morning when Ben woke up. He got out of bed and opened his bedroom door hoping to hear his mother talking to Maria, but heard nothing. He put on a pair of sweatpants and a T-shirt before going to the kitchen.

Maria was sitting at the island sipping her coffee and resting her head in her hand when he came in. Ben poured himself a cup of coffee and sat across from her.

"Did you sleep at all?" he asked. Maria kept her eyes down as she shook her head. "And you haven't heard anything from her?" She looked up, her bloodshot eyes lingering on his face for a moment, and then on her coffee.

"No," she whispered.

"I'm gonna call the cops again."

Maria sat back in her chair and ran her hand through her thick, brown hair.

"What if she wanted to disappear?"

Ben narrowed his eyes.

"Did she say something to you?"

"No, it's just that she's never done anything like this before."

"Mom wouldn't leave this house or the business."

"But what if she did something…"

Ben gripped his mug.

"That's what the cops think."

Maria's eyebrows rose.

"They do?"

"They put out an APB on her. That's something they do when they want other police in the state to look for her."

"I watch Law & Order," Maria said.

"She hated him, Maria. Everybody knew it, and they told the police."

"Everybody doesn't know her."

"Do we?" Ben drained his coffee and watched her biting her lip. He leaned forward. "Do you know where she put my dad's rifle?"

Maria sat back and looked down her nose at him.

"I haven't seen it since your father was alive."

"You were there the day he died. You saw her take it out of her bedroom closet. You must have seen where she put it."

Maria exhaled sharply, and then looked at the kitchen door.

"I remember she was in the garage."

"That shed in the garage with the padlock on it," Ben said.

Maria looked up at her mug.

"I don't know where the key is."

"But if you had to guess?"

Maria screwed up her mouth, and then looked him in the eye.

"That gold keychain with her initials, the one you gave her for Christmas when you were a boy."

"Her car keys are on that keychain." Ben glanced toward the kitchen door. "Then I'll have to see if I can break it off."

Ben got up, put on a jacket, and went out the kitchen door into the garage.

"Dear Lord," Maria prayed. "Please let it be there. Please let him find the rifle."

The shed was on the right side of the garage, and even from a distance, Ben saw that the padlock was open. He ran to the shed, took it off, and let the door swing open. There was no rifle inside, but there was a box of 30-30 Winchester bullets on the floor. Ben picked it up, slid it open, and noticed the spaces between the bullets.

"But they could have been used twenty years ago," he said.

There was a lighter, oval-shaped spot on the floor in the dust. Something had been taken away.

He closed the shed door and looked around the garage for another place she might have stored the gun, but this space, like everything else Beth Arntz owned, was immaculate, and there were no nooks or crannies large enough to conceal a long gun. Ben was thinking about the attic when he heard the kitchen door open.

"It's not there," he said.

"Then she put it somewhere else," Maria said.

He shoved his hands into his jacket pockets.

"But there is a box of bullets in there, and some were missing," he said.

"That still doesn't mean anything."

"I'm gonna look in the attic."

Ben walked past her and up the stairs to the second floor. He stopped at his mother's bedroom door and then went to the closet. None of his father's things remained, and Beth's clothes filled the entire space.

The old house had a true attic, the door to which was at the end of the hallway. Behind the door was a staircase that held small items Beth had meant to take up there such as photo albums and Christmas gifts Ben had given her that weren't quite what she wanted. He frowned when he saw them there, but went past them and up to one of two places in the house that Beth hadn't organized.

It was the typical clutter of family memorabilia, castoff toys, and trunks of clothing his great-grandparents were loath to part with after moving into the big house. As Ben scanned the area, he knew that Beth wouldn't have put the gun up here because he, as a child, would often go to the attic when he was bored. She would have kept the rifle under lock and key.

The other place Beth hadn't organized was the basement. It had been her grandfather's place to hide whenever he wanted to be alone, and her father's after great-grandpa passed away. Beth had no interest in going down there, and neither had Ben once his grandpa died.

Ben went to the other door in the kitchen that led to the basement. As he descended the steps, he flipped the switch, and light bulb fixtures lit the way to the furnace. He stared at all the discarded things that hadn't been touched in years and recalled David telling him about how he and his father had bonded over hammering nails into large blocks of wood.

"I didn't really like carpentry," David said. "But he was so happy when he showed me how to do it that I just let him think I liked it, too."

It was her father's place, and Ben couldn't see his mother putting the gun down there. No, it was more like Beth to have it where she could see it every day, or imagine it behind a locked door.

Ben went back to his room, took a shower, and got dressed. Maria was in the kitchen wiping down the counters when he came downstairs and put on his coat.

"I'm gonna stop by the police station to see if I can get a copy of the medical examiner's report."

Maria looked over her shoulder at him.

"Don't tell them what you're thinking, Ben."

"They already think she did it," Ben said. He came to her and gave her a peck on the cheek. "I can't make it any worse." He backed away and took his keys from his jeans pocket. "I'll call if I'm going to be out late."

Ben drove to the police station and asked for a copy of the medical examiner's report. The woman behind the counter printed one out, charged him for each page, and also gave him the keys to David's house.

"Does this mean the investigation is over?" he asked.

"No. It just means they've finished going through the house, and Detective Worthington thought you'd need them."

Ben looked at the report before leaving the lobby. The M.E. had determined that David was shot from behind, nothing new there, and believed that the caliber of the bullet was similar to a 30-30 Winchester. The hairs on the back of Ben's neck rose, and his hands shook. He ran out of the police station and got into his car.

He smacked the steering wheel several times. Beth went missing the day David died. His father's rifle was missing from the shed. She had hated David. He couldn't keep denying the truth any longer – his mother had killed her brother.

Had she followed David to the old mansion, or had Beth known he was going there and lay in wait for him? They had talked the night before. Had she threatened him, or was David completely unaware of what was about to happen?

As the scenes played out in Ben's mind, he wanted to get far away from the police, so he left the parking lot and drove to the crumbling manor house on King's Highway. He parked near the end of the driveway and got out so he could look at the place where David died.

The cleanup crew had left a stake in the ground where the yellow crime scene tape had been. The woods were a few feet away, which is why the police had speculated he might have been killed by a hunter's stray bullet, an idea that still offered Ben some hope.

Ben stared at the ground and thought of David lying there, his blood flowing on the ground he had held so dear. He felt his emotions welling up, left the spot, and walked toward the house.

The porch was leaning to one side, and the paint clung to the wood in patches. The windows had been broken by kids who came there after school, and the balconies on the second floors had fallen off leaving gaping holes where the French doors had been. Piles of wood and glass littered the ground beneath them. The place reeked of decay and neglect, a sad fate for a grand old house that had once seen the likes of General George Washington.

"He came to see Alastair Fenway," Uncle Dave told Ben once when they were sitting at his kitchen table. "He wanted Alastair to aid the war effort. He would act as an intermediary for the spies using King's Highway to get to Philadelphia." David had squinted and put his face close to Ben's. "Alastair had seen men die when he fought during the French and Indian War. He was just thirteen, your age, but a hardy lad. Unlike most people who built houses back then, he had them dig a cellar, and when Washington asked for his help, he had a tunnel dug going from the basement into the woods so spies could come and go without notice."

Ben wondered why this place had never been designated a historic landmark. It had been David's dream, but it belonged to Beth, and she would never do anything that would have made David happy.

Ben wandered along the edge of the house until he came to the front, and then he saw someone turning into the driveway of the house next door. He had forgotten that people still lived there.

"Alastair built that house for his son," David told him one day when he and eleven-year-old Ben were standing in the front yard of Fenway Manor. "He wanted to keep Derek close and had even planned to build a house for his future grandchildren, but he died before it could happen." David's wistful expression turned to sadness as he gazed at the house. "It was sold in 1900 when the owners needed money."

"Who lives there now?" Ben asked.

A shadow passed over David's face, and he looked toward King's Highway.

"I...I don't know them."

How different David's life might have been if he'd been able to restore the manor house.

Ben drove to David's house, and Harlan's car was gone. For a second, Ben thought about breaking into Harlan's house to see if he could find that letter but dismissed the thought immediately. He'd get the letter one day. Harlan would have to let him have it because as executor of David's estate, Ben could bring it up in court.

Ben hadn't been in David's house since he'd found the photos under David's bed. He leaned against the front door and sighed. He didn't feel like going inside. He didn't feel like doing anything. His lack of motivation was killing him, but he knew it was just his body's way of dealing with the stress he'd been under.

How long does one grieve? It wasn't like a switch you could turn off until you were able to take care of all the things that required your attention. No. There was no way to bypass grief, and as he realized this, he walked inside and assessed the current situation.

The smell of cigarettes still hung in the air. The walls would have to be washed along with every other surface in the house. The old plastic bags and newspapers would have to be recycled, and the electronic debris David collected would have to be sent to a special recycling facility. The sofa was worn and sagged in the middle, its cushions crushed and stained. The plaid recliner's footrest was wrapped in duct tape. It was all terribly sad.

The smell got to him, so Ben opened the windows and let in the crisp, autumn air. It was windy, and the curtains billowed. He let the cold wash over him like a bath, washing away the stench of his uncle's despair. It invigorated him, giving him the boost that he needed.

Ben went to the kitchen and got a garbage bag out of the cabinet under the sink. He began to throw everything on the counters into the bag. As one filled, he grabbed another, until the counters were free of clutter. He then did the same with the end tables and chairs in the living room, placing the piles of newspapers on the floor, and shoving the plastic grocery bags into a garbage bag. He then carried the newspapers to the outside bin for collection.

David didn't have cleaning supplies so Ben would have to bring some the next time he came by. He washed his hands with plain water and then locked up the house.

It was late afternoon, and he didn't feel like going home. It was Sunday, which meant football games were on TV. The Ugly Badger would be full of sports fans. He sat in his car for a moment before turning the key and heading for home.

16

SUNDAY / MONDAY

Maddie rang up another sale and took the next customer in line. She loved Sundays. The store was filled with customers and the time flew by.

At five, Maddie put Larry in the car and headed for home. As she drove down King's Highway, she thought about the boxes of textbooks in the garage and sighed because she knew how they had gotten there. Her father always fell for a hard-luck story and would take them back from kids who knew they were no longer in use. Now she would have to find a way to get rid of them.

When she got home, she fed Larry, put a frozen pizza in the oven, and then searched online for ideas regarding outdated textbooks. Some suggested putting them in front of the store in a "free" books box, while others suggested donating them to the library. She settled on putting them on the sidewalk in front of the store.

Larry was groaning as he went down on his bed. The vet said he probably had arthritis and there was little they could do for him. He suggested that a hot water bottle in the evening might help, or maybe give him the doggie version of glucosamine and chondroitin. She would have to look for some at the pet store the next time she bought his food.

Maddie had been in such a funk for so long that she'd been able to ignore the reality that Larry was getting older and would most likely die sooner rather than later. Now, the thought hit her hard. He was her last connection to her dad, his closest companion before

Maddie came to live there, and when Larry was gone, she would truly be alone. Should she consider his mortality while making important decisions about her own life such as the pet policy of her future home? Or should she stay in the house until Larry was ready to shake off his mortal coil?

Maddie walked over to Larry and stroked his head noting the gray around his snout and eyes. He seemed to smile as she ran her hand over his pate content to be alive and not wanting more than some attention once in a while.

Carl had always had a dog. He preferred them to humans, and now she understood why. They didn't require protestations of love or pledges of eternal devotion. They simply asked that you feed them, give them a warm place to sleep, and treat them with kindness.

Maddie remembered the little dog they'd owned while she was growing up. It was a Cairn Terrier named Ginger, a sweet little dog that had followed Maddie around when she came home from school. Ginger died when Maddie was fourteen, and Maddie had cried for days. Carl made her a PB&J sandwich, sat with her while she ate, and remarked that he had gotten Ginger just before Maddie was born.

"Didn't you tell me once that Ginger belonged to Mom?" Carl's face darkened. "I'm sorry, Dad."

"Nothing to be sorry about," he said. "She did belong to her."

"Do you think Mom will ever come back?"

Carl shrugged, and Maddie finished her sandwich before going to her room and crying on her bed.

Now, as Maddie stroked Larry, her mother came into her mind. Her previous search for anything about Daisy had gleaned little in the way of useful information. Daisy had disappeared before the age of the internet and before missing children appeared on milk cartons. For years it was the belief that most missing adults had chosen to leave, and therefore, didn't get the attention they deserved. With Daisy, though, the facts of the case still bothered Maddie. Why hadn't they bothered the police?

Maddie sat on the sofa and booted up her computer. She searched for sites that specialized in missing adults. She was surprised to find so many. Things had changed since 1991. Most states had government sites. Maddie put Daisy's name in the search box of each one, and then she got a hit on a site that specialized in cold case searches.

A photo of Daisy along with a short biography and her statistics were posted on the site. Her mother had been five foot seven, weighed one hundred and fifteen pounds, had dark blonde hair, and blue eyes. She favored peach colored lipstick and Shalimar perfume. Daisy's favorite foods were peanut butter and ice cream. In two minutes, Maddie found out more about her mother than she had in eighteen years of living with her father.

~

Maddie woke the next morning with Larry's cold nose pressed against her hand.

"It's Monday, Larry. I took you out late so you would sleep in."

He woofed.

She rolled onto her back and sighed. Larry put his snout under her hand and pushed it up and down.

"Please, Larry, let me have five more minutes."

He woofed.

"Ugh," she said. "All right. I'm getting up."

After taking Larry out, Maddie made a pot of coffee. She was going to try and get some of the clutter in the house organized and needed some liquid motivation. After two mugs of coffee and a slice of toast, she took a shower and got dressed.

Maddie looked around the living room. The colonial era house had high ceilings and large rooms that easily accommodated the bulky 1970s furniture she'd inherited.

Next, she peered into the kitchen. Her grandmother updated it when she moved in during the seventies, but her dad had taken down the psychedelic, geometric avocado green and silver wallpaper in the nineties and painted the kitchen yellow. He hadn't changed the avocado stove and sink, though, not even when they got a new, white refrigerator. A pedestal table sat at the center of the kitchen with four matching chairs. Larry's bed was in one corner, and the only window was over the sink. There were no curtains, not even a valance, to spruce it up.

The living room and kitchen were one half of the house. Her bedroom was behind the kitchen, and her father's bedroom behind the living room. A wide hallway separated them. A full bath was at the end of a hallway between the bedrooms. The loft was a bedroom years ago, but it was more like an attic now. Maddie didn't feel like dragging the old wooden ladder in from the garage so she'd have to check it out another time.

Cleaning was Maddie's coping mechanism, so when Carl died, she went through his room like a whirlwind but was careful not to throw anything away until she had time to see if there was anything she wanted to keep. She dusted and vacuumed, mostly Larry's fur, and put any medical equipment into one corner. As she scanned the room, she remembered that his dresser drawers were still full of his clothes. She hadn't the heart to go through them at the time of his death.

Her room was less of a problem. She'd taken most of the things she wanted to keep when she left for New York, so it was just a matter of getting rid of the furniture. The old bedroom set might do well in a consignment shop along with the girl's desk, which was still pretty solid. She took pictures of them with her phone.

Maddie thought about the garage. Her father had thrown everything in there that he wasn't using but didn't want to throw away. She'd stayed away from it until the electricity went off, and now she had to start hauling boxes of textbooks to the store. It was time to start sorting it out. She put on her coat to go to the garage, and Larry gazed at her from his bed.

"I'll take you out later."

He groaned as he put his head down.

It was drizzling as she walked to the garage and everything was damp. When she went inside the garage, it, too, felt damp. Maddie began pulling the boxes of textbooks to one side, and they were mushy. Some ripped, some lost their bottoms, and others just fell apart altogether. Fortunately, Carl had some empty plastic storage tubs stacked against another wall, and Maddie filled them with the books from the boxes before putting them into her car. It would take days to get all of them moved, but she tried to look on the bright side. At least it was getting done.

Getting rid of the book boxes made a big dent in the clutter. It was easier to move things and see what could be tossed. There was more furniture in there than in the house, most of it suffering from rot and mold. All of it would go into a dumpster.

As she moved things from one side to the other, she saw that there had been a method to her father's madness. He had created a walkway that took him around the mess to a sequestered spot at the back of the garage.

Maddie saw a small desk pushed up against the back wall in the corner. There was a gooseneck lamp on the desk and a cord duct taped up the wall to an extension cord that went to one of the bulb outlets overhead.

Maddie walked over and switched on the gooseneck lamp. Newspaper articles and photos of her long-gone mother covered the wall in front of the desk. The articles were about Daisy and other missing people. There were stories of people who had been found unconscious with no memory of who they were. A notebook sat on the desk and Maddie flipped it open. The first entry was from 1995 and the last from 2005.

"Shit," she said.

She imagined her father sitting there searching for information about Daisy. Why hadn't he done it inside the house?

Carl had an old laptop he kept in his bedroom closet, and Maddie wondered if he had used that out here, too. He didn't want her to see this stuff when she was younger, but why not move it all inside when Maddie left for New York?

Maddie sat in the old, wheeled, wooden office chair in front of the desk and read the articles on the wall. They were the same ones she had looked up online. One article dated November 11, 2001, was a Sunday supplement, the one Maddie's aunt had mentioned, about the anniversary of Daisy's disappearance. It also included a short history of Fenway Manor.

A set of metal bookends at the back of the desk held two books. One, a ledger, recorded every call Carl Brady made to the police asking if they had any new leads with the last entry written in 2017. Her father noted that the police still hadn't found her and that he had just found out he had cancer.

"...and I'm pretty sure now I will never know what happened to Daisy."

His reluctant acceptance brought tears to her eyes. All those years, he'd never given up hope, and he'd never shared any of this with Maddie.

The other book was called *Confessions of a Lady's Maid*. Maddie pulled it out and checked the inside of the cover. The publisher was in North Carolina, and the copyright date was 1820.

The cover was brown leather with gold lettering, and it had a hand-written dedication inside:

To my own Daisy Carter, I will love you forever. DLF 1988

The idea that Daisy had had other boyfriends intrigued Maddie. Carl never talked about their relationship. Daisy was beautiful. Though her father had been a good man, he was not an exciting man. He was also not what you'd call handsome. He was what Maddie thought of as comfortable.

Maddie studied the photos of her mother. They showed a pregnant Daisy. Maddie had never seen them before. She was surprised at how happy Daisy looked, especially as she held her protruding stomach. This woman was thrilled with her impending motherhood. Maddie had theorized that Daisy left because she didn't want a child. These pictures blew that theory out of the water.

There was also a photo of little Maddie in front of a sheet cake with her name written on it and two candles at the center. Daisy was standing behind her. They were both smiling broadly. Carl must have taken the photo the day Daisy disappeared.

She looks so happy, Maddie thought.

Daisy didn't look like a woman about to abandon her daughter. She looked like someone who couldn't wait to plan her daughter's wedding.

Maddie opened the top drawer and found a copy of the police report. It had been years since she'd read it, so she grabbed it as if it were the Holy Grail.

"Officers responded to a call from 1400 King's Highway at 13:33. Carl Brady stated that his wife, Daisy Carter Brady, had taken their dog for a walk and hadn't come home. He also stated that he found the dog alone and tied to the back porch of the house at 1500 King's Highway. The officers did a cursory search of the area with no results. I advised Mr. Brady that he should come to the station and fill out a missing person report."

Ofc. John Markham had written the narrative.

No wonder her father had called them a gazillion times. Maddie looked at the photo of her and Daisy in front of the cake. That woman had not run away from her family.

A cursory search – what did that mean? Why didn't the police followed up on it a few days later when Daisy failed to return? Now, most states were required to treat a missing adult as they would a child. They would have taken Carl Brady's inquiries seriously.

Maddie grabbed the book about Fenway Manor before leaving the garage. As soon as she got inside the house, she wrote down some questions she wanted to ask the police, specifically that woman who'd interviewed her about finding David Friedlander's body. She was a detective. It was her job to investigate, and Maddie was sure that if she heard the facts, she'd want to find out what had happened to Daisy Carter Brady, too.

17

MONDAY

B en slept fitfully, woke up early, and dressed before heading downstairs. Maria was still in her bedroom, so he made coffee and left some for her. When he went into the garage, he was still surprised by the absence of his mother's car.

Ben drove to Princeton and parked on Nassau Street so he could walk to the university campus. He went to the building that housed the Barrington Library. As Ben walked toward the building, he noticed an old tree that looked familiar. As he studied it, he remembered where he'd seen it - in one of the photos he'd found at David's house with David, Harlan, and "Daisy" standing in front of it.

Barrington Library housed rare books and manuscripts and was open by appointment only, but Anna Freeman had a small office nearby. Ben had been there once when David brought him in to show him something he'd found regarding the Fenway family. The office had been so cramped that there was little room for more than the large desk they shared and two chairs. Ben knocked on the door, and Anna told him to come in.

The tiny window behind her framed Anna's head like a square halo. He couldn't see her expression, but Ben smiled when he entered the room. She got up and came around the desk.

"What are you doing here?" she asked. "Why didn't you tell me you were coming?"

"I didn't know I was until I woke up this morning."

"Well come, let's sit."

She returned to her seat while Ben sat in David's old chair. He noticed a copy of *Confessions of a Lady's Maid* in the bookcase next to the desk. Anna's face didn't hide her concern.

"How are you doing?"

"I'm worried about my mother."

"Still no word?" Ben shook his head, and Anna exhaled sharply. "I'm sure she's all right. Maybe she just needed to be alone for a while. I feel that way sometimes."

"Then she should have called to let us know," Ben said.

An awkward silence followed, and Ben looked around the room. There was an old painting of Fenway Manor on the wall and museum postcards featuring portraits of each family member. Anna saw him staring at them.

"He got them in Philadelphia at that Revolutionary War museum. He was so excited when he found them. You'd think he'd won the lottery."

"I went there yesterday."

Anna tilted her head.

"To the museum?"

"No, the old manor house."

"Why on earth would you go there?" she asked.

"Because it was his favorite place in the world and I wanted to…I wanted to see where he died."

"Oh, Ben, don't do that to yourself."

Ben sat back and stretched his legs out in front of him.

"Do you think my mother killed him?"

Anna's eyes widened. "Why would you think such a thing?"

"Because I can't find my father's hunting rifle."

Anna averted her eyes.

"I can't believe she'd murder someone."

"But you know she didn't like him," he said. "And everyone liked David."

Anna folded her arms on the desk and leaned forward.

"What did the police say?" she asked.

"They're still investigating."

"Then you shouldn't draw any conclusions, not until you talk to her yourself."

Ben rubbed the armrest of the chair.

"When I went to see Harlan the day Uncle Dave died, Harlan said he came to his house the night before and gave him something to put in Dave's file. Did Harlan say anything to you about it?"

Red patches appeared on Anna's cheeks, and her jaw twitched.

"He didn't mention it to me," she said.

"Really?" Now Ben leaned forward. "We talked about it at the house after the funeral. He didn't say anything about it after I left you two alone?"

She shook her head. "No."

Ben saw her stiffen and she kept her eyes on the desk. He thought of the tree and the photos in David's suitcase.

"Do you know anything about a girl Uncle Dave might have been dating when they went to school here?"

Anna's hand trembled, and she put it under the table.

"I don't recall whether he had a girlfriend," she said.

"Harlan told me that you gave Uncle Dave his pay envelope when he became a researcher," Ben said. "You must have known him well."

"I didn't get to know him until we started working together in this office."

"You never talked to him when he was an associate professor?" Ben asked. "Wasn't Harlan an associate professor at the same time?"

"When David was an associate professor, Harlan was still working on his masters."

"Oh, yeah, Uncle Dave did say something about that." Ben sat forward. "Did either of them know a girl named Daisy?"

Anna swallowed hard.

"There was a girl named Daisy who worked as an assistant to the faculty."

"Really?" he asked.

"She was a student who needed a bit of extra cash."

"I found this suitcase under Uncle Dave's bed. It was full of pictures, most of them taken here. A lot of them were of this beautiful girl, but there were some with Uncle Dave, the girl, and Harlan. They seemed close."

"Daisy was a pretty girl," Anna said. She squirmed.

"But you don't remember if they were dating."

"I don't recall." Anna sat back and exhaled sharply. "Daisy did marry a local boy. I remember that because Harlan and I went to her wedding."

"You knew her well enough to go to her wedding?" Ben said.

"We were friendly."

Ben sat back and glanced at the wall.

"Do you remember Uncle Dave ever dating *anyone*?"

"David was so young when he joined the faculty. It's possible he went out with some of the girls, but I never heard of it."

"It's weird him having all those photos," Ben said. "It seems like he really had a thing for that girl. If I brought one of them by, would you look at it?"

"Of course."

"Okay. Then I'll stop by one day after I get his house sorted out." He stood. "It's been nice seeing you again."

Anna stood. "I'll keep your mother in my prayers."

He stopped at the Starbucks before getting into his car and watched the students walking across the street. For a moment, he missed being one of them, and that's when he remembered the job offer he'd received from the school in California. The whole thing had slipped his mind, so he dialed their number and told them that he would not be able to accept the position at this time.

18

J anet looked at the M.E.'s report, closed her eyes, rubbed the back of her neck, and sighed. The Friedlander case was a dog with no clues, no suspects save one, and she was missing. All she had was the bullet that came from a Winchester rifle. Someone had shot him, whether on purpose or by accident, and unless they came forward to confess the odds of finding them were close to nil. She put the file down and took out her notepad.

Janet's partner had retired. She and Gaines had worked together for five years, and she missed having someone to bat ideas around with. They were still in the process of finding her a new partner, but the budgetary reasons that had led to Gaines retirement were tying their hands. All they would tell her was they hoped they would have one for her before the first of the year. In the meantime, she could avail herself of a uniformed officer if necessary.

She looked at the notes of the interviews she and Gaines had done before he left on Friday. They had talked to Harlan Monteif, Anna Freeman, and Ben Arntz. The students they'd contacted all said the same thing – David was a great guy, but they didn't know him very well. So far, everyone agreed that David Friedlander was the greatest guy who ever lived and that his sister hated him.

Janet read her emails to see if anyone had found Bethany Arntz. No one had reported finding her. How had she managed to hide so well when you couldn't use a debit card to fill your gas tank without being flagged? Perhaps if she had carried cash with her, she could avoid an electronic trail.

Ben had said he didn't know where his father's rifle was. Janet logged into the county system and started searching for any gun registered under the name Arntz. It was the second time she'd run the search, but she wanted to be thorough. Guns registered under the name Conrad Arntz included a handgun that had been re-registered in someone else's name in 1981 and a Winchester hunting rifle that was registered in 1980. The bullet taken from David Friedlander's back matched those used by a Winchester hunting rifle. There was nothing new there.

She opened the file containing the missing person's report Ben had filed. Janet's gut told her Beth had killed her brother, but a jury required evidence. At this point, even an overworked public defender could make a case for reasonable doubt simply by mentioning the stray bullet theory. Janet had to find Bethany Arntz; she had to find that rifle.

With nowhere else to go, Janet dialed Ben Arntz's number and he answered right away.

"Hi," she said trying to sound casual. "I was wondering if you might have heard from your mother?"

"No. I guess that means you haven't found her."

"No."

An awkward silence ensued, and then Janet thought of something.

"I ran a check on that rifle your dad owned, and it hasn't been re-registered."

"Okay."

"It might still be in the house somewhere."

Ben thought of the shed. He took the phone away from his mouth, exhaled sharply, and then put it to his ear.

"You're welcome to come by and look around."

"You're giving your permission?"

She wouldn't have to get a warrant.

"We've got nothing to hid," Ben said.

"Great. Then I'll see you soon."

Janet wiggled in her chair with glee. She got up and went to arrange for assistance to conduct a search, and then stopped by the desk of an office clerk on the first floor.

"You find anything for me?" Janet asked.

"Maybe. It's about the property where the body was found. I also checked the calls on Friedlander's cell phone."

The young woman gave a folder to Janet, who took it back to her desk on the second floor. There were several sheets of copy paper inside. Janet looked at those pertaining to Fenway Manor first.

The Fenway property belonged to Bethany Arntz. The deed was transferred to her in 1992. There were several entries dated a year apart where a town council hearing was scheduled to be held to determine the status of a condemned dwelling. They were always either postponed or canceled. This might happen when an owner promised to bring a dwelling up to code, but Fenway Manor hadn't changed in years.

Janet went online and tried digging deeper into the notes, an entry that would give more information but was only visible to officials and law enforcement. She found none, which was strange, and she noted it in her notebook.

The last entry was docketed on October 28, and the notices for the November 28 court hearing sent out that day, which meant that Bethany Arntz had received it before her brother died. While she wasn't sure what this meant, Janet felt it might be significant considering David had died there.

Janet put this in the file that held a list of facts learned and questions she had:

1. David was born in 1964; adopted two years later by Jacob and Linda Friedlander.

2. He graduated from Princeton in 1982 with a degree in history and became an associate professor in 1986.

3. Left the university in 1991 following a breakdown and hospitalization in a private hospital in upstate New York.

4. Returned to Princeton in 1993 as a research assistant in the Barrington Library.

5. What had caused the breakdown?

6. How did he become an associate professor at 22?

7. Beth's husband died in 2002.

Janet put "Beth holds the deed to the property on King's Highway since 1992" as number 8.

She ran a search of the local paper's archives and found an article about Bethany Friedlander being named CEO of her father's corporation following his death in 1997, five years after he gave Beth the property.

Janet was still stuck on why David Friedlander had gone to the property in the first place. It belonged to his sister, a sister who, according to everyone she'd asked, hated him and had made no secret of the fact that she wouldn't mind if he disappeared forever. Would she have lured him there so she could shoot him and blame local hunters? If so, why now?

Janet thought about the notice from the town council. Was it just a coincidence that David's death had occurred within days of the notice being sent out? And why hadn't any papers been filed to stop the condemnation even though papers had been filed every year for the last twenty some odd years?

Now, Janet looked at the list of David's phone calls. Most of the calls were between David and Ben or Harlan Monteif, but she saw one call David had received from Beth's phone on Tuesday. The call had lasted five minutes. She looked for more calls between them but came up empty.

It was too much of a coincidence. Janet's gut told her that that phone call had somehow led to David's death. The murder weapon was a rifle. You couldn't conceal a rifle like you could a handgun so David would have seen her walking up to him with the gun.

Not if she hid in the woods and waited for him.

That would be premeditated murder.

If Beth had planned to kill David, why would she run away? Killers who plan their murders tend to have a strategy for what happens *after* the deed is done, too. Running away makes them look guilty. It's sloppy. If her perfect house was any indication of her predilections, Beth Arntz was anything but sloppy.

And it wouldn't be easy for someone like Beth to disappear. She had taken enough insulin for one day. If she were planning an extended trip, she would have taken more. She was a missing person. If she went to a pharmacy requesting more insulin, she'd have to give her name so they could contact her doctor. The request would have been flagged.

Nothing came up when the missing person report was filed, but Janet ran a check on Beth's credit cards again. There had been no transactions for the last seven days. How had she managed to disappear so completely?

Janet pondered the relationship Bethany had with her son. He seemed like a well-adjusted young man. He'd never been arrested, and there were no incidents of juvenile mischief. He was also young. Beth was in her sixties. She dialed Ben's number again.

"Hey, it's me again," she said. "I was wondering if you might have been adopted."

"No. My mother was thirty-seven when I was born. They never expected me to happen."

"So, you were a surprise. Are you and your mom close?"

"I guess you'd call us close. It's always been just the two of us."

The chief came to her desk, and she ended the phone call.

"Okay, well, we'll be there in a few. Please don't go anywhere."

"I'll be here."

"The team is ready," the chief said. "I hope you find something."

"That makes two of us."

Before she got up, Janet looked for Conrad Friedlander's death certificate and saw that the cause of death was an abdominal aneurysm. He was 46 years old. She also looked up the Friedlander's financial situation and found that Beth had done a great job of running the company. It had grown considerably over the last twenty years, and when she died, Ben would become a multi-millionaire.

Ben had been close to David and felt responsible for him. Perhaps the burden of dealing with a mentally ill uncle had built up resentment toward him. Maybe Ben had hidden in the woods that morning, killed David, and when his overbearing mother arrived, had shot her, too. But what had he done with her body and her car?

Now, Janet had two suspects, both with access to a Winchester rifle, but only one had a clear motive - money.

19

TUESDAY

Candy sat in her therapist's waiting room. The last time they saw each other, Candy was starting her real estate course. Now, she couldn't wait to tell Sandy about her new job.

Over the weekend, Candy had obsessed over her encounter with the ghost at Fenway Manor. She couldn't stop thinking about his face. She wanted to know more about him. She even dreamed about him. In the dream, she was lying with her head on his chest and listening to his heartbeat while he stroked her hair. She woke up alone and disturbed by the idea of sexualizing a ghost.

"You can go in now," the receptionist told her, and Candy gathered her things.

She went into the office and saw Sandy typing some notes into her laptop. Candy took her usual seat and waited until Sandy looked up and smiled.

"You look good," Sandy said.

"I feel good."

"I'll be just a minute."

Sandy finished typing something before shutting the laptop and going to her seat, an overstuffed armchair in muted colors. She liked to sit cross-legged while she listened to her clients, and Candy did the same.

"So, how have you been since I last saw you?" Sandy asked.

"I got my license," Candy said. She grinned. "I'm a real estate agent now, and I already have a listing."

Sandy smiled broadly. "See. I told you that you could do anything."

Candy was beaming. "Thank you for making me do it."

"Well, you're very welcome, but you made the decision."

"Right. No one can make me do anything. I have the power. I make the decisions."

"Do you believe that, Candy?"

Candy squirmed. "I do, a little. It's just that sometimes it feels like that if I make a decision, it isn't always what I want to do but what I can do."

"That's the way it is for most people. We can't control every situation." Sandy peered at Candy. "Is there something you wanted to talk about today?"

Candy bit her lip. She wanted to tell Sandy about her dream but feared what she might think. Sandy had worked a long time to get Candy to admit that what she had seen at Fenway Manor was not real, so if Candy admitted now that she knew it was…

"I can see you want to say something," Sandy said.

Candy clasped her hands.

"Remember when I told you about the time I saw a ghost at that old mansion on King's Highway?"

"I do."

"Well, I saw him again."

Sandy's eyebrows rose. "When did this happen?"

"The other day. I was checking out a house, and I saw him."

"How did seeing him make you feel?"

"At first, I freaked out a little, but then I told at him to go away, and he did."

"Great," Sandy said.

"It felt great, but then over the weekend, I had a dream that upset me."

"Okay."

"I dreamed about him."

"What happened in the dream?" Sandy asked.

Candy blushed. "We were lying together, and I had my head on his chest." Sandy watched Candy squirm but stayed quiet. "I don't like feeling that way about someone who's dead."

"Remind me what he looked like."

Candy screwed up her mouth before answering.

"He has long hair and soft eyes, is really good-looking, and he wears this pirate shirt like one of those guys on the covers of my mom's romance novels."

"So, you were attracted to him," Sandy said. Candy closed her eyes and nodded. "Have you dated at all since you were last here?"

Candy shook her head. "It's hard to meet people."

"Then I would say that the dream was born out of your need to be connected to someone, preferably a man."

Candy leaned forward.

"So, I need a man."

"You need a connection, and since your mind had you in a somewhat intimate situation, well, that tells me you might be ready to have a relationship with a man."

They had talked many times about Candy's inability to respond to men who had tried to have conversations with her, and Sandy had told her to give herself time. She had suffered a trauma, which included a sexual assault, and her mind was trying to make sense of the world again.

"You are so much better, Candy," she said. "You just have to believe that."

"I still get tongue-tied when I talk to men," Candy said.

"But you do talk to them, right?"

Candy smiled. "Yeah."

"Well, that's an improvement. One step at a time."

"I'm worried I might not be able to trust them."

"Trust is learned, and the only way you learn it is by doing the thing you fear. It's hard, and no one expects you to jump into a relationship. Take it slow. That's how you gain confidence."

Candy sat back and sighed.

"I am so tired of learning. I just want to be better - now!"

Sandy smiled. "I wish you could see yourself ten years ago so you'd see how far you've come."

"I guess." Candy sat up again. "But I'm thirty now. I want to have kids before I'm too old."

"You look younger than your age. And you still have plenty of time left to have children."

"So, I can get away with saying I'm what, twenty-five?"

"I'll never tell anyone." Sandy leaned forward. "Be patient with yourself. You've always been so impatient to get better."

"Do you blame me? I've lost so much time that it's no wonder I'm dreaming about ghosts."

"Don't get too caught up in this, Candy."

"You don't believe I actually saw a ghost, do you?"

"I believe you believe it."

For a moment, Candy worried that Sandy might suggest she go back on one of her meds, a drug that had made her feel awful, but then Sandy smiled.

"There's nothing wrong with indulging in fantasy now and then as long as you know what's real."

They chatted for another half-hour, and then their session ended. They made another appointment to meet in six months.

"If you feel the need to see me sooner, make an appointment," Sandy said as she saw Candy to the door.

"I will," Candy said. "Thanks."

As Candy walked back to her car, she thought about the ghost. Despite what Sandy said about her need for a connection to a real man, Candy wanted to know more about him and why he was haunting Fenway Manor. She wondered if there was something he wanted, something only a living person could provide, and as she drove down King's Highway on the way home, she glanced at the mansion hoping her pirate would appear. He didn't, and she sighed.

20

TUESDAY

It had rained overnight, flooding in the parking lot behind Maddie's store, and Larry's paws were wet when he walked inside the store. Larry left a trail of pawprints from the back room to his bed. Carl Brady had kept a Swiffer mop for just that reason, and as Maddie cleaned the pawprints off the floor, she saw Candy standing at the front door. Maddie had called her the night before and told Candy she was ready to sign the listing agreement.

Maddie moved a little faster as she pushed the mop along the floor, which left a trail as its effectiveness decreased. She propped it against the table, and then let Candy in.

"Sorry to be here so early," Candy said.

"It's okay. I was just mopping up a little before opening."

Candy shook her umbrella before closing it, and then came inside. She had a sign under her arm and took it to the table, set the umbrella on the floor, and sat. Maddie joined her.

"I talked to Ross, and he thinks you can get 160k for this place. That's what the plant store went for last year."

Maddie's eyes widened. "That would be great."

"I brought my sign." Candy held it up. "After we get the paperwork out of the way, we can decide where to put it."

"I've got that agreement in my bag," Maddie said.

She went around the counter and took the papers out of her bag. Candy took off her coat and hung it over a chair at the table.

"Here," Maddie said as she walked toward Candy. She held the papers out, and Candy met her, took the papers, and smiled.

"This is so exciting," she said. "My first listing."

"Wow. And it's for me."

Candy hugged Maddie.

"I'm so glad it happened this way." Candy took the papers to the table, sat, and filled in the information about Maddie's store. "Is there anything you want to ask me about before you sign?"

Maddie sat and watched Candy.

"It's pretty straightforward."

Candy finished filling out the form and then slid it to Maddie.

"Just sign where I put the little x."

Maddie signed her name and slid the form back to Candy.

"That's it," Candy said and then picked up her sign. "So, where do you want to put this?"

"In the window near the counter so they can see it, but it doesn't interfere with my display."

Candy glanced at Maddie's display window. The sign would have been more noticeable there, and the display was nothing more than books set at different angles.

"You do want people to see it, Maddie."

Maddie glanced at the front of the store, her eyes going from one window to the other. She slipped her hands into her jean's pockets.

"That is a pathetic display, isn't it?"

"Considering the holidays are coming, you might want to dress it up a bit and put the sign in the corner near the door."

"I don't know," Maddie said. She stood and walked over to the display window. "I guess putting it in the display window would be better."

Candy took the sign to the display window. Larry lifted his head and groaned.

"Hey, fella," Candy said. "What do you think of this sign?"

Larry put his head down.

"He couldn't care less," Maddie says. She smiled. "He's no help at all."

Candy placed the sign in the corner and put a piece of tape at the top.

"I have these mounting squares to keep it in place when we decide. Let's go outside."

Candy grabbed her umbrella and opened the door. They went outside, huddled under the umbrella, and then stared at the window.

"I can't believe I never noticed how boring it is before," Maddie said.

"You've had other things on your mind."

"The sign doesn't look bad there. I guess it will be all right."

"You having second thoughts about selling?" Candy asked.

"No, not at all, it's just that I always thought of myself as a good marketer. If I'd done this for one of my clients, I'd have been kicked out on my ass."

"Go to the dollar store and get some cheap stuff to brighten it up," Candy said.

"I think my father had a small tree in the back." Maddie sighed. "It's not my favorite time of year."

"Yeah, I feel the same way about the holidays, but my mom likes them, so I go along with it because it makes her happy."

"My dad liked them, too. God, it's cold out here. You want some coffee?"

"Thanks, but I have to get back to the office. Let me put get that sign squared away."

Candy followed Maddie inside. She took the tape off the sign and put on the mounting squares before putting it back in the window. "There." She put her coat on, grabbed her umbrella and purse, and then smiled at Maddie. "I'll be in touch."

Maddie closed the door behind her and then went to the back room to get a broom to sweep up the dried dirt. She checked around the back room for a tree but couldn't find one. She checked all the nooks and crannies, including some storage closets she had never looked into, but there was no tree.

The rain was keeping customers away, so Maddie ran across the street for coffee. When she returned, she pulled the book she'd found in the garage, *Confessions of a Lady's Maid*, out of her bag. She opened it, reread the words written by DLF, and then turned a few pages until she saw notes written in Carl's hand.

"Daisy Carter?" was written on the page where a maid named Daisy was first mentioned. Maddie searched for another note and found one twenty pages in that read, "Time travel?"

"What?" she said aloud.

Had her father been so desperate to find out what had happened to her mother that he would contemplate she had traveled through time?

As Maddie flipped through the pages, a passage caught her eye.

"*...as he explored the depths of my depravity.*"

Maddie's eyebrows rose, and she read the preceding sentences.

"*Twas Mr. Martin who turned my soul. Did he think me hand-some? Or just another wanton strumpet given to fanciful desires? Nay, I should like to stroke his heart with my loving tongue, that as he explores the depths of my depravity, he will know we are but kindred souls.*"

A customer came into the store and Maddie marked her place in the book. Her cheeks felt hot, and she wondered how her father could have thought that this Daisy was his Daisy. She asked the customer if they needed any help, and they said no, so she hurried back to the book.

"*I have naught but my own sweet soul to restrain my desire, and it is weary of the fight. It longs for rest on Mr. Martin's form and to descend upon that which gives me pleasure.*

"*But I see the Master's eyes as he visits Lady Emily in her darkest hour, as he plans his libidinous pursuit of me. And she not recovered from her travail, a poor, sickly thing still pining for a kind word from her lover. Is this to be her sad end?*

"*I ran from her room in search of Mr. Martin. He has taken refuge in the barn where naught can hurt his heart, and when our eyes meet, he comes to me, his hands upon my face, and his lips seeking to awaken my desire. My breasts long for his tongue, my lips to surround his manhood, the lash of his whip upon my buttocks.*"

"Can I pay for this?"

Maddie looked up to see her customer at the register. Heat warmed her cheeks, and her heart raced as she thought of her father reading these passages. She shut the book and went to check out her customer.

When she returned to the book, she was still blushing. Why had that woman reminded him of her mother? The mere thought made Maddie blanch. Then Maddie thought of DLF, and the cringe she felt caused her to shake out her arms.

"Oh, God, yuck."

She put the book back into her bag and retrieved the feather duster from beneath the counter. She dusted the shelves, hurrying up and down each aisle, but she couldn't stop thinking about Mr. Martin. When was the last time she'd had sex?

Maddie had come to live in Logans Grove last December. She'd slept with her roommate a week before. Maddie and Kevin had an arrangement since neither of them had a significant other, and it worked while she was in the city, but now she wasn't so sure she wanted that kind of relationship again. She'd gotten older, and wanted to meet someone she could fall in love with.

When she was done dusting, she looked at the time. It was only one in the afternoon. Maddie sat at the table and looked at the notes on her phone. She saw the one to remind her to call the detective about her mother and dialed the number.

"Detective Worthington," Janet said when she answered.

"Hi. This is Maddie Brady."

"Oh, hi, Maddie."

"Listen. I was wondering about something, and I thought you might be able to help me."

"Shoot," Janet said.

"My mother disappeared twenty-eight years ago."

"What was her name?"

"Daisy Carter Brady," Maddie said.

Maddie heard Janet typing.

"Was she living in the house you're living in now?"

"Yes."

Janet kept typing.

"The facts of the case make me wonder if…well if the police might have, well…not done a great job looking for her," Maddie said.

"I found a file," Janet said. She didn't tell Maddie that the case was marked "Closed." "What day did she go missing?"

"It was on November 9th, 1991."

"And no one has seen her or heard from her since then?"

"No."

"Let me see what I can find out," Janet said. "Give me some time, though."

"Okay. I appreciate it."

The afternoon passed slowly as the rain escalated bringing downpours that filled the gutters with rivers heading toward the drains and Maddie decided to close at four. She gathered her things, along with Larry's leash, and locked up the store. They stopped at a supermarket on the way home so Maddie could buy a pint of ice cream to redirect her sexual frustrations to guilt over consuming too many calories. She also picked up a frozen pizza. Might as well shoot the works.

When she got home, she fed Larry, and then put the pizza in the oven. She took the book out of her bag and put it in one of the bookcases before heading for the sofa. While the pizza cooked, she flipped through channels and landed on the five o'clock news. A pretty young brunette was standing in front of a video labeled, "Murder at Fenway Manor."

"Services were held for David Lawrence Friedlander on Saturday," the brunette said. "Police released a statement earlier saying that they are still following leads and are asking the public to come forward with any information they might have regarding the case." An old photo of the deceased appeared with his full name underneath. "If you know of anyone who might have been hunting in the woods behind Fenway Manor on King's Highway, please contact the Logans Grove Police Department hotline."

Maddie saw the man's name spelled out beneath his photo and her mouth fell open.

"Shit."

David Lawrence Friedlander - DLF.

21

TUESDAY

Candy left the office at 3. The rain had turned into a drizzle. As she passed Maddie's house, she thought about the ghost and wondered if he was lonely.

"He's a freaking ghost, Candy," she said, as she got closer to the mansion. "He's not lonely."

She saw him standing at the curb and slowed down. When she stopped, he didn't move, but a chill ran up her spine. She decided to take a good look at him.

The ghost was illuminated from within like one of those plastic Santas you see on people's lawns at Christmastime. He looked like a washed-out version of a living person – pale skin, watery blue eyes, and hair that might have been dark blond when he was alive. His lips weren't too full, and his nose was perfect. He looked as if he'd been ordered from a modeling agency to appear on the cover of GQ.

Candy got out of the car and stood with it between her and the ghost. She shivered from the cold this time and smiled. The ghost smiled back.

"What's your name?" she asked.

He glanced back at the mansion. Candy stared at it trying to discern what he meant when it hit her – the house was called Fenway Manor.

"Your last name is Fenway," she said. He nodded. "Then I should find you on the internet." He looked puzzled. "That's a new thing. Don't worry about it."

She blushed as he stared at her. His gaze was full of longing, and she folded her arms over her chest. He tried to mouth something, but she couldn't make it out.

"I'm sorry. I don't understand."

He smiled and shrugged. Candy moved to the end of her car.

"I'm going to see if I can find out what your first name is. Is that all right?"

He nodded and smiled broadly.

"Okay, then, that's what I'll do," she said.

The drizzle was turning into rain, and she was freezing.

"I have to go," she said. "I'll come back again."

He smiled at her, and then faded away.

Candy didn't feel like going home where her mother would ply her with questions about her day, so she decided to go to The Ugly Badger to get something to eat. She wasn't in the habit of going out alone to restaurants with bars, but she was taking what Sandy had said to heart. Candy had to meet new people, new men, in order to learn how to trust again. It would never happen if she spent every night at home with her mother.

All the way there, Candy thought of the ghost's face and the human emotions he displayed. Why had she been so frightened of him?

Maybe it was his association with her accident that had intensified the experience of seeing him the first time. He had come out of nowhere as she was running from Kevin. She had gotten drunk and almost died in an accident. The whole evening had been a nightmare, so it was understandable that she would believe the ghost had something to do with the residual fear she'd had for years. Poor man. She felt as if she owed him an apology.

She parked beside the only other car in the parking lot and sat for a moment. It was nearly four, too early for dinner, but if she went inside and just had a coke...

"Oh, for God's sake, Candy."

She got out of her car and walked to the front door. She went inside, and a young woman at the podium in the waiting area smiled at her.

"Hi," she said. "How many?"

"Just me."

The hostess glanced over her shoulder and then smiled again.

"Have you ever been here before?"

"No," Candy said.

"Then I'm gonna put you in our special booth."

"What's so special about it?" Candy asked.

"The table has been here since 1730."

Candy followed the hostess as she went toward the other end of the restaurant. They passed the bar where one patron was nursing a beer while he watched TV. He glanced at them, and Candy thought he was cute. She didn't see his eyes follow her as the hostess sat her in the last booth.

"See those initials," the hostess said pointing at the table. "They were carved by the guy who owned that old mansion on King's Highway."

Candy's heart skipped a beat. Fenway Manor. She ran her finger over the letters.

"Do you know anything about him?" Candy asked.

"Not me, but I know someone who does." The hostess glanced at the man at the bar. "If you want, I can ask him to come over."

Candy glanced at him, and her cheeks turned red. It was the second time that day that she found herself confronted by physical sensations that she hadn't experienced in a long time. She folded her arms over her chest.

"He's a nice guy," the hostess said. "He just lost his uncle. He might like some company."

"And he knows about the Fenways?" Candy asked.

"His uncle knew everything about them, and I know they spent time in here talking about it."

"Okay."

The hostess went over to the man, said something, and then he got off his stool, grabbed his beer, and came over to Candy's booth.

"Hi," he said. "My name is Ben." He held out his hand, and Candy shook it. "Do you mind if I sit down?"

"No, not at all," she said.

Candy felt heat rise up her chest and spread across her arms. Ben sat and put his beer in front of him.

"Carrie said you were asking about the Fenways," he said.

"I pass that old house all the time, and I don't know anything about them."

Candy studied Ben's features. He looked a little like her ghost with short hair.

"My uncle was the expert on Fenway history. He told me the story about how Alastair was on his way to Philadelphia to pick up his bride when he stopped here. He was young and carved those initials with his dinner knife."

"Why would he do that?" she asked.

"It was 1763. Maybe that's what they did back then."

"Like graffiti."

"Right. And he wasn't the only one. There were more of them years ago, but when they did the last restoration, they decided to keep Alastair's and buff out the others. I think my uncle had something to do with that."

He smiled, and Candy's heart skipped a beat. She began to relax. Ben was easy to talk to.

"Did your uncle know why Alastair did that?" she asked.

"He said that he thought Alastair was nervous about getting married and wanted to remember who he was."

"He really gave it some thought."

"It was his whole life years ago," Ben said. "He was obsessed with the Fenways."

Candy noticed the way Ben held his beer with both hands. She liked his hands.

"The hostess told me your uncle passed away. I'm sorry for your loss."

"I'm still trying to process it." He looked into her eyes and smiled. "So, what else would you like to know?"

Tell me about the good-looking guy.

She folded her arms on the table and leaned toward him.

"Was there a guy who lived there with long hair?"

"A guy in his thirties, right?" Ben said.

Her eyes lit up. "Yes. Do you know anything about him?"

"Sure. What do you want to know?"

"Everything."

The server came, and they both ordered something before he began reciting the tragic history of Fenway Manor.

"In 1748, Alastair Fenway was thirteen and heir to a fortune. He was always getting into mischief so his father, the Duke of Bramshire, put Alastair on a ship bringing troops to fight in the French and Indian War. He and a boy he befriended named Rupert Granger had romantic ideas about becoming war heroes. They stayed with the British army and ended up fighting right alongside them."

"And he survived."

"They both did, but Rupert ended up with a permanent limp after being shot in the leg. In return for Alastair's service, King Charles awarded his father a grant for the land in Logans Grove. Alastair cleared the land and built the house, but it belonged to his father, which is something Alastair bitched about for years."

Candy laughed. "I can see why it would bother him."

"Yeah, I can, too."

Ben stared at Candy for a moment. She blushed and averted her eyes.

"Um, so, Rupert settled in Philadelphia and Alastair in Logans Grove. By the time he was 19, he was overseeing the entire estate, which consisted of several farms. He also started an import-export business with Rupert. They remained business partners until Alastair died."

"There's a story about that I heard when I was a kid. Did he kill his entire family?"

"That's what everyone says. The truth is he killed his wife and son. His wife killed their daughter-in-law."

Their food came, and then Ben raised his eyebrows.

"If you really want to know what happened, I can give you a book about it."

"There's a book about it?"

"My uncle had it. It's called *Confessions of a Lady's Maid*."

"Oh, I'd love to read it," Candy said.

"He kept it at the university. I can grab it the next time I go and lend it to you."

They ate in silence for a few minutes, and then Ben sat back.

"Have you ever gone to Fenway Manor?"

"Actually, I was just there." Candy blushed.

"Just now?"

She nodded. "My friend is selling her house, and it's right next door."

"That's Derek's house," Ben said.

"Whose Derek?" she asked.

"Oh, shit, he's the one you asked about. Alastair's son."

"The guy with long hair."

"Yes, that's Derek Fenway."

His name is Derek, she thought.

Ben sat back with a quizzical look on his face.

"What made you ask about him?" Ben asked.

Candy put her fork down and looked out the window. She bit her lip, and then looked at Ben.

"I saw him."

"You saw the ghost."

Candy raised her eyebrows.

"You know about him?"

"I've never seen him, but my uncle did."

"And you believed him?"

"Why not?" Ben said. "Who am I to judge?"

"You don't think it's weird?"

"My uncle was weird, for sure, but he never lied to me. If he said he saw the ghost of Derek Fenway, then he saw the ghost of Derek Fenway."

Candy sat back, smiled, and then picked up her fork. They ate for a while, and then people began arriving for dinner. Candy took out her phone and saw the time.

"It's almost six," she said.

"Do you have to go?"

She looked into his eyes and shook her head. They talked till long past dinner and didn't get up until nine when the bar was filling up, and the noise made it hard to hear what they were saying. Ben walked her to her car. Before she got inside, Candy texted him goodnight so he'd have her number, and then he watched her car until it disappeared down the road.

22

WEDNESDAY

B en woke up when his phone rang. The first thing he thought of was Candy, but the ID said *Unavailable,* and he recognized the detective's phone number.

"Ben," Janet said. "We found your mom." Ben held his breath. "Ben?"

"Where did you find her?"

"She's at a medical center in Cape May County."

He sat up and put his feet on the floor.

"Cape May?" he asked.

"I'm going there now. Would you like to ride with me?"

"I'll drive down in my car."

"Then I'll meet you there," she said, and then gave him the name of the medical center and the town. Ben put them on his phone.

Ben went to the kitchen to tell Maria, who was still in her night-clothes.

"She's in Cape May," he said.

Her eyes widened, and then her expression registered her confusion.

"Why?"

He shook his head and shrugged.

"No idea. I'm driving down there now."

"I'm going with you."

They both readied themselves, and once they got on the road, it took two hours to get there. The receptionist at the hospital directed them to intensive care.

"It's family only," the woman said.

"This is my aunt," Ben said. "And I'm her son."

The woman looked at Maria with a hint of suspicion but gave them the passes anyway. They took the elevator to the second floor. The smell of the hospital reminded Ben of David's last heart attack. His mind flashed to his uncle's pale face as he lay in his hospital bed.

The rooms in the ICU didn't have doors so there was no moment in which they could prepare themselves for what they saw when they found Beth. She was on a ventilator surrounded by machines and, like David, her face was pale. There was a bruise on her forehead, which caused Maria to gasp, and then she went to Beth, took her hand, and wept. Ben went to the other side of the bed and waited for Beth to open her eyes.

A nurse came with a rolling, laptop cart and smiled at them.

"So, Beth has company."

"She's my mother."

"Have you seen the doctor yet?" she asked.

"We just got here," Ben said.

"Then I'll let him know you're here."

The nurse went to one of the machines to check something, and then took Beth's pulse. She went to the laptop and typed something into Beth's chart.

"When did they bring her in?" Ben asked.

"They brought her in last night. She was unconscious."

"Will she wake up?" Ben asked.

"The doctor can answer that better than me," the nurse said.

She left with the rolling cart, and Ben looked around the space for a chair. He found one in another, curtained room and brought it to Maria. He was about to go find one for himself when the doctor came to Beth's bed.

"Hello. I'm Dr. Singh."

"I'm Ben Arntz, and this is my aunt, Maria. I'm her son. How is she?"

"Right now, we're monitoring her. Would you come with me for a moment?"

The doctor led Ben to the Family room, a place with sofas, chairs in muted colors, and a TV on the wall. They stood near a window where Ben could see a forest of fall colors. He fisted his hands as he waited for Dr. Singh to speak.

"Your mother has suffered a massive stroke. Her blood sugar was very high when they brought her in, which we believe was the cause of the stroke." He paused as Ben absorbed the news. "Right now, there is no brain activity." Ben stared at the doctor as if he didn't understand what he was being told. "She's not going to wake up."

As the doctor's words sunk in, Ben looked out the window at the brightly colored trees. Fall was Beth's favorite season.

"You're saying she's brain dead."

"Yes. I am doubtful that she will wake up, Mr. Arntz, and a decision will have to be made." Ben stared at the floor and Dr. Singh put his hand on Ben's shoulder. "Go spend some time with her. I'll be around later to check on her, and we can talk then."

Dr. Singh left Ben in the Family room. The same comforting numbness he'd felt when he'd learned of David's death fell on him. The second anchor in his life would soon disappear. Ben had been thrust into adulthood by the loss of his uncle, and now he had to decide when to end his mother's life as well.

Maria came into the Family room and walked over to Ben. She put her hand on Ben's arm and squeezed it.

"What did he say?" she asked.

"He said she's not going to wake up," he said.

"That can't be true," Maria said.

Ben looked into her eyes.

"She's not there anymore, Maria."

"She's breathing. Where there is life, there is hope."

Ben offered her a sad smile.

"I know this is hard for you."

"She's alive, Ben. She will return. I just feel it."

Ben was too tired to argue with her about the inevitable. If Maria was unable to accept the truth, then let her have her denial.

"Let's go back and sit with her."

As they walked down the hallway, Ben saw Janet standing by Beth's room. Maria walked past her while Ben stopped to talk to her.

"I'm sorry about your mother," Janet said.

"Have you found her car?" Ben asked.

"She was registered as a guest at the Blue Moon Bed and Breakfast." She handed him Beth's wallet. "She checked in last Wednesday. The local police went through her room. Her insulin bottles were empty."

Ben's heart was pounding in his ears.

"They also looked through her car, Ben. They found a Winchester rifle in the trunk."

Ben was watching Beth when Janet said this. None of it made any sense. Beth Arntz was a responsible person. She made lists. She wouldn't have just run away.

"She had a rifle in her trunk," Janet said.

Ben kept looking at Beth and wishing she would wake up. He wanted her to tell him why she had run to Cape May.

"If it's the same caliber as the weapon used to kill your uncle..."

"Then she will be arrested," Ben said.

"She will be arrested."

"None of this makes any sense," he said. "Why would she go to a bed and breakfast?"

"If she shot David, she might have panicked. She probably got on the parkway and drove as far as she could."

"But she would have called us."

"Not if she was frightened. People do strange things when they panic."

"I can't believe this," Ben said.

"Look, I have to go back to Logans Grove. I'll call you after forensics checks out the gun."

Janet left him standing in the hallway. Ben went to join Maria beside Beth's bed. Someone had placed a chair on the other side of the bed, and he sat there. He touched her cold hand and then sat back in his chair. Beth's face was still. Her eyes didn't flutter. A machine was breathing for her and Ben knew in his heart that if he turned off that machine, his mother would die.

But that small spring of hope that dwells in everyone's heart welled up inside him. What if Maria was right? What if Beth was just sleeping? And what would Beth think if she came back only to find a police officer posted outside her curtained room?

Ben tried to remember if his mother had ever expressed her end of life choices. Had she said she wouldn't want to live on a machine? Would she refuse heroic efforts to save her if it meant she'd live in a vegetative state for the rest of her life?

He wanted to ask Maria if Beth had ever talked to her about it, but Ben feared she would lie to keep Beth on the machine. Ben's mind was in such a muddle that it took a while for him to realize that Beth's attorney would know. She always kept her will up-to-date.

Ben left the room and looked at his phone. Arthur Mantz had always handled any legal paperwork for the Friedlander family, save for David, who preferred Harlan. Arthur would have prepared Beth's will. Ben dialed his office number. He was told that Arthur was out, but he would be back later that afternoon.

Ben stood in the hallway as his mind went back and forth over the last few days. He recalled the box of bullets in the shed and shuddered. The shed had been left open. She had loaded the gun before going to meet David. She had murdered him in cold blood.

"Jesus," he said.

Ben went back to the chair beside her bed and watched Beth's chest rise and fall. He tried to remember a time when Beth had said something nice about her brother, but he couldn't remember any. David hadn't gone off the rails in years. He hadn't posed a threat to the Friedlander's public image in years either and would probably have been dead soon anyway, so what had prompted the quickening of his demise?

Beth was an advocate of the death penalty. Criminals should be punished, but New Jersey didn't have a death penalty. She could be sentenced to life without parole. The idea of his mother confined to a cell and forced to live a life out of her own control was daunting. He pitied anyone who would have to share that cell with her. By pulling the plug, Ben would most likely ensure that she would not have to pay for what looked like premeditated murder.

Was that the fair thing to do? She had taken David's life. What would David think of her getting off scot-free?

His musings were interrupted when the nurse came in to check on Beth. She asked Ben if Beth had an advance directive.

"I left a message with her attorney," Ben said. "He hasn't called me back yet."

At two, Ben's phone rang, and he went to the family room so Maria wouldn't hear.

"Hello, Ben."

"Mr. Mantz. I was calling…because my mother is in the hospital. She's on life support, and I have to make a decision. The hospital is asking for an advance directive. " There was silence on the other end. It lasted for ten seconds. "Are you there?"

"Oh, Ben, I'm so sorry." He paused, and Ben heard him sniffle. "Yes, Beth made one when we drafted her will." Ben heard Arthur typing. "How did this happen?"

"They think high blood sugar caused a stroke."

"Oh, dear God. Why I just spoke to her. She wanted some amendments added to her will. I'll have to look up her file." Ben heard him tapping on his keyboard again. "She did make a living will, and you are her health surrogate. She stipulates the following; If a physician determines that she has lost the ability to make her own decisions because her brain has ceased to function properly, then she would like a cessation of life support. She doesn't want to be kept alive artificially. She wants to be allowed to die peacefully."

"She said that," Ben said.

"She did. I remember when she made this directive. She didn't want you to have to make the decision, and with her diabetes, she often worried about how you would handle things."

"I just want to do what she wants. Can you fax a copy of that to the hospital?"

Ben went to the nurses' station and got the fax number, which he relayed to Arthur. He returned to Beth's room where Maria was praying softly. He didn't want her to know what was happening until the advance directive arrived, and then she would see that it was Beth's wish to be taken off the machine. Fifteen minutes later, the nurse came to the room and handed Ben the fax from the attorney. He looked at Maria with sad eyes.

"Mom made a living will," he said. "She doesn't want to be kept alive by machines."

He gave it to her, and she read every word seeking a loophole that would keep her lady alive. When she was done, tears rolled down her cheeks. She threw the paper across the bed, laid her head on Beth's hand, and sobbed.

At eight p.m., Ben's cell phone vibrated, and he saw that it was Janet calling. He answered it and asked her to wait while he went to the Family room.

"I can talk now."

"The bullet taken from your uncle's body was fired from the rifle we found in your mother's car." Ben sat and slumped in the chair.

"I'm sorry, Ben. I wish I had better news, but the Cape May County Sheriff's Office is sending a man over to stay by her room."

"Do you have to do that?"

"She's our suspect now. If there's the slightest chance she'll wake up, someone has to be there."

He started to say that they were going to turn off the machines and then stopped. What if they tried to prevent them from doing that?

Ben ended the call and went to Beth's room where he found Dr. Singh listening to her heart. He gave Ben a sad smile, and then Ben took him aside.

"Her lawyer sent her advance directive," Ben said. "She doesn't want to be kept on a machine."

"I've seen it," Dr. Singh said. "We can proceed whenever you want."

"I want to talk to Maria first."

Ben went to Maria and put his hand on her shoulder. Maria looked up and saw the doctor standing behind Ben.

"Just a little more time," she said.

He squatted beside her and held her arm tightly.

"Maria, the police believe she killed Uncle Dave. They are sending a cop to stand by her." He watched her face to see if she understood but saw nothing but pain. "If we don't do this now, they may try and stop us, and then she could be like this for months." She looked into his eyes. "You read the directive. She didn't want that, Maria. She wanted to die peacefully. For Mom's sake, we have to do this now."

Maria crumpled and wept. She then took Beth's hand and pressed it to her face.

"Adiós por ahora."

Maria got up and left the room in tears. Dr. Singh moved to the machine, glanced at Ben, and then turned off the machine. A nurse came in to assist the doctor as he removed her breathing tube, and then Beth was breathing on her own.

"Sometimes they breathe on their own for a while," Dr. Singh said.

"How long?" Ben asked, tears streaking his ashen face.

"We can't tell. It could be minutes, but it could be hours. Her last brain scan confirmed again that there was no activity, so based on my experience, it shouldn't be long."

Ben sat beside her as the doctor and nurse left them alone. He kept watching the hallway for an officer and felt like he was committing a crime when all he wanted to do was follow his mother's wishes.

Ben decided to focus on Beth instead and watched her face for signs of life; a smile, or the fluttering of her eyelids, but she remained still. Her chest was moving slower now, and as her body followed her mind, it slowed more and more until Beth stopped breathing and slipped away.

A Sheriff's deputy came to the edge of the curtain and looked at Beth. He acknowledged Ben and then stood near the curtain with his back to Ben. He didn't ask about the tubes being removed, or anything else about Beth's condition.

A few minutes passed, and then Dr. Singh came and pronounced her dead. Ben stayed in the room for a few minutes and then left to tell Maria. She was in the Family room looking out the window when he came up to her. She held his hand for a while and then ran out of the room.

It was late, and Ben was tired. He wanted to take Maria home. He went to the nurse's station and gave the nurse the name and number of the funeral home. He stopped by Beth's room and took one last look before heading to the elevator.

23

Maddie woke up Wednesday morning thinking about David L. Friedlander. She got out of bed, took Larry outside, and then took a shower. As the water rolled down her body, she remembered the passages in the book and shuddered. Had her mother and this man...oh, God!

"Stop thinking about it."

She got out of the shower, dressed, and went to the kitchen, but she wasn't hungry. Maddie took out her laptop and searched Friedlander's name online. She found his obituary.

"Mr. Friedlander was a gifted student who earned his doctorate in history in 1986 at the age of 22. From 1986 until 1991, he was an associate professor at Princeton University. In his later years, he worked as a researcher in the Barrington Library."

David Friedlander had been at the university when her mother was a student there. Maddie wanted to talk to someone who had known her mother, someone who would know whether she and David Friedlander had been lovers. The first name that came to mind was Anna Freeman. Maddie knew she still worked at the university because she and Harlan Monteif had come to her father's funeral and they'd talked about Anna's job in the Barrington Library.

Larry came to the door as Maddie put on her coat.

"You have to stay. I'll come back for you in a little while."

With great reluctance, he returned to his bed.

Maddie drove to Princeton and parked on the street. It was the odd, sunny day in November and Maddie left her coat open as she walked to the library. The wind blew back the flaps of the coat, and cool air chased the warmth from her skin. It felt good; it felt alive.

Swirling leaves danced on the sidewalk marking her path, and squirrels rushed about in a last bid attempt to gather acorns for the winter. Maddie had missed the autumnal procession that heralded the beginning of winter to come. When she worked in the city, she would walk to the subway and pass a local park every day; now, she drove three miles to town.

When Maddie arrived at Anna's office door, she knocked, and entered before Anna could say "Come in." She was at her desk and peered over her reading glasses. Anna smiled and then got up to give Maddie a hug.

"What brings you here?"

"I…wanted to see you," Maddie said.

"Well, isn't that nice. Won't you sit down?"

Maddie sat in David's chair. She glanced at the items on the wall, saw a photo of David Friedlander, and pointed to it.

"The truth is, this is why I came," Maddie said. "Did you know that I was the one who found his body?"

Anna's eyebrows rose, and she blushed.

"I hadn't heard that."

Maddie watched her pick at the edge of the blotter on her desk.

"Did you know him well?" Maddie asked.

"David and I worked together for many years. It was such a shock to lose him that way."

Maddie glanced at the bookcase next to the desk and saw a copy of *Confessions of a Lady's Maid*.

"Did you share this desk with him?" Maddie asked.

"Yes, I did," Anna said. "This is a small department."

Maddie pulled *Confessions of a Lady's Maid* from the shelf.

"I found this book on a desk my father kept in the garage of all places. There was an inscription on the first page. It was signed 'DLF.'" Anna's jaw twitched. "Did my mother know David Friedlander?"

Anna clasped her hands on the desk.

"Yes, she did." Anna's knuckles were white.

"Did he teach one of her classes?" Maddie asked.

"No, she worked as a clerical assistant to the faculty."

Maddie sat back. "Was this when she was working on her master's?"

"I don't remember exactly. All I remember is that she needed the money and applied to become a clerical assistant."

Anna pulled her hands apart and picked at her cuticle. Maddie put the book back on the shelf.

"I don't know much about her time here," Maddie said. "Was she a good student?"

"Daisy was smart, but she was also emotional. I think she lost her focus after a while."

"Why do you say that?" Maddie asked.

"She became pregnant."

"With me."

"Yes, and at the time I thought…"

Anna paused.

"You thought what?"

"Well, she didn't have to get pregnant, not if she wanted to earn her degree."

"So, you didn't think she took her education seriously enough," Maddie said.

"Look, Maddie, Daisy was a lovely girl, but as a woman, I knew how hard it was to get the things you want in life. Daisy was just like so many girls who put their own careers in jeopardy when they allowed a man to rule their hearts."

"So, who ruled her heart?"

"I imagine it was your father."

Maddie glanced at the bookcase again.

"But the inscription in the book I have at home says '*To my own Daisy Carter, I will love you forever. DLF 1988.*' I was born in 1989."

Anna rolled her eyes. "Oh, that god awful book."

"Have you read it?" Maddie asked.

"No, I haven't read it, but I heard about it several times. It was David's favorite book."

"Some of it borders on soft porn." Maddie leaned forward. "DLF said he would love her forever. My mother, in the inscription." Anna bit her lip. "You were her friend, weren't you? You were at the house the day she disappeared. Wouldn't she have confided in you?"

Anna exhaled. "She was closer to Harlan than to me."

"Really? So, maybe he would know?"

"He would know more than I."

"Okay. Then I guess I'll have to go and see him." Maddie stood. "Take care."

Maddie left Anna's office and walked across the campus to the history department. Harlan's office was the first door she came to, and again, she knocked and entered before he had a chance to ask her in. As Anna had, he peered over his glasses and smiled.

"Madelyn."

"Hello, Harlan."

"Come in, come in."

His office had a nice cushioned chair in front of his desk, and when she sat, she shifted a bit before settling down.

"I like this chair."

"I bought it in England. I find it helps people relax so they can talk to me without stammering."

She smiled, and then grew serious.

"I just saw Anna."

"Oh?"

"I wanted to ask her about my mother and David Friedlander."

As with Anna, Maddie noticed a subtle change in his expression and a reddening of his cheeks.

"Whyever are you interested in David Friedlander?"

"I was the one who found his body."

Harlan sat back and bit the end of his pen.

"I hadn't heard that. It must have been horrible for you."

"It was." She crossed her legs. "So, I've been going through dad's stuff because I'm going to sell the house."

"You're serious," he said.

She nodded. "I haven't decided where I'm going yet, but anyway, I found some things that made me want to know more about my mother."

Harlan leaned forward, put his elbows on the desk, and clasped his hands.

"How can I help?"

"I wanted to know if she and David Friedlander had been in a relationship."

Harlan stared at his hands. He sat back and gripped the edge of the desk.

"You want to know if David was your father."

Her eyes widened, and she sat back.

"Wow. You get right to the point."

Harlan pursed his lips. "I find it saves time, which, as I get older, is a precious commodity." He sat back. "Yes, David and your mother were in a relationship while she was a student here."

"Do you remember what year that was?"

"Well, let's see. I had just earned my masters and was working on my doctorate. It must have been '88 or '89."

"I was born in 1989."

"Then it was '88. She was a clerical assistant to the faculty, and they began seeing each other."

"Why would you think he was my father?"

"Because she was pregnant when David left for England. She married your father two months later."

"Shit."

"David had received a grant to study in England. It was offered to him in such haste that he didn't have time to tell Daisy. He was gone before she could talk to him, and he never wrote her to explain. She became distraught, and when your father offered to marry her, she accepted rather than become a single mother, which, at the time, still bore a stigma that might affect her chances at a career."

Maddie slumped in her chair.

"My father never told me any of this."

"Carl was a kind man, but he wasn't, shall we say, academically inclined. Daisy was smart. She deserved an equal partner." Harlan stared at his desk. "I think that's why we all thought Daisy might have run away."

"Did you tell the police that?"

Harlan shook his head. "We told them what we knew." He tilted his head. "We all searched for her after the police left. We called her name and went into the woods." He leaned forward and looked her in the eye. "The police have David's DNA results. If you want to know for sure, get your DNA tested and have it compared to his."

Her lip trembled. "What would be the point?"

"You would be eligible for a piece of the Friedlander fortune."

"I don't want his money," Maddie said.

"Oh, don't be foolish, Madelyn. You'd have a right to it."

"But he abandoned my mother. Why would I want anything from him?"

Harlan peered at her over his reading glasses.

"Because Daisy didn't deserve to be treated so shabbily. She'd want you to have it."

Harlan looked at Maddie as she stared at her hands. She seemed younger than her twenty-nine years. He remembered when she came to his office years ago asking about the day her mother disappeared. He felt powerless to help her then, but even more so now that he knew...

"I don't want his money," she said. "But I would like to know if he's my father. Just in case of some kind of health problem, you know."

"Maddie," Harlan said. "Carl loved your mother, and he loved you."

"I know. He never stopped trying to find her, either." Maddie eyed him. "She took the dog, Harlan. It was my second birthday. I understand why he couldn't believe she just walked away."

Harlan's jaw twitched.

"Well, you could always hire a private detective."

"I don't have the money for that," she said.

"You could have it if you put a claim on David's money."

"You're such a lawyer, Harlan."

"I can't help myself."

"Well, I can, and I'm not going after his money." Maddie stood, and then noticed the time on Harlan's mantel clock "I guess it's time for me to go and open the store."

"My door is always open to you," he said.

After she left, Harlan sat back, and then got up and looked out the window. He watched Maddie crossing the campus and exhaled sharply.

"Damn you, David," he said.

Maddie got into her car and drove home. Larry greeted her at the door. She attached his leash and took him to the car.

She felt as she had after Carl died as if some part of her had gone to sleep. Maddie didn't want David Friedlander to be her father. She wanted Carl Brady, a kind and unassuming man without a complicated history, to be her father. Those were the genes she wanted.

After she picked up Larry, Maddie was driving down King's Highway and turned on the local radio station.

"Bethany Arntz, a local celebrity and heiress to the Friedlander fortune, has died. A spokesman said she had suffered a stroke."

"Did you hear that, Larry? Can you believe it?"

The announcer said something else, but Maddie only heard part of it.

"...murder of her brother, David Friedlander."

"What did he say, Larry?"

As soon as she got to the store, Maddie booted up her laptop and searched Bethany Arntz. A lot of articles about her life came up, but it was the first one that caught Maddie's eye.

"Heiress Bethany Arntz has died. Police announce that she had been sought in the murder of her brother, David Friedlander."

24

F riday morning, Ben woke to find the media camped out on the road in front of the house. Ben had lived his life in relative anonymity due to Beth's pathological need for control and a fear that her son might be the target of kidnappers. He wasn't sure how to handle the situation.

Ben was exhausted. After contacting the funeral home, he stayed in the living room watching mindless TV shows while Maria wept in her bedroom. From time to time, he would peek out the windows to see if the media was still there or go online to see what they were saying about him. He was surprised when one of the major TV gossip shows called him "the hunky son of heiress Bethany Arntz."

Ben hadn't paid much attention to his looks as he was growing up. He'd always been a bit shy with girls, and they usually approached him. The evening he spent with Candy had been unusual in that he'd forgotten himself when he talked to her.

Ben had picked up the phone a couple of times to dial her number, but in his state of mind, he decided not to call her. He didn't want to turn her off by talking about his dead mother, the woman who killed his uncle. Ben kept dwelling on the facts and trying to find an explanation for what had happened that would put his anger to rest. He knew his mother had shot his Uncle Dave. He knew she had fled to Cape May. The police accepted her guilt, but Ben still couldn't connect that Beth with the woman he'd known all his life.

Friday passed too quickly, and on Saturday morning he again found himself donning his black suit as he waited for a limousine to pick him up and take him to the funeral home.

The limousine arrived at ten a.m. He kept his eyes on the limo as he climbed inside, and on the back of the seat in front of him as it passed those clamoring to take his picture. Maria had chosen to stay home and deal with the caterers again so she wouldn't have to see Beth in the casket.

There was media outside the funeral home, too. The limo stopped at the door, and Ben ducked inside. For the second time in two weeks, Ben found himself in the same room at the funeral home where David's viewing had been held. There were more attendees this time, more people who came to pay their respects and see Bethany Arntz laid to rest.

Ben stood by the open casket for a few minutes after the others left for the cemetery. The makeup artist had done a good job of making her look as she had in life. Ben kept expecting her to say something, and perhaps explain to him why she had killed his Uncle Dave.

Ben rode alone to the cemetery and thought about poor Maria whose guilt knew no bounds.

"I should have asked if she had her phone. I should have gotten more details about that meeting in the city."

No matter how many times Ben assured her that it wasn't her fault, Maria still believed she could have done more to save her lady.

Beth was interred next to her mother in the Friedlander mausoleum, a large, concrete structure with a Jewish star at the center above the entrance. There was room for seven members of the Friedlander family, but since David had chosen not to be entombed, there were still four spaces left. Ben's father was in another cemetery in the Arntz family tomb.

While the media stayed at a respectful distance, Morris Tidwell, the second in command at the Friedlander Foundation, offered a eulogy expounding upon Beth's contribution to the various charitable organizations the foundation supported, her tireless belief that everyone was entitled to a second chance, and her compassion. Ben's thoughts again went to David. She never felt he deserved a second chance. The hypocrisy infuriated him.

When the service ended, Harlan came to Ben and then walked with him to the limousine.

"Anna and I will come in my car," Harlan said. "Is there anything you need?"

"No."

Harlan left Ben beside the limo and went to his car, but glanced back a time or two. He saw a young lady go up to Ben and wondered who she was. He also saw the change in Ben's expression when he greeted her.

Ben managed a smile as Candy approached him.

"I'm so sorry, Ben," she said.

Ben was struck by her beauty and reached for her hand.

"Will you come to the house?" Ben asked.

"Sure." Candy blushed.

"You can ride with me."

She glanced behind her. "I have my car. I'll follow you."

"There are people in the road in front of my house. You can park in our driveway."

"I think I can handle them." She looked at the small crowd gathered a few yards away. "Have they been bothering you?"

"They were outside the house all day yesterday."

"They'll go away after a while," Candy said.

"I hope so." He held her hand. "I guess we'd better go."

"I'll be right behind you."

Ben watched her walk away and wished he could go with her. They could drive to the boardwalk and watch the waves roll in. He waited until she was inside her car before getting into the limo.

Ben stared at the gray clouds through the window, and then laid his head back and studied the interior, counting the stitches in the leather, and wishing he were anywhere but here. He winced when the driver pulled into the driveway of his home, and Ben heard the members of the media yelling questions. He ducked out of the limo and ran into the house.

Ben waited in the foyer for Candy. He took off his coat and handed it to one of the people hired to handle the needs of his guests. Harlan had arrived with Anna before Ben, and both of them wore sad expressions. They nodded to him from the living room.

Ben stood at the small windows beside the door looking for Candy's car. Instead of her old sedan, he saw her walking up the drive. She came to the door, and Ben let her in before she could ring the bell. The man took her coat, Ben took her hand, and they went to the living room.

"Did they bother you?" he asked.

"I just kept walking and didn't talk to them."

"I feel like such an idiot. I should have hired someone to keep them away."

"What, like bouncers?" She smiled. "Don't worry about it. People will just do what I did."

Ben held her hand while he greeted the people he knew. He introduced her to them and would move on as quickly as he could to the next person. Unlike those who came to see David, these people weren't there to mourn Beth. They were there because etiquette dictated that they make an appearance. They all made the same polite remarks, the meaningless things you say when you don't really know or care about the deceased, and Ben was grateful when he saw that he had greeted all those he was familiar with.

Ben steered Candy to the dining room. She looked at the food and sighed.

"The food looks great."

"We can stay here and eat," he said. "I can't listen to another person tell me how sorry they are."

"Would you like me to make you a plate?" she asked.

"No, I'm fine."

They went from one end of the table to the other filling their plates. There were two chairs by a window, and they sat in them while they ate. When Ben was done, he put his plate on the windowsill.

"When this is over, I'm going away for a while," he said.

"That's a good idea," she said. "You've been through a lot."

Candy looked at the house and imagined what it might be worth. *Stop it, Candy*, she thought.

She glanced at Ben. He looked younger than he had the night they met and she worried he might think she was a bit forward by the way she showed up at the cemetery. She couldn't believe the news when she heard that his mother had died and was surprised by the urge she had to run to his side.

Ben didn't seem to notice the looks they were getting as people came into the dining room, but Candy did. She blushed and tried to focus on the yard outside the window.

"Do you want to talk about it?" she asked.

Ben glanced at her, and then looked into her eyes. They were warm, and he felt safe, but then Maria came into the room and saw Ben with a pretty blonde.

"You have guests," Maria said.

"I know, Maria." He looked at Candy. "This is my friend, Candy."

Maria gave her the eye as she put another tray of food on the table.

"Don't hide in here," she said, and then she returned to the kitchen.

"You heard her," Ben said. "We can't hide."

"I'll stay with you," Candy said. "We'll get through this."

He took a deep breath.

"This isn't how I saw our first date," he said.

Candy smiled. "I thought we already had our first date."

Ben chuckled. "You're right, and I had a great time."

"I had a great time, too."

He leaned toward her with an earnest look on his face.

"Will you stay after everyone leaves?"

"Sure."

They walked into the living room and sat together on the sofa. Two hours later, guests started leaving, and Candy and Ben went to the front door where he accepted the last of the condolences from a woman who had known Beth in high school. When he shut the door, Ben turned to Candy, gazed into her eyes, and then kissed her.

"I want you to go away with me," he said.

Candy raised her eyebrows.

"I thought we were just going to hang out."

"Oh, we will, but I want to go away somewhere warm. Somewhere we can be alone."

Ben's eyes were bloodshot and sad as he tried to convey the urgency of his request, and she would drop everything in a heartbeat to follow him if she could.

"I can't just leave, Ben."

"Why not? It's my treat."

She shook her head. "It's not the money; it's that I just started my job."

He looked around the foyer.

"You can sell this house for me. I'll sign the contract today. How can anyone deny you some time off if you list this house?"

He was right. If she listed this house, Ross would give her whatever she wanted.

"*You've been given a second chance, Candy.*" Her mother's voice echoed in her mind. "*You can't ruin this.*"

Candy walked away from him and into the living room.

"Look, I know we hardly know each other," Ben said as he followed her. "But I could get you your own room."

She sat on the sofa and laid her head back.

"You can't imagine how much I want to go."

"Then what's stopping you?" Ben asked.

Candy didn't want him to know about her past, about her DWI, her years of recovery, and her inability to keep a job, but Sandy had told her it was best to go with the truth.

"*People find out anyway,*" *she said.* "*You might as well be honest up front.*"

If Ben found out from anyone else, it would be devastating.

He sat beside her and put his head back so he could see her eyes. She turned her head to face him and smiled sadly.

"Thirteen years ago, I was in an accident. It was pretty bad. I was in the hospital for a long time."

"How old were you?" he asked.

Candy hesitated. Ben would do the math. She closed her eyes and soldiered on.

"I was seventeen. I'd been at a party, and I'd gotten drunk. When I drove home, I went off the road and hit a tree."

"Oh my God."

"The airbags and seatbelt helped, but I still hit the windshield. Both my legs were broken. I didn't graduate with my class. I had to get my GED and then I went to the community college. I had trouble keeping jobs, which is why my mother suggested I get a real estate license." She put her hand on his. "The guy I work gave me a chance because my mother's friend asked him to." She put her head on his shoulder. "I haven't been there long. If I leave now, he has no reason to keep me on."

"I'm sorry," Ben said. "I had no idea."

"If not for that, I'd love to go away with you."

Candy touched his cheek with her finger, and Ben thought he saw a tear in her eye.

"Is there somewhere you've always wanted to go?" he asked.

"I love those commercials with the couples on loungers at the beach."

He smiled. "Do you get time off for the holidays?"

She laid her head back again. "I don't think so. Ross probably goes away then."

"Then we should go away for a weekend. Just fly to Jamaica for two days."

"I'd love that."

"Why don't we plan to go at the end of the year?"

Will we still be seeing each other at the end of the year? Candy thought.

"Okay."

"Then it's a plan?" he asked.

"It's a plan."

Ben fell back and sighed. Candy glanced at him and saw that his eyes were closed.

"Listen," she said. "Why don't we get some rest and do something tomorrow?"

"That sounds nice," he said. "What do you want to do?"

"We'll play it by ear. Call me when you wake up."

Ben put his face close to hers and kissed her again. They kissed a little more, and then a little more, and then Maria came into the living room with a crew to supervise the cleanup. She glared at Ben, and then he and Candy got up and went to the foyer. The man with the coats brought hers and Ben held it for her while she put it on.

"You have wonderful manners, sir," she said.

"Bethany Arntz wouldn't have had it any other way."

Ben went outside with her. He put his hands on her cheeks, kissed her, and then heard the clicking of cameras.

"Shit," he said.

"Try to get some rest," she said.

"I will."

He wanted to walk her to her car, but she put her hand on his chest.

"You stay here," she said. "I'll deal with them."

They tried to stop Candy as she walked by, but she waved them away. He stayed in the driveway until he saw her car drive by.

As he turned to go inside, he looked at the house. He'd never liked it. The ivy-covered walls of the gothic, brick mansion left him cold. He hadn't been kidding when he told Candy she could sell the place. It was his mother's house, and as the anger that had been simmering beneath the numbness of grief rose inside him, Ben knew he had to leave this place. It would never again be his home.

25

SUNDAY

Maria made a pot of coffee and moved around the kitchen in a trance. She didn't have to wake up Beth, make her breakfast, clean her clothes, or make her bed. For twenty years, she had served the mistress of the house, and now she felt lost. While Ben still needed someone to care for the house, Maria didn't know if she wanted to be there anymore. The memories were too hard to bear.

Ben came downstairs, saw her face, and then went to pour himself some coffee.

"Do you want breakfast?" Maria asked.

"I'm not hungry," he said.

"You have to eat. Your mother would be upset."

Ben flinched at the mention of his mother. He went to the island, sat, and then stared at the coffee.

"I want to talk to you," Maria said.

"Okay," he said.

"I'm going to leave this house."

Ben's eyes rose to meet hers.

"What do you mean?"

"I can't be here anymore. There are too many memories."

"But I always thought of you as part of the family," he said.

Maria gave him a weary smile.

"I have my own family, Ben."

"Yeah, I know, but you've always been here."

"I will find someone to replace me before I go."

"I don't care about having someone else to clean, Maria. I care about you."

A tear rolled down her cheek. Maria walked over to Ben and reached for his hand.

"You are a young man now. You need to live on your own. Close up this house and find a place of your own; a place where you can do whatever you like. You don't need a mama anymore."

Her words seemed to echo his thoughts as Ben looked at the mansion the day before. This wasn't his home, and now Ben was free to go and make his own life.

"It's time. You are twenty-three now. You're old enough."

"I could go anywhere." He wrapped his hands around his mug. "But I'd be alone."

"Not for long." She put her hand under his chin. "Look at that face. You'll be fighting the women off in no time." She pulled her hand away. "You even had one here yesterday, didn't you?"

He peered up at her. "I like her."

Maria raised her eyebrows. "She seems nice, but you be careful. It's not always easy to know who is real and who wants your money."

"I don't think Candy cares about that."

"Everyone cares about that," Maria said.

"Does that mean you too?" Ben asked.

She sighed. "No. I stayed because I loved you and I cared about your mother."

"Candy is a nice person."

"Fine. Just be careful."

Maria went to the other side of the island and sat.

"So, where will you go?" Ben asked.

"I'm going to live with my sister. She's a widow now and has a room in her house near Chicago."

"That's far away," he said.

"They have an airport, and you're always welcome."

Ben looked around the kitchen.

"I have been thinking about selling this place. I don't want to live here anymore."

Maria's eyes widened.

"It's too soon to decide something like that. Just get a place of your own and wait." Ben stared at his coffee as Maria's voice grew louder. "This place belonged to your grandparents. You can't just make that kind of decision without thinking about it."

"She killed Uncle Dave, Maria."

Maria's shoulders slumped.

"I still don't understand how she could do it."

"Mom saw him for what he was," Ben said.

Maria exhaled sharply. "What do you mean?"

"David was just another rival. All she ever wanted was my grandfather's respect. She worked hard to earn it, but whatever she did wasn't enough. All David had to do was exist."

Maria sighed. "My father didn't believe a girl should go to college. They all believed a girl would just get married anyway so why waste the money?"

"My grandfather was wrong. He just made things worse between them." Ben's eyes welled with tears. "Uncle Dave just wanted to teach. He just wanted to be who he was." He shook his head. "He was harmless. Why kill him when he was gonna be dead soon anyway?"

"I don't know." Maria got up and went to the sink. "Maybe we will never know."

Ben spied the mail basket sitting at the end of the island. He pulled it closer and started sorting through the mail. He found an envelope from Arthur Mantz' office and opened it. It contained the notice to condemn along with a form letter from Arthur's secretary.

"Maria, did you know about this?"

"About what?"

"The city wanting to condemn Fenway Manor?"

"They send one every year." She stared at the notice. "If that's a new one, then it's the second one they've sent."

"It's from my mother's attorney." He read the notice. "Did my mother get one?"

"I remember she got something from the town last month."

"Where would it be?" he asked.

"It's probably in her desk."

Ben ran up the stairs to his mother's room. The small, white desk in her bedroom sat in front of a large window. Piles of envelopes were arranged in order by date received. Her pens were kept in the top drawer so they wouldn't clutter the desktop. Her laptop was closed and occupied the left corner. Her landline phone occupied the right.

Ben sat in Beth's petite office chair and looked through the envelopes. One dated October 28 from the City of Logans Grove had been opened. It contained two sheets of paper - one, the notice Arthur Mantz had sent, the other a letter from the mayor advising that since she hadn't complied with the 1995 order to refurbish or raze the mansion, the town had filed a motion to lift stay of proceedings, and the matter would be heard on November 28.

"1995," Ben said.

Ben had driven by that old place for years and never saw a sign out front saying it was condemned. He had never heard his mother mention that the town wanted to condemn the place. David hadn't said anything about it either.

It was no secret that Beth had friends in high places. Had one of them enough clout to stay the order of condemnation for over twenty years?

This made no sense to Ben. Why would Beth use her influence to keep Fenway Manor from being torn down? Beth had never shown the slightest interest in the place. It was David who cared about it. If anything, she would have delighted in tearing it down just to see him suffer.

Ben put the papers back into the envelope. He opened the bottom drawer of the desk, the one that held Beth's files. He flipped through the tabs until he found one that said, "Fenway Manor." Inside were more than twenty years of Notices, all saying the same thing.

Ben opened Beth's laptop and waited for it to boot up. He went to the county website and looked up the docket number on the motions. Every time the town had filed a motion to lift the stay, a Judge Charles Anderson had denied the request. Ben searched Judge Anderson and found that he had retired at the end of last year. He would no longer be around to stop the condemnation from going through.

Ben shut the laptop and sat back. He looked at the stack of bills and realized he'd have to pay them. He picked them up and took them downstairs. Maria was wiping down the counters when he walked into the kitchen.

"Did Mom ever talk to you about Fenway Manor?"

"She said she hated it and wished it would fall down," Maria said.

"Then why not just let the town condemn it?" Ben said. He

looked at his phone. "Shit. I'm supposed to meet her attorney at eleven. I'd better get going." He took his jacket off the hook by the door, and then looked at Maria. "Don't go anywhere yet."

"I can't go without you," she said, and then smiled. "I need you to drive me to the airport." She shook her head at his anxious expression. "You're such a worrywart."

"So, I've been told." He smiled. "I'll be back later."

Ben got into his car in the garage and dialed Candy's number. They agreed to meet at the Italian place on Artisan Row. He pushed the button on the garage door opener, and then drove past the media as he turned onto the road and hoped they wouldn't start following him around town.

He drove to the American Hotel in Freehold. It had been built as a stagecoach stop in 1824 and rebuilt over the years into a fine hotel. Ben was able to grab a parking spot on the street and walk to the hotel.

He met with Arthur in his room. They sat at a small table near the window. A large folder and two bottles of water sat in the center.

Arthur was in his eighties but looked closer to sixty-five. He had been Jacob Friedlander's friend and attorney since the fifties and had represented Beth all her life. Arthur had handled the transfer of ownership to Beth when Jake died and knew all the family secrets. As he opened the file, Ben was eager to ask him about Fenway Manor but decided to wait until they got the legalities out of the way.

"As I said over the phone, your mother called me because she wanted to change some things in her will, but she didn't sign the final papers. I can file the original in probate as it is."

"When did you talk to her?" Ben asked.

Arthur looked at his phone. "It was almost two weeks ago on a Tuesday."

"What did she want to change?"

Arthur pulled out a sheet of paper.

"She wanted to add a bequest to a Maria Vega, and she wanted to end David's trust payments." Arthur looked up. "I tried to dissuade her regarding David, but she was adamant."

"I didn't think she knew about the payments."

Arthur shook his head. "When your grandfather died, the trust was inadvertently added to a list of his assets. My secretary at the time was working off an old list that should have been discarded when Jake requested the change, but these things happen, and Beth found out about the money. She wasn't pleased and threatened to end the payments, but Linda persuaded her to let sleeping dogs lie."

"But it's a separate trust," Ben said. "Mom didn't have control over that trust."

"Before Linda died, Beth persuaded her to put Beth in charge of the trust."

Ben sat back and shook his head.

"And Grandma went along with it." He looked at Arthur. "So, why end the payments now?"

"If you want my opinion, I think she was ending them simply out of spite."

"She didn't have to do it at all. Uncle Dave's heart was failing. Why couldn't she just leave it alone?"

"Beth was a hard woman." Arthur sipped his coffee. "Everything was black and white to her, and her feelings toward David never softened." He sat back. "Did she speak to David before…"

"They talked on the phone the night before."

"Have you any idea what they discussed?" Ben shook his head. "So sad. Well, shall we go over the will?"

"Yes."

"It's fairly simple considering the size of the estate. She left everything to you – the company, the stocks, bonds, the properties in Logans Grove..."

"How much did she want to leave Maria?" Ben asked.

"Fifty thousand."

"You're kidding. That's all?"

"It was the amount she requested."

"Maria has been with us forever."

"Ben, you're free to give her whatever you want. As I said, Beth never signed the amendments."

Arthur pulled out a copy of the letter from the town Ben had found on Beth's desk.

"I saw the one you sent her," Ben said. "Do you have any idea why she didn't tear it down years ago?"

Arthur shook his head. "I told Jake to tear the thing down fifty years ago, but he had some fool notion about turning it into a museum or something. When he made his will, I thought he would leave it to David. When Jake told me he was giving it to Beth, I didn't know what to make of it. I told him he should give it to David, but he was adamant."

Ben sat back. "And now it's my problem." He leaned forward. "Did you notice that the order to stay was executed in 1995?"

"Has it been that long?"

"Every year the town would go the court to have it lifted, and every year this judge named Charles Anderson would turn them down."

"Jake and Linda knew a couple named Anderson. He might have been their son."

"He retired at the end of last year."

"And Beth lost her connection," Arthur said. "Which means the town could file a motion to have the order lifted and nobody would stop them."

Ben glanced out the window.

"So, when they enforce the order, what happens next?"

"She was ordered to either refurbish or tear it down. They will expect you to do it now. I suggest you hire a local attorney to represent you in court."

Ben sat back and clasped his hands in his lap.

"There's something else I wanted to talk to you about," he said.

Arthur sat back and pursed his lips.

"I want to sell the company."

Arthur sighed. "It's too soon to make that kind of decision, Ben. I advise waiting at least a year before you make any permanent decisions."

"But I have no interest in it. I want to teach."

"Ben, listen to an old man. I understand how you feel, but your mother just died. You just lost your uncle. Whether you know it or not the things that have happened in the last two weeks are clouding your judgment." He watched as Ben tossed his head back and stared at the ceiling. "Let one of the board members have your proxy until you're absolutely sure this is what you want to do. There's no rush. You have money to live on, and Kirby Grant has been Beth's right-hand man for twenty years. He can handle the duties of a CEO until you decide to move forward." Arthur's avuncular smile comforted Ben. "You can teach if that's what you want, but don't throw away your legacy on a whim."

"Fine. I'll wait, but I won't change my mind."

"That is your right. In the meantime, I'll file for probate." Arthur took some papers out of the file. "I'll need you to sign as executor that you are allowing me to act as your representative."

Arthur slid the papers to Ben, handed him a pen, and Ben signed them.

"That's it?" Ben asked. "I thought there would be more to it."

"No, that's it for now. You're lucky. Beth had everything prepared. There's a lot to take care of, and she wanted to be sure it would be a seamless transition."

"I suppose I should do the same thing someday if I have anyone to leave it to."

"I can prepare something that allows you to designate a beneficiary." Arthur smiled, and then bit the end of his pen before speaking. "How are you doing, Ben, really?"

"I can't sleep, and I don't feel like eating." He folded his arms on the table. "I want to know why my uncle had to die."

"The police are absolutely sure it was Beth?"

Ben nodded and looked at Arthur.

"I feel like I didn't even know her."

"That relationship was fraught with peril," Arthur said. "But I never dreamed it would come to this."

Arthur picked up the file and slid it into his briefcase on the floor beside the table.

"I've been cleaning David's house," Ben said. "Maybe I'll find something that will explain it."

"Perhaps you shouldn't dig too deeply," Arthur said.

"Do you know something?"

"No, but I've seen families torn apart by things they discover after a loved one passes away. It might just be the old man in me, but I don't want to see you bogged down by things that happened before you were born. Forget the past. Get on with your life."

Ben smiled and then leaned forward.

"I'm working on that. In fact, I met a girl, and we're having dinner tonight."

"That's wonderful. That's exactly what I'm talking about."

"She's really pretty," Ben said. "She makes me feel happy."

"Be careful. Women have a way of turning your head, and you have a great deal of money now."

"You sound like Maria."

"Well, it's true. Money tends to draw people with evil intent, and you don't have anyone to guide you. Use caution."

"Candy doesn't have any evil intentions," Ben said.

"Let's hope not."

"So, you'll send me something when you've filed for probate?"

"I will. And if you have any questions, call me. I'm always available to you."

Ben got up, and Arthur followed him to the door. Before he left, he turned and shook Arthur's hand.

"Thank you, Mr. Mantz," Ben said.

"You're welcome. Take care of yourself."

When he left the hotel, Ben sat in the car for a while staring at the traffic on Main Street and remembering how it felt to have no responsibility other than to study. He watched the people strolling on the sidewalk. Where were those people going? Had they recently lost someone or had they just met the love of their life?

Two weeks ago, his biggest problem was telling his mother that he was quitting school. Now, as he was confronted by new obligations that he was ill-prepared for, the urge to run away to an island somewhere returned, and he had to force himself to tamp it down as he headed back to Princeton and David's house.

26

SUNDAY

Candy woke up thinking about Ben. She hadn't felt this way about a guy since high school. She was proud of herself for having told Ben the truth about her accident. He didn't cringe when she told him it had happened thirteen years ago, and he'd still asked her to go to Jamaica with him. The old fears that had kept her from getting close to anyone seemed to vanish when she was around him.

Her mom, Nina, was reading the Sunday paper at the dining room table when she came downstairs.

"I made you eggs," Nina said.

"Thanks."

"You have to eat something."

"I'm getting coffee first."

Candy went through the door that separated the dining room from the kitchen.

"You can't live on coffee alone. You look too thin."

"I haven't lost any weight, Mom."

"You will if you don't eat."

Candy took a deep breath while she tried to handle her emotions. She was thirty, and her mother still badgered her about her weight, what she ate, how late she stayed out, etc. It was time to find a place of her own, but until she sold Maddie's store, she'd have to stay in her old bedroom, and that meant being nice to Nina. As grateful as Candy was to her mother for taking care of her for so long, she wished she could get Nina to stop loving her so much and wished her mother would show Candy that she believed in her.

"They buried Beth Arntz yesterday," Nina said. "Good riddance. She was a hateful woman."

"I went to the funeral," Candy said.

"I was wondering if you were going to tell me about him."

Candy's hand began to shake. She got a mug out of the cabinet and poured her coffee out of a carafe her mother used to keep it hot. Nina didn't like leaving coffee in the coffeemaker. It burned, and then you had to make a new pot and coffee wasn't cheap.

"Candy," Nina said. "I saw your picture in the paper."

"Oh, shit," Candy said.

She stood at the door for a moment, and then she went through the door and brought her coffee to her seat at the table. Nina eyed her as she waited for Candy to speak.

"I did what you told me to do. I read the obituaries and checked out some houses that might go up for sale now that their owners were dead."

"And this is how you met him?" Nina leaned toward Candy. "Well, at least you got something out of it because that house will never be sold."

"You don't know that," Candy said. "It belongs to Ben now. He might want to sell it for something more modern."

Nina looked at Candy over her reading glasses.

"So, tell me about him."

"There's nothing to tell. I met him a couple of days ago. He's very nice."

"And good-looking. And rich."

Candy rolled her eyes as she sat.

"And that house is a legacy," Nina said. "There's no way he's gonna sell it. Rich people hold onto stuff forever."

"People are different now, Mom. Younger people are playing by different rules. Many of them are changing the way things are done, like weddings for instance. A lot of them feel that spending so much on a wedding is foolish. They don't even buy engagement rings anymore."

"Baloney."

Candy exhaled sharply. "No, it's true. I've been reading a lot about them because I'm going to have to sell houses to them, and it's true. They don't feel the need to accumulate a lot of stuff." Candy leaned forward. "They don't even buy television sets."

"Now that can't be true. Everyone has a TV."

"They watch on laptops or on their phone."

"On their phone? I'd go blind if I watched TV on my phone." Nina turned the page of her newspaper. "So, when are you seeing him again?"

"We're going out to dinner tonight."

Nina raised her eyebrows. "Is he picking you up here?"

"We're going to meet at the restaurant," Candy said.

Nina pursed her lips. "What? You don't want him to meet your mother?"

Candy threw her head back. "We just met." She brought her head down and looked at Nina. "I don't even know where this is going."

Nina screwed up her mouth and eyed Candy. She took a deep breath and then exhaled sharply.

"You know, those young people might be onto something. I've been thinking of getting rid of some of the stuff around here."

"Like what?"

"Like my old bedroom furniture." Nina clasped her hands on the table. "Do you know it belonged to my grandparents?" Nina shook her head. "It's so heavy, and I don't need twin beds anymore. I'd like a nice queen size for myself." She peered over her glasses at Candy. "Maybe you'd like to take it when you get a place of your own."

"I don't want twin beds either," Candy said.

"The dresser is nice," Nina said.

"You said it's too heavy and I agree. I want to pick out my own furniture."

"Maybe the end tables and grandma's lamps. You'll need those things and they ain't cheap."

Candy shoulders slumped. "I know, Mom. I'll figure something out when the time comes."

Nina picked up her paper, and then put it down.

"So, tell me about her funeral? I'll bet people came just to be seen. No one liked her, you know, not even in school. Her parents made her go to public school, and she never let us forget she was too good to be there. What a snotty bitch she was."

"Her son is very nice," Candy said.

"I always wondered if he was her real kid. She was old when she had him you know."

"How old was she?"

"In her late thirties," Nina said. "Who carried her to the grave?"

Candy shrugged. "I wasn't there for that. You know I'm thirty. Do you think I'm too old to have a kid?"

"Oh, don't be ridiculous." Nina smiled. "So, is that boy as good-looking in person?" Nina leaned forward.

"He's younger than me," Candy said.

"Oh, that's doesn't matter these days. Besides, you lost a lot of years. You're just starting out so you can say your twenty-five."

"The wrinkles under my eyes say I'm thirty."

"Oh, don't give me that. You don't have any wrinkles." Nina examined Candy's eyes. "Besides, you can always get a shot of Botox. They can Botox under the eyes, right?"

"I have no idea."

"Well, you should find out. It wouldn't hurt to know."

Candy finished her coffee and got up to fetch another mugful. Nina resumed reading her paper, but she also watched Candy put a plate on the table when she returned. It contained a single slice of toast with strawberry jam.

"Is that all you're having?"

"I'm not that hungry. Besides, I'm going out to dinner, and I don't want to be full."

Nina leaned forward on clasped hands. "You're gonna eat in front of him?"

Candy kept her eyes on the table.

"Oh, for God's sake, Mom. Of course, I'm gonna eat in front of him."

"Okay, you don't have to snap at me."

"I didn't snap," Candy said.

Nina sat back. "So, you went through the obituaries like I told you."

"Uh, uh."

"Did you find any other promising leads?"

Candy sat back. "Remember my first day when I told you that I had gone to see Maddie? She is going to sell the store *and* the house."

Nina frowned and sat back.

"Yeah. I remember now." Nina stared at her hands. "I thought she hated you."

"We talked, Mom. She's okay with me. That's why she's letting me sell her properties."

"That's just business, Candy. I don't see Maddie as the forgiving type."

"She's older now, and she's changed. Besides, it's none of your business, is it?"

Nina screwed up her mouth and shrugged.

"It's my business if someone hurts you."

"I'm old enough to take care of myself."

"You might think you are, but I know you, and you aren't a good judge of people."

Candy tossed her head back again and sighed.

"She really hurt you," Nina said.

"It was a misunderstanding," Candy said.

"One you paid for. What about the guy who nearly raped you? He got off scot-free, and Maddie went off to the city and had a glamorous life."

Candy clenched her teeth and gripped the edge of the table.

"Everything is fine now, Mom."

"Fine, but I don't want to hear about it if she breaks your heart again."

"I won't say a word. I'll take it to my grave."

Nina got up and took her plate to the sink. After she wiped down the kitchen, she went to the living room to watch TV. Candy nibbled at her toast and wished she could crawl into another universe where no one asked her what her plans were.

Candy spent the rest of the morning getting ready for her date. She chose an outfit that wasn't too revealing, yet was feminine and attractive – a pair of silk slacks that were part of a suit she wore for work and a long-sleeved blouse with covered buttons she left untucked.

She worried over the lines on her face for a while and stared into the mirror hoping they would dissolve into a perfect, smooth area, but that didn't work. The scar on her throat had healed nicely but was still visible. She put a little concealer over it, which lightened it some, and then tried on a pastel scarf, but she felt it made her look old. Instead, she tried on an old, gold choker with a butterfly at the center and liked the way it looked.

It was too early to meet Ben, but Candy wanted to get out of the house for a while. She went downstairs and saw that her mother had fallen asleep in front of the TV.

"Yes," she said softly.

She went to the kitchen door, took her coat and purse off the hook, and went outside. She put on her coat while she walked to her car in the driveway, got in, and drove away.

How would she kill five hours? She could go to Artisan Row and do what all the tourists did on weekends, but the thought of all those people made her cringe. Parking would be a nightmare. As she drove down King's Highway, she was approaching Fenway Manor when she decided to pull into the driveway. It was a warm day for November, and she had put on a pair of casual shoes she would replace with the heels she kept in the car for work before she met Ben. She tied a scarf around her head to protect her hair and got out of the car.

Candy walked down the driveway to the back of the house. She thought about Ben's uncle and how sad Ben was over his death. All the money in the world couldn't heal the pain of his loss any faster. It made her think of what it would be like if she lost her mother. Despite how much her mother tried to insinuate herself into Candy's life, Candy knew she'd be lost without her mom.

She thought about what Nina had said about Beth. She'd called her a "hateful woman." How had someone like that given birth to a boy like Ben? He'd been nothing but kind since she met him. She hoped he didn't have a hidden, darker side.

Candy scanned the woods surrounding the yard. Derek. The ghost now had a name, and she felt a thrill go up her spine. Now she knew his history, and this gave her something to talk about, even if the ghost couldn't talk back.

It was windy as she walked across the yard toward the woods. She shoved her hands into her pockets and looked up at the sky. The clouds were scattered and flat. They didn't look fluffy at all, and this disappointed Candy. She preferred the fluffy clouds that gathered in distinct shapes. She was gazing up at the sky when she felt her shoe hit something. She stopped and looked down. There was a piece of cement embedded in the ground. She was grateful she hadn't tripped and landed on her face. She stepped over it before looking up to continue her walk. That's when she saw him standing a few feet away.

"Derek," she said.

He smiled broadly and rushed to her so fast that it startled her. Candy gazed at the glowing figure before her and sensed his happiness. His smile didn't fade as he stared into her eyes.

"I talked to a man who knows your family history." She pointed toward the house. "He said your mother died there." Now, his smile faded. "It must have been awful for you."

He signed something with his hands, and she shook her head.

"You know sign language?" Candy said. "How did you learn sign language?"

Derek's eyebrows rose, and his expression was quizzical.

"Did someone teach you?" she asked. He nodded. "So, other people have seen you."

He nodded again and then moved closer. Candy took a step back.

"My name is Candy," she said. He smiled and mouthed her name. "Yes! I understood that. Say something else."

"I'm lonely."

"I'm sorry to hear that." She peered at Fenway Manor, and then back at him. "Why *are* you here all alone?"

Derek shrugged.

"It must be hard," Candy said. "I've been lonely, too." A brisk, cool wind blew across the yard, and she shivered. "I'm going to sit in my car. Can you come with me?"

He tilted his head forward, and then she walked away. When she got to her car, he appeared next to it.

"You can fly," she said.

Derek nodded and put out his arms.

"Like a bird," Candy said. "Like Superman."

He put down his arms and narrowed his eyes.

"He's a superhero. He flies through the air and saves people. I don't know much more about him." Candy thought for a moment. "Wait." She pulled out her cell phone and searched for a picture of Superman. When she found one, she held it up for Derek to see.

"That's Superman."

Derek studied the picture and then smiled.

Candy got into her car but left the door open. Derek kneeled in front of her as she glanced at the house.

"So, this is where you lived."

He nodded, went to the house, put his hand on the wall, and went inside. He came back out and held out his hands like a magician. Candy clapped.

"Oh, I wish I could do that, just disappear when I want to." He shook his head and frowned. "No, I don't mean I want to die, just disappear for a while."

He smiled, came to her, and then put out his hand as if to touch her face.

"Beautiful," he mouthed.

Candy blushed, turned her face away, and then stared at her hands.

"I've been told I'm pretty since I was a little girl," Candy said. "It doesn't change the way I feel. I don't feel comfortable around people. That's why I said I'd like to disappear sometimes."

Derek squatted so he could see her eyes. She looked at him. He smiled broadly and made a funny face.

She chuckled. "You're funny." She tilted her head. "Are you happy, Derek?"

He clasped his hands between his knees and looked toward the end of the driveway. He turned his face too look at her and then mouthed the word, "No."

She laid her head back and sighed.

"Is there anything I can do to help you?" He shook his head and shrugged. "But there must be some reason you're still here. If we can figure out what it is…"

He shook his head again and put his hand on hers.

"But there must be something I can do," Candy said. "It's so unfair."

Derek's wistful smile said it all – he had accepted his fate.

"You are really okay with it?" she asked.

He nodded, and then sat on the ground. Candy looked in her rearview mirror and saw the lines under her eyes.

"Can I ask you something?" Derek nodded. "I met a man. His name is Ben, and I really like him. He's very nice, but he's younger than me." She looked at him. "Do you think that matters?"

Derek got up and put his face close to her.

"He will love you."

He backed up a few steps, used his hands to outline a female form, folded his arms over his chest, raised his eyebrows, and winked at her.

She blushed, giggled, and then laughed out loud.

"Oh, my God, you're just like the men now."

He threw his head back and laughed.

"You're so easy to talk to," she said. Derek kneeled beside her again. "Do you remember seeing me before? It was a long time ago. I was inside the house. A boy tried to...and you were at the door when I tried to run away."

Derek's solemn expression as he nodded touched her heart.

"I was so scared when I saw you, but you're not scary at all."

Candy shivered as she glanced at her phone on the passenger seat. She held it up for Derek to see.

"It's a quarter to two. I'm supposed to meet my date at six." She put the phone into her purse. "I'd stay here with you, but I'm freezing. I'm going to have to leave now."

Derek stood and took a few steps back. She closed the car door and then rolled down the window.

"I'll be back. I promise."

He smiled and held up his hand to wave goodbye. Candy returned the wave before turning the car around and heading down the driveway to King's Highway.

27

SUNDAY AFTERNOON

After driving to David's house, Ben was too tired to go through the piles of junk. He checked the mail, and then he went back to his house.

The media was still there when he returned, and he averted his eyes as he turned onto his driveway. When Ben went inside the house through the kitchen door, he found Maria in her room sorting her things. He had some time before he had to meet Candy, so he went to the library and began going through his father's desk.

Conrad Arntz had died in 2002 leaving all his earthly possessions to his wife and seven-year-old son. An undetected abdominal aneurysm had burst while he was flying over Las Vegas, and he died before they could get him to a hospital.

Beth had to break the news to Ben. He remembered how he'd felt, but not what Beth had said. He had stayed home from school for a month until Beth felt it was time for him to return. Ben wondered now if it was for him or for her that Beth kept him home so long.

He pulled out the desk drawers one at a time and put all the papers on the desk. There were notes and receipts in an accordion file with a label that read, "Beth" along with journals and photographs. Ben was surprised to find so much there after all these years.

Conrad had kept meticulous records of each time he filled his car with gas or ate at a restaurant. A ledger of paid and unpaid bills was in the center drawer. Ben noticed that his bar bill was high and that he frequently ate out - alone.

As he went through one of several check-size accordion folders, Ben saw a folded piece of stationary and took it out. It was hand-written in Beth's fine hand and was dated November 5, 1997.

Dear Conrad,

I know things have been difficult between us for quite some time, but you must understand that I cannot, under any circumstances, sell, raze, or destroy the Fenway house, and you know why. That you should ask such a thing is unconscionable. I know you only want the best for Ben, and perhaps when David is gone, we can discuss this, but until then, please do not ask me again.

His father wanted to get rid of the Fenway house. Ben would have been two at the time.

"...perhaps when David is gone..."

She couldn't do anything about the place until David died. Was it possible she was trying to protect David?

Ben thought about the notice to lift the stay of proceedings and Beth's call to Arthur Mantz about making changes to her will. He felt that there was a connection between the two. She was taking away David's means to live as if she knew David wasn't going to be around anymore. Had she been planning to kill David for a long time, or was her decision prompted by the town's determination to rid itself of Fenway Manor?

Ben sat back and looked around the library. Nothing had been moved after his father died. It was dusted and vacuumed, but other-wise remained in suspended animation as if awaiting Conrad Arntz's return. Would his mother have done the same for him if Ben had died before her?

He looked at the note Beth had written to Conrad again.

"...perhaps when David is gone, we can discuss this, but until then, please do not ask me again."

Why did they have to wait until David was gone? It couldn't

have been because Fenway Manor was important to David, that he loved it more than life itself, or that he couldn't bear to see it torn down. These were the reasons Beth would have used to tear it down, so why had she blocked the efforts by the town to condemn it year after year? It just didn't make any sense.

Ben put the note back into the accordion file, shut the drawer, and then noticed the time. He had to get ready for his date, so he headed upstairs to change.

~

Candy arrived at the restaurant first and chose to wait in the lobby for Ben. She had gone to Artisan Row after all and had spent some time watching Maddie's store from the café window. She'd had one latte and had felt full, but the smell of pizza revived her appetite.

Ben came in wearing a suit jacket with no tie, his hair tousled from the wind, and his cheeks rosy from the cold. She saw him come in and felt a tingle go through her as he flashed a smile. Candy got up and met him at the podium where the host greeted them. Ben's eyebrows rose when his eyes met hers.

"You look great."

"You, too," Candy said.

They were taken to a booth near the fireplace and Candy was grateful for the heat when Ben helped her out of her coat. She sat as he hung the coat on a hook between their booth and the one next to theirs.

"I've been looking forward to this," Ben said as he sat. "I really enjoyed being with you the other night."

"Me, too."

"I also want to thank you for coming yesterday," he said.

"There's no need. I wanted to come."

"Forgive me if I talk about it. I'm still trying to process it."

"Talk about whatever you want," Candy said.

"I just can't figure out why she did it." He ran his finger along the edge of the menu. "I mean, they didn't like each other, all right, but I never thought she'd kill him."

"I don't have any siblings, but I think it's possible to get so angry with someone you love that you lose control."

"She didn't lose control. She planned…" He stopped when he saw the sad expression on her face. "I'm sorry."

"It's okay. You said you're still processing it."

Candy started reading her menu when the server came to the table and asked for their drink order. Ben ordered wine, but she ordered a coke.

"You don't drink," he said. Candy blushed, and her eyes went to the table. "Right. Sorry."

She smiled and peered at him through her lashes.

"It's okay," she said. "I don't mind talking about it."

Ben looked over the menu and made her quiver.

"I really needed this," he said. "I haven't talked to anyone close to my age since I left school."

"I'm not that close to your age," she said.

Ben tilted his head.

"Does that bother you?"

"A little."

He reached for her hand and cupped it.

"It doesn't make any difference to me, and I don't give a shit what anyone else thinks."

"Really?"

"Really."

The server returned with their drinks and took their food order.

"Okay," Candy said. "So, I told you about me. Now it's your turn."

"Okay. I'm twenty-three, I just quit school because I don't want to become a professor, and I want to teach middle school history."

"You sound so sure," she said.

"I am sure. I've already been offered a job in California."

Candy's face fell. "That's far away."

"Oh, I'm not going to take it," he said quickly. "But it's what I want to do. My mother was really pissed off when she found out I'd quit school because it was *her* dream that I become a professor." He folded his arms on the table and leaned forward. "I did everything she ever asked me to do." He looked into Candy's eyes. "What the hell was wrong with me?"

"You're an only child like me. I still have trouble telling my mother things I know will upset her."

"But I never questioned her, I never rebelled, not until the day I decided to quit." Ben glanced at the fireplace. "In fact, the only thing I ever did to rebel was to maintain a relationship with my Uncle Dave." He looked at Candy. "She tried to keep me from seeing him, but when I found out about him, I rode my bike to his house to meet him. I was eleven. I went there at least once a week. It was the only thing I ever did against her wishes."

"You must have been close to him."

"I was." He clasped his hands on the table. "I never had a friend until I went to college."

"You're kidding?" Candy said.

"I had to keep up my grades. On weekends, I studied."

"I was just the opposite. I didn't worry about my grades. My mother used to get so mad at me when she got my report card." Candy laughed. "Oh, my God, I remember one time when I was a junior how she tried to ground me for it, and I climbed out my bedroom window so I could go to the homecoming football game. I wanted to be a cheerleader so bad that I would hang out with the squad and do anything they asked me to. I just couldn't miss the game that night, but my mother figured it out and came looking for me. She yelled at me in front of everyone, and the squad wouldn't let me work for them anymore. I was devastated."

Ben's smile warmed her heart.

"I went to a private school," he said. "We didn't have homecoming."

"I thought everyone had homecoming," Candy said.

"We didn't have a football team." Candy's mouth gaped. "It emphasized scholastic achievement and rich people paid for the pedigree. They didn't need sports. In fact, the gym classes consisted of resistance training and yoga."

"Holy shit," she said. "I've never heard of such a thing."

Ben held up his glass.

"To leading a normal life."

"I agree," she said.

He sipped his wine and watched the candlelight flicker in her eyes.

"You're very pretty, Candy."

"You ain't so bad yourself."

He sniggered. "Ah, thanks." He sat back. "So, tell me about your old boyfriends."

"I didn't have many," she said "There was one during my sopho-more year. He was a senior, and it ended when he went to college. I went out with a few guys, but nothing happened with them, and then I had my accident."

"So, maybe we were meant for each other." Candy blushed and felt warm. He reached over and put his hand on hers. "Is that okay to say?"

"It's fine," she said. "It's great actually. So, what about you?"

"I dated a woman when I was in college. Her name was Jennifer, and she was from Texas. We got along well, but when she went home, she didn't come back, and we fell out of touch." He sipped his wine. "I never dated anyone else."

"You're kidding? Did you ever find out what happened to her?"

"She got married a year later," he said.

"And you never dated *anyone* else?"

"No. I just didn't have time."

"Well, I'm glad you have time now," Candy said.

The evening passed too quickly and before they knew it, three hours had passed. Neither wanted to end the date, but Candy had to work in the morning, and Ben didn't feel right about bringing her to his mother's house on their first date, so they decided to see each other again the next evening.

"I know a place in Princeton you might like," he said. "Can I pick you up?"

"I would rather meet you. I can come to your house."

He smiled. "You haven't told your mother about me, have you?"

"Oh, no, she knows. She saw a picture of us kissing outside your house. It was in the paper this morning."

"Oh, shit."

"I had to tell her about you, but I don't want you to come to my house yet. You're not ready for that."

"I can handle just about anything," he said.

"You haven't met Nina."

He got up and held her coat while she put it on.

"You'll have to tell her sometime," he said. He wrapped his arms around her and whispered in her ear. "I'm not going away."

Candy shivered when she felt his warm breath in her ear. She pulled away. Ben put on his coat and followed her to her car. She leaned against it; he came close and kissed her. It was the best kiss she'd ever had, and she didn't want to pull away. He kissed her again, sending more shivers up and down her body, and then he pulled away.

"I won't let you go if we keep this up."

"Right," she said.

He opened her door, and she slid inside. He waited until she had driven away and smiled. He felt lighter than he had in days and was grateful to whoever had sent her to him.

28

Another busy weekend ended, and Maddie was eager to get home. She wanted to look up David Friedlander online. She wanted to see his face again, to look at his nose, his eyes, or his mouth for any resemblance to hers.

Maddie stopped at a taco place on the way home. She made sure Larry was settled before setting up her laptop and her food on the kitchen table. She found a bunch of articles on David Friedlander.

Maddie clicked on the "images" tab on Google and found lots of photos of him. She stared at each for a long time before putting a photo of herself on the desktop and comparing it to David's.

The curve of his mouth was similar, as were the shape of his eyes. Maddie knew if she looked at the photos long enough, she'd convince herself that he was her father, so she filled the desktop with the Google screen and kept looking at David's pictures.

Maddie was shocked to find a picture of him with her mother and clicked on it. It was on a university alumni website and was captioned, "David Friedlander and a friend attend the 1989 reception honoring Mason Grant." Daisy was "a friend." Maddie felt a hot little ball of fire form in her stomach, and she didn't think it was the taco she'd just eaten.

She clicked on the other images and found an article about David Friedlander finding some bones at Fenway Manor.

"Friedlander believes the bones belonged to Derek Fenway, the son of war hero Alastair Fenway. At the time of the tragedy at Fenway Manor, Derek was unaccounted for. He had been away from home for quite some time and was believed to be in Missouri when his family died. Friedlander is paying for the exhumation of Angelica Fenway's remains so a DNA test can be made for comparison."

Maddie looked at the bones. They had been found near an old oak tree in the woods with a pair of leather boots. She clicked on another photo of David standing beside a gravestone.

"The remains of Derek Fenway were interred beside those of his mother, Angelica Fenway. David Friedlander provided a headstone."

A chill ran through Maddie as she looked at the photo. It was a profile, and David had a bump on the bridge of his nose. It was just like the one Maddie had on hers.

She closed the laptop and folded her arms. So many question marks hung over her head as she got up and put on her coat that they almost weighed her down.

Maddie went to the garage to look through the desk drawers again. She sat at the desk, and this time, she took the papers out and read each one. Carl had saved everything, and to Maddie's disappointment, they all said the same thing with little variation providing nothing new in the way of information. She stacked them up so she could take them outside and toss them into the trash.

Maddie looked at the book that had been set between bookends with *Confessions of a Lady's Maid*. It was an old-school tome on how to find missing relatives written in the days before the internet. There were notations in the margins. Maddie recognized Carl's handwriting. She wondered if he'd ever followed any of the steps outlined in the book.

She took folders out of the file cabinet and flipped through them. One contained letters Carl had sent to agencies in the book and the replies he'd received. Maddie kept that one to take inside.

Maddie slammed the cabinet drawers shut, and the sound echoed off the concrete walls. The reverberation hit her like a wave. Her father had wasted his life chasing a ghost, and now she was doing the same.

Carl had always been a good father, but Maddie had always felt that they were a little out of sync. It wasn't a lack of love, for Carl had loved her, but she never felt a kinship with him. In fact, Maddie hadn't felt a kinship with any of the relatives she'd met in her life, and if she was David Friedlander's daughter, it would explain a lot.

Maddie got up and pulled the photos off the wall. She put them into the folder with the letters before going back to the house. When she got inside, Maddie paced around the kitchen table. Now, the taco she'd eaten felt like lead in her stomach, and she wrapped her arms around her waist. She wished she had someone to talk to, another set of eyes to look at what she'd found to see if there was something she'd missed.

Maddie had been living alone for a while now, but this was the first time she'd ever felt the need for another person's company. The reality of her situation bore down on Maddie like a sledgehammer. She was completely alone in New Jersey.

Then she thought of something else. If David Friedlander hadn't died, would she even be searching for Daisy right now? Was this longing to find her really a need for family?

Maddie went back to the laptop and brought up her Aunt Sylvia's family tree on an ancestry website. They would compare your DNA to others to see if there was a familial connection. Would someone who ran away do something like this? Perhaps not, but their children, if they'd had any, might without knowing their mother's true history. A brother or sister would be a close match. Without hesitation, Maddie signed up and ordered a kit to submit her DNA.

Now, Maddie spread the photos out on the table. Daisy's smiling visage appeared in each one, her eyes shining, and her face glowing. She had been a beauty with a brain, a combination that would often make a woman's life more difficult.

Studies showed that good-looking people were more successful, but for a woman, good looks could be a double-edged sword. She might get a good job, but she was also expected to work twice as hard to keep it while fending off males who felt entitled to cop a feel now and then.

Maddie had heard herself described as "nice" more than once. She was not beautiful, nor did she possess great hair, a brilliant smile, or a sunny disposition. Men tended to avoid her if she was with a group of women at a bar, aiming for the obvious beauties with their fabulous hair and impeccable makeup. She would often have a drink or two and then grab a taxi home.

She had fallen into a sexual relationship with her roommate because he didn't have anyone else at the time, but she noticed that he would always turn off the lights before climbing on top of her. It was a means to an end, and now, as she looked at the glowing face of her mother, she felt ashamed she had sold herself so lightly.

Maddie had experienced little sexual harassment during her career. She'd worked mostly with women, and the men, being outnumbered, kept their thoughts and hands to themselves. Maddie had heard lurid tales of things men did in other offices and was grateful she had found the company she worked for.

Had Daisy been harassed when she worked for David Friedlander? Had he ever pushed her up against a wall and threatened her career if she didn't sleep with him?

Maddie put the photos back into the folder and glanced at Larry. Her father had spent his whole life with dogs, a path she might consider if she didn't meet someone who found her utterly irresistible.

If Daisy was pregnant by another man, why had Carl agreed to marry her? Had he been so blinded by her beauty that he didn't care whose baby it was? Had Daisy ever even slept with him?

Maddie felt terrible thinking it, but she had seen pictures of her father as a young man. Is this why he had never sought to divorce Daisy so he could find another woman who would love him the way he deserved to be loved?

Maddie was sure of only one thing in her life – that she would never marry a man unless she loved him. She wasn't Carl. She couldn't settle for just any man. She would rather raise dogs.

Maddie got up and went to her father's bedroom. She looked in the dresser drawers for more clues and found a plastic shoebox full of pictures taken while she was growing up. She searched all the drawers and under his bed, but it seemed that Carl had confined all his research to the desk in the garage.

29

MONDAY

Monday morning, Ben returned to David's house with boxes and a roll of garbage bags. He left them in the kitchen and went upstairs. All night, he kept thinking about Candy and how she made him feel, and those thoughts reminded him of David's muse, the pretty woman in the photos he'd found in the suitcase underneath David's bed.

Who was she? Why hadn't he written her name on any of the photos, or mentioned her in his journals? As far as Ben knew, there hadn't been another woman in his life, so it was safe to assume she was the love of his life, the one that got away, his true north, etc., so why wasn't she memorialized in his writings?

Ben wrestled with these thoughts for a long time before drifting off to sleep. He'd gotten up with the intention of going through David's hoard, but he also wanted to look at those photos again. When he got to David's bedroom, Ben opened the suitcase on the bed and took the photos out. Underneath the photos were several journals. He laid them in three rows - the pictures of Daisy were on top, the pictures of her and David were in the middle, and the journals written in David's hand were on the bottom.

Ben scanned the photos in the top row. Daisy was beautiful, and she was in love. The raw emotions he saw were so unlike any he had seen in his mother, and he wondered if that was what had attracted David to her. She didn't conceal her heart.

The photos of them together were sweet. David was happy; not in the strange, euphoric way he'd been during episodes of mania when his eyes would reflect his madness, but the way you look when you're hopeful about the future. David was normal in those photos, and Ben sighed. He'd never seen his uncle that way.

Ben searched the photos for another minute or two and then put them back into the suitcase, but left the journals on the bed. He retrieved the boxes from the kitchen and went back to the bedroom. After emptying all the dresser drawers and the closet into the boxes, he sat on the bed and opened the oldest journal. It was dated, "1975," and in it, David wrote about his father telling him that Fenway Manor held a treasure.

"Dad said he's going to sell the land and has to tear down the house, but he said we can look for the treasure before that happens."

They had found an empty trunk in the basement but nothing else. David was disappointed. The rest of the journal was about his classes at school and his sister, Beth.

"She's the meanest person in the world."

Ben flipped through years 1973 through 1981 but stopped when he saw David mention Princeton in the journal from 1982. David was seventeen and in his junior year. He was the youngest boy in his classes, and most of the other students didn't want him tagging along while they drank and partied. He felt isolated and powerless.

"I hate this place," he wrote. "I want to go home, but my father said I have to learn to live on my own."

Ben wondered why his grandfather had forced David to live on a campus a few miles away, and then he remembered who had raised Beth. She had done the same thing when Ben went to Princeton, but he had been twenty in his junior year.

Then Ben noticed a change in David's writing. Sometime during that same year, David began to experience strange thoughts that kept him awake at night.

"They race through my head, and I try to sort them out, but I can't keep up with them."

He'd been experiencing his first episodes of mania years before they manifested into full-blown mental illness. Ben recalled David talking about them.

"I couldn't tell anyone about those thoughts. I didn't think my parents would understand and I knew my father was counting on me to take over the business one day. Can't have a madman sitting at the head of the board."

David didn't share his fears with anyone, not even Harlan, but now Ben wondered if he had shared his fear with Daisy. Had it scared her away?

The next journal was written shortly after David left for England to teach a class at Oxford in 1990. One page was titled "Daisy."

"That *is* her name," Ben said.

"She's the light of my life," he wrote, "a star in the evening sky, a whisper that caresses my ear like a gentle breeze in summer. Being away from her is torture."

He wrote a lot of poetry about her, of his yearning for her, and the agony of being apart. Ben skimmed through it trying to find out what happened between them, but the journal ended abruptly in 1991. The last entry read:

"I've never felt this hopeless."

"Damn it," Ben said. "What happened?"

He looked for another journal, but that was the last one in the suitcase. He went around the house checking all the bookcases but found none.

At four, Ben was exhausted, so he went home. While he drove, Ben thought about searching for some of his relatives, people he knew existed but who had never been in his life. His mother spoke of a cousin in Pennsylvania, and Ben knew his grandfather had had a cousin, too, but they had dropped out of the Friedlander's lives.

He also wondered how he would find Daisy. Had she lived nearby, or was she from another state? Maybe he could hire a private detective. Ben had so many questions to ask her. He put that on his to-do list.

Maria was in her room when Ben came home, and he knocked on the half-open door. She saw him and smiled, but he could see her eyes were red.

"When are you planning to leave?" he asked.

"Not until the end of the month. We have time to talk about getting someone to replace me."

"I don't want to think about that."

Maria smiled sadly.

"So, how was your date last night?" she asked.

"It was good. I like her."

"Are you going to see her again?"

Ben leaned against the door frame.

"Tonight. She's coming here before we go out."

"Where are you taking her?" Maria asked.

"To that place in Princeton we used to go to whenever I graduated from something."

Maria's eyebrows rose. "Ooo, *costoso*."

"Well, yeah, you know me."

"I do, and you must be careful now. The girls will be looking at your money."

"Why does everybody keep saying that?"

"Because men don't always think with their heads."

Ben laughed out loud.

"It's not funny, Ben. It's true." She came to him and put her hands on his shoulders. "You have no idea how attractive you are. You must be careful with your heart."

"I'll be careful. I promise."

"This is what your mother worried about. She was afraid you'd meet the wrong kind of girl, one who thinks of nothing but money. That's why she kept you so close when you were growing up."

"She kept me close because she was afraid I'd run away." His tone was bitter.

"She loved you, Ben, more than anything."

He exhaled sharply. "That's what she always said."

"It's true. She loved you. And she didn't trust other people."

"I don't want to live that way, Maria."

Maria stepped back. "Okay. You live the way you like, but don't be fooled."

"I will do background checks on all future dates. In the meantime, I have to get ready for the one I have tonight."

"Oh, you think you're so funny."

Ben went to his room, showered, and put on the suit he'd bought for his college graduation. He looked at himself in the mirror, and his shoulders slumped. Beth had always helped him buy his clothes, but he'd never actually looked at a rack of clothing himself. It was time for him to go shopping.

He heard the doorbell ring and couldn't decide whether to wear a tie, but when he heard Maria answer the door, he threw the tie over his shoulder and went downstairs. Candy was wearing a navy-blue dress under her coat. To him, she looked beautiful, and he was happy to see that Maria was smiling.

"Hey," Ben said as he came to Candy and kissed her cheek.

"She told me to be nice to you," Candy said.

Ben looked at Maria, and then she came to him and helped him with his tie.

"She worries about me," he said.

Maria finished and patted his chest.

"Have a good time."

Ben looked at Candy.

"Shall we go?"

They walked to his car and Ben opened the passenger door for her.

"I don't see anybody in the street," Ben said.

"It's dark and cold," Candy said. "And that news cycle is over."

"Thank God."

Candy slid onto the seat and waited for him to get inside. While he was putting on his seatbelt, Candy saw Maria looking out the big window in the living room. She stayed until they left the driveway.

30

MONDAY

The drive to Princeton took twenty minutes with traffic and Candy told Ben about her boss, Ross Carpaza.

"He doesn't think I'm going to sell anything," she said.

"Did he say that?"

"No, but I can feel it."

"You said he doesn't pay you, right?" Ben asked.

"No, but he's the broker, so I need him. I'm an independent contractor. And Ross knows a lot, so I'm learning, but I think he looks at my blonde hair and makes assumptions about my intelligence."

They stopped at a light and Ben glanced at her.

"I think you should go out on your own," Ben said. "I still want you to sell my house."

Excitement rose up in Candy's chest. Her hands were shaking, so she clasped them in her lap.

"I'd have to go back to school. I'd have to become a broker."

"But you could sell my house, right?"

"Yes, I can list it, but the sale goes through the broker. I get a commission on the sale."

"Well, I'm seriously considering selling that house, so when I decide, you'll be the first to know."

They arrived at the restaurant, and when the maître d' saw Ben, he seated them right away. The restaurant had a large dining room with subtle lighting and elegant accouterments that had suited Ben's mother to a "t." She would bring Ben there to celebrate important events in his life like birthdays and graduations. Those memories surfaced as they were seated and Ben wished he'd brought Candy somewhere else, but she seemed impressed by the surroundings.

"This place is beautiful," she said.

"I'm glad you like it." He watched her read the menu. "Maybe you should pick a place next time."

"Why? Is there something wrong?"

"No, I just...remember the last time I was here. It was to celebrate my graduation." The electric lighting cast a candlelight hue. It softened the highlights in Candy's hair. She looked like an angel. Ben smiled as his eyes met hers. "I'm glad I'm here with you this time."

They gave the server their drink order, and then Ben shifted in his seat.

"My mother picked out this suit."

Why did I say that? he thought.

"It's nice," Candy said.

"Thanks, but I've never picked out anything for myself. I'd like to choose my own clothes for a change."

Candy thought of her dress, another of the suits her mother had bought for her for the new job.

"My mother picked out this dress."

Ben grinned. "Really?"

"I needed clothes for the new job, and I didn't have any money of my own. I also wasn't sure what I should wear because I hadn't been in an office for a while."

"My mother was so worried about appearances that I never got to buy myself so much as a T-shirt."

"Oh, my God. What about high school?"

"It was private, and there were uniforms," he said.

"I would have been mortified."

"It didn't bother me because everybody had to wear them, and it was a boy's school anyway, so no girls."

"Still, it's like the first time you get to try on who you want to be."

"Hey," he said. "Why don't we go shopping together? We could both get new clothes."

"I'll go with you, but I haven't made any money yet."

"I'm buying."

She shook her head. "I couldn't let you do that."

"Why not?"

"Because I like you. And I don't want you to have any doubts about that." She tilted her head. "But I'd be happy to go with you."

"You could help me figure out what to buy."

"Wouldn't that be like your mother picking out your clothes for you?" Candy raised her eyebrows. "Wouldn't you rather have a salesclerk help you find something?"

Ben raised his eyebrows. "Yeah, Mom used to tell them they were needed elsewhere."

Candy cringed. "She was a strong woman, wasn't she?"

"That's a nice way of putting it," Ben said.

"Maybe she had to be that way," Candy said.

"Why would she have to be that way?"

"Because women have to be twice as good to get half as far." She bit her lip. "I read that somewhere and memorized it."

"Well, Bethany Arntz must have memorized it, too." The server brought their drinks, and Ben took a sip of wine. "She was good at running things; I'll give her that."

"What was your father like?" Candy asked.

"I don't remember much about him. Mom told me once that he wasn't that interested in business."

"Maybe that's why she chose him."

"So, he wouldn't try to compete with her?" he asked.

Candy nodded. "What do you remember about him?"

"He liked to hunt."

At the mention of hunting, Ben recalled the rifle. He pushed the thought out of his mind. He wasn't going to let that ruin his evening.

"Did he ever take you anywhere?" she asked.

Ben shook his head. "Not that I remember anyway."

"You know, it's amazing how much we have in common. I never really knew my father either."

"What happened to him?" Ben asked.

"He died of a heart attack when I was five, which is why I try not to get mad at my mother when she gets overprotective. I think when I had that accident, she was scared to death she'd lose me, too."

There was a lull in the conversation, and Candy gazed around the room. She saw a portrait on the wall of a dashing 18th century rogue with long hair and a wicked smile. Her heart raced as she recognized him.

"Look at that portrait." She pointed, and Ben turned his head to see it.

"That's Derek Fenway," he said.

"Remember when we talked about them?"

"Yeah."

"Well, I stopped by there yesterday and saw him again."

Ben's eyebrows rose. "Oh."

"I was able to read his lips."

"Uncle Dave found his bones."

"When?" she asked.

"A while ago. He had them buried in that old graveyard near the Presbyterian Church. That's where the others are buried."

Candy looked perplexed.

"What?" he asked.

"Well, I've been trying to understand why he's stuck to that house and I remembered something I saw in an old movie about burying bones in sacred ground." She gave him a small smile. "I guess it didn't work."

"I think that's what Uncle Dave thought, too," Ben said.

"Do you think I'm crazy?" she asked.

"No. Why would I think that?"

She shrugged. "Because I see Derek."

He reached across the table and put his hand on hers again. "No, I don't think you're crazy. Uncle Dave used to say he had the sight, so you must have it, too." He squeezed her hand.

"It took so long for me to recover," she said. "It was hard for me to think sometimes."

"Do you still have trouble thinking?"

She shook her head. "I'm much better now."

"What happened to you isn't like what happened to my uncle. Don't even think that."

Their eyes met again, and he smiled just as the server came to take their order.

"I wanted to ask you if you were able to get that book you told me about," she said.

"I haven't been to the university. David might have had another copy at his house. We could go there and look through his book-cases when we're done."

"I'd like that."

In silent agreement, they ate their food quickly. Afterward, they stopped at Ben's house to pick up Candy's car before driving to David's house. When they got there, Ben sat in the car for a minute while he prepared himself to go inside. He wondered how Candy would feel about the way it looked. When they got out of their cars, they walked to the house, and Ben stopped.

"My uncle was a hoarder," he said. "It's sort of messed up."

"It won't bother me," she said.

Ben cringed when he switched on the lights. Candy went inside, and she didn't seem rattled by its appearance. At least the floor was free of debris, the magazines and mail were off the sofa, and the recliner was gone. Ben went past her to the bookcase near the stairs containing David's old history books.

"As you can see, he liked to collect books."

Candy came alongside him.

"Is it here?"

"I don't see it," he said.

Ben looked at each book in the bookcase and then moved to another one. He scanned the shelves but didn't see any title mentioning the Fenway family.

"That can't be the only copy he had."

"It's not important," Candy said.

She looked around the room and saw the pictures on David's wall. There were several paintings of historical places around Mercer County. Ben followed her gaze.

"He loved history, especially the history of this county."

Ben took off his coat and threw it onto the sofa. He came close to Candy and put his hand on her cheek.

"He would have liked you," he said and kissed her. "I like you."

He cupped her face. She leaned into his kiss and wrapped her arms around his waist. For a moment, Ben felt awkward standing in David's living room, but Candy was warm and receptive. She moved to take off her coat, and he helped her, throwing it on the sofa next to his.

They continued to hold each other and kiss until Candy started taking off Ben's suit jacket.

"Not here," he said softly. "Let's go upstairs."

31

TUESDAY

B en woke up the next morning and saw Candy sitting cross-legged on the floor with a blanket wrapped around her. She had a photo album in her lap.

"Hey," he said.

She looked up. "Hey." She held up the album to show him a photo. "That's my friend's mother. Why did your uncle have a picture of her?"

Ben sat up. The photo was one Ben hadn't seen before.

"Where did you find that album?"

She blushed. "I tripped when I got out of bed, and I saw it wedged between the back of the dresser and the wall."

Ben narrowed his eyes. "Are you all right?"

"I'm fine. I do it sometimes when I first wake up, or after I've been sitting in this position too long."

She blushed again, and he smiled.

"Well," he said, "we were up late last night."

He threw the sheet over his shoulders, got up, and went to the bathroom. Candy kept looking at the photos. It had been a long time since she'd thought about Daisy. She remembered how frustrated Maddie had been whenever she asked Carl what had happened to her because Carl would always evade the question by changing the subject.

Candy turned another page and found an artsy nude photo of Daisy sprawled on a bed. Daisy's head was tilted, and she gazed at the photographer with half-lidded eyes. Those expressive eyes revealed her soul, and Candy slammed the album shut as if she'd been caught with her hand in the cookie jar.

Daisy's disappearance was a part of the town's history. There were few details, but Maddie would bring it up now and then, usually when Candy stayed overnight at her house. They would stay up most of the night talking.

"All Dad will say is she went away one day and didn't come back. But you know what I found? I went to the library and looked up the newspapers from when it happened, and it said she left the dog tied to the porch of that nasty, old place next door." Maddie had gotten close to Candy's face and whispered. "Why would she take the dog?"

"Maybe she was going to take it with her and changed her mind," Candy said.

"She'd take the dog, but not me?"

"Yeah. That's bad."

What would make a woman with a young child take off without a word? Candy tried to imagine her own mother doing something like that, but Nina would cut off an arm before she'd abandon Candy.

Candy looked around the room for other hidden objects that might offer more clues regarding Daisy Brady. She left the album on the floor, got up, wrapped the blanket around her shoulders, and then walked to the window. She heard a loud rumble as the garbage truck came toward the house and then stood to watch them dump the trash from the cans into the back of the truck. She didn't hear Ben coming up behind her and started when he put his arms around her. He had wrapped the sheet around his waist.

"Sorry," Ben said

"It's okay. So, how did your uncle know Maddie's mom?"

"I'm not sure. Maybe they met in college."

"I guess they were close," Candy said. "There are some nude photos of her in that album."

"You're kidding?"

Ben went and picked up the album.

"They're near the back," she said.

Ben flipped to the nudes, and his eyes grew wide.

"Yeah, I guess they *were* close," he said.

Ben tossed the album onto the dresser and went back to Candy, wrapped his arms around her, and nuzzled her neck. Candy tilted her head toward his.

"This is a nice neighborhood."

"It's an old neighborhood."

She glanced over her shoulder.

"Have you decided whether you're going to live here?"

Ben lifted his head.

"I love this place. I had a lot of good times here with my uncle."

She turned around to face him.

"It could be really nice. You'd have to put some money into it, but it will retain its value because of its proximity to the college."

Ben laughed. "You're trying to sell me this house!"

Her cheeks reddened. "Oh, God, I sound like an agent." He squeezed her. "I'm sorry. I guess that's the mindset I'm in right now, but it is true."

She put her arms around him and pulled him closer as her blanket fell to the floor. As their bodies came together, Candy felt as though she were melting into him. Ben never rushed but took time to touch her face, to kiss her, to look into her eyes, and to caress her gently.

As if choreographed by some writer in one of her mother's romance novels, Ben picked her up like a knight carrying his damsel to the tower and took her to the bed.

～

As she dressed to go, Candy kept thinking *this is too good to be true*. When she smelled coffee and toast as she came downstairs, the thought persisted. She hadn't much experience with men, but she remembered how coarse the boys in her classes had been and Ben was such a gentleman. Could she trust him to remain that way?

Candy went into the kitchen and saw Ben standing at the stove. She spied the cracks in the walls, the tattered wallpaper, the ancient kitchen table, and chairs, and wondered how his uncle had let it get this way.

Ben was wearing his pants and shirt from the night before, and he smiled when he saw her at the doorway.

"He didn't care much about appearances," Ben said.

She raised her eyebrows. "How did you know what I was thinking?"

"It's what everybody thinks when they see it in the daylight."

"How long did he live here?" Candy asked.

"I think he moved in when he got out of the hospital, so, it must have been 1992 or 93."

"It looks like he never did anything to it after that."

"I've cleaned it up a few times." Ben looked at Candy and smiled. "More than a few times. The coffee's ready if you want some."

She smiled. "What are you cooking?"

"I made eggs. Scrambled. That's the only way I know how to cook them."

"I can get my own coffee."

"I've got this. Sit. You're my guest."

Candy sat and looked at the sugar bowl at the center of the table. She studied the tabletop. The surface could be refinished to remove the stains. The chairs could be replaced. She had redecorated the entire kitchen as she waited for him to sit down, and then Ben brought two mugs of coffee to the table.

"What was your uncle like?" she asked.

"He was weird." Ben put the mugs on the table. "That's how people usually described him." He glanced at her. "He was diagnosed as bipolar, but I never saw him depressed. When it came on him, he was manic. He'd get all excited. His thoughts would race, and he couldn't stop moving. It was kind of scary if you didn't understand what was happening."

He went to the stove, filled two plates with eggs, and then brought them to the table.

"Do we need anything else?" he asked.

"Milk for the coffee."

Ben got the milk from the fridge and brought it to the table.

"I used to buy him milk. He always ran out, but he wouldn't call me to get it for him. He didn't like to bother anyone. I used to tell him it bothered me more if he didn't ask because then there would be no milk for my coffee when I stopped by." Ben smiled as he sat. "He liked to talk. A lot. That's why it's so sad he couldn't teach anymore."

"Was he on disability?"

"He worked at a library on campus as a researcher." Ben eyed her across the table. "God, you're pretty."

Candy wrapped her hands around her mug and lowered her eyes.

"Stop it."

He reached for her hand.

"Do you have to work today?" he asked.

She nodded. "I have to be there in case someone comes in and wants to see a house." Her eyes met his. "I get off at five. I usually go home, so my mother doesn't think I've been kidnapped."

"Did you tell her you weren't coming home last night?"

"She thought I was going out with Maddie. I texted her that I was staying at Maddie's so we could catch up."

Ben raised his eyebrows.

"I can come to pick you up later," he said. "I'd like to meet her."

Candy shook her head and sat back.

"Oh, no you wouldn't. She will make you sit at the table, feed you pie, and badger you until you confess every sin you ever committed just so you can get away from her."

Ben laughed. "She sounds like my mother."

Ben's smiled faded, and he grew quiet. Candy reached across the table for his hand.

"How are you doing?" she asked.

"I'm okay." He looked at her. "You helped me forget about it for a while."

"It will get better," she said, "but you'll always have that thing inside you that doesn't feel right. It's like they had a place in you and it stays empty forever. You can't really fill it with someone else, but you can close the door, so you're not stuck in time."

His sad smile touched her heart.

"I like that," he said.

Ben took her hand in both of his and held it.

"I really like you, Candy."

"I really like you, too."

"Do you think…?"

"What?" she asked.

"I'm worried because neither of us has been with anyone else in a long time. Are we just making this happen, or is it real?"

"It's real for me," she said. "I feel like I've known you forever."

"Me, too."

"Then screw it. I think we should go with our feelings."

"The one thing my mother warned me against all my life," Ben said with a grin.

"Well, that might have worked for her, but you're not your mother."

He kissed her hand. "No, I'm not." He tilted his head. "So, can I come to your house later? I'm not afraid of your mother."

Candy sighed. "If you're sure, then come around seven. That will give me time to change and beat her into submission."

He laughed. "Oh, please wait until I get there."

She smiled broadly. "All right, but just this once."

They drank their coffee, ate their food, and then Candy noticed the time.

"Shit, I have to go." They got up and walked to the front door. As Ben grabbed her coat off the sofa, she glanced over her shoulder. "If you have the time, see if you can find that book."

"Oh, yeah. If he doesn't have one here, I can grab the one from his office at the library."

He helped her into her coat. Before she went out the door, Ben reached for her hand, pulled her close, kissed her, and then held her hand. She lingered for a moment as thoughts of calling in sick filtered through her mind, but Ross might call Nina. It was like being in middle school again.

"I have to go," Candy said. "I'll see you later."

Ben let her hand slide out of his as she went out the door, and then he watched her walk to her car. He waited until she had disappeared down the road before closing the door.

32

When Candy got home from Ben's, her mother was sitting at the breakfast table. Nina didn't look pleased.

"So, how's Maddie?"

"She's good. We caught up on a lot of stuff."

Nina sipped her coffee. "You want anything to eat before you go to work?"

"I ate at Maddie's."

"Ross might be upset if you're late," Nina said.

"Oh, he won't miss me. Besides, he has me filing papers right now. I can do that in my sleep."

Nina's cheeks were red. She gripped her coffee mug in two hands and shook her head.

"He's treating you like an office clerk."

"You knew that was part of the deal," Candy said.

"He's using you."

"It's not that bad, and I'm learning from him."

"He's not even paying you!" Nina sat back. "You worked hard for your license. You deserve to be treated like any other professional."

"This is the way people start, Mom." She put her hand on Nina's shoulder. "He's mentoring me." She sighed. "Besides, this was your idea."

"I know, but that's because I thought…"

"That no one else would hire me."

"You should look for a job somewhere else," Nina said.

"It would be the same no matter where I go. I'm an agent, not a broker."

Nina patted her hand. "You could go to East Brunswick."

"I don't know East Brunswick, not the way I know Logans Grove. Besides, I have Maddie's listings, and I know I can sell them." She hugged Nina. "I don't mind filing, Mom. I get to see the contracts he writes. I learn things from them."

"Well, then, I guess I'd better leave you alone." Nina squeezed Candy's hand. "But you tell me if he's treating you bad."

"I will."

Candy kissed her mother's head before going upstairs to change. As she showered, she thought about Ben. She shivered from the memory of their night together. She still had difficulty under-standing people's intentions, and despite what he had said about *really* liking her, a tiny doubt about his sincerity worked its way into her mind. Candy had given in to her feelings too quickly. She should have waited. She should have said no.

"Stop it," she said. "He likes you."

Traffic on King's Highway was murder, and it took her longer than she thought it would, but as she parked her car, she felt better about Ben. He was one of the good ones. He wasn't just using her because he was in pain.

Trini was at her desk and grinned when she saw Candy. She raised her eyebrows.

"Girl, you're looking too happy this mornin'. What you been up to, eh?"

Candy was dying to tell someone about Ben. She came up to the counter, leaned forward, folded her arms, and rested her chin on them.

"I met someone."

Trini's eyes were as wide as her grin when she got up and went to Candy. She put her hands on Candy's arms and squeezed.

"Tell me everything."

Candy blushed. "His name is Ben. He's a little younger than me, but he's so nice."

"Oh, girl, young is good. You get them young, and you can make them into anything you want." Trini laughed. "You look so happy!"

"I am happy, but I'm also a little worried. "

Trini's eyebrows met as she backed away.

"About what?"

"He's meeting my mother tonight."

Trini waved her hand and shook her head.

"You say he's a nice guy." Candy nodded. "Then you've got nothing to worry about."

"You don't know my mother," Candy said.

"I know enough about mothers to know that she wants what's best for you. I talk to her all the time on the phone. She's a good person. Everything will be all right."

Candy smiled. "I wish I had your confidence."

"You just gotta walk like you do. The rest will follow." Candy shrugged and walked away. "Stand up straight!" Trini cried, and then Candy raised her head and straightened her back. "That's it. See how that makes you feel?"

"Like I have a stick up my ass."

Trini's laughter faded as Candy entered her office. Her shoulders slumped and the anxiety she'd been fighting since she left Ben surrounded her. She didn't want to be here. She didn't want to sit at this desk all day filing papers and searching obituaries. She wanted to be with him.

This job gave her too much time – to think, to brood, to regret things she'd done in the past. Sometimes the desire to turn back the clock would overwhelm her. That would lead to a short period of self-recrimination followed by a renewed sense of putting the past behind. That would leave her with a sense of ennui. It drained her energy, so she'd drink coffee as she tried to push past the feeling that nothing she had ever done mattered. It was at this time that the same question would arise from deep inside her. Did she really want to sell houses?

The pattern was about to repeat itself when Candy walked around her desk and saw a banker's box next to her chair with a note from Ross.

"Oh, God," she said as she hung her coat on the hook and read the note.

"I need this done by four today!"

Candy looked at the exclamation point. Ross loved using them, and the sight of it pissed her off. It was his way of asserting control over her as if she wasn't serious enough or smart enough to under-stand the urgency of his request.

This was how Candy always talked herself into quitting. The

thoughts, with little variation, had arisen with every job she'd had since she reentered the workforce. She would find excuses to leave and run back home where she could hide from the world, but this time, she had to keep going no matter what.

Candy sat and booted up her laptop. There were no emails or requests from potential customers, so she opened the box and saw that it was full of slips of paper. They were the pink messages Trini left on his desk, and he wanted her to put them in order.

Candy started trembling. Rage washed over her, and she kicked the box. She closed her eyes, and her head began to hurt, sending pain down her back. She had to relax the muscles, or she would end up with a cramp that would leave her with pain for the rest of the day. It took every ounce of strength she had to focus on the breathing exercises she'd learned from a counselor, but she soon felt the pain dissipate. She waited until it was nothing but a dull ache before resuming Ross's task.

"It's just a job," she said. "Get it done and move on."

As she sorted through the mess of pink slips, she thought about Ben and kept her thoughts on him. It made her feel good, and she wanted to focus on things that made her feel good now. She'd spent way too much time and effort berating herself in the past. It was time to be nice to herself again.

33

TUESDAY

A fter looking for the book in David's house, Ben put on his coat and went to the garage behind the house. Despite his uncle's penchant for throwing things into empty space without rhyme or reason, he had kept the garage relatively free of scattered clutter. It was filled with boxes, though, none of them labeled, and all of them covered in a thick layer of dust. The cardboard boxes were soft and the edges wavy. When he opened some, the flaps would come off in his hand.

As he waded through the boxes, Ben was undaunted by the amount of stuff his uncle had accumulated over the years. After two hours though, his hands were numbed with the cold, so he went into the house and made a mug of instant coffee.

As he waited for the water to boil, he stared at the counters. They were pitted and stained from years of neglect and would have to be replaced. The floor would have to be replaced too, and the walls painted. He loved this house; it was where he felt most at home, but he could just imagine what his mother would think. She had always called it a hovel, though she hadn't set eyes on it since David moved in.

Half an hour later, he returned to the garage and started digging through the last of the boxes. He found a medium-sized wooden fruit crate filled with newspaper clippings, which he put on the back porch. By eleven, he was tired, so he closed the garage door, grabbed the fruit box, and went inside.

Ben's stomach grumbled, and he ordered some Chinese food. He took the fruit crate into the living room and put it on the floor beside the sofa. He began picking up the delicate pieces of yellowed newspaper and sorting them by dates on the coffee table. When Ben was done, he had three piles, one for each decade starting in the 1970s. There was also an envelope addressed in Beth's hand with a postmark from 1989.

Those from the seventies involved David's father and his business dealings, things that appeared in the financial section of the Newark Star-Ledger or the Wall Street Journal, and other things that Ben didn't think were worth saving. He put them back in the box. Those from the eighties were about David - his graduations, his appearance at his parents' anniversary party, his job as an associate professor, etc. Ben put them back into the box.

Ben opened the envelope and took out a newspaper clipping. It was a wedding announcement for Carl Brady and Daisy Carter. There was a photo of Daisy, and the announcement mentioned that Carl Brady owned the second-hand bookstore in Logans Grove. There was nothing else in the envelope.

Ben imagined David reading it as he sat alone in a tiny room across the pond. Was he still in love with her? Had they broken up before he left for England?

So many questions ran through his mind, especially about the relationship between Beth and David. What little he knew, though, suggested that Beth had sent it to hurt David.

Ben knew his mother wasn't the warmest person in the universe, but until she killed her brother, he hadn't thought of her as cold-blooded. She had kissed him on the forehead when she tucked him into bed as a child, had read books to him, had taken him to the city or the park like any other mother, but they were always alone. Ben tried to remember if she had any friends, and he couldn't think of one. Harlan and Anna were David's friends, and the people who came to her funeral were business associates. There was only one person who had cried for Beth - Maria, a person Beth had employed to serve her.

Ben sat back and laid his head against the back of the sofa. He stared at the tar-covered ceiling and felt a profound sense of loss. If Beth had only been this way, or if David had only been that, they would have had each other to lean on instead of simmering in their own, miserable acrimony for years. It had been pointless, and Ben vowed not to repeat their failures. Despite his introverted tendencies, he wouldn't build barriers between himself and the outside world.

Ben took a deep breath and leaned forward. There was one more pile to go through - the nineties - and it contained articles regarding the old Fenway property. They mentioned that the town wanted to condemn the property but that the actions were delayed. Article after article said the same thing, and years went by as the property fell deeper into decay.

The mystery of why Beth wouldn't just tear down the old place was bugging the hell out of Ben. It made no sense. She didn't like the place and would always threaten to have it torn down if David did something embarrassing, but she never did.

"It's how she controlled him," Ben said aloud.

Ben also found a letter from the National Register of Historic Places rejecting David's application to have Fenway Manor designated as a place of historical significance. Ben could imagine how he'd felt when he received it. He then found the article about David and Harlan finding bones in the woods behind the old manor house. It was dated November 7, 1998, the year Ben turned three. There was a photo of the bones with David standing beside them. The article was about how the bones had been carbon dated and found to be around two hundred years old.

"I believe they are the bones of Derek Fenway," David was quoted as saying. "Up until now, historians were unable to determine what had happened to Derek. They believed he was traveling out west when the tragedy occurred."

David had talked about finding those bones for years and had even taken Ben to the spot where he'd found them. That's when he told Ben he could see Derek's ghost, and Ben was disappointed he couldn't see him, too. Thinking about it reminded him of Candy, and that made him smile.

His food arrived, and he took the bag to the sofa. He switched on the TV and saw that the news was on. Ben was just about to change it when he heard something that stopped him.

"The town of Logans Grove is once again trying to have the old Fenway Manor on King's Highway condemned, and a meeting will be held on November 28th to determine its fate. For years, Bethany Arntz, who had owned the property since the early nineties, had successfully blocked the city's efforts to raze the old mansion on King's Highway. Some have speculated that with the passing of Ms. Arntz, her son, Benjamin, might take up the cause."

At twelve-thirty, Ben called it quits. After searching the house for *Confessions of a Lady's Maid* and failing to find it, Ben decided to go to David's office and grab it off the shelf next to David's desk before heading home.

34

As the first thrill of new love filled his every thought, Ben became more confused about what he wanted to do with his life. He knew he couldn't run his mother's company, but Arthur Mantz had cautioned him against making any rash decisions.

All his life, Ben watched his mother's life consumed by the family business, but Beth hadn't lost herself as she built her grandparents' company; she found herself. Beth had never struggled with self-doubt. In any given situation, she always knew what to do.

Ben had struggled with insecurity while he was growing up because Beth had made all the decisions regarding his life. It had never occurred to her that he might want something else, and he had wanted to please her. While he learned to voice his own opinion in school, it was easier to let Beth have her way at home. Ben preferred doing things the easy way, which, of course, also made Beth happy.

Now, as Ben tried to imagine himself in a corporate environment, his felt the muscles in his neck tighten. He didn't like the fast pace or spending time in boardrooms listening to someone talk about the price of company shares, and with Beth gone, he no longer had to subjugate his feelings. Ben could be anything he wanted to be. By the time he got to the campus, the confusion had cleared, and Ben had no doubt that when he told Arthur he didn't want the business, he meant it. He'd hold onto it for a year, and then instruct Arthur to do whatever had to be done to sever his ties with Carefree Garments, Inc.

As he walked to Barrington Library, Ben thought about Candy. Her reticence to accept that she was a smart, capable woman confused him, too, as most of the women he'd known had no trouble telling him exactly what they wanted out of life. Candy was beautiful, charming, and witty, but she saw herself as permanently flawed.

After listening to her talk about her mother, Ben understood that part of the problem *was* Candy's mother. After years of doing everything for her injured daughter, she was still in protective mode, but Candy didn't need a heroine; she needed someone who would push her out of the nest.

Ben wondered how he should approach Candy's mom. He'd only had one girlfriend, and her mother lived overseas. Manners seemed to impress older women, and Ben had always gotten a smile from the dean's administrative assistant when he brought her a muffin from Starbucks. Should he overpraise Candy to show his support, or would her mother think he was full of shit?

Ben chuckled. He was surprised at his desire to please Mrs. Burke, which meant his feelings for Candy were different from those he had with his other girlfriend. They were deeper, and this realization gave him pause. This was real, and he didn't feel the urge to run away. Ben wanted to get closer to Candy.

As he walked up to the office door, he recalled the last time he'd dropped by unexpectedly. Anna had been agitated. He hesitated at the door and wished he had a key to the office so he could come here when Anna was gone. Ben took a deep breath before knocking and then opened the door.

"Ben," she said as her smile faded. "What brings you here?"

"I came to grab that copy of *Confessions of a Lady's Maid.*"

She sat back and clasped her hands over her stomach.

"You're the second person within a week to ask about that book."

"Really? Who else asked about it?"

"Maddie Brady. She came to see me and saw it on the shelf. She said she has one at home."

"I don't think I know her," Ben said.

"She owns that second-hand bookstore on Artisan Row."

"Oh, yeah, I think I've seen her there."

"She also owns the house next to Fenway Manor."

"Derek's house."

Anna nodded, and Ben took the book from the shelf.

"I'll bring it back," Ben said.

"No need. Keep it. It belonged to David anyway."

"Thanks." Ben smiled. "There was something I wanted to ask you about." He saw her shift in her chair. "Do you have any idea why my mother fought to keep Fenway Manor from being torn down?"

"No."

"Did David every talk to you about their relationship? My mom didn't like to talk about it."

"It was a contentious relationship, but that's all I know. David would complain about her from time to time, but he didn't elaborate, and I didn't push him to talk."

"It's just weird because I know she hated that old place."

Anna's eyes would not meet Ben's. She clasped her hands on the desk and pressed her lips together as if a culpable word might escape without her permission. She then unclasped her hands and ran her fingers over the paperwork she had before her.

"Anna, do you *know* something?"

She sat back and clasped her hands in her lap. Her knuckles were white.

"Just that David was either having an episode or just getting over one his whole life. He was obsessed with the Fenways and afraid of Beth. More than that I can't tell you."

"Right." He put the book on the desk, his hands on the back of the chair, and then leaned on it. "It's just that I can't figure out why she killed him. None of this makes any sense."

She unclasped her hands and sighed.

"I can't imagine what you're going through."

"But the way things happened, I can't stop thinking about it. Why did she kill him?"

Anna averted her eyes. She had to know something. How could she be in this room with his uncle all those years and pretend he never talked about Beth?

"It will get easier," Anna said as she stood.

"Why do people always say that?" he asked.

Anna exhaled sharply. "Because they want to say something. They want to help make the pain go away." An awkward silence followed. "Talk to Harlan. He might be able to answer your questions."

Ben grabbed the book.

"Right. Okay, I'll talk to Harlan."

The coldness of her demeanor stayed with him as he walked back to his car. Anna knew something, and it bothered her so much that she could barely look at Ben. She had been that way ever since David's funeral. Ben remembered Harlan and Anna standing together in his living room. They'd stopped talking when he walked by. It was after he'd asked Harlan about David's letter. Shit. He'd forgotten about it again.

Why wouldn't Anna just tell him what she knew?

It infuriated him to know that she might have the answers to all his questions but refused to tell him. When he reached his car, he threw the book on the passenger seat, and something fell out of it. Ben cringed as he realized he had just thrown a two-hundred-year-old book as if it were a modern paperback and feared he had loosened some pages. When he got into his seat, he saw it was another photo and pulled it toward him. It was a picture of Daisy with her arms reaching for a young child. The girl was around two and wore a dress. Daisy was sitting on the ground in front of Derek's house, and the girl was reaching her arms out, too.

Ben puzzled over the photo for a while, and then put it back into the book. As he pulled away from the curb, he remembered the album Candy had found that morning. Why had David hidden it behind the dresser?

It was still early, and Ben wanted to see if Harlan was home. He swung by his house, but Harlan's car was not in the driveway. He parked in front of David's and went into the house. He ran up the stairs, retrieved the album Candy found and began looking at the photos.

Though he hadn't mentioned it to Candy, Ben was shocked when he saw the nudes. He felt as if he'd stumbled upon David and Daisy making love. He flipped past them now to the back and found two pages of photos. Most of them were of Daisy and the little girl. They had been taken from a distance. Some were fuzzy, and others crystal clear, but it was obvious from the way David had taken the photos that this child was important to him. That creepy feeling you get when you know something is true, but you wish you hadn't found out ran through Ben like a freight train. This was David's child.

Ben slammed the album shut and threw it across the room. He'd been his uncle's friend, supporter, and defender his whole life, and

David had never once shared this with him. How many other things had David kept from him?

Now, the house felt small. He had to get out of it and went down the stairs two at a time. When he got outside, he saw Harlan's car in his driveway, took a deep breath, and then walked over to his house.

35

TUESDAY

The old professor answered Ben's knock and hesitated a moment before he waved him inside. Harlan hoped Ben wasn't there to collect David's letter.

"I saw you were at David's when I came home," Harlan said.

"I'm still going through his stuff."

"I was just fixing myself a sandwich. Are you hungry?"

"No."

They walked to the kitchen. Ben recalled the first time he saw it when David had brought him over to introduce him to Harlan. Harlan seemed out of place in the old farm style kitchen with a built-in sideboard, old-fashioned sink with a skirt, and a wood-burning kitchen stove. It also had a built-in fifties style diner booth with red and white striped seats around an oblong Formica table. The 1860 Gothic style home had belonged to Harlan's parents. He had added his own, mismatched historical touches after they died.

Ben slid into the booth while Harlan went to the counter to finish making his sandwich.

"So, what brings you here today?" Harlan asked. "I saw that young lady leaving this morning, and I must say I was quite impressed."

"We're seeing each other."

"Do tell, dear boy."

"I like her, and she likes me. We'll see where it goes."

"As tight-lipped as ever. David always complained that you wouldn't share things with him."

"Yeah, I know the feeling."

Harlan brought his sandwich to the table, got a bottle of beer out of the fridge, and then sat across from Ben.

"I have some things I wanted to ask you," Ben said. He folded his arms on the table and leaned forward. "Do you know why my mother refused to tear down Fenway Manor?"

Harlan exhaled sharply. "I asked David once why they wouldn't just let the place go, and he did what he always did. He found a way to steer the conversation in another direction."

"She got a notice from the town right before David died."

"And?"

"I think it had something to do with what happened."

"Why didn't she just do what she always did and have the ordered stayed?" Harlan asked.

"The judge retired."

"Ahh, so, they were going to go through with it this time."

"Right, but it still doesn't explain why she wouldn't just tear the place down."

"Beth had her quirks," Harlan said.

"This wasn't just a quirk, Harlan. She kept it up for years."

Harlan sat back and clasped his hands over his belly.

"She hated that place," Ben said. He glanced out the window over the sink and exhaled sharply. "You're sure David never talked about this."

"David didn't like talking about Beth. We had an unspoken agreement to avoid the subject, and I kept to it."

"Did Daisy live in Derek Fenway's house?" Ben asked.

Ben watched the color drain from Harlan's face.

"How do you know that name?"

"I found a suitcase full of her photos under Uncle Dave's bed." Harlan stared at Ben. "There were journals, too. He was in love with her."

"He was a fool."

"What happened between them?" Ben asked.

Harlan took a deep breath.

"David received a grant that allowed him to go to England for three months to research the Fenway family's origins. If you ask me, it was his father's doing. Jake had influence with the board at Princeton. He probably gave them the money, and they gave it to David because, really, who else cared about the Fenways. Their historical significance was minimal at best. No institution would have offered a grant to study them."

"But why would my grandfather do that?"

"Because Daisy came from a poor family. It was her brains that got her into Princeton. She worked hard. She won scholarships and grants, but she didn't have the pedigree."

"So, Grandpa thought this would break them up."

"And it did, but it didn't work the way Jake had hoped it would. David was still in love with her when he returned."

Harlan hesitated.

"And?" Ben asked.

"She was pregnant when he left. She didn't tell David."

Ben sat back and exhaled loudly.

"Then why didn't he marry her when he got back?" Ben asked.

Harlan closed his eyes and took a deep breath.

"Daisy did what a lot of girls did back then. She didn't know when David was coming back and she panicked. She married Carl Brady rather than deal with the stigma unwed motherhood. She didn't want her child to be labeled a bastard." Harlan took a swig of his beer. "When David returned it was too late. She had already married Carl. David came to me in tears."

"I found a wedding announcement in one of his boxes. My mother sent it to him while he was in England."

"I think your grandfather found out about the pregnancy and wanted to keep David out of the country. Your uncle had a streak of decency that would have made him do the right thing. Jake knew this. David's grant was extended to six months."

"You really believe this was my grandfather's doing."

"I had known David a long time. I knew how Jake...handled things."

"So, what happened when Uncle Dave came home?"

"She was married to Carl by then and working at the bookstore. She could no longer hide the pregnancy. One day, David showed up. He tried to talk to her, but she told him he had to leave her alone."

"Was he ever allowed to see the baby."

Harlan shook his head. "You know how obsessive David could be. He would go to the store at closing and confront her. He kept insisting he would marry her, that he loved her, that he couldn't live without her, but all it did was frighten Daisy. Eventually, she got a restraining order, but it didn't keep him away. He was arrested, but

Jake managed to bury the charge before David was fired from his job."

"He was an associate professor then, right?" Ben asked.

"Yes, and he couldn't afford to be seen as a stalker."

"You didn't answer my question. Did he ever see the baby?"

"Daisy thought it best that he didn't. It would have been awkward for the child when it grew up. It made sense, and the Friedlanders agreed it was for the best."

"She should have let him see her."

Harlan leaned forward.

"Listen Ben. David had hurt Daisy terribly. He took off for England without a word. The grant came in quickly. He was on a plane before anyone even knew he was gone. He wrote to Daisy as soon as he got to his hotel room, but by then, her heart was broken. She believed he had placed his own interests above theirs, as he often did, and that if he had loved her, he would have turned down the grant."

Ben leaned forward and folded his arms.

"Does she still live in that house?" Ben asked.

"Daisy went missing when her daughter, Maddie, was two."

"She went missing."

"I was there the day it happened. It was Maddie's second birthday and Anna and I were invited to the party. Daisy took the dog for a walk and never came back."

"What did the police say?" Ben asked.

"They were less than helpful. Carl called them, and they took a report, but they did a shit job of searching for her, so we all went out to search instead. There was no sign of Daisy anywhere." He lowered his eyes. "She was gone, Ben. She simply vanished."

"Did the cops follow up on it?"

"It was their contention that she was an adult. They advised Carl to wait for a while and see if she returned on her own."

Ben sat back shaking his head.

"Who takes a dog with them when they plan to run away? And on her kid's birthday no less. What the hell was wrong with the cops?"

"It was standard procedure..."

"That's bullshit." Ben's shoulders slumped. "So, Maddie believes her mother ran out on her."

"It's an odd coincidence, but she came to me the other day

asking questions, too. She wanted to know if David was her father. I told her to have her DNA done while the police have samples of David's and see if they're a match. They might ask for your permission."

"I'll let them know it's okay."

Harlan leaned forward.

"Ben, you must understand the ramifications involved if she finds out."

"What ramifications?" Ben asked.

"It would mean she has a claim on the Friedlander money."

"So, she should have a claim if she's David's daughter."

"It could be messy, a public fight like that. Are you sure you want to go there?"

"God. You sound like my mother," Ben said.

"She understood how things worked in the world, Ben."

"I'm going to sell the company, Harlan. If she's my cousin, I'll give her half the money."

Harlan's eyes widened. "Do you have any idea how much money is involved?" He leaned forward. "You could have people coming out of the woodwork claiming their entitlement to your fortune."

Ben sat back, let his head rest on the back of the seat, and then closed his eyes. "Why does everything have to be so complicated?" He opened his eyes and sat forward. "I'm so tired of all this bullshit."

"It's necessary bullshit, my boy. Human beings are incapable of dealing with each other honorably. We have laws to ensure cooperation. Without them, we have chaos."

"And laws that always seem to favor one side over the other," Ben said.

"Not always. Sometimes justice prevails."

"Will it prevail for Maddie?"

"If she's David's biological child, she will have a legitimate claim on your fortune, but if you choose to share your money with her, you must do it secretly. Otherwise, the media will hound both of you relentlessly."

"They were sitting outside my house the day of my mother's funeral. I saw them a couple of times since, but they seemed to have lost interest."

"Something like this will revive their interest. If she sues, papers will have to be filed, and those are public records unless you do it privately. It might be wise to keep the DNA results to yourself until the probate is over. Once it's done, you are free to give your money away as you choose, so wait until then. Give it to her in gold bars if you want to, but do it with a private contract."

"I really hate this," Ben said.

"It's for your protection as well as Maddie's. If you were anything like your mother, I wouldn't be so trusting, but I believe you will do the right thing by her."

Ben lowered his head. "I've never had a cousin."

"She's a good person."

"I was just thinking the other day that I don't have any family around here. It would be nice."

"She might not feel the same way, you know. Don't be upset if she doesn't want anything to do with you."

"You are such an optimist, Harlan."

"I'm a realist, my boy. I've seen too much, and I know too much. I shed the patina of romanticism long ago. The world sucks, to put it bluntly."

"Right." Ben looked at the clock on the wall. "It's getting late. I've gotta go."

"Keep me in the loop," Harlan said.

Harlan breathed a sigh of relief when he heard Ben close the front door. He hadn't meant to use Maddie's DNA to distract the boy from asking about David's letter, but it had worked. He had given them both the same advice and hopefully, it wouldn't come back to haunt him.

Ben went to his car. His phone rang-it was Arthur Mantz. Ben let it go to voicemail. There were decisions to make and people to please, but Ben needed some space. He wasn't due at Candy's for a while, so when he started the car, he drove to King's Highway and headed to the Artisan Row to pick up a bottle of wine. He didn't think about Uncle Dave's letter until he was getting out of the car in the public parking lot.

36

TUESDAY

Maddie had filled the car trunk with the bins of old textbooks from the garage. She brought them to the store and dragged them into the back room. The clouds rolled in just as Maddie finished putting the last of the bins of textbooks in front of the store, affixing a "Free" sign to the front of each.

That morning, she stood on the curb and looked up as if her angry stare would send the clouds away. They looked as if they were ready to open up and send teeming showers her way, but that didn't mean they would. As often happened in the fall, the clouds would portend a wicked shower, but send drizzle instead, which would still curl paper book covers and leave the pages wrinkled. As it turned out, it was one of those days, and Maddie had to drag the bins inside an hour later.

She was keeping the store open later because of the holidays, and around four-thirty, she needed a boost to keep her going. Maddie headed across the street for coffee. She rocked as the barista steamed the milk and kept glancing out the window wishing the next hour would pass quickly. When the barista handed her the coffee, she returned to the store and found a customer squatting next to Larry petting his head. Larry was blissed out and kept urging the man to continue.

"Sorry I wasn't here," Maddie said. The man turned his head, and she held up the coffee. "Can't survive without this."

"Where did you get that?" he asked.

"Across the street. It's as good as Starbucks."

"I'll have to try them." He stood. "Are you Maddie?"

"Yes."

"My name is Ben. Candy told me to come and check out the store."

"Oh, well." Maddie held out her arms. "This is it."

Ben looked around the store.

"It's...charming."

Maddie laughed out loud.

"It's old and outdated, but thank you for being kind."

Ben smiled. "You're welcome."

"So, is there something you were looking for?"

Ben studied her face. She had David's eyes.

"I teach history." The lie reddened his cheeks. "I'd like to find something about Mercer County that kids could relate to."

"I don't have a lot of reference books here, mostly paperback bestsellers and self-help books. I also have bins of used textbooks that might have something." She took a sip of coffee. "Why don't you look around?"

Maddie took her cup to the table, took her phone out of her pocket, and sat. She looked at her Instagram page, and as Ben walked down the aisles, he watched her out of the corner of his eye. She moved her hand a certain way, and it reminded him of something David used to do. He took books off the shelf, flipped pages, and then went to the table.

"You were right," he said.

"Sorry to disappoint you."

She smiled, and he recognized Daisy's smile.

"Do you think it will rain?" he asked.

Maddie twisted her mouth, and then glanced outside.

"It might." She shifted in her seat. "Is there something else?"

Ben took a deep breath and then exhaled.

"My name is Ben Arntz. David Friedlander was my uncle."

"Oh." Maddie bit her lip and wrapped her hands around her coffee.

"Can I sit down?" he asked.

She nodded, and he sat across from her. He picked at his index finger for a full minute, and then looked up at her.

"I've been trying to figure out how to say this, but there's no easy way. I talked to Harlan Monteif earlier, and he said you might already know this, and now I'm stumbling all over myself."

"He told you about David and my mother," Maddie said.

Ben sat back. "My uncle had photo albums with pictures of you as a baby."

Maddie blushed. "Pictures of me?"

"He took them from the house next to yours, the old Fenway place."

Maddie sat back and folded her arms.

"He was stalking me."

"It was more like he was stalking your mother." Ben put his hands in his coat pockets. "He was in love with her. He ended up in a hospital from a breakdown. I don't think he understood what he was doing."

"So, did you come here just to defend his actions?" She glared at him.

"I don't really know why I came here." He clasped his hands on the table. "I guess you've heard that my mother killed him."

"It was on the news."

"I've been trying to figure out why, that's why I've been looking through all their stuff and found out about you. Harlan said you might need my permission to compare your DNA to David's. I'll let the police know that you have it." He smiled slightly. "I'm sorry. I don't always handle things like this well."

"How often do things like this come up?" she asked.

"I should have said it differently." He squirmed. "I just wanted to meet you. I don't have people, I mean family, here, and if it turns out we're related, it would be nice."

"We'd be family," she said.

"Is that all right?" he asked.

"I don't know. I have to think about it for a while."

"Okay." He stood. "Well, it's been nice meeting you."

"You, too," she said. "Give me your phone number so I can call if I decide to do the DNA."

He texted her so she'd have his number.

"Maybe I'll stop by again," he said as he went through the door. "Have a good night."

"You, too, and thanks, for the DNA I mean."

"No problem."

Ben still had time before he had to be at Candy's, so he drove to the police station. He asked for Detective Worthington at the counter, and the duty officer called her. Janet appeared in the lobby a few minutes later.

"Hey," she said.

"Do you have a minute?"

"Sure."

They went up to the second floor and sat at Janet's desk.

"I wanted to ask you if you could find out about a woman who went missing almost thirty years ago. Her name was Daisy Brady."

Janet pulled a file from the stack on her desk.

"I've already got her file. I ordered the file from the archives after her daughter asked me to look into it."

"You mean Maddie," Ben said. Janet nodded. "I just talked to her. I told her she has my permission to have her DNA compared to David's."

Janet narrowed her eyes.

"And why would you do that?"

"Because I think she's my Uncle Dave's daughter."

"And how did you come to that conclusion?" Janet asked.

"I found some old photo albums under my uncle's bed, and I talked to people who knew him. He was dating Daisy."

Janet raised her eyebrows.

"I think we found those when we searched his house but they didn't seem relevant at the time."

"One was hidden behind a dresser. That one had pictures of Maddie with Daisy."

She sat back and clasped her hands over her stomach.

"I guess we should have looked harder."

"I talked to Harlan Monteif," he said. "He told me Daisy was pregnant when David went to England."

"I saw his name in the file. He gave a statement the day she went missing."

"Harlan said the cops didn't look for her," Ben said.

"They did," Janet said. "They followed the route she took and didn't find any evidence of foul play."

"But wouldn't the circumstances indicate that this was more than a runaway wife?" Ben asked. "She took the dog. It was Maddie's second birthday. Who runs away on their kid's second birthday?"

Janet had asked herself the same questions as she read the report over the weekend. The officers had taken a report of the facts and interviewed witnesses. They had done a search. She wondered why they hadn't followed up on Carl Brady's inquiries, but it was the fact that the case had been placed in the archives two days after it was filed that really bothered her.

The officers had ignored facts in evidence, and she had spent the better part of the weekend thinking about Daisy Brady. Something about the case didn't feel right. One of the responding officers was now a detective, and the other had retired shortly after they investigated Daisy's disappearance. Was that merely a coincidence? When she got to work on Monday, she found a note on her desk from the chief. He had heard that she requested the file from the archives and wanted to see her in his office.

"Why did you pull a missing person case from thirty years ago?" he asked.

"I'm looking into it at the daughter's request," Janet said.

"Well, do it on your own time. We don't have the resources right now to work on a cold case that happened decades ago."

When she left his office, she'd been struck by his vehemence. Other officers had worked on cold cases during their shifts, so what was different about this one?

When she got to her desk, she finished up the paperwork on the Friedlander case and then started her own file on Daisy Brady, which she kept in a locked drawer.

"I can't discuss the details of the case with you," Janet told Ben. She wrote something on a yellow sticky note, tore it off, folded it, and handed it to him.

"This is my number," she said.

"I already have…"

"This is a new one. Put it into your phone when you get outside."

She stood, and then Ben got up and went to the elevator. He glanced back once before stepping inside.

Janet watched him walk to his car from the second-floor window. Ben got inside his car and read the note as he felt his phone vibrate in his pocket. The note read, NOT HERE. He took his phone out of his pocket and read her message.

Fenway Manor tomorrow morning at 10

37

TUESDAY

Ben got a text as he drove across town to Candy's house. It was from Arthur Mantz.

"I have all the paperwork ready for you to sign. Just let me know if you want me to come to you, or if you want to come to the city."

Once the papers were signed, probate could go forward, and Ben would be one step closer to selling everything that bound him to his mother's legacy.

As Ben thought about being unfettered, he thought of Candy. He remembered her sitting on the floor with the blanket wrapped around her. Her cheeks were pink and her eyes drowsy. He was besotted with her, and now he worried about his money. What if she *was* only interested in him because he was rich?

It seemed as though everyone had warned him about it, and his mother had cautioned him since birth that women were vultures who would seize upon him like a plague if he weren't careful.

"Your looks will attract them," Beth said, "but it's your money that will keep them."

Beth had been particularly hard on the girls from Logan's Grove.

"Their families have never risen above the poverty line."

It wasn't true, as Ben had discovered after he met some of them in college, but Beth's opinion never changed.

Now, a seed of doubt was trying to plant itself in his psyche, but Ben put it in a box in his mind and closed the door on it. He liked Candy. He liked her so much. He was going to trust his own judgment and live his own life.

But there was no compartmentalizing his net worth. The amount was staggering, and as Ben turned onto Candy's street, a rush of energy flowed through him. For a moment it felt good, and then it was daunting. That kind of money changed people, and it might influence Candy. If he felt unprepared for such a shift in his fortunes, how would it affect her?

Was Candy just a distraction, something to focus on because reality was overwhelming? Was his need for her blinding him?

"No," he said.

Ben wasn't an idiot. A part of him was always grounded in reality. He had felt comfortable with Candy the moment he met her, and he never felt the need to put on airs around her. His truth now was that he truly cared for her. He wanted her, and it was his decision to be with her.

Ben got to her house at ten past seven, and her mother answered the door.

"You must be Ben." Nina smiled broadly. She was wearing lipstick and blusher. "Come on in."

He came inside, and she shut the door. He handed her the wine.

"I hope this is okay."

Nina grabbed the bottle and read the label.

"Oh, I'm sure it's wonderful." She cradled the bottle as if it were an infant. "So, come on in. Don't be shy."

He followed her to the living room. The aroma of beef filled the room, along with onions and broccoli. Candy hadn't mentioned whether they'd be eating at home, but Ben got that impression when he saw the hors-d'oeuvres on the coffee table.

"Make yourself at home," Nina said. "Candy will be down in a minute. If you'll excuse me, I have to check on dinner."

"No problem," he said.

Ben sat on the sofa and looked around the room. It reminded him of David's house when it was clean, only here, the furniture was old but well kept. The chairs and sofa faced a large TV at the center of one wall. Pictures of Candy were on every wall, along with those of a white Persian cat. Ben heard footsteps on the stairs and stood up.

Candy came into the room like a ray of sunshine. Every time he saw her was like the first time, and his heart would rise to his throat.

"Hi," she said as she walked over to him. "I know we didn't talk about what we were doing, but when she found out about you, she insisted we stay here for dinner."

"It's fine. We can go out later if you want to."

She came close to him. "She's not a bad cook, but she doesn't use a lot of seasoning."

"I'm sure it will be fine." He kissed her and then held her cheek in his hand. "I've missed you."

She beamed. "I've missed you, too."

They kissed again, and then Nina shouted from the dining room. "Dinner's served!"

They both jumped, and then Candy took his hand and led him past the stairs to the other side of the house. Nina had put all the food on the table and was waiting for them with a big smile.

"I hope you like pot roast," she said.

"It's my favorite," Ben said. Candy squeezed his hand. "Where should I sit?"

"Anywhere," Nina said.

Candy pulled out a chair, so Ben pulled out the one next to hers. Nina sat across from them. She began passing the food around, and when their plates were full, Nina looked at Ben.

"I was so sorry to hear about your mother."

"Thank you."

"I never knew her, but I knew of her. She did a lot for this town."

"She'd be happy to hear that," Ben said.

"I've lived here all my life," Nina said. "My parents bought this house in 1947."

"My grandparents lived here with us," Candy said.

"My father worked at that factory over on Mormont," Nina said. "He told me this house cost him seven thousand dollars."

Ben smiled. "I guess that was a lot back then."

"He used the G.I. Bill."

"Mom, Ben is going to let me list his house," Candy said.

Nina's eyes widened. "Oh, my God!" she cried. "You're not selling that wonderful mansion, are you?"

"I'm planning to, yes."

"But it's your heritage. You can't just walk away from your heritage."

"Mom, it's Ben's decision what he does with that house."

"Well, I don't think his mother would be happy if she knew. And she's only been gone a week, right?"

The muscle in his jaw twitched, and then Ben put a forkful of food into his mouth.

"Mom, what did you make for dessert?"

Nina saw Candy's red cheeks.

"Yeah, I made an apple pie. I got the apples at Acme."

"I like apple pie," Ben said.

"My mom makes a great apple pie."

Nina straightened her shoulders.

"So, Ben, what do you do in your spare time?"

Candy closed her eyes and prayed for a bomb to fall onto the dining table.

"I…like to read."

Nina's eyes lit up.

"Really? What kind of books do you read?"

"I like historical novels, things like that."

"I love romances. I also like a good mystery."

"Did I tell you I listed that bookstore on Artisan Row?" Candy said.

"You told me," Nina said.

"This food is really good," Ben said.

Nina smiled broadly. "I'm an old-fashioned cook. I'm glad you like it."

Nina kept chattering about the neighbors, the way the town was changing, and the cat on the wall, a pet that had died five years ago.

"I loved that cat," Nina said. "He was my best friend in the world."

"I've never had a pet," Ben said.

"Oh, you need a pet."

"Maybe when he settles down, Mom."

Nina noticed Ben's empty plate.

"You want some more?"

"No, no thank you. I'm full."

"Not too full, I hope. Remember that apple pie."

Nina took the plates to the kitchen and Candy grabbed Ben's hand.

"I'm sorry," she said. "I hope she didn't upset you."

"It's okay. She's not the only one giving me advice."

Nina returned with an apple pie and new plates. She put the pie in front of her seat.

"Anybody want coffee?"

"I'll have some," Ben said.

"It's too late for me, Mom."

"But I thought you two were going out," Nina said.

"It would keep me up all night, Mom."

"Maybe you're right," Ben said. "No coffee, Mrs. Burke."

"Okay. I won't make any then."

Nina sat and started cutting the pie. As she scooped them out the slices fell into pieces as she plopped it onto a plate.

"Doesn't matter how it looks as long as it tastes good, right?"

"Right," Ben said.

Ben was surprised by how good it tasted and asked for another piece, which made Nina happy. As she handed it to him, she touched his finger and blushed.

"You are a handsome one, aren't you?"

Ben avoided her eyes and smiled.

"So, where are you two off to tonight?"

"I thought we'd go to The Ugly Badger," Ben said. He looked at Candy. "If that's all right with you."

"It's fine. I like the Badger."

"I haven't been to The Ugly Badger in years," Nina said. "Your father used to take me there. What kind of crowd is it these days?"

"There are all kinds of people there," Ben said.

"So, an old lady like me wouldn't feel awkward."

"You're not going with us, Mom."

Nina blushed. "I didn't think I was."

Candy pushed her plate away and got up. Ben wasn't sure what to do, so he pushed his plate away and stood up, too.

"It was good, Mom."

"Yes, Mrs. Burke. I really like the pie."

Nina's eyes widened. "I forgot the wine."

"It's okay. We can have it another time."

Candy glanced at him. "You brought wine?"

"I did."

She smiled and then eyed her mother.

"I don't know when I'll be back, so you can lock the door."

"Thanks for the meal," Ben said.

"You're welcome, Ben. It's been nice meeting you."

"You, too."

She followed them to the front door and watched them put on their coats. She stood at the door while they got into their cars, waved as they drove away, and then she returned to the table, sat at her place, and wept.

All she wanted was what was best for Candy, but she always seemed to say the wrong thing. And what harm would it have done to invite her along? She didn't have to sit with them, and it would have been nice to get out of the house.

When she was done crying, Nina took the plates off the table and did the dishes. She had fallen into a routine over the years, and now that Candy had a fella, she wondered what her purpose would be. And when Candy got married, what then? Would she ever come to visit her mother?

Nina wasn't sure, and that made her cry harder. Sad thoughts of her late husband and the days that followed returned, and she sat at the kitchen dinette sobbing into a dishtowel.

Candy didn't know how depressed her mother had been since she started working at the agency for Nina hid it from her. She had also hidden her suicidal ideations. As much as Nina tried to find a reason to go on, it was getting harder every day.

Candy had been her focus. Her daughter's recovery had kept her mind off her loneliness for years, but the last few evenings when Nina had been alone, the reality of her existence hit her hard. In the end, we are all alone, and we can't count on anyone to save us.

38

WEDNESDAY

B en opened his eyes and saw Candy lying on her stomach on the floor, a blanket over her, and her cell phone flashlight in her hand. *Confessions of a Lady's Maid* was open in front of her. He'd given it to her the night before, and they had gone through it, checking David's notes in the margins, and reading the end so Candy could see what had happened to Derek. The author, like everyone else in the story, thought Derek was traveling when the tragedy took place.

"Hey," Ben said. "When did you wake up?"

"About an hour ago." She got up and crawled into the bed beside him.

"Have you been reading all this time?"

"I was looking for an answer." She snuggled.

"To what?" he asked.

"I thought maybe they had added something at the end about him and we just missed it." She sighed. "How did the author know what had happened at Fenway Manor?"

"The author was Emily's personal maid. She came with her when Alastair brought Emily from Philadelphia. She wrote it in South Carolina under a pseudonym. That's where she and Mr. Martin went after they ran away following the tragedy."

Candy snuggled closer to him.

"So, Daisy Carter wrote the book. Funny she has the same name as my friend's mother."

"I met Maddie the other day when I went into the bookstore," Ben said.

Candy got up on one elbow, looked at him, and pursed her lips.

"Remember when I told you about my accident?"

Ben nodded.

"Well, that night, Maddie's boyfriend assaulted me."

"Why didn't you tell me that?" he asked.

"I didn't know you well enough," Candy said. "The thing is, he told her I let him…and she believed him. We didn't speak after that. We just started talking again a few days ago."

She put her head on his chest, and he put his arm around her.

"Is that why you had the accident?" Ben asked.

"I was really upset and drank too many beers."

He put his other arm around her and held her tightly.

"I'll never hurt you that way," he said.

She looked into his eyes and smiled.

"I believe you."

They stayed that way for a while, and then Candy thought of her ghost.

"I think Derek is counting on me to help him."

"He's a ghost," Ben said. "I don't think he's counting on anybody anymore."

"You can't see him," she said. "He looks so sad."

Ben looked up at the ceiling.

"Maybe if I tear that place down, he'll go away."

"But then where would he go?" she asked.

"I don't know." Ben turned his head toward her. "Maybe he'll go to the house next door."

"He can go there now."

Ben sat up and wrapped his arms around his knees.

"Look, I don't know anything about ghosts, and to tell you the truth, I really don't care what happens to Derek Fenway."

"Why are you so upset?" she asked.

"I'm not upset." He hung his head. "It's just that I've been listening to this bullshit about Derek Fenway all my life. My Uncle Dave thought he could set Derek free. Now, you want to help him, but neither one of you thinks about what he did during his life. He wasn't such a great guy, you know. He hurt a lot of people."

Ben got out of bed, put on his pants, and went downstairs.

Candy wrapped the blanket around her and followed him to the kitchen.

"I'm sorry," she said.

"Why are you sorry?"

"I didn't mean to upset you."

Candy stood in the doorway. He opened the refrigerator and took out a bottle of water.

"I told you I'm not upset," he said. He saw the sad expression on her face. "We're just having a discussion."

"But you sound like you're mad," she said.

"It's a loud discussion." He tilted his head. "Haven't you ever gotten into an argument with somebody where you just couldn't agree?"

"It usually ends with me storming off to my bedroom."

She tried to suppress a smile.

"Well, that happens too, but it can also end when you both decide to agree to disagree."

"Really?" she said. "So, you're not angry."

He shook his head, and then took a swig of water.

"I think Derek was an asshole. You don't. There's nothing to be angry about."

She came up to him and leaned against his chest. He put his finger under her chin and lifted her head so he could see her eyes.

"Are we okay?" he asked.

She kissed him.

"We're okay." She kissed him again. "So, what do you want to do now?"

"Let's go back upstairs."

They made love and then lay in each other's arms while the sun rose. It was getting late, and Candy had to go to work, so she got out of bed and dressed while Ben snored softly. She dropped a shoe while putting it on and he opened his eyes.

"It's almost six-thirty," she said. She sat at the end of the bed. "Thank you for getting me that book."

"Did you find anything helpful?"

She shrugged and then smiled.

"That Daisy was a bit of a slut."

He smiled. "Okay."

"I guess that's the wrong thing to say, isn't it? I guess it's my mother coming out in me. After all, I didn't exactly say no the first time you asked me to come up here."

He sat up and rubbed his eyes.

"No, you didn't." He put his hand on her cheek. "Slut."

She smacked his hand away, and he pulled her down as he fell back on the bed. She was giggling as she tried to push herself off him, but he wouldn't let go.

"Let me go!" she cried. "You can't talk to me that way."

Ben was nuzzling her neck and growling like a bear. She was laughing harder now, but she was able to free her arms and began tickling his sides.

"Stop!" he cried. "Stop, I can't stand it."

She stopped and then rolled over onto her back. They were both laughing, and she took his hand while she caught her breath.

"I'll remember that," she said.

"I'm sure you will."

Ben sat up and leaned on his hands.

"I just had an idea," he said. "Do you think your ghost might know what happened to Maddie's mother?"

Candy sat up.

"That's a great idea. He must have been there when she disappeared."

"Why don't we meet there when you get off work, and we'll ask him?"

Candy's shoulders slumped a bit. "I think he knows sign language. I was going to watch some videos on YouTube so I could talk to him."

"Sign language?"

"He knows sign language."

"I know some sign language," Ben said. "I had to learn it for one of my teaching classes."

"So, if I show you what he's saying, you could interpret it for me."

"It's a bit more complicated than that. You have to watch how he moves his head or his facial expressions."

"I can do that," she said eagerly.

"Okay. We'll give it a try." Ben looked at her clothes. "You're leaving?"

"I have to go home and change before I go to work."

"Do you really have to go now?"

She smiled. "I'm gonna try getting into my room before my mom wakes up." She got out of bed. "I'll text you when I get off of work, okay?"

"Okay. Do you want to eat first before we go look for your ghost?"

"We should go to Fenway Manor first while it's still a little light outside."

He put on his clothes before following her downstairs. As they stood at the door, she kissed him again.

"I'll see you later," she said.

He watched her walk to her car and waited until she had driven away before closing the door. He still had three hours before he had to meet the detective, so he decided to go home and change his clothes.

39

WEDNESDAY

B en got to Fenway Manor before Janet arrived, so he took a walk across the property to the edge of the woods. He had no idea where the property line ended, or how many acres there were, but it was in a prime location on King's Highway, and it had to be worth millions.

He turned, looked at the manor house, and then saw the stake left when they took the crime scene tape down. David had been facing the house when he died. It was nice to think that the last thing he saw was the thing he'd loved most.

Ben's eyes rose from the bottom of the house to the top as he thought of what it would take to tear it down and how long it would take to clear the property. He had spent some time online looking at companies that specialized in demolition. It would be thrilling to watch the whole thing ripped apart in front of his eyes.

Janet pulled up behind Ben's car, got out, and waited for him. The November wind blew into her coat causing it to balloon behind her. She grabbed the flaps and wrapped her arms around her waist as she shivered, and then leaned against her car.

"It got colder since this morning," she said when Ben approached her.

"Yeah, it has." He leaned on the car beside her. "So, why did you want to meet here?"

"I didn't want to talk in the office because I'm not sure who's listening. One of the officers who took the missing persons on Daisy sits at a desk nearby. I don't want him to know I'm looking into this case yet."

"Okay."

"Carl Brady contacted the station every year asking about Daisy's case. The duty officer would take the message and give it to a detective. The detective would look up Daisy's name to see if there was any news, and when there wasn't, they'd make a note of it in the file." She put her hands into her coat pockets. "I think Daisy deserves more, but I can't do much without someone finding out."

"So, why did you want to see me?" Ben asked.

"Because you mentioned something about Maddie's DNA. You believe David Friedlander was her father."

"I have no proof, but Harlan's pretty sure about it."

She stared at the manor house for a moment.

"My gut tells me something happened to Daisy, something bad, and whoever did it had friends in high places, people who could cover it up."

"Like the chief."

"Somebody higher."

"The mayor?"

"At the very least."

"My grandfather knew people like that."

"So, did your mother." She scanned the back yard. "This property belongs to you, doesn't it?"

"I inherited it when she died."

"And she inherited it from her parents."

"My grandfather. He used to bring her and Uncle Dave here when they were kids."

"When I was investigating your uncle's death, I found out that Logans Grove had been trying to condemn this place for years. There was an Order to Stay Proceedings executed in 1995, and the town has been trying to get it lifted ever since, but a judge named Charles Anderson..."

"Denied their motions," Ben said. "He retired, and I guess my mother couldn't find anyone else who'd do it for her."

"That's right," Janet said. "So, why did she fight it for so long?"

Ben shrugged. "There's something I didn't tell you because I didn't think it mattered at the time, but my mother got really upset when I told her I was quitting school. She blamed David. She said he talked me into it."

Janet looked at the ground.

"Did he?"

Ben shook his head. "It was gonna happen sooner or later. I'd already made up my mind. Uncle Dave just agreed with me."

"But your mom still believed it was his fault."

Ben folded his arms. "I think it was easier to blame him. She couldn't imagine I'd want something different than what she'd planned for me."

"That could go to motive. Feelings build up, she loses her connection in the courts, and now she has to deal with this. Maybe David was the one who went to the judge. Without him around, she could just have it torn down." Janet walked over to the house and put her hand on the wall. "And having him killed here was like some sort of poetic justice."

"It was his favorite place in the world," Ben said.

Janet screwed up her mouth as she stood back from the house.

"So, why wouldn't she just destroy it?" She turned around. "Wouldn't that be the best way to hurt him?"

"Yes."

"And how does Daisy fit into all this?" Janet went back to the car and leaned on it. "I've been thinking about what you told me yesterday. You think she got pregnant by David." She glanced at him. "Rich people have ways of handling things like that. They throw money at it."

"You think my grandfather offered Daisy money to what, go away?" Ben said.

"Or to have an abortion. That would be my guess. Obviously, Daisy refused, which would have pissed him off."

Ben walked up to the house and looked to the right.

"What I didn't tell you is that David was obsessed with her. He stalked her when he got back from England. He stood on that porch and took pictures of Maddie and Daisy."

"Who told you that?"

"Harlan mentioned it, and I found the pictures."

"Did she ever call the police?" Janet asked.

"Harlan said she did."

"Nothing like that came up when I ran his name through the system."

"My grandfather was also friends with the chief," Ben said.

"Which means any charges against David would have magically

disappeared." She sighed. "Poor Daisy. I'll have to go through the paper files the year before she went missing and see if I can find anything."

"And I'll keep looking through his stuff."

Janet got into her car and drove away while Ben looked at the peeling paint on the mansion's walls and imagined David standing on the back porch using a telescopic lens to stalk Daisy and Maddie. The thought of it made him cringe, and his memories took on new meaning when he began to realize that his Uncle Dave hadn't been the kindhearted soul everyone believed him to be.

40

B en spent the next hour searching on his phone for local paternity testing labs. He found one in New Brunswick, bookmarked it, and then headed to Artisan Row. He parked in public parking behind the café and stopped to get two coffees before heading to Maddie's store. He found her standing on a ladder dusting the molding on the ceiling when he came in.

"Are you nuts?" he said.

He put the coffee on the table and went to hold the ladder.

"I'm fine," she said.

She kept dusting until she got every cobweb she could reach, and then she came down and looked across the room.

"I have to get the rest of them," she said.

"I'll help you," he said. She pursed her lips as she glanced at him over her shoulder. "It will go faster."

He helped Maddie carry the ladder across the room, and then, with Ben holding it in place, she finished dusting. When they sat to drink the lattes, they were tepid, and the froth had disappeared.

"I appreciate the thought," Maddie said.

"I saw you and reacted."

"So, what's up?"

"I found a place that does DNA tests. You have to pay for it, but it won't take as long as those online sites."

"How much does it cost?"

"It's…not cheap, but I thought since it was David, that you might let me pay for it."

Maddie tilted her head forward.

"How much?"

"Four hundred dollars."

Maddie blanched. "You're kidding?" He shook his head. "Oh, my God."

"It would ease my mind to find out. I'd like to know if you're my cousin."

Maddie sat back and stared at him.

"That's right."

"So, will you let me pay for it?" Ben asked.

"Well, since there's no way in hell I can pay for it, and since it means something to you, okay."

He smiled broadly. "Great."

"And if it turns out he left money, I'm telling you right now that I don't want it. Not any of it."

"Understood. So, you'll have to go to the lab and have them do it, and I can go with you if you want."

"Okay," she said. "Text me the name of the company. I'll call them and see what I have to do, and then I'll let you know."

"Good. Great. I'll wait for your call." He tapped the table with his fingers. "Um, I know your dad died." Maddie nodded. "Do you ever not think about it?"

"No. I live in his house and work in his store. I walk his dog. It's impossible to avoid thinking about him, but it's less painful if that helps."

"My mother killed my uncle. I can't stop thinking about it."

"I can't imagine what you're going through," she said.

"I don't feel like me anymore." He sighed as a customer walked in. "Well, I don't want to keep you from anything."

"You're not. You can sit here all day if you'd like. Larry would love seeing a new face."

Larry's head went up at the mention of his name.

"Maybe I should get a dog. My mother wouldn't let me have one." He waved at Larry. "Does he like riding in the car?"

"He might have when he was younger. Now, he lays down and groans if I hit the brakes too hard."

Ben chuckled. He pushed himself away from the table, stood, and pushed the chair in.

"Text me after you call them."

"I will, and thanks, Ben."

"Anytime, Maddie."

She watched him walk across the street and into the café. She wondered what it would be like to have him as her cousin. He seemed nice, and his manners were impeccable. And he had lots of money.

"Don't start daydreaming, Maddie," she said.

Ben bought another latte before heading home to change his clothes. He needed to call Arthur Mantz to make an appointment to sign the papers. He liked Maddie. He wanted her to have something. He wanted something good to come out of David's life.

When Ben got home, he called Arthur, and they agreed to meet at the American hotel the following Tuesday. Ben went downstairs to Maria's room and saw that her bags were almost packed. She was sorting items on the bed and looked up when he walked in.

"I'm getting done faster than I thought I would," she said. Maria stood and put her hands on her hips. "My sister is looking forward to having me there. She wants me to come sooner." Her expression begged for his approval.

"What do you want to do?"

She let her hands drop to her sides.

"I'd like to go. You don't need me here, and she is lonely."

"Of course, I need you here."

Maria came to him and put her hand on his shoulder.

"You're a grown-up now. You can take care of yourself." She went back to the bed. "So, do you think you'll keep seeing that nice girl?"

"I hope so," Ben said. "She seems to like me."

"Just be careful, Ben."

"You said that before."

"I know," she said, "but I can't help it. I feel like I have to say what your mother would say."

"If you were my mother, you would have had Candy kidnapped and taken as far away from me as she could go."

"Beth wasn't that bad," Maria said.

"She *was* that bad. You just saw a different side of her." Ben said it with bitterness.

"I hope you will focus on the good memories of her."

"She killed my uncle, Maria."

"But she loved you."

"You think that was love?" Ben asked. "She didn't let me breathe without her consent."

Maria closed her eyes and shook her head.

"Okay. You're right. Now go and let me finish packing."

"You haven't told me what you decided," he said. "When are you leaving?"

"I have a plane reservation for Monday afternoon."

"Oh," he said. "You already have a reservation." Ben slipped his hands into his pockets. "Listen, I have something to tell you." He walked over to her and sat on the bed. "My mother left a bequest to you. It was for…" He hesitated. While Beth might think fifty grand was enough for twenty years of faithful service, Ben did not. This woman had been like a mother to him. She'd been there all the time, day and night, for twenty years! "She left you two hundred and fifty thousand dollars."

Maria's mouth gaped, and she sat on the bed.

"You're kidding."

"She wanted to show you how much she appreciated you."

"Oh, my God. I never dreamed."

"You should invest it for your retirement. I'm sure one of mom's brokers can help you sort things out. They must have an office in Chicago."

"I can't believe it," Maria said.

"I hope it makes you happy," Ben said. "So, then I'll plan to drive you to the airport."

Maria came to Ben and took his hand. He looked into her eyes and understood that she didn't believe for one moment that Beth had left her that money.

"You've done enough. I can take the shuttle."

"No, I want to take you. I want to be there when you take off."

"They won't let you go past the gate entrance," Maria said.

"I'll buy a ticket."

"Don't make jokes."

"I'm not joking. I'll call them today to make a reservation."

She shook her head. "Please stop. I want you to say goodbye at the gate."

"Okay, you win. I'll say goodbye at the gate."

Ben retrieved his laptop from his room and took it to the living room. He did an online search into the town's condemnation laws. Arthur was right – once a house was condemned, the owner would have to bring it up to code or tear it down. He wanted it to be his decision to destroy the damn place, not the town's. He sent an email to one of the demolition companies on his list.

At 4:01, Ben closed his laptop. He went to the kitchen, got a Hot Pocket out of the freezer, and popped it into the microwave. When the bell rang, he took it out and was headed for the island when he changed his mind. He'd never been able to eat on the sofa in the living room.

Ben felt positively wicked as he sat on the sofa, put his plate on his lap, and switched on the TV. He found an old sitcom rerun. When the commercial came on, he happened to glance at the bookcase near the front window. Ben had never taken a good look at it before; it was always just something in the living room. It was made of dark mahogany and had glass doors. Something in it looked out of place. He put his plate on the coffee table, walked over to it, and opened the glass door.

Beth liked everything to be color coordinated. This particular bookcase held books of a singular color - brown, which is why the yellow scrunchie, one of those elasticized, cloth-covered bands women used to tie back their hair, had caught his eye. It was hanging from a small, white plastic hook that had been stuck on the right wall of the bookcase.

Beth had never used scrunchies. Ben took it off the hook and looked at it for a moment as he tried to figure out why it would be there. It had been placed so that anyone sitting on the sofa might see it, and that was Beth's favorite place to sit in the room. As Ben examined it, he saw that there was something wrapped tightly around it. He ran his fingers over it so it would loosen. When it did, he took one end and pulled it until it came off. Ben held it up in front of the window and saw it separate into three, long strands of what appeared to be light brown hair.

A chill went up his spine. Ben went to the kitchen and got a Ziplock bag out of the drawer. He put the scrunchie along with the strands of hair into the bag, and then put them back into the bookcase.

Ben wondered if Maria had ever seen it hanging there. The bookcases were covered so she wouldn't have dusted them very often, but still, she must have seen it. Had she ever questioned why it was there?

Ben wanted to ask her, but Maria was so defensive when it came to Beth that he chose not to ask her about the scrunchie.

As he shut the door on the bookcase, Ben received a text from Candy. She was leaving her job on time and would meet him behind Fenway Manor as planned.

41

WEDNESDAY

B en was waiting at Fenway Manor when Candy arrived. She was wearing jeans and her heavy coat. He came to her car, waited for her to get out, and then kissed her hello.

"I'm sorry I'm late," she said. "A call came in as I was walking out the door from someone who wants to see a house. I couldn't hang up on them."

"No problem." He smiled. "When are you showing it?"

"They're gonna come by next week. They live in the city and want to move to *live in the country*. It's what they always say, and then they get here and want to know where the theaters are."

Ben laughed and hugged her.

"So, do you see the ghost?"

She looked over his shoulder.

"Not yet. Let's take a walk."

The sun was just setting as they walked across the yard. Candy's shoe hit the concrete block again, and she almost fell, but Ben grabbed her arm.

"I think they were part of the garden," he said.

"I almost tripped over it the last time I was here, too. I should have brought my sneakers with me this morning, but I had my mind on other things."

Ben smiled. "Yeah, me too."

They walked toward the woods but stopped short of going inside.

"I don't see him," Candy said.

"Should we go into the woods?"

"It's too dark." She took a deep breath and shouted. "Derek!"

"Does he hear?" Ben asked.

"He acts like he can hear."

Derek had yet to make an appearance, and it was cold, so Candy shoved her hands into her coat pockets and shivered.

"I say we go for now."

"You sure you want to give up so soon?" Ben asked.

"It's too cold, and if he were coming, he would have been here by now." She looked at Ben. "Maybe he's afraid to come out when you're here."

"Do you want me to go back to the car?"

"We'll both go and wait in there."

They went to Ben's car and got inside. He put his hand on hers and felt the cold.

"Damn, your hand is cold."

"What little blood I have goes to my heart when the temperature hits sixty."

Ben laughed and kissed her hand. Candy put her head on his shoulder.

"Maria is going on Monday," he said.

"Where is she going?"

"To live with her sister in Chicago."

"She's nice. I hope she's happy there."

"I'm gonna miss her. She's been with me practically since I was born."

"Will you get someone to replace her?"

"I'll have to. It's a big place. I mean, well, I guess I could clean it if I had to."

She moved her head forward so she could see his eyes.

"But you don't have to. You can hire people to do that, people who need a job."

"Yeah, and I really don't want to clean it, do I?"

Candy laughed. "I can just see you with the vacuum cleaner. 'How do I turn this on?'" She snorted. "Or, yelling at the washing machine like it's Alexa. 'Machine wash my clothes.'"

"Yeah, yeah, very funny. I know how to turn on the washing machine."

"But can you turn it off?"

He grabbed her and started tickling her, and then she saw a light at the window. She gently pushed Ben away.

"That's him."

Ben turned his head but saw nothing. He moved to his seat while Candy got out of the car. Derek was hovering near the side of the house, and she went toward him as Ben got out and followed her.

"Derek," she said. "I wasn't sure you'd come." She looked at Ben and took his hand. "This is Ben." She stepped closer. "We wanted to ask you a question."

Derek smiled and nodded.

"A long time ago, someone came here, a woman named Daisy."

Derek flinched, and Candy glanced at Ben.

"I think he knows the name." She pointed toward Maddie's house. "She used to live in that house."

Derek nodded, and Candy smiled broadly.

"You know who I mean."

Derek nodded again.

"Do you remember the day she was walking her dog and left him tied to the porch behind this house?"

Derek backed away, and Candy moved forward.

"Derek." Candy smiled as Derek frowned.

"What's he doing?" Ben asked.

"He moved back, and now he's frowning."

Candy moved toward him again.

"Daisy disappeared," she said. "We were wondering if you saw her that day."

Derek gestured in sign language.

"He's doing this." She mimicked Derek's gesture. "What is he saying?"

"I'm not sure." She did it again. "It looks like can't or don't know maybe."

"How can we figure out what he's saying?" she asked.

"What's he doing now?"

"He looks frustrated." She shivered. "Now he's shaking his head and moving his hands like he wants to hit someone. He's looking up and shaking his head." She put her hand out toward Derek. "I'm sorry I don't understand you."

That's when Derek vanished. Candy looked around and up at the sky as if he'd be hovering in the air, but he was gone.

"He's gone," she said.

"He left?"

"He just vanished."

"It's cold. Let's get out of here."

"I feel so helpless," Candy said.

"It's not your fault. Maybe he's just doing some sort of 18th century weird shit sign language that nobody would understand."

She giggled as they walked to the cars, and Ben stopped by hers until she was inside.

"You want to go to the Badger?" he asked.

"I'm hungry."

"Then I'll meet you there."

He kissed her through the open window before she drove off, and then he scanned the yard before getting into his. He followed her down the drive and noticed she stopped a bit longer than necessary at the turn to the road.

When they got to The Ugly Badger, they parked side by side and held hands as they walked to the entrance. Candy was quiet.

"Did you see him before we turned onto the road?" Ben asked.

"Yes. He was standing at the end of the drive." She sighed. "He's so handsome. It's such a shame he died the way he did."

"Yeah, well, nobody told him to sleep with anything that moved."

"Ben!" she cried. "That's a terrible thing to say."

"But it's the truth." He saw the look on her face, and his shoulders slumped. "Look, I know you think he's the victim here, but he was old enough to know better. I can't feel sorry for him."

"But he's been stuck here for two hundred years. Doesn't that make you feel a little bad for him?"

"Not really."

He held the door, and she walked past him. Several people were waiting for a table, so they sat at the bar until one became available. He ordered a beer, and she asked for a coke.

"You really don't think he's suffered being left here all alone while everyone else was set free?" Candy asked.

"No."

"That's because you can't see his face."

"Which you think is handsome."

She smiled. "You're jealous."

He took a big swig of his beer.

"He's a ghost."

"You are jealous," she said.

"No, I just don't have the same fascination with Derek Fenway as you or my Uncle Dave."

"I'm not fascinated by him. I just want to help him."

"Which is what Uncle Dave wanted to do."

"He and I would have had a lot in common," Candy said.

"Except you're not crazy," Ben said. He kept his eyes on his beer.

"That's not what my shrink said." She lowered her eyes and looked up at him through her lashes. "That was a joke."

"I know."

He straightened his back, and then she straightened hers.

"I was just..." she began.

"I know."

Ben grew quiet, and Candy sipped her coke. They were both glad when Ben's name was called. The host led them to a table by the fireplace, and Candy relished the warmth.

"I can't wait for spring," she said.

"I want to get away from here," Ben said.

He gazed at her across the table with the saddest look she'd ever seen.

"Okay," she said with a smile. "Which island are we going to?"

"I'm serious. I want to leave here and never look back."

Her smile faded. His mood was dark. She reached for his hand and squeezed it.

"Then why don't we go away?" she asked.

"Because you have a job and it might disappear if you take off for a week."

"But you said we'd never come back," Candy said.

"What would your mother have to say about that?" he asked.

"We'll bring her along. We'll put her in a bungalow of her own. Maybe she'll meet a rich man and get married."

Ben smiled. "She would like that."

"Oh, she'd be thrilled. Can you imagine Mom in love?"

"He'd have to like pot roast."

She was happy to see him smile.

"That goes without saying. He'd also have to like cats."

"Why hasn't she gotten another cat?" he asked.

"She can't afford the vet bills."

"Seriously?"

"Corky was a Persian. He got sick with cancer, and she couldn't afford the treatments. I don't think she ever got over that he died because she didn't have the money to help him."

Ben sat back. "God. I wish I'd known you then."

"If we had been doing what we're doing back then, I would have been arrested."

He laughed, and she glowed.

"I wouldn't have told anyone," Ben said.

"Oh, your mother would have found out."

"That's true. Nothing got past her."

His face darkened again.

I shouldn't have mentioned his mother, Candy thought.

"So, what do you say we go shopping over the weekend?" she asked.

"What, you don't like my shirt?"

"Oh, it's divine but too old for you. You need to loosen up. I want to get you some casual clothes, maybe T-shirts, too."

"I guess I could use some."

The mood lightened a bit, and they ordered their food. Candy avoided talking about Ben's mother, his uncle, or Derek Fenway. She talked about which island she'd like to visit, but Ben still remained quieter than usual.

When they finished eating, they left The Ugly Badger. Candy kissed Ben and then got inside her car. He didn't ask her to come to David's house but waited until she drove away before getting into his car and driving home.

42

W hen Janet came to work on Thursday, she logged onto the department's file server and searched for *Daisy Carter Brady*. There was one file containing a missing person's report and several notations regarding phone calls from Carl Brady. She tried searching a different way, but the results were the same.

Janet reread every word on every page of the digital file. A hand-written entry at the bottom of the first page read: No evidence of foul play, but Carl Brady admitted that he and his wife had been arguing before she left the house. Carl Brady's written statement included facts left off the narrative such as he had searched the grounds calling his wife's name and had gone into the woods.

The woman took her dog for a walk and didn't return. The dog was tied to the porch, which was a deliberate act. A woman leaving her husband wouldn't take the dog. She also wouldn't choose to leave on her child's second birthday. Even if she didn't want to take the child with her, she would still *plan* her escape. Daisy's actions felt random, and to Janet, that meant she hadn't planned on going anywhere that day.

Janet understood the officer's point of view, though. Daisy and Carl had been fighting. It might have been their contention that Daisy wanted to scare him by disappearing for a while. Give him time to cool off. It made sense, yet it still bothered Janet that they never followed up, especially after Carl called the first time.

She looked at the date on the report - November 9, 1991, and then she Googled the weather on that day - minimum temperature

55, maximum 62. It wasn't cold. Daisy could have stashed some things at the mansion and gone off on foot.

Janet saw the dates of the phone calls from Carl Brady. He had called every day in November, but there were no notes on what was said. One officer did note that he referred the call to a Lt. Dan Meissner. The name was unfamiliar, so Janet assumed he had either gone to another town or retired, but one of the responding officers still worked in Logans Grove, and she was looking at him right now.

Sgt. Tom Jarrod sat at a desk across the room. Everyone knew he had been one of the youngest uniformed officers to be promoted to detective in Logans Grove because Jarrod liked to brag about it to the newbies when they came to work at the station. Janet looked him up and found that he had been hired in 1991, the year Daisy went missing. He was promoted to sergeant at the end of that year, the same rank he held now.

"That can't be right," she said.

Jarrod had been young at the time and would have jumped ahead of older, more seasoned officers. His career had been rather lack-luster since then, so what had prompted such a meteoric rise?

Janet then looked up his partner, John Markham, and found that he had retired on December 28, 1991. He'd been on the force for twenty years so he might have turned in his badge and gun of his own accord, but the timing was suspicious. Janet grabbed her note-book and wrote down his name with a question mark beside it.

Janet sat back and watched Jarrod. He was due to retire soon. A party was being held on December 5 at The Ugly Badger. He was biding his time now and staying at his desk when he could. He was too close to getting his reward for almost thirty years of public service to risk losing it by responding to an active shooting or freak encounter with a knife-wielding assailant.

There was nothing special about Jarrod. He looked like an aging cop who'd seen too much and drank to forget what he saw. Janet didn't know much about him and hadn't cared to find out after he made certain comments regarding women detectives the day she arrived. His breed was aging out, and as far as she was concerned, it was good riddance, though she had to give credit where credit was due.

Jarrod was responsible for catching a man who had terrorized women on the campus at Princeton. The assailant would follow their cars as they drove home after stopping at a convenience store, and then pull them over while impersonating a cop. He'd rape and strangle them, and then set their cars on fire. It had been a big win for Jarrod the day he arrested the guy, the biggest in his career, and no one at the department was allowed to forget it.

Jarrod had another reason to dislike Janet. She had been brought in from the outside when the department's lack of diversity was challenged by the city council. Jarrod's son had been due for a promotion and was passed over when the Chief decided to hire a woman instead.

Janet didn't want to talk to him. She doubted he'd even remember the case, despite the strange coincidence of his promotion, and if he did, he probably wouldn't tell her anything. And if he found out she was working the case, he'd tell the chief.

Janet went back to John Markham. She couldn't find an address or telephone number, so it was possible he asked to have it concealed from law enforcement. All cops' addresses are concealed from the general public for safety reasons, even retired cops, but the department usually had a forwarding address. Was he just a privacy nut, or had something forced him to quit, something he didn't want to talk about?

Janet tapped her fingers on her desk. Markham had retired almost thirty years ago. He could be dead, or too old to remember, or unwilling to tell her anything. Still, there was something about this case that wouldn't let her off the hook.

She had a friend at the National Security Agency, a woman named Cheryl Riggs whom Janet had gone to college with, and Janet had never taken advantage of their friendship by asking for something she couldn't find on the department database. She sat forward and folded her arms on the desk. She tapped her finger on her arm and began to rock back and forth as she looked at John Markham's name on the monitor screen. Her gut told her he knew something about Daisy and she had to talk to him. She took out her cell phone and dialed Cheryl's number.

Janet was honest about the facts and Cheryl agreed that there was something off about the whole thing, which allowed her to keep a clear conscience when she searched for retired Logans Grove officer John Markham.

"He's living in Florida in a place called The Villages." She gave

Janet the address and phone number. "If I were you, I'd visit him in person."

Janet thought about making a trip to Florida on her own dime and cringed.

"I don't know if that's possible."

"Well, he might block you from calling him if he doesn't want to talk, and he'll know you're after him if you try to go there after he blocks you on the phone."

"I know."

Cheryl sighed. "Look on one of those discount sites. It might not cost as much as you think."

"But this place is near Orlando."

"It's up to you, Janet."

"Right."

They hung up, and Janet went to a travel site to search for flights to Orlando. It was November and flights to Florida cost more as Northeasterners sought warmer climes. Even those that left late at night weren't cheap, but she could make a round trip in one day if she could find a way to pay for it, and then she could go without telling anyone what she was up to.

43

SATURDAY

On Saturday, Janet sat at her kitchen table flipping through websites. She slammed down the lid of her laptop in frustration. The cost of a round-trip airline ticket and a rental car was way beyond her means. As she thought about the possible coverup, though, she knew she couldn't just let it go. She had to find a way to get to Orlando.

Her doorbell rang, and she went to the front door. It was the postman with a certified letter. She signed the slip and took the letter to the kitchen. It was from her ex-husband's lawyer, and she put it on a pile of unopened mail to be dealt with later. The thought of her ex's smirking face made her reach into her bag for a cigarette, and then she remembered she'd quit smoking, but her notepad fell when she pulled her hand out of her bag. She saw Ben's name on the page as she picked it up.

Janet bit her lip. Ben wanted her to look into Daisy's disappearance. Ben also had a lot of money. Would he be willing to pay for a round trip ticket to Florida?

"You can't ask him that, Janet," she said aloud.

But the idea wouldn't go away, and by noon, she was dressed and ready to go to his house to talk to Ben personally.

Janet turned around twice as she drove down King's Highway, but the third time was the charm. She made it to the front of his house and turned into the driveway. The worst thing that could happen is that Ben would say no. He might get angry and call the chief, but that was unlikely. He wanted to help Maddie find out what happened to her mother.

Janet parked, straightened her shoulders, and got out of her car. She rang the doorbell, and Maria answered with a smile.

"Detective."

"Hi, Maria. Is Ben home?"

"He went out early this morning."

"Do you know where he went?"

"He might be at his uncle's house."

"The one in Princeton?" Janet asked. Maria nodded. "Okay. I'll drive by and see if he's there. If he gets home before I find him, will you give him my card?" She took a card out of her pocket and handed it to Maria.

Janet got back in the car and headed to Princeton. She saw Ben's car in the driveway of David's house as she approached it and parked on the street. The front lawn was full of old furniture and black garbage bags. When she knocked on the front door, Ben answered within a minute and smiled when he saw her.

"Hi," he said.

"Hi, Ben." She rocked on her heels. "Can I come in?"

"Uh, sure." He let her pass and closed the door. The living room was full of boxes. "Excuse the mess. I ordered one of those dumpsters, but it hasn't arrived yet."

"It looks better than the last time I was here."

"Why don't we go to the kitchen?"

Janet stood at the entrance of the kitchen and scanned the room.

"Wow," she said.

"Yeah, I got this one cleaned out." He put his hands on his hips. "You want coffee?"

"Okay."

Janet sat at the table while Ben filled two mugs. He brought them to the table and set them near the sugar bowl.

"You take milk?"

"Yeah."

He got the bottle out of the fridge, grabbed a spoon out of the drawer, and sat while she gazed out the window.

"Looks like he had a garden back there."

"He grew flowers. Mostly tulips."

Ben watched her put milk and sugar in her coffee. She stirred it, and he waited for her to speak.

"I've been looking into Daisy Brady's disappearance," she said.
"And?"

"I found something that might lead us to some answers."

"That's good news," Ben said.

Janet folded her arms on the table.

"I have a lead. There's a retired cop I want to talk to. He was one of the responding officers, and he retired a month after it happened. I want to find out why."

"How old would he be by now?" Ben asked.

"It was a twenty-year retirement, which means he could have been forty. He's still alive. I know where he is, I just have to go talk to him, but…"

"But what?"

Janet tapped her finger on her mug, pursed her lips, and avoided his eyes.

"He lives in Florida, and I don't have the money to pay for an airline ticket."

"Doesn't your office pay for travel?"

She exhaled sharply.

"The chief doesn't want me wasting time on this case. I'm not sure if someone told him not to pursue it, but said we don't have the resources to work on a cold case right now. I know he wouldn't approve my request to travel."

Ben sat back, and Janet continued to plead her case.

"The thing is, the other responding officer is a detective who still works in the department. I can't talk to him without the chief finding out." Janet looked at Ben. "He was a rookie when he answered the 911 call. His promotion came a few weeks after Daisy went missing."

"And you think it's related. One cop retires, and the other gets promoted."

"Right. It's a little too coincidental."

Ben sat back and looked out the window.

"I'll pay for the plane ticket."

Janet breathed a sigh of relief.

"I was hoping you'd say that."

"Maddie needs to know what happened." He clasped his hands on the table. "So, when do you want to go?"

"I'm off tomorrow. If I could get an early morning flight and be back the same day." He took out his wallet. "And it would probably be better if I used my own debit card to pay for it."

Ben stopped and raised his eyebrows.

"Then we'll have to go to the ATM." He slipped his phone into his pocket. "Do you have time to look at something before we go?"

Janet nodded, and then followed him up the stairs to David's bedroom. Ben opened the suitcase on the bed.

"These are the photos I told you about."

Janet looked at them for a minute.

"They're good."

She took out the photo album Candy had found behind the dresser and Ben put his hand on it.

"Some are private," he said.

She glanced at him. "I'm a big girl."

"But I feel like we're invading his privacy if we look at them."

"He's dead, Ben. I don't think he cares anymore."

"I just don't want you to use them...I think it would hurt Maddie," he said.

"Okay."

She put the album back into the suitcase. She went through the loose photos, took them out, and noted the familiar locations.

"A lot of these were taken on campus," she said.

"They both worked there at the time. She was also a student, too."

"How long did they go together?" Janet asked.

"I'm not sure." Ben sat on the bed.

Janet narrowed her eyes. "Where are the pictures he took with a telescopic lens?"

Ben picked up the album with the nudes and flipped to the back.

"They're here."

Janet looked at the photos.

"He was stalking her," she said.

"Daisy wouldn't let him see Maddie."

"Maybe she had a good reason."

"He wasn't well," Ben said.

"Stop making excuses for him, Ben."

He got up and went to the window.

"He was good to me."

"I'm sure he was." She put the album and the photos back into the suitcase. "Nobody is a hundred percent good or bad."

"I can't believe he'd hurt her."

Janet went and stood beside Ben.

"Your mother was concerned about appearances, wasn't she?"

"Yes."

"Was your grandfather?"

Ben leaned his head against the window frame.

"Not as much as Mom."

"But an illegitimate grandchild might have upset him."

"He was an old-fashioned guy."

"And David was his heir. He probably wanted David to have a suitable wife and family."

Ben nodded. "And it took him a long time to accept that David wouldn't be able to do that."

"Was that when your grandfather realized that he'd have to turn things over to your mom?"

"Probably." He went back to the bed and closed the suitcase. "I think Uncle Dave was relieved. He never wanted to run the company."

"But did he want a relationship with his daughter?" Janet asked.

"He never told me about her."

"But it's obvious from those photos that he at least wanted to see her."

Ben sat on the bed. "The thing about David is that he wasn't like other people, and he knew it. I don't think he believed he could be a father to Maddie, but that didn't mean he didn't want to see her."

"Like an uncle," Janet said.

"Exactly. He loved seeing me, but I could always tell when it was time to go home." Ben lowered his eyes. "He could be scary when he was off his meds."

"Maybe he scared Daisy. Maybe that's why she wouldn't let him see Maddie." Janet exhaled sharply and looked at the graying sky. "It looks like rain again." She turned to Ben. "Shall we go?"

Janet followed Ben to the ATM. He gave her the cash and then wished her luck.

"Let me know what happens," he said before getting back into his car.

When Janet left Ben, she went to the station. The floor was quiet on weekends, which meant she could poke around the files on the QT. She logged onto her computer and went back to David Fried-lander's file. When he'd been found dead, she had searched for any files they might have had on him, but nothing turned up. The files before 1998 hadn't been digitized yet. They were in the basement.

Janet got on the elevator. The basement system was well organized and kept that way by a retired cop who volunteered on weekdays. She didn't have to look far to find the folders for last names that started with a C in 1989. The box was only half-full of files, and she found Daisy's right away. It had been filed under Daisy June Carter. There were three reports - one for each incident.

The first one was dated June 10, 1989. Daisy had been granted a restraining order against David Friedlander.

The second one came in on June 15, 1989. David had shown up at Daisy's wedding and had to be restrained before officers could get him off the premises. There was no arrest report in David's file.

The third complaint came in on September 20, 1989. David had been spotted outside Carl and Daisy Brady's house at 1400 King's Highway, Logans Grove. Officers responded and picked up the suspect, but no arrest was made.

Janet was angry. There was no mention of the incidents in David's file, not even a footnote referring to Daisy's file in the archives. The files had been buried.

David had been menacing Daisy for months. Maybe she tried to ignore him or give him the benefit of the doubt before she got scared and went to court. She was a single, pregnant woman who'd been forced to make a choice she probably didn't want to make because she didn't know what else to do. David's family was rich and powerful. The stress must have been overwhelming.

The more she thought about it, the more convinced Janet became that David had something to do with Daisy's disappearance, that it had been covered up, and then she also realized that she'd better watch her back.

44

S hortly after her plane landed in Florida, Janet picked up a rental car before heading to the Villages. She'd never been out of New Jersey and was surprised when the sun hit her eyes.

How can it be brighter down here? she thought.

And while she may have expected warm temperatures, she wasn't prepared for the humidity. As she walked to the parking lot to pick up her car, sweat began trickling down her forehead. By the time she reached her car, her blouse was clinging to her.

"Why would anybody live down here?" she said as she got into the car.

It took five minutes for the air conditioning to acclimate in the economy sedan, so she took those minutes to map her destination on the GPS. She was approximately 45 minutes away from the sprawling 55+ community.

As Janet drove, she focused on a list of things she wanted to ask John Markham. First, why hadn't anyone followed up on the missing person's report? Depending on his answer, she was ready to ask him why he had retired a month later. It might have been planned, but she didn't believe that. If he refused to answer or danced around the question, she'd ask him if someone had ordered him to leave. She hated the idea of grilling a fellow officer and was worried that he, like other, older male officers, wouldn't take her seriously, and would adopt the misogynistic attitude still prevalent among older officers. She had to be prepared.

Maybe that's what it was - a misogynistic attitude - that had caused them to dismiss Daisy's vanishing act. She was just another irate female who revolted against the natural function of a woman so she could go off like some modern day Brunhild, leaving her poor husband to raise *her* child while she went off to "find herself."

Janet had suffered male fools gladly hoping it would smooth the way to an ever-higher position, but as she grew older, the constant need to salve bruised male egos was getting harder to handle. She often found herself yelling at a male, uniformed officer in a way no man would ever do. She'd had to clench her teeth against an expletive aimed at a superior officer who would casually mention a female officer's generous proportions. Janet had been subjected to harassment and had grown weary of the battle. As she braced herself for what might be another confrontation, she turned onto the road that would take her to the Villages. As Janet pulled up to the gate that barred her way, she stopped and showed the guard her badge and ID.

"I'm here to see John Markham."

The guard looked up John Markham's phone and called him to ask if he was expecting anyone. The guard looked at her ID and read it to the person on the other end of the phone. He glanced at Janet, hung up the phone, and opened the gate.

"Turn left at the end of this road," he said.

Janet followed his instructions and found John Markham's house about a mile inside the community. It was a ranch style house with a palm tree at the center of the yard. Janet parked on the street and walked up the painted driveway to a small walkway leading to the door. An elderly man was at the picture window watching her, and she smiled. He left the window and was at the door in less than a minute.

"Hi," she said. She showed him her badge. "Are you John Markham?" He didn't answer. "I was hoping we could talk for a few minutes."

The man's expression didn't change, and he remained silent. She noted a slight tick under his left eye, but otherwise, John Markham was unexceptional. He took a deep breath and looked her in the eye.

"Why?" he asked.

"I want to ask you about Daisy Brady."

His eyes softened. His eyebrows rose a bit. He stepped aside so she could come in, and then he led her to the living room.

"I don't have anything but water to offer you," he said.

"I'm fine, thanks."

He sat in a broken-in, brown leather chair with a matching footrest. On top of the footrest were a remote with large numbers, a TV Guide, and a pair of reading glasses.

John crossed his legs and turned down the sound on the TV as Janet sat across from him in an upholstered chair. He clasped his hands over his stomach and didn't appear to be rattled in any way. Janet took out her notebook and looked at the questions she'd prepared.

"You and Tom Jarrod responded to the 911 call the day Daisy Brady went missing."

"Yes, we did. Tom was a rookie they'd assigned to me."

"Did you two get along?"

"Fair to middling. He was full of himself but willing to listen."

"The report said you did a cursory search, but there was no evidence of foul play…"

John held up his hand.

"Stop. I know what you want to know." He uncrossed his legs and sat forward with his hands between his knees. "The day we went there, the husband was frantic, so we walked over to the old mansion. We looked for drag marks going into the woods and at the entrances to the house, but the whole thing was padlocked, and the locks were closed. There were footprints on the steps, but kids went there all the time to drink and do drugs, so there was no way to discern when they had been made. We didn't find any clothes or other items to indicate she'd been assaulted, so we went back and told the husband to file a missing person report."

"And you retired the next month. Was that planned?"

John's mouth quivered. He sat back.

"I'd done my twenty. My wife wanted to move south. She had rheumatoid arthritis."

"But had you planned to leave then?"

John's shoulders slumped; he laid his head back and stared at the ceiling.

"The chickens always come home to roost," he said.

"What?"

He looked at her. "The truth will not be silenced for long. It's something my father used to say whenever he caught me lying. I wasn't a very good liar."

"So, what is the truth, Mr. Markham?"

"The truth is rich people have powerful friends, and they stick together as long as it's worth their while."

"You're talking about the Friedlanders."

A sad smile creased John's lips as he lifted his head.

"I read about David Friedlander online."

"Did you read that his sister Beth was the one who pulled the trigger?"

"She killed him?" John shook his head. "Damn. I can't imagine her in jail."

"She's dead. She went into a diabetic coma and died."

"Of course, she did." John shook his head again. "Seems like they always get the easy way out."

"I wouldn't call that easy," Janet said.

He tapped the arm of the chair with his finger.

"That family. The father used to come into the station like he owned it. I'd see him enter the lobby whenever I was on desk duty, and he'd walk right past us to the elevator." He sighed. "It didn't surprise me when they asked me to leave."

John pushed the things on the footrest aside, and then sat back and put his feet up.

"I wanted to get into that house and look for Daisy," he said. "I never believed she ran away. When I asked to investigate it, the chief said it had been given to a detective. When I asked the detective if I could assist, he told me he could handle it. When a week passed, I asked him how things were going, and he said the case had been shelved pending new information. I said what information, and he said he'd gotten a phone call from the girl asking them to back off. She'd run away from her husband, who was abusing her, and she didn't want to be found."

"That wasn't in the file," Janet said.

"Damn right it wasn't, because there was no such phone call. He handed me that line of bullshit to get me to stop asking questions. It was right after that the chief called me upstairs and told me it might be better if I retired."

"What did you think when Jarrod got promoted."

He waved his hand. "That shitfaced asshole. He played ball, and they made him a detective!" He looked at the ceiling and shook his head. "The older guys complained, but nothing came of it." His eyes met hers. "Some threatened to go to the mayor, and one did, but the mayor told him to back off. That's when I knew for sure."

"Knew what exactly?" Janet asked.

"That the girl was dead, and the cabal had closed ranks."

A chill went through Janet's body.

"Why didn't you just go to Fenway Manor and knock the doors down?"

"Because I had a sick wife who needed insurance." He took a deep breath. "They had me by the short hairs, and they knew it."

"But they might have covered up a murder."

John gazed out the picture window.

"Is it still there?" John asked.

"What?" she asked.

"Is Fenway Manor still there?"

"Beth's son owns it now. The town is trying to condemn it."

"It should have been condemned a long time ago."

"It would have been, but Bethany Arntz always got them to back off," Janet said.

"Is the son anything like his mother?" John asked.

"He's a decent kid. He wants to find out what happened to Daisy, too."

"Tell him I'm sorry I didn't do more," he said.

Janet looked at the lines on his face and wondered how long his wife had been gone.

"Did you have any kids, John?"

"Two girls. They still live in Jersey. It's too hot for them down here."

"I agree with them."

John chuckled. "My blood has thinned. I feel comfortable now."

"Well, I appreciate you talking to me," she said.

"What are you gonna do?" he asked.

"I'm gonna try and find out what happened to Daisy."

"If you do, will you let me know?"

"Absolutely."

Janet stood, and John got up to walk her to the front door. He shook her hand and wished her luck.

"I hope you get 'em," he said.

"I'll do my best. Her daughter deserves to know what happened to her mother."

John bit his lip. "I forgot about the kid."

"If it helps at all, she's turned out all right."

"It does." He took another deep breath. "Please tell her I'm sorry."

John stood at the door and watched her get into her car. He stayed until she drove away. He looked small to Janet as if he'd been compressed by the weight of his decisions, and it occurred to her that what had happened to John could happen to anyone.

No cop was immune from the corrupt systems that still plagued local police stations. The moneyed would always demand special treatment, and if circumstances were just right, a normally honorable public servant would buckle under their demands - for a price. Once they did, the demands would continue until one of them died.

Bethany Arntz had died. The chief who had been there when Daisy disappeared was long gone, as were several mayors, and the judge who had helped her was retired. Beth had run out of options.

The house would be condemned, and Beth would have had no choice but to tear it down. *This* had been the impetus for her actions. Something she and David knew, something important enough that it had driven her to murder, was going to come to light and that must have scared the shit out of her.

Janet had a 3 o'clock flight, so she went back to the airport and turned in her car. She had time to eat something and make a few phone calls, so she found a comfortable spot away from people and called Ben. She asked him to meet her at Fenway Manor in the morning and to bring the keys to the padlocks.

45

SATURDAY/SUNDAY

B en had kept to himself for a couple of days. Thursday, he drove down to the beach to walk on the boardwalk, and then down to Cape May. He stood in front of the B&B where his mother had stayed and wondered why she had chosen to go there after she killed his uncle.

Friday, he finished cleaning out David's house and put everything but the boxes that would go into the dumpster on the front lawn, except the kitchen set and David's bed. When he took the last garbage bag to the curb, he felt ready to move on.

Ben spent Friday evening with Maria. They ate dinner together, and then they sat in the living room and watched TV.

When he woke up on Saturday, he thought of Candy. Ben always knew when he needed to be alone for a while, but now he missed her terribly. He dialed Candy's number, and she answered on the first ring.

"Are we okay?" she asked.

"We're fine."

"You're sure? Because it's been a while since we talked."

"Everything is fine." He smiled. "I've been cleaning out David's house, and I lost track of time." Ben took a deep breath. "I do that sometimes. I get so focused on something I forget everything else." He thought of her face and remembered how she'd looked when she thought he was mad at her. "Call me if you don't hear from me. I need a nudge once in a while."

"Okay. I can do that."

"So, I called to see if you felt like going to that Italian place you like for dinner."

"Sure."

"Or we can go somewhere else if you want to. Whatever you want to do."

"The Italian place is fine. When do you want to meet?"

"Around six."

"Okay. I'll see you then."

Ben got to the restaurant before Candy and sat in a booth next to the window. He ordered their drinks from the server, and then he looked at the menu. He glanced at the window and saw her car pull into the parking lot, and then watched her walk to the entrance of the restaurant.

Candy's cheeks were rosy, and his heart pounded. There was just something about her that was different from the other women he'd known, and that something made what he felt for her special. As he watched her walk inside, he couldn't imagine a life without her.

Candy waved when she saw him, walked to the booth, took off her coat, and then slid onto the seat across from his. She smiled broadly but noticed the dark circles under his eyes.

"Hi," Ben said. "You look cold."

"I think the temperature dropped as I was driving over here." She picked up the menu, and then looked over the top. "I'm glad you called me."

"I hope you don't mind that I ordered your drink," he said.

She furrowed her brows.

"It's fine."

Ben sat back. "That detective came by earlier, the one who worked on my uncle's case."

"Oh?"

"She's looking into Daisy Brady's disappearance," Ben told her about their conversation. "Janet thinks somebody covered up her disappearance."

"But why would they do that?" Candy said. "Daisy wasn't rich or famous."

"But David was – rich that is. They were dating, she got pregnant, and I don't think my grandfather liked it."

"Holy shit," Candy said. "But that would mean that David is

Maddie's..." Ben folded his arms on the table and leaned forward while Candy sat back. "Does Maddie know?"

"She knew before I did," he said. "I told her she has my permission to have David's DNA compared to hers."

"Oh, poor Maddie."

"She took it pretty well," he said. "Better than I would have."

"And how *do* you feel about it?"

"It would be nice to have someone in my family."

"So, you'd be okay with it," Candy said.

"Why not? It's not her fault. Besides, I always wanted a cousin."

"I always wished I had a cousin, too."

"Do you have anyone besides your mom?" Ben asked.

She shook her head. "It's just the two of us."

"Like me." He sat back. "Um, I wanted to talk to you about something."

"Okay."

He hesitated as he ran his finger through the puddle surrounding the base of his beer glass.

"I know what I want to do with the land after I tear down Fenway Manor."

"Really?" she asked.

"I've been thinking about it for a while, but this morning I read that the town has the money to build a new high school, they just can't find a property in town that's big enough. Well, I have a property that's more than big enough, and I want to donate it to the town."

Candy's eyes widened.

"Have you any idea what that land is worth?"

He grinned and held up his hands. "Not a clue. I just want the kids to have a better school." He put down his hands and looked into her eyes. "Those kids are trying to learn while sitting in trailers behind the old school. It's cold, and it's cramped. I just can't let things stay that way."

She leaned forward.

"I love that you think that way."

"But?" he asked.

"But nothing. I think it's a great idea. I just wonder what will happen to Derek. I wish there was some way we could set him free."

Ben tilted his head forward to see her eyes.

"You know that's not really our problem."

"I know, but seeing him, seeing his face when I asked about Maddie's mom, it was just so sad. He's real to me, Ben. He may have been bad when he was alive, but I think he's changed, and he deserves to go wherever you go when you die like everyone else."

When the server brought their food, Candy picked at hers while Ben woofed his down. When he was done, he sat back and watched her move her food around the plate.

"I'm sorry," he said.

"For what?"

"I know how real he is to you."

She sat back and put down her fork.

"He knows something about Daisy," Candy said. "I could tell by the way he acted."

He reached across the table and took her hand.

"I've missed you. Can we talk about this tomorrow?"

She smiled and shook her head.

"I thought you cleaned out his house."

"I did. I left the bed though."

She laughed, and then Ben signaled the server for the check.

On Sunday morning, Ben woke up and looked at his phone. It was almost one in the afternoon. He turned toward Candy to see if she was awake, but she was still snoring lightly. He smiled, got up, put on his pants from the night before, and then went downstairs to make coffee.

As he went past the living room, he remembered that the dumpster would be delivered the next day. The thought made his brain tired. He felt like he'd been cleaning up David's shit forever, and then a thought eked its way into his mind. Why was this his responsibility?

"Because he left you the house," Ben said out loud.

He left his mess to you, too - his crap, his plastic bags, his nicotine-stained walls, and his erotic photos of Maddie's mother. He left them all to you without once considering whether you wanted them.

In his whole life, it seemed that no one had considered whether Ben wanted something or not, and now that he had a choice, he imagined waking Candy, getting her outside, spreading gasoline over the walls, and then setting the whole damn thing on fire.

Ben was not prone to violent thoughts, but the rage that had been brewing under the surface since he'd found out his mother had killed his uncle was displaying itself in short bursts of anger. He'd felt contentious with traffic on the road, and with people in lines at the supermarket. If he didn't come to terms with it soon...

He set up the coffeemaker. He put the coffee bag back into the cabinet and then slammed the cabinet door shut. He leaned his head against it for a moment and rubbed the back of his neck. How long had he listened to their bullshit - his mother's constant complaints about everything under the sun, and his uncle's whining because no one understood him? Two needy people who clung to him, their hands grasping, their minds focused on one thing – Ben's attention - Ben, who was always the good boy, the good son, and the good nephew.

He punched the cabinet, and then sat at the table and put his head in his hands. An idea that had been lingering at the edge of his mind forced its way through his defenses, bringing with it shame. He had to look at it, had to admit it was true, and nothing would assuage the guilt.

I'm glad they're dead.

He sat up and looked at his hand. His knuckles were bleeding where he'd hit the cabinet, and he got up to wash them in the sink. Welcome numbness set in salving his honesty so he could go on with his life as the reality of his confession sunk in. What would Candy think of him if he told her the truth? What would Maria think?

What do I think?

He put his hands on the counter and looked out the window at Harlan's house. Harlan would understand. He would tell Ben that it was perfectly natural to feel that way after all the years he had cared for his uncle.

"*And your mother was a beast,*" Harlan would say.

But Ben couldn't let go of his guilt. He really didn't want to feel that way, to remember them as burdens. He wanted to remember them as people who'd loved him.

Candy appeared at the entrance to the kitchen wearing Ben's shirt. She went to him and put her arms around him.

"Whatcha looking at?" she said.

Ben looked over his shoulder.

"Nothing. Just waiting for the coffee."

"You want me to make something for breakfast?" she asked.

"I'm not hungry."

Candy noticed the kitchen clock.

"Holy crap. It's after one."

"We sort of overslept," Ben said.

"I'll say. So, it's lunch we're talking about."

"I'm not hungry for that either."

"Then what are you in the mood for?"

Ben smiled, turned around, and gave her a long, lingering kiss. She pulled away with a devilish smile, backed away, and then ran to the stairs. Ben switched off the coffeemaker, and then followed her upstairs.

Almost two hours later, Ben's phone rang, and he looked at the caller ID. It was Janet Worthington asking him to meet her at Fenway Manor.

"Okay," he said. "I'll be there."

Candy put her hand on his stomach as he hung up.

"Who was that?" she asked.

"That detective. She's on her way back from Florida, and she wants me to meet her tomorrow morning at Fenway Manor with the keys to the house."

She snuggled against him.

"Did she say why?" she asked.

"No, but it must have something to do with Daisy because…"

Candy sat up with her eyes wide.

"She wants to get inside the house."

He exhaled sharply and put one arm behind his head.

"Right." Now his eyes widened. "She wants to get inside the house."

"We should try talking to Derek again," Candy said.

"Okay, but not until we eat something."

"Oh, now you're hungry."

"I'm starving," Ben said. "Let's go to the diner. I'm craving grease."

"Not me. I want something light."

"You can eat my garnish."

"I'll give you garnish," she said smacking him playfully.

He pulled her close and kissed her.

"We'd better stop now," Candy said. "Or we won't go anywhere."

They showered together and then dressed. Ben took the keys to the padlocks off David's keyholder on the kitchen wall and put them in his pocket. He gathered David's flashlights before they put on their coats and went to the car. As they drove away from the house, Candy had a thought and grabbed Ben's arm.

"What if Derek has been guarding something?"

"Like a sentinel at the mouth of hell?"

"No, like something, or some*one,* who needed him."

"Can we talk about this while we eat?" he asked.

She smiled. "As long as we eat fast."

46

A fter they ate at a diner on Route 18, they stopped at a convenience store and bought batteries. Candy filled the flashlights with them as they drove to Fenway Manor.

It was a true autumn day, and as they stepped out of the car at Fenway Manor, they caught the scent of burning leaves in the air. The sun filtered through the trees casting a golden glow on everything, and a gust of wind lifted Candy's hair sending it in all directions. She pulled it away from her eyes and then saw Derek standing near the woods.

"He's here."

"Why don't you go and talk to him while I see if I can open the padlocks?"

Ben took a flashlight from the car and went to the back porch as Candy walked across the yard toward Derek. Derek's eyes were on Ben as he walked up the steps to the back door. As Candy drew near to him, she saw the beginnings of a smile, but it faded quickly.

"Hi, Derek," she said. He smiled when she said his name. "Ben and I are going inside the house. Would you come with us?"

Derek glanced at Candy for a moment, and then looked at the porch. She followed his gaze and saw that Ben had gotten the door open. She turned back to look at him, and Derek's expression had changed. He was backing away.

"What is it?" Candy asked. "Tell me, Derek." She narrowed her eyes. "Are you afraid to leave this place?"

Derek fell to his knees. He appeared to be in pain.

"Help me understand," she said.

He lifted his head as Candy kneeled down.

"Is there something in there you don't want us to see?"

He stared at Candy for a moment, and then his shoulders slumped.

"This is frustrating," she said. "I wish you could talk to me."

He held up his head and smiled, but it was with resignation rather than pleasure.

"Maybe I should stick to yes or no questions." She tilted her head. "Do you remember Daisy?"

He nodded.

"Do you know what happened to her?"

"Candy," Ben shouted from the porch. "Are you coming?"

"Will you come inside?" Candy said to Derek.

Candy stood and waited for Derek to stand, too. When he remained on the ground, she walked away from him, went to the car, grabbed another flashlight, and went up the steps to the door. She turned once to see if he was following her, but hadn't moved.

Ben was in the kitchen scanning the room with his flashlight when she came inside. It was darker than she thought it would be, so she switched on her flashlight. The kitchen windows were grimy. Dust along with leaves that had blown under the door covered the floor. Old appliances that had been left by the last inhabitants were sad reminders that once this room had been the heart of the home. Old bottles of Lysol and kitchen floor wax were on the counter along with an old pair of rubber gloves as if the lady of the house was about to return at any moment. The furniture was gone. The basement door was leaning against one wall. The kitchen was just a wide, empty space.

"I don't remember it being this big," Candy said.

"I don't know where to start."

She held her light on the floor and saw loose floorboards.

"It's not safe to walk around in here," she said.

Candy saw the room lighten and turned to see Derek on the porch. She smiled when she saw him.

"Where do we go now, Derek?" she asked. Derek wavered as he took a step forward. "It must have been a grand house when you lived here." Derek smiled, but when his eyes moved from her face to the open basement doorway, his smile faded. "I'll stay with you." His shoulders slumped, and he closed his eyes.

"What's he doing?" Ben asked.

"He just came inside."

Derek stared at the room as if he were trying to memorize it. He looked at the large fireplace along the outside wall. He looked at the servant stairwell and took another step inside. He glanced out the window over the sink at the field between Fenway Manor and Maddie's house. After a moment, he went to the basement doorway.

"He's standing at that doorway," Candy said.

"That goes to the basement," Ben said.

Candy pointed the flashlight on the floor as she walked toward it and was careful to avoid the loose boards. When she reached the door, she looked over her shoulder and saw Ben on the floor with his arms around his knees.

"Are you all right?"

Candy went to him and put her hand on his shoulder.

"What's the matter?" she asked.

"What do you think we'll find down there?" he asked.

"I'm...not sure."

"But what do you *think* we'll find?" Ben grabbed her arm. "If we find what I think we'll find, then it means he's a murderer, too, and I don't think I can handle that. He's all I have left. I can't...it can't be...don't you see? None of it was true."

"Ben, I..."

"It was all lies, Candy, my whole life. If sh...if that's why they couldn't let go of this house, my God, what kind of people were they?"

She kneeled down, wrapped her arms around him, and rocked him.

"What kind of person am I?" he asked. "Do you know what I was thinking this morning? I was glad they were dead."

"It's all right," she said.

"No, it isn't. God, they never let me have one minute's peace."

"Ben, it's okay."

"And now, if I find out that they kept this secret all this time, that they knew..."

She pulled away.

"You're not like them," she said. "You are a good man."

"I'm her son. If she was capable of this..."

Candy put her face close to his.

"You are not your mother. You are a good man. I've never believed something so much in my whole life."

She kissed him, and then pressed her forehead against his.

"You don't have to go down there," she said. "Derek will come with me."

"But it's my responsibility."

She put her hands on his face and looked in his eyes.

"It's not *your* responsibility. It's just something *we* have to do for Maddie."

"I can't, Candy. We have to let it go like it never happened."

She pulled away, stood, and then put her hands on her hips.

"And you'd let Maddie believe her mother abandoned her for the rest of her life? Is that what you want to do?"

"No."

"Then get off your ass and come with me."

She held out her hand. Ben stared at her in surprise, and then a small smile began to crease his lips. He grabbed her hand, and she helped him up.

"You can be pretty scary when you want to be," he said.

"I learned from the best."

She gave him a small hug, and then looked around the room.

"So, where's your ghost?" he asked.

"Maybe he went downstairs."

She went to the basement doorway and saw Derek at the bottom of the stairs.

"He's down there."

Ben came to her and stared into the darkness. He held his flashlight up and saw the steps.

"They don't look too sturdy," he said.

"Maybe we should go down one at a time."

"Then I'm going first. If you fall…"

"It will make you look bad, I know, my manly man."

She smirked at him as he went around her and took the steps slowly. Once he was at the bottom, she followed.

Ben ran his flashlight over the crumbling structure surrounding him, and he wondered what David had seen when he looked at it. When Candy reached the floor, he took her hand.

"Did you tell him why we came here?" Ben asked.

"Sort of." Derek stood in front of them. "So, Derek, where do we go now?"

Derek's face was a mask of pain. Candy held out her hand, and then pulled it away.

"I'm not sure he wants us to do this," she said.

"That makes two of us," Ben said.

"Wait. He's moving now. He's going that way."

Candy pointed to the left corner of the basement.

She took a few steps with Ben trailing behind. Candy noticed that Derek was changing. His brightness was fading.

"What's happening?" she asked.

"Who are you talking to?" Ben asked.

"Derek. He's fading."

"Ask him to show us what to do."

"He's almost gone," Candy said.

"Then ask him quickly."

Derek put his hands up against the paneling on the wall and showed her how to push on it.

"He's pressing his hands against the wall." She held up the light. "It looks like that wood paneling in my mother's dining room."

"It's wainscoting. Alastair had a tunnel built into the wall so that Washington's spies could escape to the woods if the Brits showed up at the door. He was always entertaining some high-ranking British officer, and sometimes the spies would show up just as they were sitting down to dinner."

"God. You're a walking history book," she said.

"One of the panels should open when you push it."

Ben held up the light as he looked at the panels. Cobwebs were strewn everywhere. As he moved forward, he brushed them out of the way, and they stuck to his hands.

"Shit," he said as he wiped them off on his pants. "Is he still there?"

"He hasn't moved," Candy said.

Ben went up to a panel, bent forward, and pushed against it. It didn't move.

"Is he here?" Ben asked.

"Yes," she said.

"What's he doing?"

"He looks like he's about to fall asleep." She smiled. "Derek!" Her voice roused him, and he stared at her. "Which panel opens?"

Derek placed his hand on the one in front of him.

"It's further to the right," she said. Ben moved a few inches. "More." He moved again. "You're right in front of him."

Ben held the light up but couldn't see the edge of the panel.

"I'm not sure where to push," he said.

Derek banged his hand against the panel in front of Ben.

"He's smacking the panel in front of you," she said.

Ben put down his flashlight and put both hands on the panel.

"He's using his hands to push against it," she said.

"Like this?"

Ben pushed, but the panel didn't move.

"It's not moving," he said.

Ben tried again, but the panel wouldn't budge. He put up his hands in surrender.

Candy ducked under the cobwebs and came up to Ben. She put her hands on the side of the panel.

"Like this."

She shoved it, it popped open, and then she backed away as a terrible smell filled the air. They both coughed and their eyes watered. She moved behind Ben.

"Oh, my God, what is that?" she said.

Ben pulled the panel toward him. Candy stayed behind him with her eyes on his back and her hand over her nose for the smell was overwhelming. Ben held up his flashlight.

"Shit," he said.

"What?"

"Call 911."

47

The ghost of Fenway Manor stood outside the Brady house and peered through the kitchen window. His passion for the lady of the house, fair Daisy, had grown, and he was always happy to find her without her husband by her side. As he moved through the wall and into the house, Derek Fenway noticed a festoon hung over the kitchen window that read, "Happy Birthday!"

Daisy was putting the finishing touches on a cake. Her face was a mask of uncertainty as she placed two candles at the center. The child she had borne twenty-four moons ago was celebrating the anniversary of her birth, and Derek marveled at how quickly the time had passed. The girl's name was Madelyn, but her mother called her Maddie.

Daisy's marriage to her husband Carl was less than amicable, but he had risen above his earlier, drunken ways to become a reasonably good father. He would play with Maddie while her mother worked in the house, and would read to her at night before they put her to bed. The only fly in the ointment had been the contentious relationship between Daisy and Carl's mother, Ann, who always found fault with Daisy. The best day of her marriage was when her in-laws finally bought a house in Florida and moved away.

Maddie was a lively, boisterous little girl with light blonde hair and a smile that lit up her face. On this gray morning in November, however, Derek heard her, but he didn't see her.

He glanced at the old clock above the sink. It was near noon, but the sun rose on the other side of the house, so the kitchen was dark. The overhead light was on, and Derek loved the way the light played on the golden highlights in Daisy's hair. She had secured her ponytail with a yellow band that matched her blouse.

Daisy was also wearing navy-blue pants, which 18th century Derek found unsuitable; nevertheless, he understood that this was an acceptable form of dress for a modern woman. Despite her masculine attire, to Derek she was Venus rising from the sea illuminated by the sun.

As Derek lost himself in the romantic image, Carl came into the room. He had the forlorn look of a man who knows his wife doesn't love him, but that didn't stop him from going to Daisy's side. He tried to kiss her cheek, but she ducked and took the utensils she'd been using on the cake to the sink.

"Your parents will be here soon," she said.

Her tone reinforced her disdain for his parents, and Carl exhaled sharply. His face was grim. When his parents moved away, he thought it would improve his relationship with Daisy, but all it did was highlight how little they had in common. Their poverty and the long hours Carl spent at the store were all that kept them together.

Derek loved to watch Daisy play with her daughter in the yard, or read to her, or simply spend time with her, and he always knew when Carl was due to arrive home. Daisy would become agitated and rub her hands over her arms. She'd forget that she left a pan on the stove and burn their dinner, or become absorbed in a television program and forget to cook dinner altogether. Carl would come home to find no dinner, they'd argue, and she would lock herself in their bedroom with Maddie.

"Everything looks great," Carl said, his voice as dull as his expression.

"She won't think so."

Daisy rinsed out a sponge and wiped the sink.

"Why do you worry about what she thinks?"

She stopped. "Because she hates me, Carl. She always has."

"She doesn't hate you, Daisy." He went to her and tried to put his arms around her, but she moved away and wiped the table. "It will be fine. They love Maddie. This is her day."

"I know they love her," Daisy said. "But I also know that they wonder every time they look at her if she's yours." Daisy threw the sponge in the sink. "Go get Maddie. I want you to take a picture of us in front of the cake."

Carl lumbered off to fetch Maddie while Daisy looked around the room. She closed her eyes tightly and took a deep breath. A moment later, Carl appeared with Maddie in his arms.

"Put her in her chair and get the camera," Daisy said.

Carl obeyed and then went to the living room. He returned with the camera and waited for Daisy to tell him what to do.

"I'm gonna stand behind her and when she smiles, take the picture," Daisy said.

Carl held the camera up and looked through the lens so he'd be ready when Maddie smiled. Daisy bent over, put her head near Maddie's, and smiled.

"Say cheese, Maddie," Carl said.

Maddie smiled broadly, and Carl snapped the picture.

"Take her out of her chair and watch her while I straighten the living room," Daisy said.

Carl picked up Maddie. He followed Daisy and watched as she straightened the pillows on the furniture and wiped some crumbs off the table.

"I wish you wouldn't eat in here," she said.

"I was trying to stay out of the kitchen." His response was barely audible.

"She's going to say something about those pillows," Daisy said.

"So, we have a kid who likes to chew on the edges," he said. Carl smiled. "It's no big deal."

Daisy glared at him.

"She's gonna blame me for not watching her."

She sat on the sofa and held her head in her hands.

"I don't know if I can do this today," she said.

Carl put Maddie down and squatted near Daisy.

"Your friends are coming, you know, that guy you used to work for."

"Harlan." She scowled as she looked at him. "His name is Harlan. You should know that by now."

"Right, Harlan." Carl stood. "So, you won't be alone. I promise I'll deal with her if she starts anything."

Daisy put her hands on her knees, closed her eyes, and shook her head.

"You never see it, Carl. You don't see what she does, and you won't *deal* with anything. You'll just go outside with your father and drink beer." She stood and scanned the room. "She doesn't criticize everything you do."

Daisy went to the kitchen. Ginger, their little brown terrier, was standing at the kitchen door. Daisy heard a car coming up the driveway and shuddered.

"Someone's here," she said.

Carl looked out the living room window.

"It's my parents," Carl said.

"I'm gonna take Ginger for a walk before we start the party."

Daisy took her sweater off the hook near the door, grabbed Ginger's leash off another hook, and attached it to the dog's collar.

"You have to say hello first," Carl said.

"I'll wave as we walk by."

"Daisy," Carl said as they went outside.

While his parents were getting out of the car, Daisy waved at them as she walked across the driveway and past the stonewall that separated their house from the mansion's property. She pulled Ginger along, and the dog had to run to keep up. When she got farther away, she slowed her pace.

Derek stayed by her side as she walked. Daisy held her arms close to her sides. She glanced toward the old mansion, but kept moving, stopping only to let Ginger do her business. Normally, Daisy would stop before she reached the back yard of the mansion, but this time she kept going. Ginger looked up at her as if she were asking why they were going so far.

As Daisy neared the mansion, she kept an eye on it as they walked to the edge of the woods. She followed the line to the other side while Derek was indulging in his favorite fantasy of escorting her around his property while a ball was in progress.

Daisy was a cunning beauty who held her fan over her mouth to entice him, and when they were in the garden, he would fall to one knee and ask her to be his wife. She would drop her fan and abandon the flirtatious pretense she had employed to ensnare him, put her arms around his neck, and kiss him. He was lost in the fantasy when they reached the side of the woods behind the mansion, and she changed course.

Daisy never went near the mansion. She had avoided it because it was the one place *he* would come to spy on her, and Derek wondered why she was walking around the perimeter of the woods, which would take her within feet of the old house. Perhaps she felt it was less dangerous than seeing her mother-in-law's reaction to the damage done to the sofa pillows.

Daisy began to take smaller steps and shoved her hands into her pockets. As she approached the mansion, she slowed down and stopped to let Ginger sniff the ground, all the while keeping a close watch on the house. When Derek saw tears roll down her cheeks, he was truly baffled.

"Shit," she said. "I can't do this anymore."

Her shoulders slumped as in defeat, and she sighed. Within a minute, though, she straightened her shoulders, ran her hand over a loose strand of hair, and held her head high as she looked across the field toward the Brady house. Her face changed before Derek's eyes. The worry lines around her mouth were softer, and she seemed to have shed the air of gloom that had followed her about for months. She said nothing, but Derek understood. Daisy was going to leave Carl.

Derek didn't want her to leave. In his fantasy, he had imagined Carl dying so that Daisy could be alone in the house with Maddie. Derek would then have Daisy to himself. He hadn't envisioned a future without her though, and the prospect filled him with grief.

"Don't leave," he said, though he knew she couldn't hear him. "I can't face this existence without you."

"We better go home and face the music, Ginger."

She gave Ginger's leash a gentle tug as she started to walk across the yard. She was within feet of the back porch when Derek sensed someone watching them.

"Hello, Daisy."

Daisy stopped, and Derek saw the color drain from her face.

"Shit," she whispered.

She kept her eyes on the ground. Derek knew that this was why she always avoided the house, why she stayed in the field when she took Ginger for a walk.

"I didn't see your car," Daisy said.

Derek saw David Friedlander standing on the porch. The last time Derek saw him, the police were taking David away.

David took a step down from the porch.

"You look beautiful," he said.

"Run," Derek said. "Go, now!"

But Daisy stayed where she'd stopped, while Ginger barked at the stranger.

"I have to go home," she said.

Derek was surprised to hear the anger in her voice, but he was glad. It showed she had gumption. Perhaps her new attitude would send David away.

"I just want to talk to you."

"I really don't have time."

"It will only take five minutes."

Daisy raised her eyes and then turned to face him. Derek thought he saw something akin to desire on her face and it confused him. If she cared for him, why call the police and have him taken away?

"David, I really don't have time."

Her tone was softer this time. It encouraged David to take another step down.

"Why did you shut me out when I came back?"

"You already know why," she said.

He took another step down.

"No, I don't."

"You're lying."

David took another step and was on the ground.

"Why didn't you tell me?" he asked.

"We're not going to do this now," Daisy said.

"Then when? You've got a restraining order."

"You were scaring my parents," she said.

"You wouldn't answer my calls," David said. "I thought we were in love."

"I thought we were, too, and then you accepted that grant without telling me anything. You made all the arrangements before I even knew you were going!"

She spun around and started walking away, but David grabbed her arm.

"Did you know before I left?" he asked.

Ginger was barking at him, and Daisy saw some movement near her house.

"They're going to see us," she said.

"Then let's go inside."

Derek saw Daisy's reticence falter as she looked into David's eyes. None of this made sense to Derek. She should go home to her daughter. It was her birthday. Derek went and stood between them, and even though he knew he couldn't stop anything from happening, he knew David would see him. David let go of Daisy's arm.

"Five minutes. That's all I'm asking for."

David had a strange look in his eyes, and Derek's apprehension grew. He seemed different, sort of far away. There was a subtle shift in his personality, but Daisy didn't seem to notice.

When Derek was in Philadelphia, he'd seen sailors with that same look in their eyes. They'd endured long stretches at sea, and when they showed up at brothels, the women saw it too. The prostitutes called it sea madness, and they knew that a wrong word spoken in innocence might set off an uncontrollable rage.

"Don't go with him!" Derek cried in vain.

Daisy looked toward the Brady house. Derek wished her mother-in-law hadn't come for Maddie's birthday. He wished it was just another day and that Carl was at the store, but as he watched her put the end of Ginger's leash over the newel post, he wished more than ever that Daisy could see him.

David went up the steps and Daisy followed. Derek blocked the entrance, but David ignored him as they walked through him. Derek then moved to the center of the room and stood between them, but David kept his eyes on Daisy. She went to the window and folded her arms over her chest.

"So, talk, David."

"Did you know you were pregnant before I left?" he asked.

"I found out two months after you were gone."

"Why didn't you write to me? I would have come home."

She turned her head to face him and gave him a defiant look.

"I went to see your parents," she said. "They were very polite, but they were on their way to New York for the opening of a new museum." She lifted her chin. "And then Beth showed up at my parent's house and offered me twenty-five thousand dollars to have an abortion."

Several emotions played on David's face - disbelief, understanding, and rage.

Daisy glared at him. "So, you have nothing to say?"

"Beth wanted you to have an abortion?"

"Don't you understand? It was *her* reputation on the line, her money, her future, and she wasn't going to let some poor girl's little bastard muck it up."

David grabbed her shoulders and pulled her close.

"You should have come to me when I came home. Why didn't you come to me then?"

"Because I imagined a lifetime of dealing with her and decided it wasn't worth it."

His pained expression gave her pause.

"Not worth it?" David said softly.

She backed away. "I didn't mean...I'm sorry. I didn't mean you weren't worth it. I just couldn't stand the thought of having to deal with Beth for the rest of my life. Instead, I have a mother-in-law who hates me." She chuckled. "And everyone always told me how smart I was."

David was quiet. His eyes darted around the room, and Derek tried to get his attention, but David was lost in his pain.

"Carl had a crush on me when we were in high school," Daisy said. "He always asked me out, and I turned him down, but then I saw him in the bookstore. I was so scared, David. I've never been so scared in my life. I couldn't tell my parents. I couldn't tell anyone..."

"But you said you loved me," David said softly.

"I did love you." She relaxed her shoulders. "I still do, but now Carl is Maddie's father. She's too young. She wouldn't understand if I brought you into her life."

"But she's my daughter."

"And maybe someday she will want to meet you. In the meantime, you have to promise you will stay away." Daisy folded her arms across her chest again. "It has to be her choice."

Derek saw the madness return and then fade. His impotence to warn Daisy infuriated him.

"You are my reason for living," David said. "Sometimes I wake up in the morning, and nothing seems real."

"Please don't say that," she said.

"But it's true." He came to her and put his forehead against hers. "Since the first day, I saw you."

She pulled herself away from him and lifted her chin.

"Then why didn't you take me with you?" She glared at him again. "You know what I think, David? I think you're full of shit. I think your sister wrote to you and told you about me. I think you decided you didn't want any part of it. Isn't that why you ended up staying in England for six months instead of three?"

Derek saw David's eye twitch. Daisy noticed it too and backed away.

"What's wrong?" she said.

"Beth did send me something, but it was too late." David smiled and then narrowed his eyes. "If only you'd waited for me."

"I couldn't wait for you. I was going to have a baby. I didn't know when or if you were coming home!"

David laughed and shook his head.

"Daisy, Daisy, Daisy. My silly love." His smile faded, and he peered her through half-lidded eyes. "You went to my parents." He came close to her and put his hands on her shoulders. "What did you think they would do?"

"I thought they would care about your child," Daisy said.

Tears formed in her eyes and she turned her head away.

"If you had written to me, told me what you were going through, I would catch the first plane home to be with you. Nothing would have stopped me." He backed away, and Derek saw the strange look in his eyes. "Did you even know me?"

Daisy backed away again.

"I didn't know where you were. You didn't tell me where you were going." She backed away slowly. "I have to go now."

Daisy turned to leave, and David grabbed her arms so she would face him. He pulled her close and put his face near hers.

"I would never have left you if I'd known," he whispered. "I would have moved heaven and earth to be with you."

He tightened his grip and swallowed hard.

"David stop," she said as she squirmed. "You're hurting me. What's wrong with you?"

"I did my best all my life. I was the boy; I was the one who'd run the family business. That's what they wanted when they adopted me." His voice grew loud. "Nobody gave a damn about what *I* wanted."

Daisy was trembling.

"Please let me go," she said softly.

He shook his head.

"My mother was a drug addict. She gave me up for a fix." His smile was cruel. "That's my legacy, Daisy. I'm the son of a drugged-out whore." He pressed his cheek against hers. "That's the man you say you love." He suddenly pulled his face back and stared at her with one arched eyebrow. "I saw a helicopter land on the front lawn. It took my father away."

Daisy's face reflected her fear and confusion. She was trying to pull her arms away, but David had a strong grip on them. He was distracted by something behind her and smiled broadly.

"Ah, Derek, old boy. You're looking well." David laughed. "Weren't looking so well two hundred years ago, eh, old boy?" David raised his eyebrows like a villain in an old, silent movie. "Had a touch of the pox now, didn't you?"

As David talked to Derek, he loosened his grip, and Daisy moved her arms slowly until they were nearly free of his hands, but then David tightened his grip around her wrists.

"I tell them all the time, but no one listens," David said. He rolled his eyes. "The custodians, Derek. Keep up, old boy."

David moved his hands up her arms and put his face near Daisy's.

"She thinks I don't know, but I know *everything*."

Tears rolled down Daisy's face, but David wouldn't let her go.

"Listen," he said. "Can you hear them?"

"I don't hear anything," Daisy said.

"They sound like Beth, droning on and on. What a busy little bee she is."

David wrapped his arms around Daisy and held her close.

"I don't want to be David Friedlander." He spoke softly. "I want to be your husband."

Daisy closed her eyes, and her lip trembled. David suddenly pulled away from her, and his eyes were wide.

"We can get married." He smiled broadly. "I can blow up balloons, and we can get flowers from my garden. Tulips! Oh, Daisy, and you can wear that dress, the one you bought at the flea market. You looked like an angel in that dress. And I'll tell my parents. I'm old enough to make up my own damn mind now, aren't I?"

Daisy saw the madness in his eyes and forced a smile.

"It sounds wonderful," she said.

Derek noticed a quiver in her voice, but David was unaware of her discomfort. He was ranting about the wedding he saw in his head, and as he did, Daisy took a few steps back.

"We won't invite Beth, no, she can go to hell. We hate her anyway." He laughed hysterically. "Oh, God how I hate her."

Daisy kept taking a step back, and David winced.

"That buzzing." He noticed how far Daisy had moved away from him and closed the gap between them. "Don't you hear it?"

"I don't hear anything, David," Daisy said. "Just the wind."

His eyes widened, and he grabbed her arms.

"We can hide in the basement."

David pulled her by one arm toward the basement doorway. They were a few inches away when he stopped.

"The noise is coming from upstairs," he said. "We have to go down to the basement."

"David," Daisy said. "Why don't you let me go down first?"

He stopped and turned to look at her.

"Why?"

"So, I can find a place for us to hide."

He thought about what she said and let go of her arm. When Daisy turned to run to the back door, David grabbed her by the ponytail and pulled her back.

"We have to go to the basement!"

Derek stood at the basement doorway with his arms outspread like some sort of avenging angel.

"Daisy, come," David said. He wrapped his arms around her from behind. "Don't leave me."

He held her for a few seconds, and she wriggled to get out of his arms.

"Please," he said.

Daisy clawed at his arms and pulled at his hands, but David wouldn't let her go. His eyes were closed, and he seemed immune to her pleas. Derek saw him shaking his head and then watched as David turned around and pushed Daisy down the basement steps.

"I have to save you!" David cried.

She fell onto her back and went headfirst down the steps. Daisy screamed and tried to grab the railing, but was unable to get a hold of it as she tumbled down the stairs.

Derek went to the bottom of the stairs. He heard something snap as Daisy's head hit the ground. For a moment as her soul left her body, she saw him. She hovered near her body, stared at him in wonder, and smiled. He watched her fade away as she went through the veil.

"David!" Derek shouted as if his vehemence would bring sound to his voice.

Derek went to the kitchen where he found David sitting on the floor with his back against the cabinets. He was breathing hard and looking at his hands.

"Beth always said I was useless," David said. "That I can never do anything right."

Derek screamed at him, but David just stared. Derek went to the basement doorway. He waved his hands, and David saw it from the corner of his eye. He turned his head.

"Are you asking me to follow you?"

Derek nodded, and David got up. He went to the doorway.

"I'd forgotten how dark it is down there."

David took a lighter from his pocket, flicked it on, and held it above the steps. A look of horror came over his face.

"Oh, God," he said. "Oh, God."

He went down the stairs and kneeled beside her.

"No, no, no, oh God." He looked at Derek. "Why, how?"

Derek stared at him in disbelief. David didn't remember what had happened just moments ago.

"Oh, God, Daisy, no." His eyes met Derek's as the memory returned. "*I* did this."

David sat back on his heels and moaned. He kept shaking his head and wringing his hands.

"No, no, no. Please, God, no."

He went to his knees again and grabbed her hand.

"Please, Daisy, wake up." He kissed her cold hand. "You must wake up."

But Daisy didn't wake up, and David stared at Derek.

"I have to go. I have to get help."

Derek watched him run up the stairs. His sanity had returned, but it was too late for Daisy. Now, Derek knew rage, and he wished he could kill David, but nothing would return Daisy's spirit to her body.

Derek stared at Daisy recalling the moment she saw him, and he hoped it had comforted her. Shortly after David left, Derek heard voices outside and went to the yard. Carl was there with his parents along with a chubby, balding man. They were calling her name and walking along the edge of the woods. Not one of them could see

Derek, and he wished they had brought Maddie with them, for all children had the sight until they reached their fifth year, though she was much too young to understand him.

As the others searched the woods, Derek returned to Daisy. He paced the basement floor trying to find a way to bring the others to her but found none. When he returned to the yard, they were gone, and the sun was setting over the trees in the western sky.

He stayed with Daisy and recalled his fantasy about asking her to marry him. If there had been a woman like Daisy around when he was alive, he would have married her and been a faithful husband. He never would have visited the brothels in Philadelphia. He wouldn't have gotten the pox. He would have had a daughter like Maddie, and they all would have lived in the house Alastair built for him. It would have been a life he could be proud of.

But as in all his other fantasies with the women he'd known over his years as a spirit, it left a bitter taste in his mouth. In truth, he hadn't deserved a woman like Daisy. He'd been a cad with nothing to show for his life but the disdain of the women he'd wronged.

A lot of time passed before Derek heard someone coming into the house. He went to the top of the stairs and peered into the kitchen. He saw a beam of light moving toward him.

The person came to the basement door and scanned the stairs with the light. They wore a black stocking cap, but as they passed Derek to go down the steps, he saw who it was – Beth Friedlander. She had visited the manor as a sullen teenager with her father and her brother, David. She was wearing a black jacket, pants, and tight gloves.

Derek went to Daisy's side and put his arms over her. He remembered how Beth had treated her brother and knew she had not come to help Daisy.

Daisy's legs were on the last step, so Beth walked around them to get to the floor. She stood where Derek kneeled and stared down at Daisy's face.

"Shit," Beth said.

She held the flashlight up and toward the corner until the light illuminated the panels on the far wall. She put the light down so that it stayed on the panels, and then went to each one until one of them gave way. She pulled it out as far as it would go, and then went back to Daisy.

"Are you happy now, Dad?" she said. "Do you see what he's done?"

She went to Daisy and grabbed hold of her feet. Beth pulled them down the stairs and around, so they were pointing toward the panel. She grabbed them and pulled, but Daisy must have been heavier than Beth had anticipated. It took a long time to get Daisy across the room, and she muttered to herself as she pulled.

"You wanted him to run your company. Do you see what he is? He's an imbecile. He's out of his mind. And when you die, he'll be my responsibility, but I've got news for you. I won't spend a penny supporting him. You're precious David will die on the streets alone, drooling on himself."

She laughed at this and seemed energized by the fantasy. It seemed easier for her to pull Daisy, and soon, she had her in front of the space.

"Old Alastair had a good idea, didn't he, Daisy? This should do nicely."

It was difficult getting Daisy inside the space, but Beth managed it by sitting Daisy on the edge and then shoving her inside. Beth pushed Daisy and crawled in after her until Daisy's feet were past the edge of the opening. Beth backed out of the tunnel and put her hands on her hips.

"You should have taken the money, Daisy."

Beth pushed the panel shut. She stopped once before climbing the stairs to pick up something off the floor. It was the yellow band from Daisy's hair. Beth shoved it into her pocket, and then Derek followed her up the stairs.

She went out the back door, and he went to the porch. Beth replaced the padlock and walked away. Derek followed her down the drive. Her car was parked behind a large bush near the road. He waited until she drove away before returning to Daisy.

Derek went inside the tunnel, lay beside her, and then put his hand on hers. Over the next few days, he stayed with her. When she stopped looking like Daisy, he left her and went to her house to watch Maddie play. He'd smile at the girl when she saw him, and even though he knew she would lose that sight someday, seeing Maddie's face, with a smile so like her mother's, helped ease his pain.

48

SUNDAY

After Ben asked her to call 911, Candy searched for Derek. Panic rose in her chest as she climbed the rickety steps. She went to the back yard and called his name, but she didn't see him anywhere. In her heart, she knew that he was gone forever, but she wasn't prepared for the ache that accompanied the realization.

When the police came and questioned them, Candy kept looking over the officer's shoulders to see if Derek might be lingering near the woods, but he wasn't. When they got into Ben's car to go home, she kept looking in the side mirror for him, but Derek wasn't there. When Ben dropped her beside her car at David's house, she got inside and followed him home.

Candy parked next to him in the driveway. He was out of his car before she opened her door.

"Are you okay?" he asked.

"He's gone," she said as tears streamed down her face. "Derek is gone. I couldn't find him anywhere." She looked up at Ben. "He stayed for her. It must have been terrible for him."

Ben reached for her hand.

"Come inside for a while."

She got out, and they went inside. Candy let him take her coat, but she felt numb.

"Are you hungry?" he asked. She shook her head. "You want a drink?"

She nodded, and they went to his father's study. Candy sat on the large, leather couch while Ben opened a bottle of whiskey and poured two glasses.

"Do you need ice?" he asked.

"No," she said.

He brought the glass to her and sat beside her. They were quiet as they sipped their drinks and let the warmth spread through their bodies.

"I shouldn't do this," Candy said.

"You can stay here tonight. We have six bedrooms."

"No, I shouldn't drink." She put the glass on the end table. "I should go to Maddie."

"The cops will do that," Ben said.

"But she needs a friend."

"Candy, we don't know for sure that it's Daisy. We have to let the police take care of this. If you go to her and it turns out that it's not Daisy, it could really hurt her."

Candy laid her head back, and Ben put his glass on the end table. He laid his head back, too.

"I want to do something. I want to fix this somehow."

"Yeah, like I wanted to fix my uncle."

"He was gone the moment we found her," Candy said. "I can't believe I'll never see him again."

He's been dead for two hundred years, Ben thought. *Most people never saw him in the first place.*

"But this is what you wanted," Ben said. "He's free now."

"You're right. It's exactly what I wanted."

She snuggled against him and sighed.

"Poor Maddie," Candy said. "Daisy might never have been found if that place had been torn down years ago."

Ben glanced at her.

"No, they would have found her. The demolition tears the house apart. Then they clean it out."

Ben didn't need the DNA results to know they had found Daisy Brady, but he wondered what had happened the day Daisy disappeared. Had David seen her and lured her inside? Had he pushed her down the stairs or was it an accident? Whatever happened, Beth had to know there was a body in the old tunnel beneath that decrepit old mansion.

"My mother had to know Daisy was in there. That's why she fought so hard to keep the town from condemning Fenway Manor."

Ben thought about the skeleton and remembered its long hair. It was the same color as the hair he'd found on the scrunchie.

"Shit," he said.

"What is it?" Candy sat up.

"Wait."

He got up and went to the bookcase in the living room, retrieved the scrunchie, and brought it to Candy.

"I found it hanging on a hook in a bookcase in the living room. It had long hair wrapped around it."

"It's yellow like the blouse she was wearing," Candy said.

"I wonder if the cops are still there." He pulled his phone out of his pocket and dialed Janet's number. "Hi, listen, I found something in my house that might be important. Are you still at Fenway Manor? Okay. I'll come over right now."

"Are we going back?" Candy asked.

"You don't have to come with me. I'll be right back. You can watch TV in the living room if you want."

Ben felt wired. He put on his coat and left the house. He returned forty-five minutes later and found Candy asleep on the library couch. She was in the same position as when he'd left her.

He went to Maria's room and saw light coming from underneath her door. He knocked, and she told him to come in. She was on the bed surrounded by her luggage.

"What time am I taking you to the airport tomorrow?"

"My flight is at three. I have to be there at one."

Ben stood at the door for a moment and wondered if he should tell her what they had found, but decided Maria had already been through enough.

"Remember, my sister has a spare room," she said. "She said you are welcome anytime."

"I know, but you won't be *here* anymore."

Maria came to Ben and put her hand on his arm.

"When I left my mama, I was younger than you. I survived. You will be fine."

"I know. It's just that I'm gonna miss you so much."

"And I will miss you."

"So, we should leave here around noon," Ben said.

Maria nodded.

"And those bags on the bed are the ones you're taking?"

She nodded again. "I might leave some if you promise to send them to me later."

"I can do that. Just leave notes on them to remind me." An awkward moment followed, and then Ben reached out and hugged her. "I'm gonna miss you so much."

"And I'll miss you," she said.

She began to cry, and Ben held her until she calmed down. He left her to go and check on Candy and found her lying on the couch now. He went upstairs, grabbed a blanket off a bed in a spare room, returned to Candy, and wrapped it around her. He then went to the living room and called Nina to tell her what had happened.

"Oh, my God," Nina said. "Is Candy all right?"

"She's fine. She fell asleep on my couch."

"Poor baby."

"I don't want to wake her so I wanted to let you know she might not come home tonight," Ben said.

"Well, thank you for that," Nina said. "You truly are a gentleman."

"I'll let her know I talked to you."

Ben went to the living room and switched on the TV. He searched for a fantasy, something that would take his mind off the events of the past two weeks, but all he could find were ghost stories and murder mysteries. He shut it off and looked at the time. Ben wanted to go to Harlan's, but it was too late for that. He'd have to go first thing in the morning. He wanted to get David's letter, and this time, Ben wasn't leaving Harlan's house without it.

49

W hen Ben knocked on his door the next morning, Harlan was still in his robe and pajamas. He didn't seem surprised to see Ben.

"We need to talk," Ben said.

"Of course. Come right in. I was just waiting for my coffee."

They went to the living room. Harlan had been watching the news, and they were showing a scene behind the mansion.

"Do you want coffee?" Harlan asked.

"I'm good."

Ben followed Harlan to the kitchen and sat at the table while Harlan got a coffee mug from his cabinet.

"So, they found a body at Fenway Manor," Harlan said.

"It was in the basement," Ben said. "Candy and I found it."

Harlan was about to pour his coffee when he stopped. He turned to face Ben.

"How on earth did that happen?"

"We followed Derek Fenway, and he showed us where she was." Ben watched Harlan put his mug down. "I came to get that letter Uncle Dave left me."

"Yes, of course, I'll be right back."

Harlan went to retrieve the letter and returned a few minutes later.

"David was very agitated when he came to see me that night," Harlan said as he handed it to Ben. "He told me the town was going to condemn Fenway Manor and Beth hadn't been able to stop them." Harlan sat. "He was sick, Ben. He knew his time was running out and he wanted you to know what had happened in his own words."

Ben held the envelope for a moment before taking the letter out. He recognized David's handwriting but was surprised to find that what he had written was clear and concise, not the muddled ramblings Ben was used to in David's emails.

"Many years ago, I met a woman named Daisy. We fell in love, and I wanted to marry her. I would have, too, but then I was offered a grant, the one I've told you about. I wanted to see Daisy before I left, but there was no time. A plane reservation had been made, and the first lecture was the following day. Years later, I discovered that my father had financed the grant. He wasn't pleased with my relationship with Daisy and felt that if I went away, Daisy and I would simply fall apart. He didn't understand how deeply in love we were.

"I broke Daisy's heart when I left. I didn't know she was having my child. Beth sent me a wedding announcement, and I nearly went mad because I couldn't get home before Daisy wed Carl Brady.

"When I returned, Daisy refused to talk to me, and I was devastated. I had been experiencing odd thoughts and strange dreams for some time, but I'd never lost touch with reality. Then, obsessive thoughts began to fill my mind. Some days I would be fine, and then I would wake up in the midst of a manic episode and run about the house ranting about this or that. It frightened my poor mother to death.

"I was able to maintain my position at the university, and then a colleague dropped by during one of my lectures. He told me that I had made little sense and that perhaps I should see a doctor. That's when I began seeing a psychiatrist.

"All this time I would watch Daisy from afar. I would stand on the porch behind Fenway Manor and wait for her to come out of Derek's house. I never stopped loving her. I kept thinking that if she would only talk to me, that I could turn back time and change things so we would be together.

I continued to watch her when Maddie was born. I took their pictures and developed them in a dark room I'd created in the basement of my parent's house. I kept the photos in an old suitcase down there so no one would see them.

"On Maddie's second birthday, I went to Fenway Manor that day to see my daughter. I was having a bad day. I'd been prescribed

medication, but when it wore off, the manic thoughts would return. I had left the house without taking my pill, and I felt fine. My mind wasn't racing, and I felt good. When I saw Daisy walking her little dog toward the house, I took it as a sign that I should go to her and tell her that I still loved her.

"I hid inside the house until she came near the porch, and then I called her name. We talked, and she was afraid her husband would see us, so we went inside. Derek was there. He kept his eyes on me as I spoke to her. I was simply trying to find out why she hadn't waited for me to return, and as she spoke, I started to feel out of sorts. Nothing she said made sense. I kept asking why and pleading with her to marry me, but Daisy wouldn't listen.

"Things happened so fast, Ben, so fast. Derek came to me and took me to the basement doorway. I saw Daisy at the foot of the stairs and ran to her side. I didn't know how she had gotten there, and then I remembered pushing her down the stairs..."

"He pushed her down the stairs," Ben said.

"He was out of his mind, Ben."

"He killed her and left Maddie to grow up thinking her mother had abandoned her."

"He was mentally ill, Ben. The medication helped, but it didn't work as well as what he'd been taking before he died. David would never have hurt her if he was in his right mind."

"He pushed her down the stairs."

"He didn't know what he was doing," Harlan said.

"He pushed her down the stairs!" Ben cried. "And then he went on with his life as though nothing happened."

"He would have gone to prison."

"For how long, Harlan? It was an accident, and as you said, he was mentally ill. How long would he have gotten for manslaughter? He probably would have been sent to some cushy mental hospital for rich felons. At least Maddie would have known that Daisy didn't just walk away."

Ben threw the letter at Harlan.

"Finish it, Ben," Harlan said.

"I can't."

"Then I'll tell you what happened."

"Don't."

"He went home to his parents. He wanted them to go with him to the police. He wanted to confess, but Jake wouldn't hear of it. He called a doctor and had his son committed to the hospital that night. The doctor gave David a sedative, and your grandparents drove him to upstate New York. When he woke up, he was in a room with bars on the windows."

"Why didn't he go to the police when he got out of the hospital?" Ben asked.

"He was on antipsychotic medications. I went to see him, and he barely recognized me." Harlan sat back and exhaled sharply. "When he was released, Jake moved him into the house next door. I couldn't believe they were going to leave him on his own, but they were so devastated by his illness that they had become completely dependent on Beth. They went along with whatever she wanted."

Ben still refused to look at the letter.

"You should read it," Harlan said.

"I'm finished with him," Ben said.

"It was Beth's idea to hide the body in Fenway Manor." Ben's jaw twitched. "She did it while your grandparents drove him to the hospital."

"I don't want to hear anymore," Ben said.

"David wanted Maddie to know the truth."

Ben shook his head. "No. He's not gonna clear his conscience at her expense."

Ben stood up.

"You shouldn't have kept this from me," Ben said.

"I was just trying to protect you."

"Then you should have taken me away from them years ago." Ben glanced out the kitchen window. "She kept a trophy, Harlan, a yellow scrunchie Daisy wore in her hair. She hung it in the bookcase in my living room. All these years, it was there where she could see it and remember what she'd done."

"Dear God," Harlan said.

Ben left the house and went to his car. As he passed David's house, he knew that he could never live there. He would tell Candy the next time he saw her that she had another listing.

50

Maddie loved Mondays. It was the only day she didn't have to work, and she loved sleeping in. Even Larry seemed to understand that he'd have to wait a bit longer than usual to go out, but today, he came to Maddie's bed and nudged her hand. She grumbled, and he nudged her again.

"Please not today, Larry." Now he grumbled. "Okay. I'll get up, but I'm not getting dressed."

She'd been up late the night before watching the flashing lights at the mansion. It reminded her of the day she found David Friedlander. Something was going on there, but when she turned on the local news, there was nothing about the old mansion.

Larry started barking as she put on her coat and she shushed him. When he refused to stop, she peeked out the kitchen door window and saw Detective Worthington coming toward her door.

"Shit," she said. "Shush, Larry."

Maddie opened the door before Janet could knock and held onto Larry's collar. The detective looked grim.

"Hi, Maddie," Janet said. "Can I come in?"

"Sure. I just have to take Larry out. Why don't you take a seat at the table and I'll be right back?"

While Maddie took Larry to the back yard, Janet sat at the kitchen table and put her purse on the floor beside her. Her shoulders slumped as she gazed around the kitchen noting the distinct seventies décor. When Maddie returned, she went straight to the coffeemaker.

"Coffee?"

"No thanks. This won't take long."

Janet watched Maddie pour some kibble into Larry's bowl. She clasped her hands on the table and focused on the dog while Maddie made coffee.

"I saw the lights at the mansion last night," Maddie said.

"Actually, that's why I'm here."

A chill went up Maddie's back as she turned on the coffeemaker.

"It wasn't another shooting, was it?"

"No, nothing like that," Janet said.

"Because I didn't hear anything."

Maddie sat across from Janet and their eyes met, and then Janet took a deep breath.

"Yesterday, a body was found in the basement of the old mansion." She let that sit a minute while Maddie held her breath. "It was a female. The M.E. thinks she might have been in her twenties. From the clothes she was wearing, we determined that she had been put there sometime in the late eighties or early nineties."

Maddie felt the muscles in her throat tighten.

"We have to do a DNA match..."

"She's not dead." Maddie shook her head. "She left. My father told me they had a fight. She ran away."

"Which is why we want to do a DNA match. We need a sample of your DNA. We need to find out for sure."

"She ran away!" Maddie cried. She slapped her hand on the table.

Janet reached inside her purse and took out a vial shaped like a test tube. She pulled the top off and held it out to Maddie. It held a stick with a cotton swab on the end.

"We have to be sure. You have to be sure."

"She's not dead," Maddie said softly. A tear rolled down her cheek.

"Just brush it against the inside of your cheek."

Maddie turned her head away. It was better to live in the fantasy than to learn that your mother had been in the basement of that awful old place all these years.

"Please, Maddie."

Maddie's head dropped, and she started to cry. Janet pulled her hand back and let her have a minute before holding it out again.

"Maddie."

Maddie took the swab from Janet, held it for a few seconds, and then brushed it against the inside of her cheek before handing it back.

"It shouldn't take long to get the results back. Do you want me to call someone?"

Maddie shook her head.

"I'll be fine."

"Call me if you need to talk." Janet got up. "I'll call you as soon as we get the results."

After Janet left, Larry came to Maddie's side as if he knew she was in pain and rested his head on her knee. She stroked his head as she sobbed.

Janet dialed Ben's number as soon as she got into her car.

"I just saw Maddie, and she's pretty shaken up."

"Did she give you the DNA?" he asked.

"Yes, but it wasn't easy. I think I just killed her dearest fantasy."

"Just remember to match it against my uncle's, too."

"Right."

She hung up and sat for a moment. Finding the body was going to bring up a lot of questions regarding the way things were handled when Carl Brady reported his wife missing. While she understood the solemnity of the situation, she couldn't help but feel good that Jarrod was about to be exposed, and that his boast of being the youngest cop in Logans Grove to become detective would be seen for what it truly was - an ill-gotten reward for a crooked cop.

Janet dropped Maddie's DNA off at forensics, and then returned to the mansion. The team was finishing up, and she went to the van to take a look at what they'd found. The clothes were female - blue Jordache jeans, a dingy yellow Henley T-shirt, Ked's sneakers, and a white cardigan sweater. The bones were concealed in a black body bag, but the M.E. had left his clipboard next to it, and she read his short narrative.

"The victim, a female, had been placed in a tunnel concealed by a panel in the basement. She was on her back with her legs stretched out in front of her. Hair was lying in clumps on the shoulders, behind the skull, and on the ground around the skull. Photos will show the placement of the victim.

"The bones collapsed as soon as they were moved, and samples of dirt were taken from underneath the remains and on all sides. A cursory examination shows a break at the base of the neck."

Someone had broken her neck. Janet had been in the cellar, and now she believed that the victim could have fallen down the stairs by accident, but then someone moved her body to the tunnel. If it was an accident, why the cover-up?

While she had no proof, Janet firmly believed it had something to do with David Friedlander. It was the only thing that made sense. It would have motivated his parents to call the mayor or the chief right away and get the two uniformed cops on board.

Janet followed the van back to the station. Jarrod was reading a newspaper at his desk. She noted his nonchalance and wondered if anyone had told him about the discovery at Fenway Manor. If they had, his body language gave no clue that he was the least bit concerned.

Janet went to the archive to get the original file on Daisy Brady. When she returned to her desk, she opened a new one without a name until they knew without a doubt that it was Daisy. Janet sat back and rubbed her neck. She kept thinking of Maddie's face and tried focusing instead on what she had seen when she arrived at Fenway Manor the night before - the victim, reduced to hair and bone, waiting for someone to find her.

Janet waited until late afternoon to go to the M.E.'s office and see what progress had been made. He had begun assembling the bones and was nearly finished when she came in.

The M.E., an older man who'd been with the department a long time, looked up when he saw her come in.

"Detective."

"Hey. So, do we have a cause of death yet?"

"A broken neck. I have to wait for pathology before I can make an exact determination."

"She could have been pushed down the stairs," Janet said.

"Or strangled, but it would take a great deal of pressure to break those bones."

"A strong man."

"Most likely, but I think you're right. She either fell or was pushed. In order for her neck to snap that way, she'd have landed on her back at an angle, her head would have hit the ground, and the weight of her body would have snapped her neck."

Janet pondered this for a moment. Would the victim have been aware after the fall?

"Did she know she was dying?"

"It's hard to tell. She could have been conscious for a second, but the trauma would have been significant, so it's doubtful."

"I brought a DNA sample," Janet said. "I'd like it tested for a match. I'd also like it tested against David Friedlander's DNA."

The M.E. raised his eyebrows. "You think they're connected?"

"I think it's possible. His nephew asked me to confirm it."

"I'll let you know."

~

Janet put David Friedlander's file in her "Closed" basket. Jarrod wasn't at his desk yet. She wondered what would happen when they identified Daisy's body. Would internal affairs investigate what happened, or would Jarrod simply retire without a word being said?

She sat back, tapped her pencil against the edge of her desk, sighed, and then saw Ben Arntz's number on her phone.

"Hey," she said.

"Hi."

"I put that scrunchie with the other evidence," she said.

"I think that scrunchie was a trophy."

"Why would you think that?"

"Because my uncle killed Daisy, and my mother stuffed her body in that tunnel behind that panel."

Janet's eyes widened. "You sound like you *know* what happened."

"My uncle wrote me a letter confessing everything."

She leaned toward him. "Holy shit. I need to see that letter."

"Harlan has it. You can ask him for it."

"Why does Harlan have it?" she asked.

"Because I didn't want it."

"I guess I can understand why. Well, thanks for the information."

Janet looked at Jarrod wished knew how broken Ben was, but would he even care? She doubted it. She doubted Jarrod would care about anything but his pension.

~

Maria's bags were in the foyer when Ben arrived, and she was in the kitchen making him a sandwich.

"Is that you?" she said, her voice echoing across the tiled foyer.

"It's me."

Ben went to the kitchen and saw her fixing the sandwich. A wave of emotion washed over him. This was his mother; this was the woman who raised Ben, tucked him in at night when his mother was away, read him bedtime stories, and came to take his temperature when he was sick.

"You can't leave me," he said softly.

Maria turned and tilted her head.

"Oh, Ben."

"I need you."

He went to her and threw his arms around her. He wept into her shoulder, and then Maria started to cry.

"You will come and see me anytime you want," she said.

"I'll be there every month."

"And you'll bring that pretty girl with you."

He pulled away and looked into her eyes.

"Do you like her?"

"I do. I think she's good for you."

His sad smile warmed Maria's heart. He still cared what she thought.

"You should eat before we go," Maria said. "Sit."

Ben did as he was told while Maria took her bags to his car. When she returned, she found him sitting at the island in front of the half-eaten sandwich staring at the notice of the meeting to condemn Fenway Manor.

"It's time," she said softly.

He snapped his head back.

"Right. Let's go."

They spoke little as they rode to Newark International Airport. Monday traffic on the turnpike was fierce, but they made good time. As they approached the airport, Maria put her hand on Ben's arm.

"I don't want you to come inside."

Ben looked at her. "I have to come inside."

"I don't want an emotional scene in front of all those people." She sighed. "Someone might recognize you." He frowned and rolled his eyes. "I will call you as soon as I get off the plane. We can talk about Christmas." She squeezed his arm. "I love you, Ben.

He choked back his feelings.

"I love you, too."

He pulled into the departing lane and went to take her bags out of the trunk while Maria went to get a baggage cart. Before they parted, Maria hugged him.

"You call as soon as you land," Ben said.

"I promise. You take care of yourself. Eat. Sleep. Don't let yourself get sick."

"I won't.

Maria squeezed him tightly before pulling away from him. Ben felt the cold air dissipate the warmth of her body. She grabbed the luggage cart, waved at him, turned, and then went inside the terminal without looking back.

51

After he dropped Maria at the airport, Ben went to Carpaza Realty, and when Trini saw him, she grinned from ear to ear. He was one good-looking boy.

"Hello," she said.

He came up to the counter and folded his arms on it.

"I'm looking for Candy," he said.

Trini's eyebrows went up.

"She's here. Let me see if she's available."

Ben paced around the lobby for a moment, and then Trini returned. Candy was behind her.

"Hi," Candy said. "Come with me."

Ben followed her to her office, and once they were inside, Candy wrapped her arms around him.

"I missed you this morning when I woke up," she said.

"I went to see Harlan."

She pulled away. "You all right?"

"I got to read the letter. It was a confession."

"Holy shit," Candy said. "What did it say?"

"Can I tell you later?"

"Sure. Come in. Sit."

She went behind her desk and watched him as he gazed around the room.

"I didn't think it would be this small."

"I'm low on the ladder right now," Candy said. "So, is there a reason for this visit, or did you just miss me?"

"I always miss you. But that's not why I'm here."

"Okay. I'll let that pass for now." She smiled.

"I want to sell both my houses."

"Both houses."

"I don't want to live in either one," Ben said. "I want to put them on the market now, today."

Candy's hands shook. "You're sure about this. This isn't just a reaction to what happened yesterday."

"No. I've made up my mind. I want to get rid of them, and then I'll let you find me another one."

She sat back and gripped the edge of the desk.

"Okay. I'll ask Trini to make up the listing agreements."

Candy got up and went to Trini's desk. Her legs felt wobbly, so she grabbed the counter.

"He wants to sell both of his houses," she whispered.

Trini clapped her hands. "Oh my, God! Good for you."

"Ross will be pleased. He might even respect me a little."

"Oh, he'll be pleased all right. You landed a big fish, Miss Candy. Ross will be overjoyed when he hears what you did" Trini saw the gleam in Candy's eye. "Well, I better get on those agreements. You give me the addresses."

Candy went back to her desk.

"She needs the addresses, and then she'll type them up."

A half an hour later, Ben was signing two listing agreements that named Candace Burke as his agent.

"I have to do a walk-through and get the assessment, have a title search done, and then Ross and I will come up with a figure. The listing agreements will say that I agree to represent you in the sale of your properties. When I get all the facts, we'll make up a more detailed contract for you to sign."

"Great."

Candy smiled broadly. "Okay. Well, that's done." She sat back. "So, do you feel like going out later on?"

"I was hoping you'd ask."

"How about that Thai place near Artisan Row. I've never been there."

"I could go for Thai. I'll meet you there around six."

They walked to the lobby, and Candy watched as Ben went to his car. He looked so lost she wanted to cry.

"He's something," Trini said.

"He's really great," Candy said. "I'm worried about him, though."

"What's to worry about?"

"You heard about that body they found in the news, didn't you?"

"The one in that awful mansion?" Trini said.

"That was Ben and me."

"What?"

"We found it. Ben owns that mansion."

"Why didn't you tell me when you came in? Oooh, girl. You went inside that place?"

"Yup."

Ross came through the door and frowned.

"Trini," he said. "Don't you have work to do?"

She turned to her computer and began typing. Candy stood straight and looked him in the eye.

"I signed two listings today. The Friedlander mansion and a Queen Anne in Princeton."

"The Friedlander mansion?" Ross said. "I didn't know they were looking to sell."

"I know Ben Arntz, and he asked me to handle it for him."

"Come to my office," he said.

Candy followed Ross down the hallway to his large office in the rear. He sat behind his desk and waited for her to settle in her chair.

"So," he said, "is this for real?"

"He signed the listing agreements."

"Well, then I'm impressed. And you're sure he's serious about selling?"

"He wants something smaller. I think after what's happened, he'd like to start over somewhere else."

"Wonderful, wonderful. So, you know what you have to do. Just run everything by me before you put anything in writing."

"I will."

"You screw this up, and it will affect your entire career. People will see your sign in front of that place, and they *will* remember, especially if it's out there a long time. Everyone who passes it will see your name."

"They would see your name, too," Candy said.

"Exactly, so we have to do this thing right."

"I will cross my T's and dot my I's."

"That's what I like to hear."

She left his office walking on a cloud. She was smiling so broadly her cheeks hurt. Candy went to her desk, opened her laptop, and sent Trini an email asking for the number of the property inspector and photographer Ross used.

When Candy got home from work, Nina was pleased to hear about the listings, but she warned Candy it might affect her relationship with Ben.

"That old saying about not mixing business and pleasure ain't for nothin'. You be careful."

"Don't worry. Ben and I are fine."

"I know, just be careful."

"I'll remember."

As Candy went up the stairs, she noticed some empty cereal bowls with spoons next to her mother's chair in the living room. When she came back down, she picked them up to take them to the kitchen. That's when she saw empty potato chip bags shoved in chair cushions along with wrappers from chocolate bars, but the worst of all were the two empty whiskey bottles in a magazine rack that hadn't held a magazine in ten years. She got a trash bag from the kitchen and bagged everything she found.

After putting the trash bag outside, Candy looked at the stove, counters, and sink. Everything had a greasy residue. The pots and pans in the cupboard still had bits of food stuck to them, and Nina had been using paper plates and plastic utensils to avoid having to wash them. Candy had a lump in her throat as she tried to figure out what had happened to her fastidious mother.

She was thinking of canceling her date with Ben when Nina came down the stairs. She came into the kitchen and found Candy wiping the counters.

"Do you have a date with Ben tonight?"

"We're supposed to meet at that Thai place."

"Oh. I've never been there."

Candy wanted to ask Nina if she was all right, but it was hard finding the words because Nina had always been her rock. It was her turn to be the strong one now.

"I found some dishes in the living room," Candy said. She waited for a reply from Nina, but none came. "I also found some bottles in the magazine rack." She turned to face Nina. "Are you feeling okay, Mom?"

"I'm fine." Nina went to the kitchen table and sat.

"When did you start drinking?" Candy asked.

"What are you talking about?"

"Two empty whiskey bottles, Mom, that's what I'm talking about."

"I just take a shot at night when I can't sleep."

Candy narrowed her eyes.

"How long have you been having trouble sleeping?"

Now, Nina glared at Candy.

"I don't know. A while maybe."

Candy sat across from Nina.

"Did you ask the doctor about it?"

Nina sniffed. "All they do is give you pills. I don't need any more pills."

"But it might be something physical. You really should get a checkup."

Nina glowered at Candy.

"I don't need a checkup. I'm just fine."

"But this isn't like you," Candy said.

"How would you know what I'm like, huh? You have your own life, you're out every night, galivanting around town with a guy half your age. What do you know about anything?" Nina stood, put her hands on the table, and leaned toward Candy. "My whole life I took care of you. I have no friends, no job, and no future once you leave, and you will leave someday. So, don't go telling me what to do, okay? I'm perfectly capable of taking care of myself."

Nina was walking away when Candy got up and grabbed her arm.

"Why haven't you talked about this before?"

"I'm your mother. I'm not supposed to talk to you about this stuff."

"That's ridiculous. I'm thirty. I'm old enough to listen to you for a change." Candy let go of Nina's arm. "And Ben is not half my age."

Nina hung her head.

"You have your own life, Candy."

"And you are part of it. You always will be."

"You don't get it," Nina said. "You never will."

"Not if you don't talk to me."

They stood across from each other for a minute or two, and then Nina sighed.

"I don't want to be alone."

"Why would you be alone?" Candy said.

"Because you will get married one day. You'll have a place of your own. At first, you'll visit, but after a while, you'll get too busy. You'll call me and say you can't make it, or your husband has a thing, and you have to go away for the weekend."

Candy tilted her head.

"You don't know that."

"It happens all the time."

"Well, it won't happen to us."

Nina exhaled sharply.

"Candy, as much as I wanted you to get better, I dreaded the day you would finally be whole again. I knew you would have to have a life of your own and it killed me inside. You have no idea how hard it was for me to let you go out into the world again."

"I have a pretty good idea. You didn't exactly hide how you felt, Mom."

"And now you'll have money. You'll go off with Ben, and that will be that."

"I love how you have my whole life planned out for me," Candy said. "Yes, I like Ben, and yes, we will probably be seeing each other for a long time, but who knows if it will last?" She sat back. "You have no idea how important you are to me. I could no more leave you behind than I could my cell phone."

"And that's saying something."

Candy put her hands on Nina's shoulders.

"Mom, I love you, and I need you. Please don't ever doubt that." She saw the sadness on Nina's face. "I think you should talk to your doctor about getting some help."

Nina looked Candy in the eye.

"I'm not crazy."

"I didn't say you were crazy. I said you need some help with these feelings. I've been in therapy, Mom, and it really helps."

"I don't need therapy. I need you."

"And you have me, even if I move away, you'll go with me."

"No, I won't," Nina said. "Don't be ridiculous."

"Mom, there's a big world out there and like you said, I'll have money. We sell this place, and then we can live anywhere. I can sell real estate anywhere."

Nina's eyes lit up.

"You'd actually take me with you."

"I couldn't imagine not taking you with me. I like you."

Nina blushed. "And you think you could sell this house?"

"Of course, I can sell it. It's structurally sound and relatively clean." Nina screwed up her mouth. "And it's near town, schools, and the university. We might have to spruce it up a bit, but it will sell."

Nina scanned the kitchen.

"We could do this."

"I still think you should talk to someone," Candy said. "Promise me you will talk to your doctor."

Nina nodded. "I'm sorry to make you worry about me."

"Don't be. Just talk to me the next time you have something on your mind." Candy moved away from Nina and picked up the sponge. "So, start thinking about what you want to do here to get things ready, and I'll help you."

Nina smiled. "This is real."

"Yup."

Nina came to her side and put her arm around Candy's waist.

"I didn't let myself dream anymore."

Candy stopped wiping the counter. She put her head on Nina's.

"You should never stop dreaming, Mom. Your life isn't over."

"It was for me."

Nina burst into tears and Candy wrapped her arms around her mother's shoulders. She held her until Nina had shed all her tears, and then Candy kept holding her so Nina would know she would always be there to catch her mother's tears.

52

The results of the DNA tests were on Janet's desk when she got to work the day after Thanksgiving. She was staring at them when her phone rang. It was Ben. She hesitated a second before answering it because she knew she should talk to Maddie first but hit the button before the last ring.

"Hey," she said.

"Hi. I was wondering if you got the results yet."

Janet tapped her finger on the paper, and then sat back in her chair.

"It was Daisy."

"Have you told Maddie yet?" Ben asked.

"I haven't had the chance to talk to her yet."

"And what about my uncle?"

"That's also a match. He was Maddie's father."

She heard him breathing for a few seconds.

"Will you let me know after you talk to her?" he asked.

"I will." Janet saw Jarrod across the room. He was cleaning out his desk. He had been scheduled to leave on Dec 5, the day of his party, but it had been canceled when Jarrod was asked to leave ASAP. Janet bristled at the sight of him. "I have to go. I'll talk to you later."

Chief Keene came out of the elevator and glanced at Janet before walking over to Jarrod. He handed him some paperwork and then headed toward her. His grim expression was worrisome, and Janet braced herself.

"We are preparing a statement for the media. If anyone tries to talk to you, you are to tell them 'No comment.' Are you clear on that?"

"I am."

He looked over his shoulder at Jarrod.

"He was a good cop, you know." Keene exhaled softly. "That's all I wanted to say."

He returned to the elevator, and Janet watched Jarrod carry a banker's box across the room where he joined Keene. They didn't exchange words, and Keene let Jarrod take the elevator while he chose to take the stairs.

The narrative that was going to be released had not been circulated yet, so she wasn't sure what they would say about Jarrod and Markham's investigation. The top brass had been in conference since Daisy's body was discovered and Janet went to Keene to remind him that the original investigation had been less than thorough. That's when she confessed that she had gone to Florida to talk to Markham.

"John Markham wanted to do more, but he was told to retire. Jarrod was promoted in his rookie year." She had thrown Daisy's file on Keene's desk. "The chief was complicit in covering this up."

"You don't know that," Keene said.

"I know that he was friends with Jacob Friedlander and that there had been several calls to the police when his son violated Daisy Brady's restraining order."

Keene had rubbed his head with both hands and then stared at her for a moment.

"And you disobeyed me when I asked you to leave it alone. You defied a direct order."

"I went on my own time."

"You weren't supposed to go at all!" he cried.

He got out of his chair and went to the window.

"Jarrod is retiring. Brigham is going to decide what to do about you."

That was before Thanksgiving, and now she breathed a sigh of relief. She would not be suspended.

The other guilty parties responsible for the cover-up were gone, leaving behind an unquenchable desire for justice. What would she tell Maddie? How would she feel when she knew that no one would pay for Daisy's death?

Janet could argue that David Friedlander had paid. He'd been mentally ill his whole life. His own sister, who had then died a horrible death herself, had murdered him. Jacob Friedlander's actions had cursed his children. Perhaps that was the justice fate had conjured to ensure that no one would go unpunished.

Janet put the paper with the DNA results into her purse, put on her coat, and grabbed her car keys. It was time to tell Maddie that her mother was never coming home.

~

Janet stood in front of the bookstore and watched Maddie dusting the shelves. She saw the old dog asleep in his bed and braced herself for Maddie's reaction to the news. She looked at the café across the street and thought about buying coffee, but it would only delay the inevitable, so, Janet took a deep breath and went inside.

"Hi," Maddie said. "How was your holiday?"

"Quiet. I went to a movie."

"Yeah, me, too, only I got my movie from On Demand, and then Larry and I had some turkey."

Janet eyed the "For Sale" sign.

"Maybe next year you'll be somewhere else."

"I hope so." Maddie put the duster under the counter. "So, I'm assuming you got the results."

"Can we sit?" Janet asked.

They went to the table and sat across from each other. Maddie clasped her hands on the table while Janet took the papers out of her purse. Maddie was biting her lip.

"David Friedlander was your father," she said. "And…the remains were those of your mother, Daisy Brady."

Janet handed Maddie the results. Maddie read them and put them down.

"Okay, so that's it. There's no mistake."

"They both are a match to your DNA."

Maddie sat back.

"Do we know who killed her?" Maddie asked.

"David Friedlander wrote a letter to his nephew before he died. He confessed to killing Daisy."

"Oh, my God."

"His sister put her in the space where we found her."

Maddie was numb. There were no tears or emotional outburst as she thought about this news. She kept looking at the graphs as if staring at them might change the results.

"Does Ben know?"

Janet decided to lie. "I thought you should be the first to know." She leaned forward. "This might change things for you."

"What do you mean?" Maddie asked.

"You are the biological daughter of a Friedlander. You have a claim on their fortune."

"I want nothing from them."

"There's a lot of money, Maddie, and they owe you for what they did."

"My father left me this store and my house. It will be enough."

Janet sat back and gazed around the store.

"So, what are your plans when you sell?"

"I'm going to spend some time with my aunt in South Carolina. She's my dad's little sister. She came up for his funeral and told me I could come and stay with her for a while. I've got cousins I hardly know so it will be nice."

"I'm glad you have family to stay with. I've heard the beaches there are nice, too."

"Yeah, well, it will be nice to be somewhere else for a while."

Janet glanced at Larry.

"And what about him?"

Maddie smiled. "Oh, he'll go with me."

"Will he be able to adjust? He's kind of old."

"I'll talk to the vet and make sure he's well enough to travel. I can't stand the thought of losing him."

Her sad tone was heartbreaking.

"Well, if there's anything I can do, just call," Janet said.

"Thank you, for everything."

Janet got up. "Take care."

Maddie watched her go out the door, and then the tears began to fall.

53

A week later, Ben came into The Daisy Chain with two lattes. With Christmas fast approaching, the Row was full of shoppers, but the bookstore looked sad. Maddie hadn't put up any decorations.

He came inside and found Maddie sitting on the floor taking books off the "Science Fiction/Fantasy" shelves. He smiled when she looked up, and then came over to her.

"How are you?" he asked.

"I'm okay." She saw the coffee cups. "Is one of them for me?"

He handed it to her, and then he sat on the floor. He looked at the titles and smiled.

"I've read every one of these."

"I never had the time or the interest."

"I wasn't allowed to go outside when I was a kid. I started reading books like these when I was eight. No one seemed to care whether what I read was appropriate or not."

She stopped pulling books and drank some coffee. She sat cross-legged on the floor and rested her elbows on her knees.

"Why are you here, Ben?"

"I wanted to say I'm sorry."

"You didn't do anything."

"I know, but my family did, and I'm the only one left to say it."

She kept her eyes on the floor and sipped her coffee.

"Maddie, I wanted to talk to you about your inheritance."

"I don't want it."

"I thought you would say that, but think about it. There's so much money, I had no idea, and..."

"I don't care," Maddie said. "I want no part of him."

Ben held his coffee with two hands.

"Okay. I can't make you take it, but is there anything you'd like me to do with it?"

Maddie tilted her head. "Like what?"

"Like give it to charity."

"I never thought of that."

"I'm going to put some of mine into education. Maybe you want to help the Cancer Society, or missing and exploited children."

"I used to give to charity when I worked in New York. I used it as a write off on my taxes." She tilted her head forward and smiled at Ben. "I was so selfish back then. It might be nice to give a big donation to some deserving cause."

"Just let me know where you want it to go, and I'll take care of it. You'll get a letter from my attorney with the details, so you know everything was taken care of."

She looked him in the eye.

"Don't let that money change you."

"I'll do my best." He exhaled sharply. "I don't have anyone left around here. Did you think about what I asked you before about being my cousin?"

She narrowed her eyes.

"You were serious."

"I've never had a cousin."

"I guess we could see each other on holidays, that is if I ever come back to New Jersey."

"Where are you going?" Ben asked.

"I'm going to South Carolina as soon as I sell this place and my house."

"But you'll keep in touch so I can invite you over for Hanukkah."

"I've never been invited to celebrate Hanukkah. It might be interesting."

"It used to be interesting when my grandparents were alive. We even went to temple then. After they died, we sort of let things slide, but my mom always insisted we light the menorah the week of Hanukkah."

Maddie recoiled at the mention of his mother, and Ben reached for her hand.

"I'm not my mother."

"I know. It's okay." She pulled her hand away. "You are a good person, Ben. I know that, but it might take some time before I'm able to be your cousin, if ever."

She got up, picked up her coffee, and put it on a shelf. She folded her arms and waited for him to get up. When he did, he saw something on a shelf and pulled it out. It was a hardback copy of *Lord of the Rings*.

"I want this," he said. He took a hundred-dollar bill from his wallet. "Do you want me to leave this on the counter?"

"It's yours. Happy Hanukkah."

He put his money back in his wallet. After hesitating a few seconds, he reached for her hand, and she let him take it.

"I hope you have the best of everything, Maddie. If you ever need anything, anything at all, please call me."

"And I hope you have a great life."

When he left the store, he turned and looked at the sign above the door. The Daisy Chain's lettering was faded, and the daisies surrounding it were dull and dirty. Just like Fenway Manor, everything starts out so bright and hopeful, every rusted car, every dilapidated house, and every failing business was once someone's dream.

David had dreamed of opening a learning center. He never made his dream come true. Ben always wanted to be a teacher. His desire to break away from his family was always foremost in his mind, but now that he *was* his family, he wanted to redeem his family name. He wanted to create a new legacy, one that wouldn't be sullied by events of the past.

His great-grandparents had survived the Holocaust. What would they have thought of Beth? Ben shivered as he walked across the street. He couldn't imagine what they'd endured or what they'd sacrificed to walk out of a work camp with nothing but their souls.

Their granddaughter was an affront to them. Beth never had a noble dream or a desire to help anyone but herself and her son, who was nothing more than an extension of herself. As he walked to his car, Ben suddenly knew what he wanted to do with his life.

The house was empty now with Maria gone, and dust had settled on the fine furniture Beth had chosen so carefully. When he got home, Ben went to his room, grabbed his laptop, brought it to the island in the kitchen, and then began a property search.

54

The dumpster at David's house had been filled and taken away a couple of times, and now Ben had a crew cleaning the walls, floors, and any other surface they could find. He didn't bother to look through things before they were hauled away. He didn't want any of it.

Ben also had a crew cleaning out the mansion, but he went through the family things himself. He wanted to keep photos of himself, his father, his great-grandparents, grandparents, uncles, and aunts. He threw all photos of Beth away save for one.

That afternoon when he got home, Ben went up to the attic. He found a trunk full of things his great-grandparents, Abram and Klara, had brought with them from Europe following World War II. Like Anne Frank, they'd been in hiding through most of the war and had been arrested just before the war ended. There was a photo of Abram after his camp was liberated. He had a shaved head and was nothing but skin and bones. Abram and Klara had been separated after they were arrested, but Abram had found his Klara's name on a register of survivors in Belsen, Germany.

Jacob had shown Ben photos of his parents and Ben had noticed the tattoos on their arms. He'd asked Jake why they had numbers instead of a picture, and Jake had steered him away from the subject as he often did when things got too real. Now, Ben looked at the photos and the numbers with the understanding that he could never forget what had happened to them. He put everything back into the trunk and labeled it so it would come with him when he left the house.

Another trunk contained the remnants of Abram and Klara's life when they came to America. Abram was a tailor and struck upon an idea for a clothing business. With the help of some sympathetic investors, he and Klara had forged ahead with little else but determination and hard work. They made money and invested it wisely.

One of the dresses they made became famous when it was worn by an actress, and then she began to order from them exclusively. Soon, more famous people wanted their fashions, and they hired talented designers to create new styles. It was as if God wanted to repay them for all their suffering, and they were grateful.

Ben had inherited a grateful heart, but it had been bruised badly. Spending time with their memories reminded him that he had much to be thankful for and he hoped they were proud of him.

Another trunk held his grandfather's memories. Jacob Fried-lander had been sent to live with his aunt in New York when Abram saw what was happening in Germany. He was three when he arrived and had no memories of his parents when he met them in 1946. All he had was a small photo of them in a sterling silver frame. Ben took it out and looked at Abram and Klara before the war changed them. They looked so young and hopeful. Ben wished he had asked his grandfather to tell him more about them, but he was too young to know he'd never get another chance.

Ben came upon a small, pink suitcase with his mother's name written in script on a gold nameplate adhered to the suitcase. Inside were some toys and a small photo album with plastic inserts. The album had "1963" in embossed gold letters on the cover. Ben opened it and found a photo of his grandmother, Linda, and Beth sitting on the steps of a house. Jake was on the porch behind them in a rocking chair. Beth was smiling, something she rarely did, and seeing it saddened Ben.

He flipped through the pages and found more photos of her - romping on the beach, making sand castles, riding on a carousel, and always with her mother. This was before David, and it was clear that Beth adored her mother. Near the end was a photo of the house again, only this time, he saw a sign over the porch that read, "Rose Cottage, 16 Seagull Way." He took it out of the insert and read the back. "Our new summer house in Cape May."

Ben had never heard anyone talk about a place called Rose

Cottage, let alone a summer home in Cape May. He stared at it as if it would pull some buried memory from his psyche, but nothing came forth, so he took out his phone and searched for it online.

The home was now a bed and breakfast called The Blue Moon, and Ben recognized it instantly – it was the B&B his mother had gone to after she killed David. It was a place she had been to before her parents adopted a boy to replace her, and perhaps the only place she had ever been truly happy.

He pulled the first photo of the family out of the album, and it became the only photo of his mother he kept.

55

B en called Candy when he finished bringing the boxes downstairs.

"Are we still on for tonight?" he asked.

"Of course," she said. "Listen, I wanted to call you. Ross had a call from some high-end broker in New York, and they have a client who wants to see the mansion. They're coming down next weekend, and I will get to show it to them!"

"Really?"

"So, we need to celebrate," Candy said. "Did we decide where we were going tonight?"

"We didn't. Where would you like to go?"

"Someplace you haven't taken me to before."

"Okay. I'll think of something." He looked out the living room window. "It's snowing."

"Then maybe we should stay close to home."

"This place is pretty empty," he said.

"You still have your bed, right?" She giggled. "I could pick something up on my way over."

"I still have the sofa in the living room. The TV, too."

"So, then we'll stay home. You can take me someplace nice another night."

When Candy arrived at the mansion, she let herself in and brought the bags of food to the kitchen. She heard the shower running overhead and got some plates out of the cabinet. When he came downstairs, he smiled.

"Hey," she said.

"That smells good."

"It's from Alphonso's. I got what you ordered the last time we were there."

"Good. Let's fill our plates and take them to the living room."

Candy got a large spoon from the drawer and started putting the food on the plates while he poured some wine. She grabbed a bottle of water out of the fridge. Ben took his glass to the living room, and then came back for his plate.

"It's not too bad out there," Candy said. "They sanded the streets already."

"You're staying tonight, right?" he asked.

"I planned to."

They grabbed their plates and went into the living room.

She glanced at the TV and saw the seven-day forecast. It would be warmer by the end of the week, which would melt all the snow, leaving everyone's yard nice and mushy.

"Janet got the DNA results," Ben said. "It was Daisy. And David was Maddie's father."

"Wow," Candy said.

"I went to see Maddie."

"Did she know?"

He nodded. "Janet told her."

"How's she taking it?" Candy asked.

"She's said she doesn't want any money. She's going to give it to charity."

"I'm worried about her. I haven't had any inquiries about her properties. I don't think anyone wants to live near that place now."

"Even with Fenway Manor gone?" he said.

"It's not gone yet, and people remember what happened there."

Ben finished his food and put the plate on the coffee table.

"It's going down at the end of the month."

"That's great."

Ben noticed that Candy was picking at her food.

"You all right?" he asked.

"I'm fine."

"You seem a little anxious tonight."

"I'm not anxious, just a little excited about that agent I talked to."

Ben moved closer to Candy while she finished eating her food. When she was done, she put her plate next to his and then snuggled up to Ben. She unbuttoned his shirt and ran her hand over his chest, but he put his hand on hers.

"I want to talk about something," he said.

"Okay."

"I have an idea, but it would mean lying to Maddie." Candy tilted her head to see his eyes. "What if I buy her house and the store anonymously. You tell her you have a buyer, somebody who wants to give her more than the property is worth, a speculator."

"And I'd be the one lying to her." Candy pulled away from Ben and sat up. "And what if she finds out? She'd feel I had betrayed her and it would be just like it was thirteen years ago."

Ben sat forward and put his arm around her shoulders.

"No, it wouldn't." He kissed her forehead. "You would say someone contacted you, maybe an agent like the one who called about this place."

"You would have to go to another agency and ask about them."

"I'd get someone to do that for me like an attorney from Mantz's office."

"And she wouldn't recognize their name."

"And she'd never know who was buying them. Arthur would know what to do."

"It could work," Candy said. "She'd be free of those places, and she'd have enough money to go anywhere she wanted to go. But what would you do with them?"

"I'd leave your sign on them until somebody bought them." He smiled. "So, we can do this?"

Candy nodded and then threw her arms around his neck.

"I'd wait a while, though," she said. "Maybe a year. Otherwise, she might get suspicious."

They kissed, and then Ben laid back on the couch. Candy snuggled up to him. They watched TV for a while, and then Ben sighed.

"I realized something when I was going through the attic this afternoon. My great-grandparents went through a lot. I want to do something that will honor their memory." He glanced at her. "I want to build a school."

"A school?" she said softly. "What kind of school are you talking about?"

"David used to talk about having a place where kids could learn the basics like art, music, civics, stuff that gets cut out of the public curriculum because of money. It would also have the usual subjects like history, math, English, social studies, but I'd also make them take vocational courses in making stuff with wood, or building electronic equipment, or mechanics. And normal gym classes. I want to offer scholarships to kids who would never have the opportunity to go to a private school."

"It's a wonderful idea," she said. "But where would the scholarships come from? If you use your own money, you might run out and then everything you worked for would fall apart."

"I'm gonna talk to the head of the Friedlander Foundation about scholarships, and there's nothing saying I can't have kids who parents can pay for a private education."

"So, you've got it figured out."

"Yeah, I guess I do."

She snuggled against him.

"Ben, do you still feel the same way about me?"

"What?"

"Do you still feel the way you did when we first met?"

He pulled away and looked at her.

"What brought this on?"

"I don't know, I guess I'm just worried because this house is almost empty and you're ready to go off and have a great life."

He chuckled. "Candy, not only do I feel the same way, I never stop thinking about you. You make me happy. You keep reminding me that life is worth living." He put his hand on her cheek. "And I need you. My great life wouldn't be great without you."

Candy's emotions swelled, and her eyes filled with tears.

"Oh, Ben."

They kissed, and then she put her arms around him, pulled him close, and slid onto her back.

56

ONE YEAR LATER

H is best man, Steve, adjusted Ben's tie.

"Will you stop moving," Steve said.

They had met when Ben was hiring teachers for his new school in a small municipality near Morristown. The location was steeped in the history of the Revolutionary War, a time Ben wanted to focus on as a teacher, and the building had been a boy's school during the Victorian era. The two-story building had thirty classrooms, three large bathrooms, a kitchen, dining hall, community room, and gym.

Behind the main building was a medium-sized Victorian Gothic style house with a wide, wraparound porch. There were three bedrooms, each with its own bath, and Ben and Candy had claimed the largest as their own.

Steve stepped back and shrugged.

"It looks okay."

Ben looked in the full-length mirror.

"What are you talking about. It's great." He stood up straight. "Well, I guess we'd better get downstairs."

"Is Candy the kind of woman who will get mad if your tie isn't perfect?" Steve asked.

"No. I was raised by a woman like that. I couldn't marry one."

Steve had learned not to ask too many questions about Bethany Arntz after he had asked Ben about Fenway Manor. Ben had clammed up and wouldn't speak for a while, and then explained that he didn't talk about his mother, and to please not bring her up again. Whatever Steve knew about her he'd found on the internet, and that's when he found out about the murder and Ben's Uncle Dave. He kept it to himself and did as Ben had asked him to.

The venue Ben and Candy had chosen for their wedding was a lovely, out-of-the-way place called Whispering Meadows. The room they rented was a large, open space with hardwood floors and stucco walls. Candy had the florist create small bouquets of yellow roses and baby's breath for each table as a concession to her mother's wish for large sprays of roses decorating the walls.

"I don't want the place to look like a funeral home, Mom."

"But it's so drab. Aren't you going to put anything up there?"

"No. We're doing this for you. We wanted to elope."

"Oh, who wants to elope?" Nina said. "You want a wedding you can remember."

"As far as we're concerned, we're already married," Candy said.

"Not until you're in the will."

Candy had agreed to the table flowers, so Nina kept her mouth shut even when Candy bought an ivory wedding gown. It was a simple sleeveless silk dress with touches of embroidery, a modest neckline, and a plunging back. It was important to Candy that she did everything right because Ben had invited people from the foundation and they knew nothing about her. She didn't want them to think she was just some poor girl from the sticks.

The tablecloths were white linen, the plates rimmed in gold, and the flatware sterling silver. Nina was overwhelmed when she saw the tables and hoped she wouldn't embarrass Candy by using the wrong fork. She expressed her concerns when she came to see Candy in the dressing room before the ceremony.

"They won't notice, Mom. They'll be busy watching me to see if I make any mistakes."

Nina had grabbed her daughter by the shoulders and put her face near Candy's.

"Don't talk like that. You're my daughter, and he's lucky to have you."

"Don't make me cry," Candy said. "I just got my makeup on."

They hugged, and then Nina left her to go and find Trini.

When her properties sold, Maddie moved to South Carolina, and Candy asked Trini to be her Maid of Honor. She was thrilled when Trini agreed. They had become close friends, and after Candy gave Ross her notice six months ago, she offered Trini a job at the school.

So far, Trini had resisted saying she didn't like the commute, but Candy would find a place for Trini to live nearby if it killed her.

Maddie came to the door of the dressing room and saw Candy standing by the full-length mirror.

"Wow," she said, and Candy whirled around.

"Maddie!" Candy cried and ran over to her old friend.

"You look beautiful."

"Thank you. I feel beautiful. Oh, Maddie, I'm so happy."

"Ben is a great guy. I'm sure you'll be happy together."

"So, how are things in South Carolina?"

"They're good. My aunt and cousins keep me busy, and it's nice to feel like part of a family again. And Larry is happy, too."

"And that's the most important thing," Candy said with a smile.

"Absolutely." Maddie looked at the door. "Well, I'd better go. I'll see you later."

After Maddie left, Candy looked at her reflection in the full-length mirror and checked her makeup and hair one more time. Trini came to the room, and her face lit up when she saw Candy.

"You look gorgeous."

Candy's hair was swept up, and tiny flowers adorned the back. She looked like a fairy princess.

"Thanks. I hope I don't fall when I walk down the aisle."

Trini shook her head as she came to Candy and gave her a small box.

"You will be fine," Trini said. "This belonged to my mother."

Candy opened it and saw a small brooch. A blue bird with outstretched wings was alighting on a single white rose.

"I figured it's old and it's blue," Trini said.

"It's beautiful."

"I didn't think about the silk. Maybe you don't want to put a hole in it."

"I don't care. Pin it on me."

Trini pinned it to the right side of Candy's bodice, and then they stood in front of the mirror for a moment.

"You ready?" Trini asked.

Candy nodded, and they went out the door. Candy walked behind Trini to the entrance of the hall where her mother waited to give her away.

She saw Ben and Steve standing at the altar. A canopy had been placed there in honor of Ben's Judaic heritage, and a rabbi would perform one part of the ceremony while the pastor from Nina's church would perform the other.

As Candy walked toward him, Ben got a lump in his throat and swallowed hard to keep from crying like a baby. She was so beautiful, inside and out, and he felt like the luckiest man on Earth.

ABOUT THE AUTHOR

A.L. Jambor lives in Florida with her husband, Hans. Amy began writing at the tender age of fifty-eight when she was inspired by a photo of her granddaughter. The result was But the Children Survived, an apocalyptic story about how a pharmaceutical company's greed led to the destruction of North America. From there, Amy began writing fantasy mysteries that incorporated both her love of puzzles and her humor. Nick Dandino and Lord Percival Plep are two of her protagonists – the first a PI in heaven, the second an English lord reincarnated as a pudgy terrier named Libby. She has also written an historical time travel series and a dark crime thriller. You can find all her books on Amazon.com.

For more information go to:
www.aljambor.weebly.com